MW00608835

# TIME
## UNINCORPORATED
### THE DOCTOR WHO FANZINE ARCHIVES

Vol. 2: Writings on the Classic Series

**mad norwegian press**

Des Moines, IA

Also available from Mad Norwegian Press...

Jacket & interior design by Christa Dickson.

ISBN: 9781935234029
Printed in Illinois. First Edition: May 2010.

*For Julie, for everything – including putting up with my*
*time and space travelling hobby*
*GB*

*For Shoshana, for everything else*
*RS?*

# TABLE OF CONTENTS

## 6. Love and / or Monsters

## 7. The Ones Who Made Us

## 10. There are Worlds Out There...

# INTRODUCTION

**by Matt Jones**

Richard Smith opens the introduction to his essays on gay men and music by writing that "Pop music's a bit like boys. I mean, I just really, really love it" and then he gives a list of all the records, lyrics and great pop moments that have meant so much to him since he was a kid.

Now I love Richard Smith's writing; it's so good that, despite never having met him or even seen his face, I've had a crush on him since my mid-twenties. (Yeah, his prose is that good.) I like pop, I love some of it, but I remember reading his list of all-time great music and wondering why I was never that passionate. And then I realised of course that it's simply that my passions lie elsewhere, in a somewhat battered, old British television programme that has been my constant companion since I was six years old.

Let me tell you about some of the things I love...

The maggot stalking Jo in *The Green Death*; my first memory of being scared. The Doctor's tears at the end. Shitting bricks at the pterodactyl attack at the end of episode one of *Invasion of the Dinosaurs*. The TARDIS dying in *Death to the Daleks* and the luxury of spending all that time in the console room at the beginning. The end of *Planet of the Spiders* and the hot tears on my young cheeks. I'd met him you see; Jon Pertwee opened a co-op supermarket in Leicester and my mum took me to meet him. I loved him and I forgot him five minutes into *Robot*. Tom is my Doctor: yesterday, today and tomorrow. The way he answers the phone – "I'll speak to anybody!" – takes the piss out of the Brigadier's racism, solemnly pronounces the indominability of the human race and mourns his burnt scarf.

I love *Genesis of the Daleks*. Particularly the audio version which has been script-edited down to essentials and has lulled me gently to sleep on those nights when the blues or heartache have threatened to keep me awake. The fourth Doctor quipping to Broton that the Earth might be a bit big for just the six of them. And the gag about having to wave a tentacle.

Every moment of *Pyramids of Mars*; literally, I love every moment of it. And to think I almost missed episode one when my mother insisted I went up the road to Sarah Lord's birthday party. My stubborn seven-year-old self wouldn't leave home until my mum promised I could come back in time for *Doctor Who*. She was so sure I'd forget all about it once I joined in the party games, but of course I was back sitting in front of the telly for the opening titles. Afterwards, exasperated, my mother asked, "Well, was that really worth leaving the party?" Apparently I looked at her and with total sincerity said, "Oh yes!"

I love the moment in *The Android Invasion* when Tom turns to Liz and, clutching a branch of a perfectly ordinary tree, says something like 'This isn't real wood, this isn't the real Earth, you're not the real Sarah!' One of the best special effects in the entire history of the show and we did it all with our imaginations.

The soldier walking with the gas-masked pony in *The Deadly Assassin*. All of the dialogue in *The Robots of Death*, but particularly "Oh I thought it was a rhetorical question, yes it's just a coincidence" and how D84 fails the Turing Test by repeating "I heard a cry" ("that was me!").

Tom's dark mood in *Horror of Fang Rock*. Petulantly demanding a holiday in *The Androids of Tara*. The reason he works out that the White Guardian is actually the Black Guardian in *The Armageddon Factor*.

*City of Death*; I love these four episodes of *Doctor Who* more than I've loved some of my boyfriends. The dialogue sings: "You're a beautiful woman, probably", "No one could be as stupid as he seems" and on and on and on. The bit at the end on the Eiffel Tower, the art critics watching the TARDIS dematerialise, the most important punch in history.

The Doctor's dismissal of Tryst at the end of *Nightmare of Eden*, "Go away, just go away." The whole atmosphere of *Logopolis*, the show already mourning its coming loss. And the opening lines to the novelisation.

"You can't mend people!" in *Kinda*. The story's bonkers and I've no idea what it means but it's got so much confidence and such great characters that I don't really care. Davison's heroism in *The Caves of Androzani*, the adultness of Jek's desires for Peri, and the way the whole story feels like it's sitting on a tinderbox, which of course it is.

Going back as an adult and discovering the black and white stories. The brilliant mystery of Susan Foreman in the very first episode. The service-with-a-smile Daleks in *The Power of the Daleks*; how brilliant an idea for a story is that? The chilling villains I've only glimpsed in the telesnaps of *Fury from the Deep*. The imaginative leaps of *The Mind Robber* and the epic ending of *The War Games*.

Discovering the New Adventures in my twenties. Paul Cornell's *Timewyrm: Revelation* was the first *Doctor Who* story that felt like it was written by someone of my generation and referenced my life (The Cure, gay rights). It also made me want to write.

I love that Russell T Davies brought *Doctor Who* back for girls as well as boys. The genius decision to make emotions as much a part of *Doctor Who* as the monsters. The wondrous leaps of imagination. A hospital on the moon! The *Titanic* as a spaceship! And, best of all, Martha as Tinkerbell, do you believe in the Doctor? The wit and razor-sharp plotting of *Blink*; "It's the same rain." Boy am I looking forward to Series Five! And I love that a whole new generation of children, including my nieces, are getting to have "their Doctor" with Eccleston, Tennant or Smith, just as I did with Tom.

Sarah hugging the Brig goodbye in *Enemy of the Bane* brings a lump to my throat. These fictional characters have been having adventures together for over thirty-five years – and they're only the supporting cast!

Most of all, I love the indestructible nature of *Doctor Who*. The format just refuses to die. And surely it has to be its lack of cynicism and its optimism that we seem unable to live without? A hero who travels in time and space in a battered, blue police box. A man who never carries a gun, who loves his friends but cares as much for his enemies, who is never cruel or cowardly, and – whilst frequently caught up in violent events – is a man of peace.

*Doctor Who*'s a bit like boys. I mean, I just really, really love it.

# FOREWORD

One of the great debates we had in formulating this collection was not the title but the subtitle: "The Doctor Who Fanzine Archive". Truth to tell, it doesn't quite fit: a good chunk of Lance Parkin's work in Volume 1 was material taken from novel pitches and a blog, which aren't quite within the mandate of fanzine reprinting. In this volume, Volume 2 (and in Volumes 3 and 4 coming up), we not only reprint online material but quite a number of essays were specially commissioned for these books.

Of course, that also begs the question: just what is a fanzine?

There have been science-fiction fanzines (fan magazines) since the 1930s. The first known *Doctor Who* fanzine – a newsletter of the fledgling Doctor Who (William Hartnell) Fan Club – was published in 1965, but the *Doctor Who* fanzine really came into its own in the late 1970s and early 1980s. Nowadays, we think of fanzines as a place for discussion of ideas. But if you look back at the fanzines of the early 1980s (and zines outside Britain well into that decade), there's an overwhelming sense of lost opportunity for future generations. At the time, the fanzine served the same function as websites like Outpost Gallifrey (and its successor, Gallifrey Base): to disseminate *Doctor Who* news. Which makes sense, but it's retrospectively disappointing. Here was a time when they had a TV series actually on the air – something fans in the 1990s could only dream about – and yet they filled pages upon pages primarily with news, interviews, profiles, lists and newspaper clippings. Some of this is deathly dull, while some of it is fascinating. The obituaries in particular make for sobering reading, as they come thick and fast, each more devastating than the previous one. Ian Marter. Robert Holmes. Patrick Troughton.

As the 1980s progressed, however, another strain of fanzine was being created. Something irreverent, thoughtful, anarchic. These were mostly British zines produced by fans who came of age as *Doctor Who* reached its apogee of popularity with the British public and stuck around for the decline. Virgin Publishing's *Licence Denied*, edited by Paul Cornell in 1997, documents these fanzines, produced by a generation of fans as they grew into actual writers, because it was no longer good enough just to be journalists. Articles became deeper and more thoughtful, in turn inspiring other fan writers to strengthen and justify their arguments, and build a case for their theories. This trend gradually became more global. As the

1980s ended, there was less and less *Doctor Who* to report about: first there were reduced seasons and then there was no *Doctor Who* at all. The 1990s, as a result, saw the rise of the fan as writer – and not just because this was the decade that saw many fans writing novels, television and movies. In the absence of a television program, *Doctor Who* fans looked for thoughtfulness, critique and strength of argument instead of the latest on-set gossip.

The rise of the internet could have killed the fanzine entirely – and almost did. The sort of rush a fanzine used to provide of facilitating discussions between fans over a several-month-long conversation about *Doctor Who* through several issues of letter columns can now be fulfilled instantaneously by posting to *The Doctor Who Forum*. And yet, the fanzine still survives. Far, far fewer in number – but it still holds its own in this online age. In many ways, the internet actually saw the quality of the fanzine flourish. There's a simple reason for this: while the latest news or press clippings or interviews with the stars could all be found online, what the online world found so difficult was reasoned and thoughtful opinion. The internet was built for knee-jerk responses or instant reactions, but it couldn't compete with the power of enlightened, long-form writing, best served in print.

The collection that you are reading celebrates the best of this tradition. It is not a "pure" fanzine reprint collection, but it seeks to at least emulate the spirit of fanzines by printing (and reprinting) the diversity of the thoughts and opinions of *Doctor Who* fans.

Functionally, we see these collections as the literary successor to *Licence Denied*. Thus, for the most part, we have tried not to tread on that volume's ground, which covered late 80s and early-to-mid 90s British fanzines. We have instead concentrated on fan writings in zines from the 1990s onward – though we do make a few notable digressions from this, such as Jan Vincent-Rudski's sequel to his infamous *Deadly Assassin* review (which appeared in *Licence Denied*).

One weakness in *Licence Denied*, which Paul Cornell acknowledged at the time, was that it avoided looking outside of British zines. Perhaps inspired by this, throughout the 1990s and 2000s, the creative, thoughtful tradition begun by British *Doctor Who* fanzines has been kept alive by zines outside Great Britain. As a result, a little more than half our contributions and contributors are from Australia, Canada and the United States. We think this only emphasises the important truth that *Doctor Who* is a British program but a global phenomenon.

There are some things we have left out. The Doctor Who Appreciation Society, the progenitor of all *Doctor Who* fan clubs, has published a number of zines since its formation in 1976, but DWAS has its own avenues for publishing and for the most part we've left it to them. Outside the UK, one of the most influential zines published over the past twenty years is *TSV* (*Time-Space Visualiser*), the fanzine of the New Zealand Doctor Who Fan Club, but it's hoped that *TSV* will get a future volume of *Time, Unincorporated* all to itself. The same is true for *Matrix*, which was one of the best fanzines in Britain in the mid-to-late 1990s. Meanwhile, mundane concerns like copyright have forced us to avoid all the fiction zines – which is a shame, as so many people currently working on *Doctor Who* began by writing adventures of the Doctor in those fanzines.

Like *Licence Denied*, we have divided this volume into thematic sections. These sections are only loose containers; with the diversity of thought, how could it be anything else? Unlike *Licence Denied*, we offered authors the chance to edit or rewrite their original articles. Aside from a few minor corrections, surprisingly few of them took us up on it, most preferring to let the work stand as it was. However, a few of the republished articles have been expanded and all have been tweaked for style.

This volume you are holding, Volume 2, was produced under the overall theme of "Backwards In Time". Our focus has been essays about what we now call the "classic series" of *Doctor Who*, or what aired between 1963-1989 (and for a night in May 1996). These essays have been written in fanzines from 1978 to the present day or were specially commissioned for this volume by the editors. Volume 3, "Forwards In Time", will feature fan writing about the new series and its spinoffs, while Volume 4, "Sideways In Time", will feature fan writing about the universe of *Doctor Who* (including non-televised versions of *Doctor Who*).

Once, during a radio interview, a reporter suggested to Tom Baker that *Doctor Who* fans were "not ordinary people". To which Tom replied, "No. *Doctor Who* fans aren't ordinary people. Ordinary people grow tired, they grow disenchanted with the things they love. *Doctor Who* fans are superior. They never stop loving."

We think this volume demonstrates this boldly and vividly. Enjoy.

# BEGINNINGS

Beginnings are important in *Doctor Who*. Except, of course, for when they are not.

On one level, beginnings are important in *Doctor Who*. Who could ever forget the sight of gas-masked soldiers being mown down in the fog in *Genesis of the Daleks*? The last of the Jagaroth attempting – and failing – to launch his ship in *City of Death*? The TARDIS opening its doors to the petrified jungle of the dead planet in *The Daleks*? The start of a *Doctor Who* story – suffused with mystery, wonder and jeopardy – is often the best part.

Terrance Dicks knew this. That's why often the best lines of his *Doctor Who* novelisations were the first ones: "Through the ruin of a city stalked a ruin of a man" (*Doctor Who and the Dalek Invasion of Earth*). "It was a place of ancient evil" (*The Five Doctors*).

And yet, on a much grander scale, beginnings aren't important to *Doctor Who* at all. Where does the story of *Doctor Who* start? Leaving aside the four versions that exist of how the Doctor and Susan met Ian and Barbara (between the pilot and broadcast versions of the first TV episode, *Doctor Who in an Exciting Adventure with the Daleks* by David Whitaker and Terrance Dicks' *An Unearthly Child* novelisation – and that's ignoring the Peter Cushing film *Dr Who and the Daleks*), the ongoing saga of the Doctor begins *in medias res*: in the middle. No secret origin, no backstory, just an old man and a time / space machine bigger on the inside than out. (The new series takes it one step further by introducing the Doctor midway through an off-screen adventure fighting the Nestene.)

It's no surprise, given the propensity for American TV adaptations to provide an origin story that just about every attempt at an American TV pilot for *Doctor Who* wanted to put the Doctor's backstory on the big screen. But that misses the point: *Doctor Who* is rarely about the why or (in spite of the title) the who: it's about the what and the where and the how. (The when is incidental.)

As fans, we would like to think there are traceable beginnings for *Doctor Who* behind the mythos and in the making of the television program. No television series has ever had more scrutiny given to its creation and early years as *Doctor Who* – to the point where some fans insist on using story titles only used in internal BBC paperwork. But, even then, tracing the beginning of *Doctor Who* is not so easy to pin down. *Doctor Who* wasn't dreamed up by one man on a sleepless summer's night the same way Jerry Siegel dreamed up Superman. *Doctor Who* was one of the biggest flukes in broadcasting history: created by committee, born out of an internal BBC study on science fiction, shepherded into production by a maverick Canadian, written into an outline by a man called "Bunny" and then produced by a woman who fought internal indifference to get the show made. And even that misses out the incredible nuances, like how that maverick Canadian's work in Canada influenced him, or how radical a TV series the first Doctor's era was, or how little regarded the Patrick Troughton tenure as the Doctor actually was.

*Doctor Who* teaches us that beginnings are not simple and are often elusive. For most fans, the one place where *Doctor Who* truly begins – and we can see this in the eyes of children and adults even today – is the moment when a continuity announcer says...

"And now... *Doctor Who*."

# My Adventures

**by Paul Magrs**
*From Time and Relative Dissertations in Space, 2007*

My best friend moved away from our street. His dad worked with mine; both were policemen. They kept in touch. My best friend's family hadn't moved all that far away. Just across town. Darlington's suburbs, where the tall houses turned into bungalows and the town itself gradually thinned out into farmland; into gentle hills of churned-up mud and brilliant yellow and green.

They thought a lot of themselves, living out by the countryside. I was six, but well aware of the ripples and currents of bragging and condescension all that afternoon of our visit. (They had an avocado bathroom suite! A downstairs loo!) The purpose of our visiting was so we could see how settled in they were, and to let us boys see each other again, because we'd been such good friends, hadn't we? Back in that busy, noisy street in the middle of town, where we still lived.

My friend's name was Tom. He had a younger, toddler brother, same as I had. Tom was keen that we went to look at the den they had made in their new back garden. We could see it from their kitchen window. The windows (double-glazed! It was evidently a far more up-to-the-minute police house than ours!) were all silvery and dripping with rain. It teemed down all that Saturday afternoon. We stared out, waiting for a gap in the weather: ready to dash out, to examine that clump of trees at the back. The heaped branches and twigs; the sheets of cardboard; the bits of old carpet that Tom had lumped together and called a den. I wasn't all that impressed by it.

I think we went out. I think we had a desultory poke around, looking at the camp he had built. I think the skies opened and I think we got soaked. And, of course, that didn't matter to us. Not to us. There's only so wet you can get, isn't there? After that, it doesn't count. And we loved getting soaked and standing under all that dripping, shivering greenery: listening to the bronchial roar of thunder approaching from the north.

"It's better than the den we used to have, isn't it? On the wasteground? It's better than the one before. Cause – look – this one is mine. It's in our garden. So it's all mine. It belongs to me."

Tom was really showing off. He was really keen on having his den, and all his adventures, right in his own backyard.

Someone (my dad, his mam, my mam, his dad, one of the adults who'd grown bored of chatting with the others) had drifted to the window, and seen us standing there, dripping in the rain, clothes growing heavier and heavier, pudding-bowl hair plastered down to our skulls.

"What on earth are you doing out there...?"

They couldn't believe it. They called us in. We'd catch our deaths, otherwise.

It was teatime. Cake and chocolate biscuits in silver wrappers, set out in geometric designs on plates and doilies. Petals of Kit Kats, Blue Ribands and Penguins. (Tom's mam trying hard to impress her first Saturday teatime guests in her new house. Putting on – as we used to say – a good spread.) Bird's Eye trifle standing at the ready, chilling in the fridge. And, with clean towels rubbed through our hair, we were made to sit quiet on the intricately and verdantly patterned living-room carpet and watch the telly.

*Doctor Who* was coming back on. The start of a new series. It was that time of year again. We would have to be quiet and watch. Give the grown-ups some peace. This was what kids like us liked to watch, wasn't it? The grown-ups all started talking about watching this programme back when they were kids, when everything was black and white, when it was all very frightening and he was an old man then, but he was much younger now, wasn't he? With those boggling eyes and that mad scarf.

I could just about remember some of last year's adventures. They came from prehistory, from winter teatimes when I was five. They came back in lurid, hallucinatory glimpses. Back then I'd been parked in front of the telly: Watch this! There's Daleks in it this week! And I remembered dank caverns dripping gold; brilliant white rooms in outer space; Daleks painted greeny blue with flashing eyes; that withered-up man in the wheelchair shouting; the potato-faced troll with his head deflating like a burst football. I remembered my dad on a rare weekend home from police-training courses, watching this with us, and him laughing aloud at the monster's squashed face – and all of us joining in with the laughter. Deflating the horror. Making it funny again.

I wasn't sure I wanted to watch this programme now.

But this was a visit. You had to be polite. You had to do what everyone else wanted to do. And this wasn't like visiting grandparents. You couldn't kick up a fuss. These were friends-of-the-family, near-strangers now in their new, big house in the suburbs with its avocado suite. You had to behave, and sit quietly on their junglelike, swirling green and brown carpet. You had to watch the tumbling blue of the time tunnel and remember that howling, thundery theme tune. You had to watch these monsters, that looked bloody and babylike, dripping with slime and baked-bean juice, living under a lake and keeping dinosaurs as pets. Hissing angrily at each other and sucking out people's minds.

You had to watch it all, and it was fantastic.

And after that...

Every den you ever built had to be the monsters' secret base, or the villain's deadly lair. Or the interior of the Doctor's marvellous TARDIS, with its six-sided console and hatstand for slinging your hat and scarf onto.

And every game you ever played when you played out – no matter who you played with – was always *Doctor Who*. The other kids were companions, villains, monsters. Your brother was always a robot dog.

And every story you ever wrote. That was always *Doctor Who*, as well. At home, unashamedly so. You turned out tales too broad, too deep, too ludicrous for the small screen. And these stories were so exciting you couldn't even bring yourself to finish them off. Those adventures went on and on and on. They were the adventures in which the Daleks and the Cybermen and the Zygons all invaded Gallifrey and Victorian London and prehistoric Earth, and they set about attacking the Silurians and Sea Devils and Dinosaurs and Time Lords and Sherlock Holmes and Queen Victoria and EVERYONE! And all the Marvel superheroes and Planet of the Apes and Dracula somehow became involved. The Fantastic Four declared war on the Cybermen, and Galactus – much to the chagrin of Davros (who had teamed up with Dracula to breed vampire Daleks!) – was threatening to liquidate Skaro. On and on and on and on and on, and you were drawing all the pictures, too.

And all the stories you ever wrote at school, they were *Doctor Who*, too. When your class read *The Hobbit*, the Daleks invaded Middle Earth and that was the end of that. When you fell in love with *The Lion, the Witch and the Wardrobe*, the Master joined forces with the wicked queen of winter and the Doctor was called for by Aslan, and his various incarnations were sprinkled in time throughout Narnia's long centuries. And then your teachers were telling you to stop, stop, stop! They told your parents you were a mite obsessed. Well, quite a bit obsessed. In fact, far too obsessed. You had to be stopped. You couldn't have time machines and monsters in every story you wrote. You should try to make up stories for characters of your own. You shouldn't allow your own characters to simply escape from the confines of their lives by stepping aboard a battered blue Police Box and travelling elsewhere. Your characters should stay at home and learn about real life. It didn't do – it really didn't do at all – to be so obsessed with something as silly as *Doctor Who*.

*

The point of this essay isn't to suddenly go: How wrong they were! Hahahahaha!

I think the point of it might actually turn out to be... They were right! They should have stopped him! They should have stopped him watching it! And reading all the books again and again! And having posters on his walls! And talking Daleks and model Tom Bakers and Top Trumps cards and Weetabix collectible stand-up figures! And buying *Doctor Who Weekly* on its first day of publication! And begging, begging, begging for day trips to Blackpool to visit that subterranean, sepulchral holy of holies: the Doctor Who Exhibition! Shabby old costumes and props standing in cupboards with multi-coloured lights flashing round them! Brilliant! Buying LOADS of merchandise and feeling dizzy and sick with candyfloss and excitement. All of it, all of it, far too exciting! Thrilled with your own knowledge and expertise in the *Doctor Who* universe... and what a vocabulary it gave you. Capacious! Voluminous! Dimensionally transcendental! Neutron flow! Vortex! War of attrition! Serendipity!

Yes! Stop him now! Go back in time and prevent it ever happening! They were right! It was true!

He did ruin his life!

*

"The whole wide world doesn't revolve around *Doctor Who*, you know. You might think it does. But it doesn't. You should get out more. Broaden your horizons."

Oh dear. I got this again and again. Mam would get exasperated with me. And with my brother, too. We were both obsessed.

The high point of it all – and the most exasperating period for everyone around us – was probably between 1980 and 1985.

In 1980, there was a collision of things that made sure that we became completely obsessed. First, there was the start of *Doctor Who Weekly*, and then there was our discovery of the Target novelisations.

We bought both from Stevens, a narrow, rather dark newsagent in our town centre. The old, good type of newsagent that sold cheap toys and novelties and the more arcane kinds of sweets. The comic cost 12p and gave these alluring glimpses of the creatures and characters inhabiting the mass unconscious of the recent past: the Zarbi, the Yeti and the giant maggots with gnashing jaws. We had never seen these beings in – as it were – the flesh, but our parents had. They stirred up the old ancestral memories.

The novels, too, made available to us in lucid, concise prose, all those adventures that occurred in the Doctor's life before we were even born. At that point, Target novels cost 75p. It all started off when my brother discovered the recently published *Doctor Who and the Destiny of the Daleks* and determined to buy it for me for Christmas. He needed to borrow 15p from me in order to do so. (I think he actually wanted it for himself, as much as he wanted to buy it for me. But that's how it always was: we shared this stuff. That was important. *Doctor Who* was the region in time and space where sibling rivalry didn't exist.) Mark stood there, hiding the slim paperback behind his back: hand out, palm up, waiting for change.

After that: no stopping us. Each weekend, we frequented WH Smiths in Darlington, Clarkes in Durham. And we discovered quite how many *Doctor Who* books there were. A tiny fraction, of course, of how many there now are, but at the time it was a dizzying profusion of brightly coloured covers. We couldn't buy them all immediately, but we were making a good start on building a collection. (*Doctor Who* fans love having collections.)

Newton Aycliffe town library helped, too. It was very modern and glass-walled. A tiny place, really. They seemed to have one whole wall of hardbacked WH Allen *Doctor Who* novelisations. Covered in sticky-backed plastic, their spines opening with that satisfyingly fresh cracking noise. They were under the "D" section in the library, making it the widest letter in the fiction alphabet: D for Dicks and *Doctor Who*.

There were so many you needed never to read anything else, other than *Doctor Who*. You went back and reread favourites. Rather like kids do nowadays, with Harry Potter.

You read the Dalek stories first. Then the ones featuring other recognisable monsters (Ice Warriors, Cybermen, troll-faced Sontarans) and then you read the ones that seemed to have humanoid enemies and often, more complicated plots. Last of all, you read the historical adventures. Only later, in the eighties, would you turn to those, and fancy yourself a bit literary and intellectual for seeing the merit in these tales: the ones in which people dressed extravagantly, bellowed in archaic tongues and drew swords on each other.

The advent of the fifth Doctor on TV kept us hooked, too. This was our Doctor. He could belong to us in a way that Tom Baker never did, though we wanted him to. Tom was doing that typical actor's trick – leaving a role we loved him for – and turning his back on our love. He even looked massively depressed and hungover in his last few autumnal, then wintry stories... Tom was being an actor and an artist and looking for new challenges. He was doing what actors always do and "returning to the stage". A couple of years later we felt betrayed all over again by him, when he failed to return for *The Five Doctors*. He was really rubbing our noses in it. He had left it all behind. He had learned to grow up. Why couldn't we? Tom had gone off to find art and life and fulfillment. There'd be no more messing about in Police Boxes, running up and down corridors and laughing in the faces of ludicrous space villains. He had outgrown all that stuff.

By the time Peter Davison was in, I was twelve. He was playing it straight. A real character: a believable, bewildered hero, one that was occasionally miffed at a perplexing universe. As I say, he belonged to us. Even if his stories did seem bereft of some of the more thrillingly schlocky moments of *Doctor Who* madness. Even if some of his more SF-type stories didn't make a lot of sense... We still loved it all.

And we kept on loving it, tenaciously, throughout the eighties, and then the nineties, as things got pretty rocky and strange.

Tenacity is another quality the fans of *Doctor Who* always have.

*

But, if I'm asked, these days, why I have written *Doctor Who* stories, novels, scripts, in amongst my more "mainstream" efforts, my more "literary" output, I end up saying that I write these things because I have always written them. I've always been right in the middle of *Doctor Who*: as viewer and reader and writer.

Another very good reason I give is that *Doctor Who* is the longest piece of continuous prose narrative featuring one ongoing character.

In the world. Ever.

And something like that... well, you've got to be involved in it, haven't you? As a writer, you've just got to stick your oar in.

I'm talking here not about the TV series, the audios, comic strips, anything else. Just words on the page. The fiction. The novels, beginning with David Whitaker's deliriously wonderful John Wyndham / Edgar Rice Burroughs pastiche, *Doctor Who in an Exciting Adventure with the Daleks*, through the Targets, the Virgins, the BBC books, up to the very present day and beyond.

Seriously. The longest story in the world. Longer and more outrageously complex than any other story cycle in any culture. *Doctor Who* keeps the same lead character: the stories don't fritter off into arabesques like the *One Thousand and One Nights*, or into portmanteau form like the *Decameron*. The Doctor is always the Doctor, with a cumulative and capacious memory of all his adventures. All of this stuff has all happened to him: to all of him. His are regenerations – not reincarnations or reinventions. He is always he.

So, although Batman, Robin Hood, or Sherlock Holmes might be said to rival him in volume of text and story, these are characters for whom the "reset" button has been hit countless times. Those characters don't carry their baggage like the Doctor does.

\*

As a kid, one of the most alluring things about *Doctor Who* was the gaps. Bits of it were missing.

I was too young to have watched and read from the very beginning. There was always a glamorous, strange and grainy prehistory going on before. The Target books and *Doctor Who Weekly* let you know tantalising bits of what you had missed. And you were also aware that actual episodes were missing from the BBC archives. They'd trashed them! They'd burned and frittered away the only master copies! Those elusive spools of film had been sucked right through a gap in the Very Fabric of Time and Space!

So... this is important: *Doctor Who* is never complete.

It is about a lack. A need. A hunger.

And it is unending. There's that old cliché about the elasticity and infinitude of its format. Which is kind-of true, but it's truer that its consumers don't half enjoy repetition and recurrent patterns.

Like the Arabian Nights. Arabesques of infinite variety. Fulfilment of the design being infinitely deferred. Stories opening out into other, further stories... The nights of prevarication and story-telling go on and on and on. Just as the Doctor always finds a new companion, a new incarnation, a new adventure to have.

But, as we go on, the audience, the reader, the fan-consumer is always aware that we are missing something. We all always vaguely remember that there was an old Doctor. Now he's long gone. And there were others before him. They are in our memories like family members who died or who went abroad when we were small. And one day, maybe, they will come back...

Oooh, Lacunae! Absences! Gaps! Let's get all Lacanian.

Or not. But I am sure that my sense, as a kid, of the endlessness of the *Doctor Who* narrative, and perceiving the gaps and holes in its fabric, were what set me off wanting to contribute to it. (This is why the ridiculously long, multi-coloured scarf was a beautiful, perfect object for the Doctor to wear. It's a metaphor for the storyline itself.)

I think others have the same response. The show requires a response. It invites us to contribute. Somehow.

Some of the fans want to complete the narrative. They construct continuity guides and canons. They want to plug the gaps. The completist wants to collect, restore, arbitrate on hefty canonical debates. They catalogue things, rather like Time Lords.

No, my impulse is always to further complicate matters.

The idea of "completism" terrifies me. What happens when it's all complete? What goes on then? Where do you go? It sounds a bit dull to me. (Remember when the Doctor eventually got to the Eye of Orion? His much-vaunted "most peaceful place in the universe"? It was rubbish. It was boring and you could tell he was only pretending to enjoy it. It was wet and there was sheep shit everywhere.)

*

Is it just me? – I doubt it – thinking: This is the last time I'll write for *Doctor Who*. No more audios. No more stories. Doesn't matter who asks. And then I've pulled back and recanted and gone into it all over again. Why? Why can't you leave it alone?

If you want to write the last word – your last word – on *Doctor Who*, well, then it might as well be your last word on your own childhood.

So you are drawn back again and again. Timescooped. As last words go, they're inexhaustible.

It's actually very hard work writing *Doctor Who*. You don't want to let anyone down. You don't want to let yourself down. There's so much to say. You feel very complicated about it. You feel silly about it. And you still feel caught up in it. At least, in a universe of your own, no one really cares if you bugger it all up.

*

There are various metaphors that persist, to do with the writing of fiction related to the "*Doctor Who* Universe". Often, these metaphors evoke the toys and games of childhood. Authors refer to "playing in the sandpit" or "playing with someone else's Lego".

The gist of these metaphors – often used by authors in interviews, introductions to novels, or web-based discussion groups – is usually that the author is saying that it's a pleasure and an honour to be allowed and sanctioned to play with toys that don't really belong to them. With toys that they feel are the best in the world. They have actually been allowed to lay their hands on them... at last.

"At last! At LAAASSST!"

Like any deluded super-villain – any Mehendri Solon or Magnus Greel – with their devilish fulfilment in sight, the fan-turned-professional writer of *Doctor Who* stories can hardly believe his or her luck.

The metaphors are infantilising precisely because of this. This is wish-fulfilment stuff. This is taking part in the *Doctor Who* universe.

It is literally true, of course, that the writer has been permitted to enter this universe. Or, in the case of fan fiction, not permitted, but perhaps tolerated. Permission is granted or withheld and is of import because we are talking about writing copyrighted characters, situations and concepts. Characters and concepts that belong to someone else. They belong – legally and literally – to a grand corporation. In every other way, of course, they belong to a huge, global and transhistorical audience. And it is they who, through endless tale-spinning in one form or another, have kept the story going.

It is a very odd business, this stepping-into the *Doctor Who* universe in order to write. To give these characters adventures and to put words in their mouths. Words and deeds they didn't actually say or do first time around. (Do opera buffs dream about penning sequels to their faves? Do Dickensians busy about knocking off prequels or alternate-universe versions of *Great Expectations*? Do Jane Austen freaks want to dwell in her world and invent more men and more balls and more frou-frou shenanigans? Ah yes, they do. They have done! Like the Holmesians, the Trekkers! Like any driven fans. Fans, it seems, like to produce. To respond. To get carried away and eventually turn professional.)

*Doctor Who* fans are notorious for knowing everything about the mythos, backstory, history, development and trivia to do with the show. Any serious discussion of the ongoing narrative of *Doctor Who* has, at some point, to get itself into laborious questions of canonicity, authenticity, apocrypha.

If you watch and read *Doctor Who*, you are already very used to the idea of alternate timelines, divergent realities, side-steps and missing adventures. Contrasting and contradictory narratives proliferate and abound – even from the start of the series. (Look at how *An Unearthly Child* differs from its pilot, from the first Peter Cushing film, from the David Whitaker novelisation, from the Terrance Dicks novelisation.) Not even the ostensible "beginning" is stable and fixed.

So... participants in this ongoing narrative have tacitly agreed that new, hitherto untold stories can "take place" between already known tales. Rather than taking a well-earned break between dashing off the end of *The Key to Time* saga, and arriving on the blasted surface of Skaro to meet the Daleks and Davros once more, the fourth Doctor and Romana could actually have had a whole load more adventures. We just didn't get to see them at the time. Hurray!

A whole spate of other fandangos, debacles and farragos might have occurred in that interstitial gap. And still could!

Maybe the winter of 1979 just went on and on and on... forever.

This came about partly as a result of the show's TV hiatus, between 1989 and 2005. Novels, stories, audios, comic strips and a TV movie flooded in to fill those gaps. To fill any gap. But only because this stuff had already and always happened with *Doctor Who*. We were used to the proliferating canonicities and the variant versions. We all wanted a universe – surely? – where the fourth Doctor could be having the TV adventure *City of Death* and the marvellous comic strip story *The Iron Legion* at precisely the same time. I know I did. And I didn't see it as a problem of quantum whatsits, or a continuity problem of theological proportions. I just saw it as fun! More stories! More adventures! Hurray!

It has become the job of the *Doctor Who* writer to weigh in there and to invent the missing hours, days, years. Those in the past, and those in the future.

Time is necessarily elastic to the *Doctor Who* writer. We have the TARDIS, naturally, and the whole panoply of time-travel technology and dimension-bending storytelling tropes available to us – in order to stretch time; to make it endless; to mash it up; to pull it apart. To do all kinds of mad stuff to it... simply in order to write our very own *Doctor Who* stories.

This is what we have been doing. For years, some of us!

And I used to tell myself very grand theories, to do with British SF and post-post New Wave SF, and magical realism and Queer Realism and all sorts of literary critical and theoretical nonsense... in order to justify messing around with this stuff.

But maybe the answer and the real reason is that by playing with these tropes and this Lego, and by learning to stretch time and credibility and canonicity like this... we are all finding out how to revisit our childhoods. We are finding out how to travel in time.

Perhaps the answer is as easy as that.

Tom Baker said something along those lines in a recent interview. What's wrong with being a fan of anything, if it makes you happy and doesn't hurt anyone else? And it makes you happy because it reminds you – strongly and viscerally – of a time in the past when you were happy. Returning to it, again and again, obsessively, creatively – whatever it is – seems to make you happy still.

*

This whole essay seems to be as if in reply to the question: "Why on earth do you want to write this *Doctor Who* stuff anyway?" At times, people have asked me this incredulously, as if involving myself in this universe was a way of deliberately sabotaging my literary reputation. (I've tried pointing out "respectable" precedents: Kingsley Amis wrote James Bond! Doris Lessing wrote science fiction! Ah yes, comes the solemn, literary reply: but she wrote very serious science fiction. Nothing about gun-toting poodles.)

Anyway. My answer is that, if you were that kind of kid, in that particular time and country – Britain in the seventies – you can't imagine not wanting to write *Doctor Who* stories in later life.

I found my 1982 diary in 1998. We were moving into our new house in Norwich and I had been lecturing at the University of East Anglia for a year by then. For the first time, I had my crates and crates of books together. For the first time, I was reunited with all my very many capacious and voluminous diaries. 1982 was the earliest surviving record of what I was up to on this planet on a day-to-day, mundane basis. And guess what? My days at the age of twelve were much the same as when I was twenty-eight. I was writing my roman-a-clef in the morning, dealing with correspondence from publishers at lunchtime, and writing my *Doctor Who* novel in the afternoon. At twelve and twenty-eight and every year between! And since!

That afternoon in 1998, sitting on the chintz in our lovely new house, I didn't know whether to feel foolish, or relieved and reassured.

In the end, I found those continuities immensely satisfying and consoling. It made me feel like I was writing *Doctor Who* stories – at twelve and twenty-eight – in order to make the world around me familiar and safe. I was writing in order to organise, reshape and reinvent my world and my imagination. 1998 was the year I finished writing my first published *Doctor Who* novel. *The Scarlet Empress* is such a long book – a romping, ridiculous, well-nigh plotless road movie. And I was writing it through a very disorienting year when I moved cities and jobs, and there was a lot of drama and brouhaha amongst family and friends. It was a terrible time!

But writing *The Scarlet Empress* dragged me through it. Getting on the red double decker bus that was meandering through the perplexing deserts of Hyspero. Trying to make magic and sorcery and outrageous camp work in a *Doctor Who* context.

I was taking it all very personally, as I have – I hope – all the *Doctor Who* stuff I've done since.

*

I had never heard the delicious term "Fanwank" until I started looking at the reviews and discussions of *Doctor Who* books and audios on the internet. I was delighted and amazed by the extent and the sophistication of the discussions, and I loved the term, which seemed, more often than not, to be levelled at the material produced for the marketplace by so-called "professional fans" or, rather, "fan-professionals".

"Fanwank" sounded naughty and silly but, as I read on, deeper and deeper into the world wide web, I started to gather that it was a phenomenon to be avoided – by both writer and discerning fan. Some writers were being routinely dismissed and even castigated for being "too fan-wanky".

But what did it mean?

I had to find out.

It seemed to be part of my job. I'd unearthed a method of literary critique I felt sure was unknown to the mainstream. "Fanwanking" or "fan-wankery" was something I needed to investigate, as part of the ongoing and wayward exploration of writing in all its forms that I seem to have devoted myself to. I love all forms of writing, but I especially love the fictional languages and forms that exist around us in our present day and age. It seems to me that fiction is everywhere: transmitted through airwaves and buzzing through cables underfoot; downloaded in stupendously huge text files; lent and borrowed from libraries in millions of cities... the print large and black on the yellowing pages; large enough to be read by myopic story junkies like me. Fiction is everywhere: cheaper, freer and less contaminated than either our water or air.

It is my job – as this writer / critic / reader / teacher thing I have made myself into – to pull and tease at these floating strands of fiction, and to ravel them up. I explore where they come from, and where they're going to. It's my role to become aware of and be fascinated by new mutations and innovations and departures.

And so, I love things like genre fiction, franchise fiction, spinoffs, fan fiction, slash fiction and even "fanwankery". These tales and texts seem to spread robustly like wild flowers between paving slabs; disrupting continuities and copyrights as they proliferate (just as, apparently, the common weed can crack pavements and tarmac in its humble tenacity).

Fankwankery and slash fiction alike have a saucy, masturbatory association, if not function. I'm sure people really do get off on reading and writing this stuff. And that's an important part of it. That's about writing fiction itself. Fiction *is* saucy and sexy. Whether these readers / writers are getting off on a Dalek / Cyber War, or a fifth Doctor / Turlough shag, I don't really care. To me, it all sounds wonderful. And, naturally, as a teenager, I was writing precisely those stories.

Still, I don't know why this "fanwankery" is despised by the fans at large. Perhaps because it's infantile. The kind of things you would write when you were fifteen. Not now, though. Not now that we're so mature and grown up and different. (Ah, but are you sure you're not secretly repressing that desire to witness a Dalek-Cyber War? A multi-Doc and old companion gangbang?)

Another reason people might despise this fiction that reveals the oddity of the fan mass-unconscious is that it is sometimes gloriously badly written.

But I love bad writing. Like some people collect garage paintings, art brut, naïve art, outsider art, I can't help picking up prime examples of bad writing – both amateur and professional. I mean good-old-fashioned, godawful, nasty, plain bad writing that doesn't even know how good it isn't. I love it.

I love the despised, the forgotten, the neglected. All of them touch my heart. Sometimes, there's more truth in the bad faith of our poor art than in the heightened and often false consciousness of that which we consider our best. Old paperbacks tossed into cardboard boxes at car boot sales, or on shelves in old charity shops... they make me itch to buy them up. They're like puppies in the pet shop. Looking doomed and smelling of wood pulp, pee and abandonment. There I was this afternoon, in a basement book exchange off Piccadilly in Manchester, weighing up *Bouquet of Barbed Wire*, *The Cylon Death Machine*, Alice Thomas Ellis' first novel and *Doctor Who and the Ribos Operation*. I had to gently talk myself out of blowing another whack of cash on another pile of tat.

As a writer and critic I am meant to – I am trained to – know the difference between what is good and bad. What is worthwhile and what isn't. What is usefully good and interesting, what is trashy and interesting, or just trashy and dull. It's a very nimble, sophisticated balance, I suppose, now that the Western Canon has been so successfully exploded. All we're left with is a rubble of old paperbacks – hurray!

I can always find something in the rubbish. Something worthwhile and adventurous, that makes me glad I saved this particular piece of writing from the brink.

Even the diabolical can be illuminating, is what I'm saying.

I feel much the same about my own writing. I find it all very hard work, but I gear myself up to do it by telling myself that it is an act of rescue. Of salvage and intervention. I tell myself: no one else will do this writing for you. Without you, it will never get done. And so, you are dooming these memories, ideas and images; you are damning these made-up adventures to nothingness, if you don't get them down on paper now.

They'll vanish! Into the Phantom Zone. Writing them down will make them real. At the least, it will give them the tiniest purchase on a chance of canonical existence...

It seems to me that Fanwank is the worst thing that the fan-consumers can think to call these latterday *Doctor Who* novels and audios. Because what they mean by that is: "Just like something I could have written. Something like I'd have written when I was ten. As crappy and as self-indulgent as that. Of course, I'd never do that now. Oh, no. I'm much more grown-up and discerning than that now..."

Such self-hatred.

They want the pros to be better than that. To resist the need for fan-wanking. To do it modestly and without overt-seeming relish or pleasure.

Ha! What's the point of writing modestly? Of writing without pleasure and relish?

It's a curious irony, I think, in a series with a rabble-rouser as a hero, and in a narrative about multiverses, alternities and possibilities, that the fans of this very show seem to want to close possibilities down. Sometimes, it's as if the fans want reality dictated to them – definitively. Canonically. They want parameters setting and concretising around them. Maybe they want a stable universe after all...

\*

And now?

I feel I need to apologise to all my friends, who have been dragged into the *Doctor Who* world with me. When I was growing up, they had to share my obsession for as long as our friendships lasted. I'll never forget the feeling of shame and betrayal from when I was thirteen, and Michael told me he'd grown out of *Doctor Who* at last. He took up body building and, as if to prove several points at once, ripped up all one hundred and twenty of his Target novelisations in his back yard. In front of me! And some of them I didn't even have!

My poor brother has never left the *Doctor Who* universe behind. He was too young to know about it, when I first wandered in.

And my poor friends who couldn't really care less about *Doctor Who*, and how they have to be interested and pleased when I give them copies of my *Doctor Who* books. And then they have to read them and become weirdly expert in the whole thing.

My family and friends are used to me going on as if all of it is real. Like it was when I was 10, 14, 21, 29...

This is just what novelists do. To a novelist, it's all very real.

Sometimes, I think I've found a way to believe it's all real, forever. And to remember precisely what it's like to be a kid.

If that means getting patronised en route, so be it. It's even happened in recent years. When *Buffy* Studies became all the rage in the Academy. Even then, *Doctor Who* could still be seen as a little bit freakish and odd by comparison.

But... no more!

I think we're at the start of *Doctor Who* Studies. And it really is about time.

I think it's to do with a freakish generation of talents growing up at the same time.

Salutations to Russell T Davies and the current cast and crew! You seem kind of respectable and legitimate!

*

I don't actually know if I have written what I set out to write.

But that's how I've always gone about this scribbling business. So yes, this essay is all shards and fragments. It consists of half-developed thoughts and mangled, discordant themes, with flashes of memories and ideas and inspirations crossing our meandering path here and there, seemingly at random.

Maybe it was *Doctor Who* itself that taught me to be wayward and brave like that. It seems important to brave out the sense of yourself. The untidy truth of yourself.

Maybe writing an essay *should* be like running through dark woods, batteries on your torch running out, fearful fiend treading hard behind you, screaming at the top of your voice...

I always liked it in stories when the Doctor created some kind of device: knocking together a load of disparate items: electronic circuitry and miscellaneous junk. They were always called "unstable-looking lash-ups" in the books.

He created these machines – these lash-ups – to defy science and logic. He switched them on and they lit up and juddered and shook. They made an unholy racket and out shot blue sparks. But... in the very last instant they would go and do something miraculous.

*Doctor Who* taught you to disobey rules. To knock together devices that would be like artworks, like pieces of statuary, rather than usable machines. It taught you to brave out the stares. Taught you to be proud of seeming, looking, sounding eccentric.

So – my writing career has been just like this. Writing just as me. Even in academic essays. It's important that my stories, essays, whatever, don't feel or sound or get shaped like anyone else's.

Well. There's next to no chance that that could happen. I've tried to shoehorn my work into other people's shapes in the past. It doesn't work. For some people it does. Not me.

So... this isn't a very tidy essay.

It's a lash-up. And here I come, running into the control room, skidding on the metallic floor in the last, fraught seconds of this adventure. As the countdown to deadly danger creeps closer to the end, here I come, with coat-tails and scarf ends flapping, dragging all my bits and pieces of tatty junk with me. I've got one huge armload of ideas and associations, and I'm ready to fling them all down, right here, in the madly fervent hope that these components will fall happily into the shape of something worthwhile. A device which – if it doesn't save the day and all our necks – will at least take us all somewhere else; somewhere unexpected, familiar, fun.

# An Old Man in Strange Skins

**by Robbie Langdon**

*From Shockeye's Kitchen #17, Spring 2006*

*Editors' Note: sadly, Robbie passed away at a* Doctor Who *fan gathering mere days before we could contact him about including this article in this collection. Robbie's friends, however, agreed that this would be a lovely tribute to someone who was there from the beginning, and his estate generously granted permission for us to include it here.*

It is fitting that, at a time when *Doctor Who* is poised to ascend to new and magnificent heights, it should take time to examine again its roots. And *The Beginning* boxset does that in a very splendid way. But don't judge a book – or this boxset – by its cover. Look inside and you will see, as Carter said when first peering into Tutankhamun's tomb, "wonderful things". You get three versions of the first episode, the whole of *An Unearthly Child*, *The Edge of Destruction* and *The Daleks* plus masses of good documentary stuff and a presentation of *Marco Polo* on three DVDs.

A DVD in itself would have seemed like science fiction back in 1963. Let's take a few moments to consider the viewing environment into which *Doctor Who* burst. I'm ancient. I was there. I remember. I saw it!

Do you know the magic number 405, children? That was the paltry number of lines which made up a television picture back in those days. Later, we moved up to 625 lines and to colour pictures, and now we use electronic gimmickry to make that number of lines work overtime, so we can have huge pictures smeared across most of a pub wall and still looking just about passable. Soon we will be going high definition, and won't that be fun! But back then it was just 405, and a 14-inch screen was big and nine inches was still not unusual. (Measured from corner to corner diagonally, that is; the actual screen width was rather smaller.) But it all comes down to retinal image. The picture we saw in our heads was probably the same size as we see today: we sat nearer to the box. (And the next generation will get used to seeing hi-def TV on screens that fit in the palm of their hand, but are viewed very close up.) No smaller an image, then, but with decidedly less detail.

If the television sets back then were much smaller, the television cameras were huge and clunky. You may well be reading this on a computer to which a very small web-cam is attached – and that is much larger than the size cameras can be reduced to now, when surgeons can give you one in a pill to examine your innards. Back then, they were the size of a fridge mounted on top of a Mini. They had a series of fixed lenses on a turret, but no zoom. If you wanted to track in on the Doctor soliloquising in front of the TARDIS console, you had to physically move this leviathan across the studio floor. Not an easy task in a confined space with cables stretching everywhere, and some of the tracking shots were a bit of a bumpy ride. (Though the audience of the time were so used to this kind of thing that the bumps would probably pass unnoticed.) The lighting equipment, too, was pretty rigid and inflexible compared with what is available today; in the studio where early *Who* was made, it was all hung overhead and they had no lighting console.

But, in spite of these limitations, they aimed for and achieved far more innovative lighting and camera effects than they could be arsed to try in the technically far more advanced colour studios, with their harsh, supermarket lighting and clamped-down, eye-level camera most of the time. Partly this is because if you are working in black and white you desperately need to add "colour" via lighting effects and camera work. Partly it's because innovative camera work and lighting costs money – and needs more technical rehearsal time – and the later stuff was made on the cheap.

Not that this mattered. Most TV sets then were atrociously set up by our modern standards. They were out of focus and not properly tuned in. They contained valves like milk bottles that took an eternity to warm up and were variable in their efficiency. You had interference: sound on vision and vision on (monophonic!) sound, plus any passing car or neighbours' gadgets. The picture could start rolling at the drop of a hat, so you had horizontal and vertical hold controls on the front of the set in order to re-adjust it. The images you see on screen now on DVD, thanks to the ministrations of the *Doctor Who* Restoration Team guys, are far better than what was seen on the average domestic TV set at the time of first transmission. (And, of course, you are probably seeing it in finagled wide-screen, rather than the narrower aspect of the original transmission.)

But, apart from the quality of the equipment, television viewing was a different matter in other ways. It was still an event; it hadn't become wallpaper. Although the broadcast of the Coronation had put a television set into most homes, there would only be one of them there. You chose to watch something; you anticipated it mentally; you prepared yourself or your family group; you switched the set on and paid attention to it. It was still special.

Television was far from ubiquitous. The transmissions were limited to a few hours a day. In those days, there were only three channels: BBC, ITV and OFF. OFF was probably the one that had the highest (non) viewing figures. Radio was still king, and "breaking news" meant there might be something on television about it the following night. This was the case with the Kennedy assassination. I heard of it on the radio on the Friday night, and we were gathered in my landlady's living room to watch the television the following night. (I was a student in digs in those days.)

And that, children, is how I came to see this new programme, *Doctor Who*, for the first time.

The first episode: we just didn't know what to make of it. There hadn't been much of a preamble; apparently, the *Radio Times* were originally going to feature it, but then switched to puffing Kenneth Horne and Co. on radio instead. What is it? A school story? A mystery story? Horror? The opening credits and music told us we were in for something rather unusual. Mist and a policeman; Dockson of Dick Green? It continues blandly enough with a couple of schoolteachers, then gets odder and odder. Strange girl. Strange figure in misty darkness. And the TARDIS (not that we had a name for it back then)...

We're so used to it now that is very difficult to recapture the eerie surprise of our first entrance. We're so used now to it being bigger on the inside, but can you imagine how it felt to discover that for the first time? Wow! And what was it? A ship? What could it do?

And who is this creature in charge of it? Is he a goodie or a baddie? That's a question that doesn't really resolve until quite a few episodes have passed. The original specifications for the Doctor included the word "malign" and there's certainly a fair dollop of that in what we see. At the end of it, we are certainly asking ourselves what on Earth (or perhaps elsewhere) is going on.

And, when you start watching the DVD, you may be well asking yourself the same question, because instead of seeing the first episode you will see the first first episode. Rather odd of them to have put that pilot in the main story-viewing sequence; there are rough cuts of it elsewhere on the DVD. But it certainly is compulsive; better camera work than the actual transmission and a much more malign Doctor. On balance, the second version is a better start to the series, better acted and with a more Doctor-like Doctor. Very instructive to see the difference, though.

Actually, I didn't find out what happened next until some years later. I didn't get to see the Tribe of Gum episodes when they were transmitted. But I did get to see *The Daleks*. This time, the *Radio Times* was giving the series the roll of drums. I was at home, so viewing it should be possible and I was full of anticipation. Then disaster struck: I was under orders to take something urgently to my aunt and uncle who lived some way away and at the top of a steep hill. Aaargh! On yer bike, mate, and if you pedal like a bat out hell you might just manage to see a bit of the end of it. The relatives in question did have a television, but there was zero chance that they would want to have a piece of children's television science fiction on. It was with a heavy heart I busted my guts trying to get up that hill without having to get off and walk as I usually did.

I arrived, covered in sweat, and wanted to make a quite get away – at least I could freewheel down the hill coming back. But no – I was told to go in and sit down and shut up. And then they turned the television on and started to watch, amazingly, *Doctor Who* with almost religious attention. It turned out that one of the actors in it – Philip Bond, who played the cynic Ganatus – was a family friend. How they knew he was in it, I don't know; perhaps his mother rang. He didn't appear until much later, of course, and what they eventually made of him bleached blond and wearing daring, slashed black leather S&M chaps I don't know. But at least I got to see it, and all the subsequent episodes. Then it was *Marco Polo*, which was "educational" so I could see it with my landlady's children.

And no problems after that, because the nation was hooked...

# Half Canadian
# on His Father's Side

**by Graeme Burk**
*From Enlightenment #97, March / April 2000*

It is quite surprising that *Doctor Who* is considered a purely "British" creation and a purely "British" icon. Nothing is born in a vacuum. *Doctor Who*, in its initial stages, was born out of the experience of a Canadian and was, arguably, born out of a Canadian ethos as well.

Sydney Newman, one of *Doctor Who*'s creators – in fact the person who came up with idea in the first place – was a Canadian. And yet, this is something which is largely uncelebrated and, even more surprisingly, unexamined – even by fans from Newman's home nation-state.

When Sydney Newman had arrived at the BBC in 1963, he had spent five years working for the CBC. Before then, he had apprenticed under John Grierson – a highly regarded pioneer of the documentary film – at the National Film Board (an organisation Newman would eventually become the head of after his tenure at the BBC). Upon arriving at the CBC at the outset of its television service in 1952, he began as a line producer for a number of programmes and eventually became the supervising producer of television drama, a role that he maintained until headhunted to ITV in Britain in the late fifties.

Newman's time in the formative years of the CBC is often overlooked in historical accounts of the creation of *Doctor Who*; usually, they start with Newman's arrival at ITV. Which is a shame, as he was instrumental in the very invention of Canadian television. Newman produced everything from current-affairs programmes (he is credited with having innovated on-the-spot television reporting in Canada) to sports (Newman was the first producer of *Hockey Night in Canada* – a Canadian institution as beloved as *Match of the Day* or *Wide World of Sports*). He also produced drama, training many of the first drama producers in Canadian television. With story editor Nathan Cohen and executive producer Mavor Moore, Newman helped foster what has long been considered the golden age of Canadian TV drama.

One has to remember that US programming didn't appear in earnest on Canadian television until the late fifties. This left Newman and his colleagues with the task of creating original programming without US competition (aside from "border" US stations), constrained only by CBC policy and the mores of the day.

All this is necessary background to bear in mind for when, in 1963, Newman decided to put together a brief for a series to fill a teatime slot between *Grandstand* and *Juke Box Jury*; a programme with children as its primary audience. Obviously, Newman had his own career in British television to draw from – he had produced some successful science fiction with his ITV series *Pathfinders to Venus* – but he also had his CBC work to reflect on as well.

In 1953, during Newman's tenure at the CBC, the Corporation aired *Space Command*, a science-fiction series for children that starred a young, pre-*Star Trek* James Doohan and William Shatner. As the entry in the Directory to CBC Television Series website explains: "The series followed one character, Frank Anderson, through the different divisions of the space command: the transport division, the satellite division, the investigative division, the exploration division, and so forth. The stories emphasised dramatic action, but were purported to have an educational basis, as the fiction grew from conditions that were known about outer space and speculations about what life would be like beyond the earth." This is not to say that *Space Command* was terribly dry. From the extant footage that has been aired in modern times (usually as proof of the sordid Canadian past of "Scotty" and "Kirk"), it was – for its day – a lively, fast-paced drama.

Newman did not produce *Space Command*, but he almost certainly had a hand in its devising, being under his purview as supervising producer of drama at the CBC. (He had the same role with the CBC's 1952 adaptation of *20,000 Leagues Under the Sea* and is inaccurately credited by many fan historians as producer.) What is interesting is that its basis is not a million miles away from Sydney Newman's original brief for his unnamed teatime children's science fiction series, especially in its idea of what science fiction should be.

Newman was, as most people are now well aware, against "Bug Eyed Monsters" in science fiction. He wanted stories rooted in contemporary science, or thinly disguised parables using scientific trappings. *The First Doctor Handbook* shows contemporary documentation from Newman that indicates this is at the forefront of his thinking. Criticising the series format document written by C.E. "Bunny" Webber in 1963, Newman noted that "it doesn't get across the basis of teaching of educational experience – drama based upon and stemming from factual material and scientific phenomena." The sort of thing Newman felt this new series should emulate is perhaps demonstrated by the fact that the numerous versions of the script for the pilot invariably involved the central characters being shrunk to six inches in height. As with *Space Command*, the fiction grew from conditions that are known or from "reasonable" speculation.

Years later, Newman still believed the series should adhere to this principle. Howe, Stammers and Walker's *The Eighties* documents that when Newman was asked to provide BBC upper management with ideas on reformatting *Doctor Who* in 1986, the freelancing former Head of Drama made it very clear he felt the series needed to return this same footing. In fact, he even suggested, once again, the literal shrinking of the main characters in order to witness how cancer cells worked on the human body, followed by fantastic adventures on the space shuttle or a Polaris submarine. As he wrote then: "Our Earth, both present and past, is just as exciting as outer space, when creatively explored."

Even so, the science-fiction aspect of this new series was a secondary concern. Newman first and foremost wanted his teatime series to tell stories set in human history, with a very distinctive educational slant. As Newman later recounted in an interview in *DWB* in 1985: "I definitely put into the (series brief) that we mustn't lose the children, this is BBC, we've got to be clean and educational. That's why I wanted (the series central concept) to be a time machine, to go back into history and dramatise history with our contemporary characters observing and being part of the changes."

Certainly, as Newman himself admitted, this focus on education was a part of the BBC ethos in the early sixties and well ensconced in the Broadcast Act. However, could it not have also come from Newman's own roots as well?

Mary Anne Miller's foundational 1987 history of CBC Drama, *Turn Up the Contrast*, points out that, in the 1950s, the links between Canadian and

British television were quite strong. The medium was so new, there was a more level playing field between the US, Canada and the UK. Much of Newman's work from the CBC wound up being imported to British television. Miller is particularly keen to emphasise that Newman's much-praised emphasis on more naturalistic drama – which came to be known as "kitchen sink" drama in the UK – had its origins in his work on Canadian television. Miller writes that Newman "understood that a good story which provoked argument around the dinner table afterwards would gain and hold audiences. To succeed, [programming] had to concentrate on the recognisable and the relevant." This use of the familiar and recognisable was a hallmark of his live dramas at the CBC. According to Newman, before his promotion to head of drama, scripts were often "Canadianised" Broadway plays. Newman's main work at the CBC was bringing in Canadian writers to write about believable people in a believable context for Canadians.

Certainly, this desire for the recognisable and the relevant was key to the original concept of Newman's teatime family series. Newman rejected the more fanciful suggestions that producer Donald Wilson and writer C.E. Webber kept handing him in favour of keeping it closer to something more naturalistic to ensure viewer identification. Newman further required recognisable and relevant characters, including a young girl and two schoolteachers with backgrounds in history and science. The grounding in the familiar as a jumping-off point for the fantastic was a Newman trademark: it was the same thing he had done with the original conception of *The Avengers*. And yet, it has its origins on the other side of the Atlantic.

The connection isn't just through Newman's work, however, but the Canadian culture itself. Certainly, the early CBC modelled itself after the BBC; in fact, legislation enabling Canadian Broadcasting was based in part on what the "mother country" had done previously. Both countries' broadcast services were mandated to educate their listeners and viewers; however, broadcasting in Canada has always placed special value on education, and has tended to integrate an educational message even within its drama. Perhaps this is because the CBC has had a unique role to preserve and promote Canadian heritage in the shadow of an entertainment monolith south of the border. It has often been joked that the CBC produces "television that is good for you" and there is a great deal of truth in that. The idea that television drama should inform and educate as well as entertain is a value that has been a unique part of the CBC since its inception. It should be therefore no surprise that Sydney Newman, who came out of both the CBC and the National Film Board, should place great value on entertainment which emphasised social relevance over mere escapism.

Canadian culture has also had a high regard for what can be best described as a benign learning of history. We can see this in the popularity in Canada of historical journalism, popularised by people like Pierre Berton (who was publishing his first works in this field during the 1950s), the fascination with the docudrama as a television genre (one which Newman had a hand in creating), and the need to "popularise" history (best seen today in the "Heritage Minute" public-service spots). These are all a part of a Canadian cultural heritage that emphasises that history is important and should be taught to the masses in the most benign ways possible. It could be argued that devising a programme that would "go back into history and dramatise history with our contemporary characters" is at least indirectly connected with this part of the Canadian cultural identity.

Of course, once the programme moved into other people's hands, the teatime serial that became known as *Doctor Who* quickly departed from the format that Newman had set forth. During the first production block, though, one can certainly see Sydney Newman's legacy to the series: educational but dramatic history lessons (especially in *The Aztecs* and *Marco Polo* – both written by John Lucarotti, a former CBC writer). Science-fiction stories as parables (*The Sensorites*) or scientific explorations (*Planet of Giants*, which finally fulfilled the ambition to make the central characters six inches tall). It is only with *The Daleks* that we see the beginnings of the departure away from Newman's format. This departure was pretty much complete by the second production block, with its emphasis on naturalism-eschewing comedy (particularly in the historical stories) and, of course, more Bug Eyed Monsters.

While this is something that requires closer examination, it is certainly safe to say that the series' Canadian connections in its early days are far stronger than just the involvement of former CBC employees, or almost producing a story where Erik The Red discovered Newfoundland. Sydney Newman's work and roots in Canada probably made a significant contribution to the gestation of the series. One could possibly even make the claim that, conceptually, the first season of *Doctor Who* was as much a Canadian product as a British one.

# Backwards, Forwards, Sideways, Hmm?

**by Robert Smith?**

*From Enlightenment #104, June / July 2001*

The time has come. We've been scattered and disorganised for far too long, but it's time for us to rise up everywhere and proclaim our love for an era of the show that has been criminally neglected. Hear me, siblings! We've whispered in the corridors, we've held secret meetings and we've denied everything when questioned, but I call on you now to stand firm with me. Together, we can be strong. Together we shall have mastery over other fandoms throughout all of Spain! Er, space.

Hello, my name's Robert and I'm a William Hartnell fan.

I'm not afraid to say it. I really, really like the Hartnell era. No, not just the early anti-hero phase, not just renewed interest in Ian and Barbara during the nineties, not just the Daleks when they were a force to be reckoned with, not just the tantalising backstory that's so close to the surface without quite being revealed – I'm talking about the whole package. The scope. The potential. Even *The Web Planet*. I love it all.

What's astonishing about the Hartnell era is the way it keeps playing with the format. The series was built on three basic templates: backwards, forwards and sideways, but the Hartnell era keeps tinkering with that. We might think we've got *The Romans* pegged as the historical story slotted between the futuristic *Rescue* and the alien *Web Planet*, but the series was doing its first all-out comedy story and shamelessly mixing slapstick with clever wordplay while sending Ian into slavery. *The Ark* seems like a fairly bog-standard future story, but there's that astonishing cliffhanger to episode two that only the Hartnell era could get away with.

The early historical stories are rightly famed for their attention to detail and effective use of the BBC's best resources. It doesn't get much better than *The Aztecs*, one of the most solid stories ever produced, which manages to be visually impressive to boot. *The Crusade* is so strong it has parts of dialogue in iambic pentameter. And just when we think we're in for a history lesson about Vikings and King Harold, one of the Doctor's own people pops up, complete with a TARDIS.

The "sideways" stories vary greatly, but on the whole they're exceedingly interesting. From tense psychological drama and macabre games to high-concept ideas like shrinking the crew and jumping a time track to pad out an otherwise average story, the era kept trying to surprise the viewers. Today, *The War Machines* is one of the more polished Hartnell stories and the one most in tune with what we think of when we imagine a *Doctor Who* story, but compared to everything around it, it was quite a departure for the series. Interestingly, that makes both present-day Hartnell adventures (not counting the first episode itself) "sideways" stories, where the series was attempting something it had never done before.

The futuristic stories are grand in their scope, even if they've dated a little now. There's a deliberate "all aliens, all the time!" story in *The Web Planet*. There are chase / quest stories like *The Keys of Marinus*, *The Chase* and *The Daleks' Master Plan*, which manage to stretch the meagre budget to a different location every episode. Something like the city on Mechanus would have taken an entire story in any other era, if for no other reason than budgetary, but in *The Chase* it's just one backdrop among many.

Oh, and just when you think you've seen it all, they throw in a one episode Doctorless story... that has absolutely nothing to do with the next story to be screened. That's astonishing.

There's only one base-under-siege story and that's the final one. It set a template for the next era of the show, which would in turn set a formula for the series that would become synonymous with "good". Yet, although later eras worked out that all they had to do was find something that worked and stick to it (monsters infiltrating isolated bases, UNIT action, possession and Hammer horror, soap opera character studies etc), the Hartnell era kept moving. For an era usually dismissed as slow and boring, its developmental pace was light years ahead of the rest of the series.

Hartnell himself is quite unlike any of the other Doctors, despite the attempts of many later actors to emulate his portrayal. He's the most human Doctor by far: he's full of very human feelings and emotions, he gets tetchy when people don't listen to him, but he also laughs in sheer delight when he overhears Vicki talking about how amazing he is in *The Rescue*. He's irascible, he's arrogant and he's frequently wrong – but he's loveable. He's a cross between your loveable old granddad and that crazy guy who lives down the street you you're not supposed to talk to. When Jon Pertwee or Colin Baker try the same thing, they just come across as rude.

It's interesting that those who saw the series on first viewing are invariably diehard Hartnell fans, but the rest of us keep placing him somewhere near Colin in our favourite Doctor polls. Hartnell couldn't make the transition to the video generation the way the other Doctors did – but he was never meant to, of course. The series was supposed to be watched one episode at a time, once a week. And viewed like that, it works far better than we'd think. Take *The Sensorites* (please). Few can argue with its reputation as a yawning plodder, where our heroes are threatened by old men who can't stand loud noises and are afraid of the dark. And yet... I caught episode five on its own on TV one day, when I wasn't expecting it. I already had the story on tape, I'd seen it once in a single sitting and hadn't exactly been enthralled – but episode five had me riveted. Hartnell wandering around the caves talking to himself was great. Watched in isolation, the way it was originally structured, even the dull episodes of the Hartnell era are enjoyable.

Hartnell's comic timing is fantastic. *The Gunfighters* works precisely because Hartnell is so good at carrying off the jokes. His interactions with the Monk and Nero are hilarious. When all is said and done, *Doctor Who*'s greatest strength is its humour and the Hartnell era can hold its own. Richard Hurndall tries hard to create his own version of the first Doctor in *The Five Doctors*, but the opening scene with Hartnell in it only shows up how much better the real first Doctor was in his prime. That's a beautiful speech and one of the show's finest... and, of course, it was almost entirely ad-libbed by Hartnell himself.

Surprisingly perhaps, there's still life in the Hartnell era – in the form of the novels. The books have been quite polarised in terms of character-isations: the first, sixth and seventh Doctors have thrived in the transition to the page, whereas the other Doctors have eluded most writers. The seventh Doctor could move forward in the NAs and the sixth Doctor had a large gap that writers could explore, but it's the first Doctor who has survived best in his original form.

Partly this is due to the pacing: novels aren't action set-pieces, like in the Pertwee era, nor do they live or die on the personality of the lead actor, as in the fourth Doctor's era. They have a steadier, more thought-ful pace, where investigation and characterisation are far more promi-nent – which suits the Hartnell era magnificently. We've seen the revival of the Hartnell Historical as a literate style and it's just as powerful now as it was then.

The Hartnell era presents us with a universe of almost limitless scope. It's often said that *Doctor Who* is a show where anything is possible, which makes it even more of a shame that the series relies on formula so often. The Hartnell era looks like an anomaly today, but it's perhaps the closest realisation of just what *Doctor Who* could be when it really wants to. It's enormous, it's loopy, it's funny, it's dated, it's downright strange sometimes, but I can't help loving it.

# The Forgettable Doctor

**by Jim Sangster**

*Doctor Who* fans rarely view the matter of wiping of old programmes with anything other than indignant fury. Recycling the tapes to enable new ones to be made simply doesn't compute as anything other than "cultural vandalism". Like it or not, it was out of sheer necessity that the BBC – and most of the ITV franchise holders too, it must be noted – systematically refreshed their stocks by wiping programmes that were no longer wanted. As we look back on the decision to wipe these "classics" with our "on-demand" twenty-first century attitudes, it's nigh-on impossible to comprehend the make-do-and-mend mentality of a post-war generation who'd only recently come off rationing.

The knock-on effect of this is that there are entire stories from *Doctor Who's* past that haven't been seen by anyone in forty years, including the majority of Patrick Troughton's tenure as the Doctor. We still have the audio recordings made by fans, and the telesnaps – those teeny pictures taken of a TV monitor by John Cura through most of the 1960s episodes. What we don't have is any way of knowing with any certainty what *The Space Pirates* actually looked like beyond episode two. We can't be sure whether *The Web of Fear* was as impressive as its soundtrack would suggest. What we have left are a few scant complete stories and a selection of random episodes.

Which prompts the question: how come Troughton is so revered among fans, almost all of whom haven't actually seen him? Surely *The Dominators* or *The Krotons* can't have been so influential as to convince us all to ignore a time in the programme's production that was increasingly formulaic and, it has to be said, lacking in the kind of risk-taking and innovation that had defined his predecessor's stories?

In the June 1999 edition of *Doctor Who Magazine*, four fans were set the challenge of watching every episode of broadcast *Doctor Who* – 698 at the time – from the very beginning. The gimmick was that they had to pretend to be seeing them for the first time, and for a couple of them this wouldn't have been so difficult. For the missing episodes, they used fan-made reconstructions that combined those telesnaps with the audio recordings to make a blurry slide-show with the occasional flurry of movement when a surviving clip came into play. In January 2008, having acquired copies of these reconstructions, I decided to have a go at this myself.

Doing "the pilgrimage" is something I think all fans should try to do, but it surprises me just how lazy fans are nowadays. Back in the 1980s, when I first joined a fan group, we didn't have the internet. We didn't even have official VHS tapes; only *Revenge of the Cybermen* had been released and the tapes were way outside the reaches of my pocket money. I met fans who'd secured pen-pals in Australia, where the episodes were still repeated regularly. Which meant watching eighth-generation copies that kept dipping from black and white into colour (especially confusing for stories that were supposed to be monochrome in the first place).

It really is so much easier nowadays; even if you only restrict yourself to wholly legal sources, every story has been released in some commercial format, whether that be DVD, VHS or audio CD. I hear of things like "torrents" but I have to admit they're beyond me. All I know is, "the kids today" manage to catch up with all their favourite programmes months before they hit British TV screens.

You might be one of the rare fans who've seen every surviving episode, heard the audio recordings and maybe even seen these fan-made reconstructions of the "missing" stories, but I'd be willing to bet very few of you have taken the trouble to watch them in the context of a continuing series. I know I hadn't. *The Dominators* had only preceded *The Mind Robber* because that was the order in which I bought the VHS tapes. Probably. By the 1990s, the fragmented way in which I – and everybody else – viewed stories made *Doctor Who* more of an anthology than an ongoing story. One where the cast changed every so often and it flicked from black and white to colour in ways that hadn't been seen in the UK since the early 1970s.

I mentioned earlier how formulaic the Troughton era was. If submitted to interrogation, at some point most fans would use the phrase "base under siege" to summarise his episodes. It's as effective a shorthand as "exiled to Earth" is, but it does help illustrate just how repetitive Troughton's time as the Doctor really was.

Some of the supposed classics do indeed stand up to modern scrutiny. Were it possible to wish episodes back into existence, I'm sure *The Web of Fear* and *Fury from the Deep* would top my list just as much as they do for everyone else. I was completely taken aback by how enjoyable *The Underwater Menace* was – and how out of context that much-shown clip of Zaroff actually is. And, considering it was stuck right in the middle of a supposed "monster" season, *The Enemy of the World* stood out head and shoulders above almost everything else, with well-formed characters (including Milton Johns as possibly the nastiest henchman in the series' history) and a couple of genuinely surprising twists.

Sadly, Season Five also gives us Victoria. Much as we adore Deborah Watling and can't fault her performance, the character as written really is

the worst of the lot. She cries and moans, rarely has anything constructive to bring to the story and clearly doesn't want to be there from day
one. Yes, she's just lost her father and been whisked away to dangerous
adventures by two mad loons, but really – would we tolerate someone
that whiny today? Conversely, Ben and Polly might echo Ian and Barbara
in their quest to get home but, like their predecessors, they have the
strength of character to get on with the task and make the best of things.
Which makes their departure story all the more surprising; they disap-
pear halfway through and don't return until a filmed insert in episode
six!

And then there are those bases. On the moon, in the frozen tundra, up
a mountain, down a tunnel... there hadn't really been that many of them
prior to 1966. Soon after, there was very little else.

Once I'd completed the Troughton era, I wanted to find out what people thought about him at the time. Luckily, through my day job in BBC
archives, I was able to sneak a look at some of the audience-response
reports compiled at the time from samples of the viewers. What surprised me most was how polarised the audience seemed to be, right from
the start. For every respondent who said they enjoyed a story, another
would dismiss it as rubbish. In the BBC's audience-response report for
*The Seeds of Death*, one reviewer describes it sneerily as "juvenile science
fiction", another as "silly, boring and ridiculous", while a third noted
that: "It all seems so obvious. Dr Who enjoys a charmed life even when
deprived of his only destructive weapon." The report concluded that
"even allowing that they were intended for children, it was high time in
their opinion that Dr Who was given a well-earned rest".

Troughton himself seemed to be popular, mostly. There were many
criticisms during his time that his more comic portrayal didn't sit well
with everyone, though most thought he seemed "just the right blend of
brains and eccentricity". Even in *The War Games*, which was dismissed by
one contributor as "the usual rubbishy nonsense", many took time out to
commend the lead actor as he bowed out of the series: "The talents of this
fine actor," a respondent wrote, "had been rather wasted here."

It's difficult to compare *Doctor Who* with what was being broadcast
around it. As is often stressed, there's nothing quite like *Doctor Who* and
when other teams try to imitate it, they very rarely come close. BBC TV
Centre was full of productions that used the exact same techniques as
*Doctor Who*: dramas like *Adam Adamant!*, *Paul Temple* and *Z-Cars*; sitcoms
like Johnny Speight's taboo-breaking *Till Death Us Do Part*; factual and
documentary series like *Tomorrow's World*. And which programme looks
like *Doctor Who* the most? *Top of the Pops!* The groovy light shows and
video effects were the same ones being used to enhance "death by radio-

phonic effect" up on the moon.

The programmes we're thinking of here – indeed the Troughton era I've just watched with my own eyes – is not the Troughton era that has topped polls and been vaunted by fans as an era chock-full of "forgotten" classics. Too many voters work by assumption. We can be certain of this if only because the 1998 *Doctor Who Magazine* poll had two Troughton stories placed in the top 10 that haven't been seen since 1967. Had *The Evil of the Daleks* turned up complete in a vault ("in HONG KONG!"), might we be witnessing the lukewarm response that *The Tomb of the Cybermen* seems to get nowadays, as viewers had the chance to see for themselves how small the Emperor Dalek's chamber looked, how horribly padded the middle episodes were and how overtly racist it was to have two consecutive stories to feature a mute black slave as the only non-white character? Did the Pertwee era score so lowly in the same *DWM* poll because of a combination of Dudley Simpson's electric organ and too great a reliance on experimental blue-screen, or did the enforced Earth-bound nature of his stories really alienate so many fans?

The truth is, we can't be sure. But I have my suspicions that one of the reasons Troughton has had this reputation for so long is that he was followed, eventually, by two easier targets.

Nobody likes the idea of rejection. To have your paranoia confirmed and discover that you're not as popular as you'd like to be is a horrible realisation to go through. In these days when not only is *Doctor Who* the number one TV programme in the UK, but it's actually socially acceptable to admit to being a fan, younger viewers might like to imagine a time when the public just weren't interested and the BBC bosses weren't falling over themselves to be seen as anything other than 100% supportive. This, more than the quality of the shows, is why the sixth and seventh Doctor's adventures come in for more abuse and general disregard than any other; when outside forces were telling us the object of our affection was below par, it felt like a personal attack on us.

In 1988, there was the ever-constant *Doctor Who Magazine*, always trying to put a positive, upbeat spin on the external forces trying to kill off our hero. But there was also a fan publication called *Doctor Who Bulletin*. Nowadays, it'd be a blog or a messageboard, claiming to be the voice of the fans and demanding "RTD MUST GO!" *DWB*, for reasons best known to its editor, Gary Leigh, began orchestrating an openly hostile and personal campaign to oust John Nathan-Turner from the producer's chair.

Curiously, while attacking the current series, *DWB* also switched its focus to celebrate the series' past, notably the episodes broadcast during the 1960s. It was around this time that John Cura's collection of telesnaps

– photos taken of a TV monitor during transmission – gave us our first views of many episodes that had long since been deleted. Over-excited news stories promising us fresh leads to archives in Africa ultimately came to nothing but *DWB* succeeded in raising interest in those stories that had been shown too long ago for many fans to have seen. Most importantly of all, the magazine's readership was, largely, not in a position to question their authority. The contributors to the magazine had done their research and had access to sources we didn't. Some of them had seen the episodes at the time, and had since spoken to such luminaries as Sydney Newman. If the man credited with creating *Doctor Who* was writing Sylvester McCoy off as rubbish, who were we to argue?

Here's where the myth of the "golden age" really began. Reinforced by apocryphal anecdotes from the cast and crew (many of which have since been debunked), we began to believe in a version of the series that had never truly existed. While the *Doctor Who* of 1988 was up against the country's most consistent ratings winner, in some weeks it was still outperforming episodes from Season Six. The lowest-rated episode of the McCoy era was only a few hundred thousand viewers shy of the lowest-rated episode of *The War Games*.

Back in 1988, there simply weren't enough viewers still watching who could convincingly make a fair comparison between what JN-T was offering us and what had been shown twenty years earlier. The vast majority of us had seen less than a handful of stories, and it felt very strongly as if those who had seen Troughton on first broadcast had a very definite agenda that meant we couldn't always trust their judgement.

JN-T's comment that "the memory cheats" is partly the key: stories viewed as a child could never compare to those the older viewers were now watching as jaded adults. But it was the scarcity of those older episodes that gives them an added allure. Our own imagined version of Troughton's Doctor could never compare to the reality of what went out on BBC1 twenty years before.

Perhaps it taps a tendency deeply rooted in *Doctor Who* fans, who more than any other fan group are aware of the production of *Doctor Who*. We know the roles of the major players like the writers, directors, producers and script editors. To my knowledge, *Doctor Who Magazine* might get its fair share of crazies, but none of them ever expect to be able to phone up and speak to the Brigadier. Ask anyone who works on one of the many magazines dedicated to soap operas and you'll see a marked increase in people who don't quite get that *Coronation Street* isn't real – that phoning up the editor of a magazine to ask him to let Sally know that Kevin is cheating on her isn't entirely rational.

Perhaps unsurprisingly, *Coronation Street* fans also debate their favourite eras, with names like H.V. Kershaw and John Stephenson in place of Philip Hinchcliffe and Robert Holmes. They pore over the limited DVD releases and unfavourably compare the 1960s to the 1980s. And, for many of them, eras might even be divided into who was the licensee of the Rovers Return rather than behind-the-scenes personnel. One thing they don't tend to do – as there's no need for them to do it – is restoration. Our own cultural history sports gaps and is affected by changes in format holdings, from videotape to monochrome film prints to digital copies. Restoration in *Doctor Who* terms, like many aspects of being a *Doctor Who* viewer, has led to a number of viewers growing up to become industry professionals. Kids who watched *Doctor Who* have grown up to work for The Mill on the new series. They're also working on the DVD releases or developing processes like VidFIRE: a means of transforming blurry telerecordings on 16-millimetre film into something approximating the sharpness of the original videotape. They restore the soundtracks to remove hiss and crackle. Occasionally, they replace original model effects with new CGI ones – and, naturally, some of us wish they didn't. Not because the CGI is necessarily below par, but because the old effects are a perfect reminder that the show involved – as it always had – people simply trying to do the best they could with limited resources.

I've been hard on the Troughton era simply because it's the one that's far too easy to re-imagine as something better than what it was. The truth is, it has as many clunkers as any other era and for all the same reasons. What my own Time Team pilgrimage left me with was a realisation that I was right not to just accept "the wisdom of the ancients" in their appraisal of the 1960s stories over those of the late 1980s. And the experience has made me an evangelist – especially to newer fans for whom the stumbling block of black-and-white television might be just as great as the problems some have with any multi-camera, studio-bound drama made on untreated videotape. The fact is, until recently at least, there was always a sizeable proportion who would have dismissed any *Doctor Who* story as "childish rubbish", whether it was made by Douglas Camfield or Chris Clough. Alison Graham in the *Radio Times* keeps catching herself each time she reviews a new episode enthusiastically; she can't resist adding "it's all nonsense of course". To which I just shake my head and look forward to her being wrong again.

# INTERLUDE

## The Key to a Time Lord - 1

**by Scott Clarke**

*From Enlightenment #120, February / March 2004*

*So picture it, I'm sitting at my computer plunking out my latest* Enlightenment *column about, oh I don't know, John Leeson versus David Brierley: who would make a better Gollum (or was I counting dust bunnies under my computer desk?). Suddenly, a blinding light suffuses the room from the crack under my bedroom door. I throw open the door to find my editor, Graeme Burk, perched at the end of the hallway in a Pier Import wicker chair, a Margarita raised in greeting. In his other hand, he grasps a copy of* Enlightenment #119.

*"Mr Clarke, what is this aimless hogwash about* Meglos. *Get a grip. You're losing your way.*

*"Well, I..."*

*"I have a task for you. A quest if you will. Find me the magic, the skill, the craftsmanship in this thing we call* Doctor Who. *Over the next six issues, I want you to take a specific element of good storytelling and apply it to a given episode of televised Who. Uncover what makes it tick..."*

*"Well you see I've got this K9 / Gollum article and..."*

*"You can't ignore this Mr Clarke..."*

*"And if I do?"*

*"Nothing."*

*"Nothing?"*

*"Nothing... ever."*

*"You mean I'll cease to exist?"*

*"No I mean there's nothing I can do. I'm only a fanzine editor, for God's sake. There are limits to my power."*

*"Yeah, yeah." I retreat back to my room. Note to self: look into a home security system.*

### Episode One: Mystery

Episode one of *The Daleks* provides an excellent template for how to construct mystery and suspense in *Doctor Who* (or any television series).

The master himself, Alfred Hitchcock noted, "There is no terror in a bang, only in the anticipation of it." Handy advice when working with a shoestring budget in black-and-white era television. Terry Nation's script draws on a series of very simple, yet effective, techniques to this end: believable characters ensure that an audience makes the necessary leap of faith, disorientation and deflection of expectations will heighten tension, and, most essential, less is more: what you don't see is more potent than what you do.

Whereas *An Unearthly Child* played with the audience's expectations of the familiar (police boxes, junkyards, grumpy grandfather, etc), the second story chooses to disorient from the get-go. After a short reprise of the previous episode's cliffhanger (involving the radiation dial), we are confronted by a negative image of the petrified forest on Skaro. One has to strain to make out exactly what is being presented, to the same effect as a darkened room or an optical illusion. It's accompanied by bizarre, "concrete" music, which heightens the sense of alienation. As the time travellers explore the mysterious forest, Nation raises only questions via Barbara and Ian. The dispersal of answers is carefully controlled.

On a number of occasions, Nation deflects our attention from the threat with moments of familiarity or humour. When Susan discovers a flower, it's a small moment of innocence and beauty, a trace of something familiar, broken by the discovery of the petrified reptile. Later, Nation repeats this tactic during the scenes in the TARDIS. He tries to lull us back into a feeling of comfort or safety. Some might argue that these are needless padding (let's have a cool science-speculation moment with simulated bacon and eggs), but what it really does is dry us out before dunking us under the water again. The banging on the outside of the TARDIS is that much more ominous because our attention had been deflected elsewhere. Following this, when the camera moves in on the scanner, we strain to make out the image of what's outside the TARDIS. Have we missed something lurking in a far corner?

We're presented with the aftermath of some terrible Armageddon: white ashy soil, petrified, crumbling tree branches. Are these the signs of post-nuclear winter? In the context of cold war 1963, this fear has real weight. Has the TARDIS landed on a devastated Earth in the future? Or a mere few years ahead? The possibilities are intriguing and haunting. What kind of creature could exist amidst ash and radiation poisoning?

Susan feels a hand on her shoulder, but sees nothing. The time travellers hear a rapping noise against the TARDIS, but no one's there. Where did the mysterious vials come from? Later, when the Doctor and his companions happen upon the Dalek city, in all its wondrous spectacle, more questions are raised. Apparently, the people of this planet are civilised enough to build such a refuge. It's the post-war dream. Or, alternatively, has this civilisation finally concocted its own downfall with the help of weapons of mass destruction? There is no sign of activity, save the watchful "cameras" inside.

The frenetic pace with which Barbara becomes enmeshed in the corridors of the Daleks' city is truly sinister. One is reminded of *Alice in Wonderland* or an unwilling participant in a house of mirrors as she stoops to make her way through one identical, slanted doorway after another. One can feel the speed of the lift as our heroine is taken further into the bowels of the city.

Of course, none of this would mean squat if we didn't care about these characters. Watching the episode now, we have the benefit of hindsight, knowing that successive Doctors were usually in control to some degree, possessing some knowledge of a given situation. Original viewers had no such assurances. We don't see a Dalek until episode two, but we feel their presence like an unpleasant breeze across our shoulders. In many ways, it was all downhill from there. Most brilliantly conceived is our first glimpse of the Dalek sucker at the end of the episode. All of the momentum and restraint built up in the previous half hour is trained on that encroaching, obscured toilet plunger. George Lucas or Peter Jackson couldn't possibly have created anything to fulfil the sheer terror on Jacqueline Hill's face.

Television viewers held their breath until the following Saturday and perhaps the greatest sense of mystery ever generated by *Doctor Who* lived in that week.

It's that sense of mystery that lives on through all *Doctor Who*. Witness the opening to *The Ark in Space*. We follow the point of view of an "inhuman" eye as it moves in on an unsuspecting sleeper. Wham, the scene cuts to the Doctor, Sarah and Harry arriving. It's a brilliant exercise in economy: unknown terror, mounting questions, emotionless voiceovers and all in a studio with only the three principal actors.

Look at *Invasion of the Dinosaurs* or *The Android Invasion*. Empty London streets and peculiar "twitchy" UNIT soldiers disorient us and play with our expectations. *Remembrance of the Daleks* bewilders us with the idea of Daleks in 1963 and then heaps the questions – what is the Hand of Omega? who is that creepy girl? – like whipped cream atop a blockbuster sundae.

Of course, the very format of *Doctor Who* works so wonderfully well at creating mystery 90% of the time. After all, when you have a blue box that can go anywhere in time and space, there are very few expectations. Add to that the financial restrictions of the day and could it really have been anything else?

# THE LAND OF FICTION

We think the makers of *The Mind Robber* on DVD missed a trick. We think they should have plumped for the extra budget to add CGI and a new dialogue track so that when Hamish Wilson's ersatz Jamie stands atop a giant letter and looks out to the forest of words he doesn't read out a series of pithy aphorisms but rather, "...with a wheezing, groaning sound, the TARDIS departed... On the storm-swept surface of Karn, an insect-like Mutt staggers from the crash site of its spaceship... Everyone turns to the computer WOTAN and it speaks. 'Dr Who is required...'"

Okay, it wouldn't add much to *The Mind Robber* but it would nonetheless be pretty cool.

*Doctor Who* is more than a forest of words though: it's a universe of them. With a format that can go forwards, backwards and sideways in time and space, gleefully taking on any genre and story it pleases for inspiration, the only limits are the imaginations of those creating it (including the imaginations of those minding the budget). That gives *Doctor Who* a storytelling engine – the aspects of characters, mythos and setting that drives a story – that is almost perfect.

Such a storytelling engine, though, requires constant fuelling. That's what makes *Doctor Who* fan writing so engaging: because they're fascinated with how that happens. They're willing to discuss how the storytelling structure influences the story, or how the mystery and mythology of the central character informs the story, or how the series relies on common ideas, symbols, genres, even downright tropes to get by, or how the series espouses one point of view when in fact it believes in another entirely.

That *Doctor Who* can be appreciated on as many levels and points of view as there can be stories is quite incredible when you think about it. Then again, how many television series have their protagonists visiting a Land of Fiction with a forest of words, never bother to explain its existence, and then blithely move on to a Cybermen story set in near-contemporary London?

When it comes down to it, that's the magic of *Doctor Who*...

# What Has Happened to the Magic of Doctor Who?

**by Jan Vincent-Rudski**

*From TARDIS volume 3, issue 3, 1978.*

It is often the case that people say "things are not what they used to be" and this complaint is being directed more and more towards *Doctor Who*. Is this justified?

To me, the striking difference between the original style and the present style of *Doctor Who* is that all the "magic" of the programme has gone.

When it first began, we knew nothing about the Doctor except that he was an alien from a very advanced culture. Although the Doctor was bossy and sometimes bad-tempered, he radiated warmth, compassion and kindness to all his allies. There was very little we found out about William Hartnell's Doctor. We eventually found out that he could regenerate and earlier on that he was not the only one from his planet able to travel in time (the Monk). Right at the beginning, we also knew that he was an exile from his own planet, and a Wanderer in Time. Apart from these few tantalising details, the Doctor was a man of mystery. We all wondered who he was, where he came from, but this was what was so exciting about this Time Wanderer.

In Patrick Troughton's days, we learnt some more. In *The Tomb of the Cybermen*, we learnt that the Doctor had a family. In *Spearhead from Space*, we learnt that he had two hearts, but in *The War Games*, things began to move. Here, we learnt he was not only an exile, but a renegade. He had stolen the TARDIS from his own people, the Time Lords. The Time Lords, we were told, were a race that had learnt to control their own environment, live forever – barring accidents – and had the secret of Space / Time travel. But they were a reclusive race, content only to observe and gather knowledge.

Episode nine of *The War Games* was a memorable episode. Here, the Doctor found he was unable to cope with the situation and had to call in the Time Lords. Neither the aliens or the War Chief were happy about this and made it quite obvious that, once stirred, the Time Lords were a force to be reckoned with. As the Doctor tried to flee from the War Games planet, the ominous groaning / rushing noise harkening the approach of the Time Lords was heard, and one by one all the captured people were returned to their own place and time; no mean feat! Apart from this splendid display of power from the depths of Time and Space, the Time Lords also placed a force field around the Aliens' planet, imprisoning them forever. Certainly, the Time Lords were very powerful.

The introduction of the Time Lords did not destroy the mystery of the programme, as the Time Lords themselves acted in a quite alien and mysterious fashion, and after *The War Games* they were again just some mysterious race far out in space.

However, during Jon Pertwee's days, the mystery gradually lessened. The Doctor was still a character full of warmth, compassion and emotions, but now we learnt more and more about him. Slowly but surely, he was becoming less and less a mysterious character. We even began to lose the homely feeling of the TARDIS. No longer did we even see people entering the TARDIS and being awestruck by it. No longer were we able to share their awe, or the Doctor's pride. In fact, over the years, it would seem there has been an attempt to brainwash us into thinking the TARDIS is useless and no good.

We returned once again to the Time Lords for a while in *The Three Doctors*. Here, they were not so mysterious, but still seemed normally a very powerful race. After they granted the Doctor's freedom, they should have faded back into obscurity and remained these mysterious beings we'd seen.

With the arrival of Tom Baker and a new production team, the programme took another turn. The character of the Doctor changed. He became less compassionate and kind, and even slightly callous. Basically, the character became inhuman. The Doctor was more alien. The programme itself took a deep breath and began to delve into areas of *Doctor Who* that all fans had their own strong ideas about.

Having reduced the role of the TARDIS to practically a mere antique piece, it was an easy step to introduce another control room. This step was not too well received, but it was a clever idea. On the same subject, in *The Invasion of Time,* the interior of the TARDIS was seen in greater detail, but what a surprise. It looked exactly like some Earth factory. A bold step, or just another part of the *Who* legend shattered?

Another possible shattering of the basis of the programme was the further views of Gallifrey, and the reduction of the Time Lords to degenerate old fools. *The Invasion of Time* raised the status of the Time Lords, but they will never be those strange mysterious people far out in space again.

The mystery has gone from the programme. Every story this year, we've heard that the Doctor is a Time Lord, and now with a Time Lady companion we're not likely to forget. If, in the eyes of the characters the Doctor meets, he is once again a mysterious character, maybe we will be able to join in with some mystery.

At the beginning, I said that we often hear "things are not what they used to be". Perhaps there are a few main reasons. The first is that there is less scope for stories. In William Hartnell's and Patrick Troughton's days, we had three, then two companions, and we had a kind of "family" in the TARDIS. In Jon Pertwee's days, the family moved to include the members of UNIT. But now, there is only one person.

Perhaps what is missing most of all is any warmth in the stories. Even when Leela left, it was pretty quick and we only had a sentence or two of slight remorse. Each story is short and sharp. We hardly have time to grow fond of the characters before they've gone. It is time to make the Doctor show some real emotion, be happy, be sad, angry and not just patter along in the same clownish way unique to this incarnation.

Let's have happy, sad, even crazy stories, with new writers, not the same bunch year in, year out, and bring back some humanity to the stories.

Every story moves along in the same way, with a strange sense of "sameness" about each story. There is a kind of dull feeling about the past season, or maybe "numb" is a better description. Although in themselves most stories are well made and good, the "magic" of the series as a whole has been lost. Forever? I hope not.

# Doctor Who and the Computers
## by Simon Guerrier

Midway into the first episode of the 1989 story *Battlefield*, one of the characters mutters that the phone in his car isn't working. On top of all the other strange phenomena so far in the story – strange bangs, the broken down nuclear convoy and the men in armour scrapping with laser guns – it's another sign that Something Odd is happening. Any minute now, the Doctor will be facing war with men from space.

But it's also more than that. Back in 1989, a carphone counted as a gag. Like the references to expensive drinks and a £5 coin in the same episode, it's a nod to the audience that this story's set "a few years" in the future.

It's sobering how recently a portable telephone was considered a really neat, space-age idea. Now mobiles are commonplace; an everyday nuisance whenever you use public transport. In fact, why would anyone bother with a phone exclusively for the car? But, back in 1989, when *Doctor Who* was a regular television fixture, wireless telephony was outlandish science fiction. They did that sort of thing on *Star Trek*.

When the Doctor's visits "the present day", there are any number of clues that we're actually a little bit in the future of the story's transmission date. Rather than using devices and brand names we, the viewers, might go out and buy as soon as the credits roll, the Doctor's got his hands on outlandish gadgets still beyond the dreams of the Innovations catalogue. It's true of the carphone in *Battlefield*, and the International Electromatics radio in *The Invasion*, twenty years before; *Doctor Who* remains one step ahead of modern technology.

What, though, do we mean by modern technology? Former *Doctor Who* script editor Douglas Adams had a characteristically witty way of putting it: "How do you recognise something that is still technology? A good clue is if it comes with a manual."

When you buy a computer, a DVD player or a particularly clever mobile phone, you need to have read the manual before you can use it. You can try pushing a few buttons and icons, and puzzle it out for yourself, but sooner or later something will get stuck or crash, and then the manual's the first thing you reach for. That or the telephone. Another dead giveaway is that technology comes with a helpline.

For my purposes, I'm going to define modern technology as those electrical devices for better processing information and communications, to improve on the limited human resources evolution has otherwise provided. You know, the sorts of things the Doctor has fought against for years.

In *The War Machines*, the first Doctor stops a clever computer based in London's Post Office tower from making nuisance phone calls. In *The Mind Robber*, the second Doctor and his companions get themselves written into the virtual reality of the Master Brain computer and have to break their way out. In *The Green Death*, the third Doctor fights big industrialists and giant maggots who were under the thrall of the machine mind, BOSS. In the fourth Doctor's first story, *Robot*, he calls computers "highly sophisticated idiots" and soon destroys an artificial man.

The fifth Doctor kills his own AI companion, Kamelion, at the end of *Planet of Fire*. The sixth Doctor rages against cocky computers in *The Two Doctors* and *Slipback*. It's one of the world's earliest computers that threatens to unleash terrible death on all mankind in the seventh Doctor story *The Curse of Fenric*. The eighth Doctor breaks the world's most sophisticated clock by stealing one of its chips.

So what is it the Doctor finds so objectionable? Let's take that first example: the first Doctor's adventure with the War Machines. Yes, WOTAN is a noisy, room-sized machine that chatters print-outs across the floor, and its War Machines are equally cumbersome and only seem good for bashing up cardboard boxes. In retrospect, as far as the technological hardware is concerned, it's a bit silly and naïve.

And yet, the Doctor fights to save the fashionable, modern people of London from a computer virus spreading down the telephone line. Today, computer viruses are a common blight in our lives, continually costing companies a fortune and getting in the way of us emailing our pals. What's more, the virus here hypnotises humans, and is the first stage in a programme to make the species extinct. The Doctor fights to save humanity from the aggressor.

What's more, WOTAN's virus working on humans isn't so unfeasible. Neal Stephenson's modern tech novel, *Snow Crash*, makes the same plot a plausible threat to the computer industry, something portrayed as a real-world danger, rather than the funky, modish fantasy it seemed in 1966. It's not the computer the Doctor has problems with; in fact, he seems quite impressed with it. It's WOTAN's invasive, misanthropic plans the Doctor finds "evil". That, and it referring to him as "Doctor Who".

It's also interesting that part of WOTAN's plan is ultimate global domination – and not just NW1, as it seems on screen. Though WOTAN may seem quaint and clunky now, compared to what was going on in the real world at the same time, it was pretty cutting-edge technology. Made up, but cutting edge.

What we know today as the internet first appeared in recognisable form in 1969: four computers in the US were connected to the ARPANET – though the very first user got as far as the letter "G" when trying to type the word "login" before the system crashed.

It was created on the understanding that a network of connected computer stations would survive, say, a nuclear strike. One of the system's multiple locations might be destroyed, but the others would continue. This was back in the days when nuclear war was a major concern, and the system was only going to be used by the military and academics – for purposes far more worthy than episode guides and pornography.

As a result, there wasn't exactly a rush to join up. By 1971, the system was connected to fifteen computers. The first email program was written the following year. And in 1973, ARPANET went international – connecting to a computer at University College London (just down the road from WOTAN).

At this point in the *Doctor Who* universe, the best technical minds were a little further ahead.

In *Doctor Who's* 1973, the Doctor fought another computer with designs on the world, and the cause of *The Green Death*. We only discover BOSS is a computer (!) at the end of episode four, two thirds of the way through the adventure. The computer is the epitome of Stevens' inhumane, inhuman project. Again, BOSS will seize power by linking itself to all computers across the world. However, it doesn't seem motivated by the need to ensure it is safe from any single system crash or nuclear strike, thus achieving immortality. Rather, like the economists who built it, its intention is to grow, to expand its market share and to consume everything it can.

It may be a clunky, cumbersome old computer, and the programme's production values have dated considerably, but, these days, the premise seems more relevant than it was when the episodes were first broadcast. Stevens is a greedy man with international business objectives who is happy to ignore the ecological damage he's causing. Instead, he freely pollutes the countryside with slimy chemical toxins in the name of efficiency and profit. It's a particularly unfeeling business mogul who makes BOSS evil, not so much the fact that it's a computer.

That said, the beginning of episode five sees the Doctor refusing to concede that BOSS is anything more than a neat idea, a jumped up digital watch. It reveals a lot about what the Doctor thinks about computers – of which, much more later.

The Doctor and some dirty, hippy chums living in a commune team up and stop BOSS. Battling the unfeeling computer is an outlet for political activism. If Llanfairfach had had a McDonalds, they'd have probably trashed that, too.

Two years after the economic villains of *The Green Death*, *Robot* sees a political group trying to conquer the world via technological solutions. With its Cold War plot and the nods to Women's Lib, the story has dated far more than *The Green Death*. But its arguments about technology, and the Robot itself, are fascinating.

As well as reckoning they could govern the planet better than the current world leaders, the humourless Scientific Reform Society also feel that the emergent technologies they themselves have had a hand in developing are being unwisely applied.

What's interesting is that a lot of the story is based around technologies that are specifically not meant to be used. The U.S. and U.S.S.R. are at a perfect stalemate with their nuclear weapons. The problem at the beginning of the story is not that the K1 Robot exists, but that it is out and about doing things. Later on, when the Brigadier gets hold of a fab new ray gun, his mistake is to pull the trigger.

So what is the Doctor fighting against here? It's not, when it comes to it, either the computers, or the giant robot. No, as he says while deftly averting nuclear disaster, computers know not what they do; they're only able to do what they're programmed, no matter how dangerous or silly. The real villains are the humourless, prejudiced humans who've made the robot do bad things. It's not the ethics of the robot that's up for debate, it's the human villains who really threaten the world. Just because SRS members tend to be good at crossword puzzles and number games doesn't give them the right to dictate other people's lives.

That's made explicit when Sarah taps into the robot's feelings. It's not a bad robot, it's just ill-equipped to cope with the dodgy moralities of its masters. It's more like a child; unquestioning of its mentors and eager for their approval. It may not be as wordy as WOTAN or BOSS, but it has the capacity to learn, to feel, to move a companion to tears, and so has far more of a claim to artificial intelligence than its forebears.

But while Sarah may fret over the robot's feelings, the Doctor (equally irrational, newly born and erratic in this story) breezes over the ethical debate of robotic consciousness and self-will. He may attempt to make friends at the end of episode two, but that's part of the bluff in his efforts to escape. He ultimately kills the robot with an ecologically sound virus, to much cheering from his UNIT chums. It's only in the novelisation that Sarah seems genuinely moved by the robot's death. It's a caring, thoughtful soul the Doctor's seen off so deftly, but as long as he's killed the friendly metal man with a green product, it seems to be okay. The robot was only a machine, after all.

Ten years later, the Doctor shows the same regard for Kamelion (and in the new series episode *School Reunion*, he does the same with K9 3.0). Again, the debates about the robot's self will and the way intellectual argument can change its mind – discussed at various points on screen – are glossed over at the end. For the Doctor, it's convenient that Kamelion's an artificial person because it means it doesn't really matter when he kills him.

So, is the problem that the Doctor doesn't like machines, or that he doesn't feel that machines have rights? Well, if that's the case, what about *The Robots of Death*? Like WOTAN, Taran Capel thinks humans inferior and unworthy – though, as a human, he sees himself as their liberator from enslavement. What's fascinating is the Doctor's attitude to the robots. He's positively charming to them while everyone else is rude. When Poul admits that robots make him uneasy, the Doctor responds that many robots feel the same way about humans. But that's not to say the Doctor here is on the side of the robots.

Rather, he's able to put an alternative point of view. In the second episode, when the humans accuse each other of the murders so far, he's the one to say, "There is one other possibility you seem to have overlooked." He's the one, having told Leela that "robots are programmed to help people, not hurt them", who suggests what none of the other humans is prepared to believe: that the robots could be the killers.

We're well into episode three before the Doctor can convince Poul and, though the logic is irrefutable, it's only when Poul can touch the bloodied robot's hands that he finally believes. Toos and Uvanov, similarly, don't believe until the robots try to kill them.

That conceptual failure on the part of the human characters is made explicit by the fact that we, the audience, know it's a robot doing the killing; we see it, right at the beginning of episode one. But, as the story proceeds, we learn that the robots are killing because, again, a human tells them to. The reprogrammed, murderous robots are not in command of themselves. They stutter, repeat orders over and over (which none of the robots do when running the ship), and have fuzzy eyes. Reprogammed, they're also unable to tell the Doctor apart from another robot in a hat and scarf.

Taran Capel's reprogramming is, then, not really any kind of liberation. It's just substituting one pair of chains for another. He tells the Doctor his next task will be to give the robots ambition, but what exactly will that achieve? To make the robots more like the hatefully irrational, greedy humans aboard the Sandminer, surely.

The Doctor's not got much time for the Sandminer crew either. In fact, the crew are just as vacuous and unimaginative as their machines; worse, because they all have something to hide. While they are selfish, waspish and quick to jump to conclusions, the Doctor's a charmer. The Doctor's justification for dealing with the Vocs so pleasantly is just good manners.

But, again, that doesn't mean he's on the robots' side. He still battles against them to save the Sandminer crew and their society. More so, there are telling moments that suggest more about the Doctor's attitude to the machines. In episode one, SV7 tells the Doctor and Leela to remain in a room. The Doctor's first act when the robot's gone, to Leela's surprise, is to get out and have a quick scout round. Two episodes later, when Poul tells the Doctor and Leela to stay where they are, Leela's ready to go scouting again, but the Doctor says no, and does as he's told.

When SV7's instructed him, the Doctor's only motive for leaving the room is to find the TARDIS; not to escape, but just so he knows where it is. When Poul's instructed him, his motive is... what? To wait for the killer robots to come find him? To let some of the minor characters get killed? To give Taran Capel more time to reprogram robots? Or is it because in one case a robot's asked him to do something, and in another it's a human who has asked him?

The one exception to the enslaved robots, and ironically the one robot to fight against Capel, is D84. While he shares the other robots' analytical intelligence, there's something more emotional about D84's responses. When he makes a silly blunder in his calculations – overlooking that Taran Capel could be doubling as one of the other humans onboard – you can hear the dejection in his tone. And when the Doctor tells him that that's okay, that "failure's one of the basic freedoms" and then asks D84 if he'd like to accompany him pursuing Capel, D84 replies, "Yes, please." And the "please" isn't just him being polite. He's delighted.

Robots are supposedly emotionless, unfeeling, logical machines – that's what makes them so eerie in the story, and causes the debilitating Grimwade's Syndrome. But D84 can be poetic when describing the functions of the Laserson probe and, when the Doctor asks "Are you sure?", replies – despite his logical, analytical robot mind – "I think so."

Other robots just do as they're told, but D84 seems genuinely keen to help. When the Doctor ignores Leela's shouts for help, D84 insists, again and again, "I heard a cry." He offers to go help Toos, and he's quick to find Poul and make sure he's safely with the others on the bridge. When he sacrifices himself to save the others, his last words are "Goodbye, my friends." D84 is the only robot to have friends, the only robot whose death is mourned; the Doctor's clearly aghast. It's a real shame he died; he'd have been a great companion.

But that's the problem. Capel is reprogramming the robots because he believes robots are stronger, smarter and more worthy than the humans. D84 proves himself to be quicker, stronger and more concerned for the humans' welfare than the Doctor. And the Doctor treats him like one of the kids who asks him stupid questions: an assistant. He chides and teases him. He doesn't treat D84 as an equal. He doesn't acknowledge his strengths. When D84 hears Leela's cry, the Doctor doesn't want to know. "That was me," he insists. Surely, his effort to not acknowledge D84's better hearing (I'm assuming that's what it is) actually leaves Leela to be throttled. But the Doctor won't be told. Not by a robot.

Robots come second, that's the conclusion of the story. What, ultimately, is the Doctor's argument against Capel? "Robots would have no existence without humans. Don't you see that Dask?"

Not long after, the Doctor meets his second-best friend. K9 is a friend the Doctor can make himself, who can do calculations and has a ticker-tape printout. In fact, K9 famously threatened to be more popular than the Doctor himself. He's the only character in the classic series the BBC ever allowed a full, proper, TV spinoff. So obviously, if the Doctor is best pals with a robot, he can't have a problem with them, can he?

Or can he?

The Doctor continually argues with K9. And for exactly the same reasons he usually argues with his companions: they are right about something, and he's got it wrong. K9's encyclopaedic knowledge, total recall and ability to judge the outcomes of the Doctor's latest plan – often correct to two decimal places – make him infuriating as far as the Doctor's concerned. Their playing chess may be a nod towards questions about the achievable intelligence of computers (the same gag's done in *Robots of Death*), but much more it reminds us how defensive the Doctor is about his own intelligence.

Like D84, K9 comes into his own when he's at his most un-robot-like. That's where the Doctor can show him genuine affection. When he bickers. Or sulks. Or gets laryngitis. As the Doctor wonders, in another beautifully put bit of techno-humour from Douglas Adams, for what reason would K9 need laryngitis?

K9, least equipped of all the Doctor's companions to defend himself from the teasing, is the one the Doctor bullies the most. In those stories where K9's not been left behind in the TARDIS, the Doctor is often telling him to shut up or get a move on. When he's stranded in the moat at the end of *The Androids of Tara*, the Doctor just laughs at him.

And there is something decidedly odd, even sinister, about a companion the Doctor can build himself. It's played as such with the revelation about the Doctor's companion Antimony's true nature as an android in the 2001 webcast, *Death Comes to Time*. But, with K9, the fact that he's a machine means that the Doctor messing with his insides doesn't matter. The Doctor spends most of Season Fifteen working over Marius' K9, before deciding he can do better by starting from scratch.

Perhaps giving K9 Mark I to Leela is less the elegant gesture to a departing companion as it is palming off the old model. Even in Season Eighteen, K9 Mark II still needs tinkering with. And then, having finally got shot of the mutt, the Doctor goes and makes an entirely new model in a different colour. But not for himself. This version of K9 is never seen beside his master (until *School Reunion* – and, er, *Dimensions in Time*). He's immediately dispatched to old pal Sarah. It's not K9, then, the Doctor has particular affection for. It's the tinkering.

In *State of Decay*, the Doctor admits that he "dabbles" with science – and that's exactly what he loves to do with technology. He doesn't want to read the manual, he just wants to push buttons until the thing works. He fixes the broken computer in the same story not through technical knowledge, but by hitting it. It's a trick he makes use of in several stories. Look at all the strange gadgets the Doctor builds: things to confuse Daleks and upset the Master's time experiments. He's not piously progressing technological innovation, he's mucking about.

So maybe he spends *The Robots of Death* merely toying with D84, and then three years toying with K9. And his attitude to WOTAN and BOSS, and even to the K1 robot, is that they're toys gone wrong. That's certainly what seems to be going on in *The Green Death* episode five, scene one. Villainous technology is the stuff he can't show off with.

What is the Time and Space Visualiser, but the earliest example of BitTorrent, with the Doctor downloading bootleg copies of Beatles gigs to prove to his young crew he's still hip? And he is, when it comes to technology. It's no coincidence that when he's battling WOTAN he also has time to stop by the disco, and when battling BOSS he's hanging out with the groovy hippies in the commune. That said, if the Doctor's not too bothered about stealing music, it's no wonder he doesn't get lucrative product placement from Apple.

Without a PowerBook, the Doctor has to use a BBC Micro to redesign the TARDIS. And what is the TARDIS but a great big internet site, a virtual portal to other worlds and times. The TARDIS is even driven via a console room; between *The Five Doctors* and *Dimensions in Time*, a console room where the controls really are comprised of different monitors and keyboards. Sometimes, the places the TARDIS takes him to are tawdry and silly, and sometimes they're really rewarding. Every now and then, he meets something really disturbing and frightening. It's like spending any amount of time on the web.

Is, then, the TARDIS technology? It has a manual, first seen in Douglas Adams' *The Pirate Planet*. In episode one, the Doctor hasn't read it, and he still hasn't read it by the time of *Vengeance on Varos*, though he admits he at least started once. Romana's interest in the manual isn't because the TARDIS is technology. "The Type 40 capsule wasn't on the main syllabus, you see," she says. "Veteran and vintage vehicles was an optional extra." She's reading the manual because the Doctor's TARDIS is an antique.

More than that, it's somehow more than merely technology. The Doctor has a symbiotic relationship with his TARDIS; perhaps part of his imprimature as a Time Lord. His first regeneration is eased by his being in the TARDIS. "Without it, I couldn't survive," he tells his astonished companions. After a later regeneration, it's the TARDIS' Zero Room that soothes the post-regenerative trauma. But that in itself doesn't stop the TARDIS being technology.

There's a Professor at Reading University who has bits of computer inside him that recognise when he walks into campus buildings or when he goes to the loo. Any number of people have "intimate" relationships with pacemakers and artificial implants. But the Doctor also anthropomorphises his ship. He refers to her as "old girl", pleads with her and explains to Tegan that "The TARDIS is more than a machine. She needs coaxing, persuading..."

While it may have been explored more in the New Adventures, there's only one television story where we're encouraged to look at the TARDIS in terms of computers. The word "Logopolis" is often translated as "City of Words", but "logo" more accurately means "symbol" in Greek, or "code". Thus we derive "logic"; as Doctor Judson acknowledges in *The Curse of Fenric*, the language of computers. So it's not surprising that the City of Code is populated with dumpy, beardie, balding men all muttering to themselves. It's the planet of the computer programmers.

*Logopolis* may go on about monitors, registers and bubble memory, but when it comes to the all-important Block Transfer Computations which mend the universe and fix the TARDIS, it has to be admitted that a computer just can't cope. "Only the living mind," insists the Monitor, is agile enough to manage the reality-warping computations. Not only is that another affirmation of the human mind over the computer, it also implies that the TARDIS has some constituent living element. The TARDIS really isn't an "it", but a she. QED. I think.

And that's also backed up by the fact that the Doctor's mind can't be contained in a computer. It breaks out. In *The Face of Evil*, it leaves Xoanon schizophrenic and so causes no end of mess. With Salyavin's mind-eating gadget in *Shada*, gobbling up the Doctor's mind (or a copy of it) just gives the Doctor access to take over and stop the villain's scheme. It's similar when he's patched into the artificial brain in *Time and the Rani*: trying to contain his mind in something artificial just isn't going to work.

So what *is* the Doctor's take on computers? He uses them, he plays with them, he takes them apart. He's comfortable using technology, but not with the power of technologies. And while he can begrudgingly admit a machine's intelligence or usefulness, he never forgets that technology is a tool. A machine may be equally good at chess, but it's not equal.

It's actually not far from Jaron Lanier's concern that computers are a way to bring people together, an aid to real human experience, not a replacement of it. In an interview with *The Guardian* in 2001, Lanier – who created Virtual Reality and is now something of a tech guru – said: "If we allow our self-congratulatory adoration of technology to distract us from our own contact with each other... then somehow the original agenda has been lost."

The Doctor won't be told what to do by a computer. So much so that, when Tom Baker and Lalla Ward starred in a 1980 series of adverts for a cumbersome, room-sized PRIME computer, it's not just Doctor Who getting married that's funny. The real gag is that he's doing so because a computer tells him to.

And who is it the Doctor's fighting? More often than not, humans and aliens who want to be more machine, more robotic, less emotional and real. There are endless baddies who go on about rationality and logic. The Sontarans tell humans that cloning is far more efficient than our binary reproductive system. The Cybermen slag off emotions. The people who aid the Cybermen – the Nietzchean neo-Nazis, the amoral businessman Tobias Vaughan, and the coldly sinister Brotherhood of Logicians – are "following their example", as the Doctor says.

Despite what he says in *The Robots of Death* about "to the rational mind, nothing is inexplicable, only unexplained", the Doctor has always had a problem with logic. The second Doctor is disparaging of Zoe's faith in logic, and she herself later talks the super-computer running the reception at International Electromatics into suicide.

Vicki of all people does something similar in "The Search" (episode three of *The Space Museum*). Her immediate reaction to the impregnable computer is to laugh at it. Then she tells her chums, "Help me get the front off." Within a couple of moments, she's handily "fixed it so I only had to answer the truth, I didn't have to give the correct reply". It's a childishly simple solution to an uncomplicated logic puzzle.

Often, that's what the Doctor's adventures are; simple logic games he's solved with his supposed brilliance. In the following episode ("The Final Phase"), the Doctor escapes brain-death from the cryogenic process by, as he says, thinking like a "mechanical computer".

While the Doctor may claim to be a scientist, he's far better at illogic and the irrational. He confuses robots and confounds monsters, and in *The Invasion of Time* purposefully fills his head with gibberish about tea to keep the telepathic Vardans out. His most effective weapon against the Daleks is the discombobulator he builds in *Remembrance of the Daleks* – a technological equivalent of what he spends his travels doing anyway.

Oh yes, the Daleks.

More than Nazism, the Daleks stand for the terrible amorality of science. Nazism is key to just some of their stories. Central to their every appearance are the abuses they perpetrate in the name of science, the fact that technology is the key to their power. With their special casings, they can survive a nuclear holocaust. With little radars on their backs, they can invade Earth. With their own DARDIS, they can chase the Doctor through time and space. They have keen research projects looking to exploit Thal radiation drugs, the Human Factor, invisibility. The Doctor's even able to use their need to have and use great technology, and somehow lets them hear of a remote stellar manipulator he may accidentally have left lying about.

One Dalek story doesn't quite get it right. *Revelation of the Daleks* is one of the series' strangest, darkest and most horrific stories. In one of their most appalling schemes yet, the Daleks exploit helpless, dying people. Most they turn into processed food, but some they turn into Daleks. But what horrifies the Doctor most of all is that now, through Davros' clever, technological machinations, the Daleks can reproduce anywhere.

It's actually quite funny when you think about it. From now on when we suddenly, unexpectedly find them underwater or buried in sand or invisible in a forest, they'll be in pairs...

The thing is, it may be a "technological" solution they've come up with, but it only makes any sort of sense if we've some idea how they reproduced before. I mean, we've glimpsed the Dalek production line in *The Power of the Daleks*, but surely that was just for the casings. If it's such a liberating thing for them to breed anywhere, they must have had a system even more complicated and unwieldy than our own inefficient binary method.

But it's a bit of a stretch, isn't it? When it comes to it, the moralities in *Doctor Who*, especially where technologies and computers are concerned, are all a bit of a muddle. The show can be witty and erudite and prescient about technology, but it's not very consistent about what it actually thinks.

In *The Two Doctors*, the Doctor's evidently proud that Dastari wrote out his theories with pen and ink, rather than using a computer. There are key plot elements about the dangers of new technology and scientific experimentation, and how security systems can be made to lie. But then, the sixth Doctor is hugely jealous of his other self's Stattenheim Remote Control. And, for someone who protests about computers so much, he does know an awful lot about them, how to bypass them, how to make them play his way.

But that's where *Doctor Who* differs from a genre show like, say, *Star Trek*. *Star Trek* loves its computers and technology; the ships are all decked out in wipe-clean controls and the cast continually solve problems by running programmes and inventing new bits of kit, or laws of physics.

*Doctor Who* is a lot more wary about technology being necessarily a good thing. In fact, the conflict between the new and the old, the futuristic and the historical, is one of the basic foundations of the series. When the show began, it purposefully alternated between stories set in the past and stories set in the future, with the Doctor's new companions – one science teacher, one history teacher – able to note the significance of the events and peoples encountered, and come to some sort of judgement.

More than that, the Doctor's an old man who's also young, and yet a young man who's also old. He lives in an old police box (made almost obsolete as a result of walkie-talkies and more convenient communications technologies), but inside it's actually a whizzy, futuristic spaceship. His adventures mix the past and future, and delight in depositing aliens with ray guns in seventeenth century London or getting members of the Jacobite rebellion or bystanders at the battle of Troy onto spaceships.

It's continually playing with the problems, the worries of technology. And never quite making its mind up about it all.

We can even rework that definition of technology, now. "We notice things that don't work," Douglas Adams once said. "We don't notice things that do. We notice computers, we don't notice pennies. We notice e-book readers, we don't notice books." We tend to think of technology in these terms, yes. But pens and books were also invented to improve our communication and quality of life. You still need lessons to use them. What are schoolbooks, but manuals for reading? All these things are useful tools.

Technology, then, is a tool we don't yet know how to use. Nothing more complicated than that, and nothing that can in itself be fought against. Because it's not the machines themselves the Doctor needs to be wary of, it's the people these tools empower...

# "Science, not Sorcery, Miss Hawthorne"

**by Hugh Sturgess**
*From The Doctor Who Ratings Guide, August 2006*

*"It was all about disproving magic, finding the truth; which was what* Doctor Who *had always been about. In Hammer Horror, mummies are mummies – they are cadavers brought back to life. In* Doctor Who, *they're robots."*

—Gareth Roberts,
on the Hinchcliffe era in "Serial Thrillers",
on the *Pyramids of Mars* DVD

Now, this statement is probably what many fans wheel out to prove how nice *Doctor Who* is. It's about a group of people, led by a man who is proud to be called a scientist (Jon Pertwee's Doctor gets into a bit of a tizz when someone suggests that he isn't one: "If I were a scientist? Let me tell you, sir, that I am a scientist, and have been for several thousand..."), who solve scientific problems with scientific methods. It's a show about empiricism, exploration and experimentation, which is what science is all about.

But, really, if you watch it, you realise the series really isn't about science at all. As Lawrence Miles and Tat Wood realised to their horror in *About Time 4*, the entire medium of television, and *Doctor Who* in particular, is on the side of... well, magic. Magic, that dreaded anti-Doctor, which the Doctor can always debunk with ease, and all adherents of which are deluded loonies. Magic is completely against the ethos of *Doctor Who*, isn't it?

No, actually. Really, "hardcore" SF only works in books, where you can stop the action halfway through and devote huge passages to cutting-edge scientific theories to explain certain McGuffin plot devices (Stephen Baxter, anyone?). On TV, you have to keep going, faster and faster, with little or no time to stop for scientific discussions (which is why *Quatermass* looks so shockingly slow to modern eyes). Really, it's much easier in TV to not explain events at all, to simply have them look right. TV's about images, not words, and science is about words, not images. TV is about magic. After all, magic is just science taught badly. No, really; even magic tricks on stage, like the "disembodied head coming out of table" trick uses laws of reflection to work, it just doesn't bother to explain this is the case. *Doctor Who* – and TV itself – has been using magic in its dramas since it was created, but no one felt like naming its own specific genre because it made sense: magic performed in a medium made entirely of magic.

If I can just first consider the first season of *Who* in 1963, you can see this truth in action. CE "Bunny" Webber (no, I don't know why either) said that the TARDIS was "the dear old magic door", and people have been saying for years that it's basically the wardrobe from the smug Narnia books. Webber also had a list of ideas for future stories (including, weirdly, that the Fairy Godmother was Dr Who's wife pursuing him through time) that seemed more like something from a Yuletide panto than a "serious" programme about science. The much-maligned director Richard Martin had the "theory" that the TARDIS interior was a force of will, which is essentially dressing up "an act of faith" in stolen pseudo-scientific robes. Sydney Newman calmly dismissed all this as "nuts", but the man who ended up in charge of establishing the tone of the scripts (and thus the series, to a degree), David Whitaker, had an attitude towards "hard" science that suggests he couldn't tell a galaxy from a biscuit. The stories written by him have a Victorian fairytale quality to them, and no one found this odd, because no one would have thought of *Doctor Who* as a "Science Fiction" show at that time.

*An Unearthly Child* shows the TARDIS, as has been previously mentioned, as a magic door. No explanation is given as to the Ship's dimensional transcendence (and it'll be about ten years before the concept even gets a pseudo-scientific mask) or its remarkable abilities of time travel and shape-shifting. The phrase "any sufficiently advanced technology is indistinguishable from magic" comes to mind. The rather lame way of avoiding questions – "where does time go?" – is flagrantly saying "it's all so advanced that we can't understand it, so deal with it". They even make the following three episodes a case in point, juxtaposing the "primitive" Ian and Barbara's incomprehension of the Doctor and his bigger-inside-than-out box of tricks with the cavemen's awe of the Doctor's matches. And the Doctor himself is blatantly Prospero, Shakespeare's magician from *The Tempest*. Any science, poorly explained, is magic.

*The Daleks* shows the TARDIS to be just like any other spaceship, which is more "scientific" than anything Chris Bidmead says about the Ship, and yet it's viewed with embarrassment today, as it feels so out of keeping with the rest of the show. But it also shows magic food-bars that taste like eggs one bite and slightly-too-salty bacon the next, machines possessed by evil spirits powered by static electricity, evolution as a force, and reveals that the TARDIS relies on mercury for its flight, not simply because of its power to make intermittent connections, but because of its mysterious, "magical" properties. Really, the whole "Daleks powered by static electricity" thing, often wheeled out to show how scientific the series is, comes off as a magical "allergy", like silver to werewolves, dressed up as "respectable" science.

*The Edge of Destruction* is, essentially, an attempt to make the TARDIS magical. The point of the story, rather than being "d'oh, the switch is stuck", is that the Ship itself has some kind of spooky intelligence. It re-enforces the idea of the TARDIS, not simply as a means to reach more petrified jungles and trippy cities, but as a world in itself, where magical things can happen. People usually say that it's a haunted-house tale, and they're not wrong; the TARDIS becomes, to all intents and purposes, for one episode only, a haunted house. Spooky silence, claustrophobia, pseudo-POV camera angles and, on one memorable occasion, even boom shadows looming over the characters all contribute to the idea of the Ship as a beast, a thing consciously conspiring to drive our heroes insane. The other title attributed to this adventure (although never actually used on screen), *Inside the Spaceship*, is ironic because this story, more than any other, tries to prove that the TARDIS isn't one.

The rest of the stories really are just part of the formula, and the rather low quality of effects mean that there are few opportunities to include "magical" events, though some do stand out; Marco Polo mentions levitating mystics, and he is the sort of person, we are encouraged to believe, who always tells the truth. The Gobi Desert is presented as a creature, a single organism, actively trying to kill the characters. The episode synopsis included in contemporary copies of the *Radio Times* is unwittingly appropriate. It mentions the Doctor "outwitting" the Gobi Desert, and the desert is presented a thing to defeat, as if the passage through it is almost a battle of wills.

However, the last big thing is in *The Aztecs*, where Sydney Newman phoned up crying, and had the lines changed to "glorify the occupation, etc, of an engineer". The Doctor mentions that he is an engineer, and sorts out the problem by making a dodgy wheel and axle by hand. Now, this has to be considered key; the title "doctor" implies learning, but not scary learning, and is not as dissociated as a professor. Also, a doctor is someone who fixes things, while a professor just thinks and makes airy pronouncements about things he's never seen. So, rather than being a series about science, is *Doctor Who* a series about engineering?

The "magic" elements of the series remained prominent throughout the next eight years, and most notably surfaced in the Animus (husky female voice controlling slaves via gold, voodoo-like), the Celestial Toymaker (Oriental magician-genie living outside space and time) and the Great Intelligence (similarly disembodied – this time, male – voice controlling furry beasts with fangs and claws via crystal balls). And while it isn't noticed today because it seems so obvious, the revelation that the Yeti are robots is entirely out of keeping with the series as a whole. If they had simply been genuine animals, controlled by the Great Intelligence, then nobody would have batted an eyelid, because *Doctor Who* was never about reducing the magical and wondrous to humdrum reality. But the Time Lords were the most magical element of all; wizards who watch over the universe, who made deals with spirits to travel anywhere and live forever. Gallifrey even looks like a wizard's castle. No one really made such a big fuss about science and, as the Doctor played by magical rules, this never clashed with any other elements. It was doing what the series always had done; dressing up magic as science.

But, with the third Doctor's era, and the removal of that pesky TARDIS, the production team got it into their silly little heads that *Doctor Who* is about science, and that the Doctor is a scientist. It's interesting to note that, before the arrival of Barry Letts as producer, the Doctor, wearing a T-shirt and mouth full of wiring as he repaired a nuclear reactor in *Doctor Who and the Silurians*, seemed more like an engineer than ever before. However with Season Eight, this "science is automatically good" idea came in with a vengeance. The Doctor proudly claimed to be a scientist, something that he had never done before.

This felt... well, wrong. Not just aesthetically – though the sight of the authoritarian Doctor as a scientist is, unconscionably, ugly – but in terms of ethos. The Doctor, really, is a chameleon, shifting what he believes in – magic or science – whenever he needs to play by different rules; witness his acceptance of the Ship's sentience immediately after using scientific methods to sort out the Daleks back in 1964. And, similarly, it just feels wrong to have the Doctor going on and on about science when the medium he exists in is based on magic. Try watching *The Daemons* immediately after seeing the Brigadier and Jo take shelter from a nuclear explosion in *The Claws of Axos* by hiding behind a jeep, and then returning to the danger zone seconds after the explosion.

*The Daemons*, is, undoubtedly, the very worst offender. The first scene is of a raging storm, thunder and lightning illuminating a churchyard with splashes of grotesque light. A man chases after his dog and finds it dead, and then sees something so terrible that he dies (it is never explained what it is, as Azal is safely locked in his barrow, Bok is still a gargoyle at this stage rather than a fat bloke in a body stocking and the Master is hardly that ugly). Then, in the very next scene, we have Miss Hawthorne face a local-bobby-possessing freak storm which she dissipates with a magic spell.

After all that, the Doctor waltzes into the story, busily dismissing Jo's allusions to "the occult and all that magic bit" as nonsense and claiming that things with built-in technobabble are somehow automatically better. He feels like a sod, and a party-pooper, when he tricks Jo with his little remote control and says "science, not sorcery". It doesn't matter that the Doctor's unlikeable, misogynistic and an authoritarian. It does matter that he pooh-poohs magic, when he uses poorly explained science as a crutch. And poorly explained science is...? To fit Bessie with the means to be driven by remote control, he would have to take her apart and rebuild her from the bottom up. When he triggers the horn by remote control, the horn bulb actually depresses, like someone is squeezing it. How does it work? It's magic.

The story's primary flaw is its belief that it can simply tell us that it's on the side of science, and we never have to actually see the Doctor doing anything in defence of it. Simply saying "science, not sorcery" isn't going to convince us.

The hypocrisy doesn't just stop there. One of the story's most memorable characters, the gargoyle Bok, is a scientific impossibility. How is he animated? Some kind of "psychic science". But how, exactly? Stone is brittle, so to move that fluidly it would have to be red-hot. And Azal; how does he shrink and grow and so forth? The production team should be acknowledged for including the snap-freezes and heat waves when Azal grows or shrinks respectively, but we never learn how he does it. It's seemingly a mind-controlled process, but it's never explained. Also, Azal and the Devil's Hump are treated with occult reverence throughout the story; the Daemon will appear three times, and will destroy the Earth on the third, while the script makes sure that the Hump is opened at the heart of a raging storm.

Really, they could explain every element of the story with real science, but they simply can't be bothered. They could say something like "the particles in the stone are so agitated that it acts like a fluid", or say that Azal has a handy device that turns mass into raw energy and vice versa.

But they don't. Now, a story that did this would have about three extra episodes of talking, and I'd probably be bored by it, but in a story that states several times that it's on the side of "science, not sorcery, Miss Hawthorne", you expect some real science. The idea of a living gargoyle is a great idea, but it's a fantastic idea, in the literary sense of the word, not a Hard SF one. Similarly, the programme-makers assume we'll see Azal as so powerful because of what he symbolises: the Devil, the oldest, most powerful villain possible (he is consciously set up as the biggest threat the Doctor has ever faced; see the Doctor's comment that Azal is more powerful than the Daleks and the Axons), and so simply becomes a big, hairy bloke who shouts a lot when you try to present him as an alien scientist.

Of course, I couldn't continue without mentioning the technobabble the Doctor uses to defeat the heat barrier. Even adherents of the story find it a problem, but explain it away as "the series was never about real science anyway". Well, someone should tell the scriptwriters that. But not only is the technobabble mesmerically meaningless, it doesn't even make grammatical sense, as many sentences are joined by completely the wrong conjunctions. So, Osgood builds a machine that... does what? Oh, something to do with air particles and a nonsense word, diathermy. Why didn't the Doctor just wave the sonic screwdriver about and say "abracadabra"? But let's look even closer at this; the Doctor says a series of nonsense words that don't seem to make any logical sense, which defeats an "evil" force. What does that remind you of? (Clue: magicians are justly famous for casting them.) Really, that's the story in microcosm: lots of people doing magic, but only some of them admitting as such.

Thankfully, as the series progressed, Barry Letts and Robert Sloman and their entourage moved on, and a conscious decision to be more "science fantasy" came in, and with it came a distrust of scientists. A look at the Hinchcliffe era shows this: the Scientific Reform Society is a group of fascists; scientist Noah is shown as inhuman while engineer Rogan is personal and argumentative; experimenter Styre is a sadist; genius Davros created the most evil beings in the universe; Sorenson tampers with the forces of creation in a bid for fame and recognition; Solon is a fanatic; Styggron is a warmongering bogeyman; Eldrad is a tyrant; electricity is used by the Rutan as a weapon; and the scientists in *The Seeds of Doom* and *Image of the Fendahl* are petty and insular.

The stories, too, took on a different bent; scientists aren't always right, and the mystical prophecies invariably come true. The eponymous planet in *Planet of Evil* is a wonderful horror concept, and antimatter makes an aesthetic sense even if it's scientifically loony. Sutekh may be an alien war criminal, and mummies may be robots, but take away his toys and the Osiran is still a demigod because of what he symbolises. (If we want to make things simple, we could think of science fiction as the drama of the relationship between humanity and its tools, while fantasy is the drama in the relationship between us and our symbols.) Here, tools stop being the issue, and it becomes about symbols.

*The Masque of Mandragora* is *The Daemons 2: This Time It's Personal*, and works to the same rules (magic bad, science good), and while representing the Helix as inexplicable – because it symbolises superstition – may be aesthetically appropriate, there's a lot here that isn't: the Doctor mulling over the positions of the stars, Hieronymous' prophecies coming true, etc. The pivotal moment comes when Guiliano – who's scientific and therefore "good" – suggests that Hieronymous has summoned up something from "beyond". He may have heard the Doctor's half-baked explanation of the Helix, but he's basically switching "demon" with "mass of ionised plasma". And if you think that's bad – and it is – the Doctor then applies "science" to defeat the Helix; basically doing something terribly technical and shorting the Helix out.

*Image of the Fendahl*'s titular adversary doesn't have any toys at all. The Fendahl doesn't deliberate, or shout; it isn't Azal, but Death, ancient and inescapable. You know that the rules have changed when the Doctor ignores the scientists, asks local witch Ma Tyler for advice, and gives three explanations for the Fendahl: one pseudo-mystical, one scientific, and one putting it all down to an amazing coincidence. But what really shows that *Doctor Who* is about symbols now is the way standard nightmare-fare is paraded before us, as if for the first time: the Doctor is chased by something, but finds he can't move his legs; giant slugs ooze down corridors; and a glowing skull "proves" that a man who thought he was safe has been manipulated all along.

The ultimate "magical" element of the series, the one that makes very little scientific sense – yet perfect aesthetic sense – is that of the Guardians. *The Key to Time* series essentially has the Doctor going on a quest for a series of "magical" artefacts, and has to outwit numerous "magical" and other obstacles such as dragons and seers, walking menhirs who drink blood, Celtic goddesses and flashy spirits, corrupt lords, and servants of the Black Guardian, clad in black robes and bone-masks. But the inspiration goes beyond Heroic – in the Classical sense of the word – quests, and into religion: the White Guardian responds to the Doctor's inquiry as to his identity with "do you really need to ask?", takes the form of an old man with a beard and can stop the TARDIS in a blaze of light; furthermore, in *The Armageddon Factor*, when the Black Guardian drops his disguise, he seems to burn in black flames.

Season Eighteen, rather than being "real science", is simply hooked up on aesthetics. Let's look at the stories; the Recreation Generator on Argolis can make you old, make you young, duplicate you, mix and duplicate multiple people, and even do all that and make them young again. It's essentially a great big shiny, magic wand, something that Bidmead apparently loathed. It might not make scientific sense, but it does make aesthetic sense: the Doctor was horribly aged in the Generator, so it's inevitable that when lots of masked men get out of it at least one is going to be his younger self.

Then we come to *Meglos*, and the much-feted chronic hysteresis. The Doctor and Romana may not apply rational science to the problem, but the way they escape makes perfect aesthetic sense, and fits everything we know about the hysteresis.

The E-Space trilogy is a great example of this: *Full Circle* presents evolution, as *The Daleks* did, as a force, constantly running in cycles, while *State of Decay* is just so sublime a balance of styles that the term "science fantasy" seems made for it: the Giant Vampire is presented as an ancient, inexplicable symbol of terror, but the Doctor can defeat him because he knows how to manipulate the controls of a spaceship well enough to drive this colossal artefact through the creature's heart. That this story seems like a greater victory for "science" than *The Daemons* should tell you something about the nature of television as well as the nature of the programme itself. TV works best dealing with symbols, and *Doctor Who* is no different. The Doctor is "science", and thus uses technology, while his enemy is "superstition", and is thus the Vampire King of an ancient race that clashed with the Time Lords when the universe was still young.

*Warriors' Gate* is probably the only magic realist *Doctor Who* TV story. The term "magic realism" has been bandied around quite a bit, but this is an honest-to-God example of the genre. Events, such as the cliffhanger to episode three and the monochrome garden, aren't explained, which many people take to mean that the story is about hard science that they can't understand; the truth is that the author is just making it all up as he goes. The crew of the Privateer are normal, plodding folk: they don't want to take over the universe (or even work hard), don't understand how the space-machinery works, and just want to get their bonuses.

However, the cargo they have is hundreds of "leonine mesomorphs", as Romana calls the Tharils, "with a lot of hair" – lion-people to you or me – who want to escape to the ruins of a church so that they can pass through an indestructible mirror into a black-and-white garden. Any doubt where this story's origins lie ends when the Doctor compares talking to Biroc to talking with a cheshire cat, and later alludes to "the right sort of nothing".

Season Eighteen makes science a kind of "ethos" rather than a series of principles. It may be powered by an artificial device grafted onto a sun, but the fairy-tale kingdom of Traken is ruled by a genuine wizard, and evil turns to stone inside its walls. (The notion of a talking statue exploiting the sadness of a lovelorn young women for its own ends is pure Grimm fairytale, as well.) *Logopolis* depicts entropy as an "anti-life" force, and it is held in check by a planet of chanting wizards in long, flowing robes.

Magic made a resurgence after the more conventional Seasons Nineteen through Twenty-Four. The Time Lords become sorcerers once more in *Remembrance of the Daleks*, and the Hand of Omega bears a striking resemblance to the Ark of the Covenant from *Raiders of the Lost Ark*. *Silver Nemesis* has a material that can cause "bad luck", and a medieval sorceress and her servant use a magic potion to travel through time. *The Greatest Show in the Galaxy* has the Doctor performing magical tricks, and a circus is revealed to be run for the entertainment of three stone gods in a netherworld. However, Season Twenty-Six has the greatest amount of magic: *Battlefield* has knights and witches coming into our world from a universe built from magic, and the Doctor is revealed to be Merlin himself; *Ghost Light* has dead beetles returning to life and an angel awaking in a stone spaceship to burn the Earth; *The Curse of Fenric* has the Doctor battling an echo of evil, essentially fighting evil itself; and *Survival* has those two polar opposites – the Doctor and the Master – fight to the death with bones (and the famous image of the Doctor holding the skull aloft is strangely reminiscent of a similar shot in *An Unearthly Child*) as the world tears itself apart around them.

*Doctor Who* works with magic, not science. It's a universe of wizards, goblins, evil spirits and heroes. So it's good to see that the new series, for the most part, plays by those rules, not feeling the need to explain how time works in *Father's Day*, showing the Gelth and the werewolf as magical, and the first series ends with Rose becoming, in essence, one with God, but is saved from burning by a kiss. And that's great. Because if everyone keeps screaming "look, this is science" at us at every turn, we'll invariably shout "no, it's stupid" right back at them.

# Everything You Know (Could Have Been) Wrong

**by Robert Smith?**

*From Enlightenment #102, January / February 2001*

> *"The children of my civilisation would be insulted."*
> *"Your civilisation?"*
> *"Yes, my civilisation. I tolerate this century but I don't enjoy it. Have you ever thought what it would be like to be wanderers in the fourth dimension, have you? To be exiles...? Susan and I are cut off from our own planet, without friends or protection. But one day, we shall get back. Yes, one day..."*

> —*An Unearthly Child* (transmitted version)

Six years is a long time in television. Most shows are lucky to get that sort of run today; even mega-hits like the various *Star Trek* incarnations or *The X-Files* don't last long beyond that expiry date. And if they do, they've usually run out of steam around the Season Six mark. It's not much different in Britain either: *Red Dwarf* managed six years of continuous production, then struggled to tag two extra seasons on the end, some years later.

*Doctor Who*, on the other hand, managed to do a lot better than that. Only *Mr Squiggle*, an Australian children's show featuring an alien from the moon who would visit his Earth friends every day and draw upside-down pictures based on random squiggles (erm, it's a lot better than it sounds), managed to outlast it in the science-fiction stakes. (It ran from 1959 to 1999.) Yet, for the first six years, *Doctor Who* was a very different show, and not just because you couldn't tell that the console was painted green.

There were no Time Lords, no backstory, no Master. Food came out of a machine, you watched your surroundings on a little TV screen hanging from the wall and you would tell the time on an ormolu clock that would conveniently melt if you'd pressed the wrong button on the console. Aye, lad, those were the days.

By the time we got to the Eric Saward years, everyone and their Terileptil had heard of the Time Lords, and often the Doctor as well. Double-heart jokes were a staple of the Pertwee years and *The Five Doctors* even reinstated the Doctor's status of being "on the run from your own people in a rackety old TARDIS". The Doctor stares into the distance, saying "Why not? After all, that's how it all started."

But did it? For the first six seasons, we didn't know about Time Lords, or Gallifrey, or Type 40 TARDISes. Even regeneration was called "rejuvenation" when it first appeared (although fortunately its ability to regenerate clothing was reused in *Castrovalva*; a clever and subtle piece of continuity). The entire premise of the series was that the central character was a mystery and intended to remain so. However, there's a fair amount of on-screen evidence to suggest that the early production teams had their own ideas about where the Doctor came from.

In the pilot episode, Susan tells Ian and Barbara that she was born in the forty-ninth century. In both pilot and transmitted episodes, she claims to have made up the word "TARDIS" from its initials, while the Doctor later claims to have built the TARDIS in *The Chase*. (I realise that *The Chase* also has studio lights in the jungle and a Dalek with a cold, but let's ignore that for the moment.)

Furthermore, the 1966 film *Dr Who and the Daleks*, co-written by David Whitaker, the series' original script-editor (and hence the man responsible for much of the ongoing vision of the early stories) has the Doctor as a very human inventor, who builds the TARDIS. Sound familiar? Okay, so he's not from the forty-ninth century, sports an appalling moustache and later gets an extra grandchild, but I think there are more than a few hints in the Hartnell era itself to suggest that the Doctor was not quite the alien we all thought.

For one thing, he doesn't have two hearts, as verified in *The Edge of Destruction* and *The Sensorites*. (The former is a bit dubious, since it's Ian who checks and the Doctor is unconscious at the time, but in the latter it's the Doctor himself who says that a blow under his heart could kill him.) Furthermore, in *The Sensorites* he says "Cats can see in the dark, unlike us humans." However, most telling of all is *The Savages*, which sees Hartnell in righteous fury telling the Elders "They're men! Human beings like you and me!"

*The Savages* is an interesting story for other reasons (not least of which is Frederick Jeager's incredible impersonation of the Doctor; he was extensively coached by Hartnell himself). The humans there have evolved to a level where they have some affinity with time and are able to watch the Doctor's exploits throughout time and space (maybe Ian Stuart Black was suggesting that *Doctor Who* fans will become the dominant lifeform in the future). The Doctor gets very chummy with them, almost as though he's feeling right at home with humans from the future living on an alien planet.

The Troughton years are a bit more cunning. Regeneration obviously ups the alienness of the lead character, so the Doctor is far more evasive whenever it comes to medical tests (*The Wheel in Space*) or the question of how many hearts he has. (The Dulcians have two and the Dominators measure Jamie to determine he has one but the Doctor narrowly avoids being tested himself.)

The Doctor's backstory in *The War Games* proved to be a satisfying and durable one. It broadly fit the facts, at least as far as the viewer could remember. Even with the advent of video, there was enough doubt that fans could theorise to their hearts' content, coming up with inventive theories to explain the problem with the number of hearts and Susan naming the TARDIS. The durability meant multiple reappearances of Gallifrey and the Time Lords over the years, and incorporation of the ideas into merchandise and factual books (helped enormously by *The Deadly Assassin*, of course, which ironically ignored a great deal of what went before it).

Furthermore, every attempt to make a movie felt the need to show us this backstory, or at the very least explain it for the viewers (thus missing the point of the series' title entirely). Jean-Marc Lofficier's history of unmade *Doctor Who* films and TV pilots, *The Nth Doctor*, is full of tales about the Doctor starting on Gallifrey and fleeing on some mission or other. Even *The TV Movie* felt the need to throw us fact after fact in a massive infodump, as though where the Doctor came from were the most crucial thing new viewers could need (and maybe that's true of American audiences).

I think *The Savages* is the closest suggestion to what the early production teams had intended for the Doctor and Susan. Namely, that they were human colonists from the far future who had fled their home (possibly due to a war), and explored time and space. It's an interesting speculation, although what we ultimately got was much, much better.

The series had six long years with barely a hint of an answer to just who the Doctor was. It probably couldn't have dragged on without explanation forever and was massively revitalised when Season Seven began. It's something of a shame that we can't go back to that, but one of the keys to the series' longevity is its flexibility. This means that just about anything is possible, including re-injecting some of the mystery, as seen in the McCoy years, or the alienness of the fourth Doctor (which was highly praised by Verity Lambert). And, despite all the explanations we think we have, it would be quite poetic for the series to turn around and tell us that what we think we know isn't it at all. It's that unpredictability that puts the "Who" into "Doctor Who".

Let's hope it stays that way.

# Symbolism

by David Carroll, Kyla Ward and Kate Orman

*From Burnt Toast #3, June 1990*

Fiction, and indeed art, in its most basic form has two objectives: to be entertaining and to be meaningful. These criteria can both be interpreted in many different ways, leading to the multitude of forms in which we express ourselves. The importance of each of these objectives also varies widely, depending on the structure or the author of the piece. Symbolism is simply one of many (and possibly the subtlest) ways in which "meaningfulness" can manifest itself. Like good mathematical notation, a literary symbol can summarise a great deal of connotation in a simple framework and, if used properly, it can enhance a story without drawing overt attention to itself.

*Doctor Who*, with its many producers, writers and script editors, has redefined its use of symbolism constantly over the years. The normal "brief" for a *Doctor Who* writer seems to be to entertain, to provide a story that can be followed by anyone and submerge as much symbolism as desired under the storyline. Thus, we have stories ranging from the relative simplicities of *The Visitation* to the deeply ingrained Buddhist imagery of *Kinda*.

What follows is a look at symbolism within *Doctor Who* over the years, from the series' overall "mythology" to individual stories, and even lines. It's a big job, and we've undoubtedly made many omissions, so write in if anything's too blaringly missing, or indeed wrong.

**Duality:** Perhaps the most important, and certainly most used, piece of symbolism throughout the show's history, this involves two states, structurally similar, but ideological opposed, and with no middle ground in between. This motif comes up again and again; a short list goes something like: Good / Evil (both by implication, or more explicitly as in White / Black Guardian), N-Space / E-Space, Matter / Anti-matter *(Planet of Evil)*, Man / Beastman *(Inferno, Planet of Evil, Greatest Show)* Aggression / Pacifism *(The Daleks, The Dominators, Survival)* Intellectualism / Simplicity *(The Daleks, The Savages,* Gallifreyan Society, *Kinda, The Mysterious Planet)* and Beauty / Ugliness *(The Daleks, Galaxy Four, Ambassadors of Death, The Claws of Axos)*. And, of course: Doctor / Abbot of Amboise, Doctor / Salamander, Doctor / Meddling Monk, Doctor / Master, Doctor / Gallifreyan society, Doctor / Valeyard and Doctor / Fenric. Note that this simply isn't a listing of doubles in the show: the Doctor coupled with either the Daleks' robot or Kraal's android, or the Rani and Mel, or the two Nyssas in *Black Orchid*, have more relation to plot development than any symbolism. The most interesting of these is perhaps the Doctor / Master relationship because of its variability. The fifth Doctor / Master was obviously Good / Evil whilst seventh Doctor / Master is closer to Sanity / Insanity. As for the pre-*Keeper of Traken* Master, there seems to exist a far more complex relationship which goes beyond the scope of this discussion.

**The Crystal...** symbolises desired power. One has only to look at a well-used device of sci-fi, for example in *Star Trek IV*, where the ship's power comes from a crystal and a dangerous quest must be undertaken to find a replacement. The power can be more esoteric, as in *Enlightenment* where Turlough is offered the glowing crystal in exchange for the Doctor's life. The blue crystals of Metebelis III are also a dangerous stimulator of mental powers; through them the Great One seeks to dominate the universe. And, in *The Time Monster*, the Master seeks to use the Crystal of Kronos, in which the monster is imprisoned, to control its power. The crystal also required a quest, through the maze of the minotaur. In these last cases, the power embodied in the glowing crystal is delusive. Mere possession of it does not bring the wisdom and ability to use the power, but destruction. For Turlough, "enlightenment was not the diamond, enlightenment was the choice".

**Morality Plays:** A more "entire" form of symbolism, this sort of structure gives related meanings to each part of the whole, relating them to a moral stance. Stories such as *The Daleks* and *The Claws of Axos* are examples of this, but the best case within *Doctor Who* has to be *The Two Doctors*. Here, the Androgums are representative of ourselves whereas the humans are representative of the animals we kill to eat. This theme carries right through the story, including characters representing the amoral animal researcher, military interest in animal research and of course Oscar, who kills simply to admire his beloved moths (and gets pinned himself as just desert).

**The Web:** "There he sits, like a spider at the centre of a great, metal web," said the Doctor in *The Sun Makers*, a story notable for its "science fiction" look. This indicates that webs have another meaning than "here is a Gothic mansion", though in *State of Decay* and *Warriors' Gate* it is used as one of the standard gothic props. But, even there, what does it signify? Recall the scene in the Lugosi *Dracula* where the Count glides up a web-filled stairway. When Harker tries to follow, he is entangled by them. Webs are also a warning, the premonition of a trap closing. As the

Doctor parts the web of *Warriors' Gate*, he moves deeper into danger, the danger being entrapment rather than death. Web imagery also occurs in *Castrovalva*, where the web is the imploding city, with Adric imprisoned at its heart.

**The Question Mark:** One of the most obvious symbols of the show, the "?", has been a trademark of John Nathan-Turner's reign. After letting the audience get used to it as the Doctor's emblem, it has recently become more noticeable thanks to the seventh Doctor's coat and umbrella, not to mention the card from *Remembrance of the Daleks*. (It is strongly suggested in the *Remembrance of the Daleks* novelisation that the question mark is actually the seal of the Prydonian chapter on Gallifrey. And, talking of strong suggestions, go out and read this book, it is the best piece of printed *Doctor Who* ever.)

At its most simple, the symbol simply summarises the mysterious nature of our hero and its greater prominence parallels the Doctor's recent enigmatic nature. However the use of the "?" is more widespread than is perhaps first apparent; for example, the Doctor's mourning cloak in *Revelation* contains question marks worked into the detail and, far more interestingly, Omega's costume from *Arc of Infinity* has a pair of stylised question marks in the same position as the Doctor's. It is this, along with the fact that the question mark appears on the Doctor's card, that suggests it is more than a piece of English notation but also a character or symbol of Gallifreyan origin, perhaps a mark of rank or family from the Dark Times.

And, since we have been talking about Gallifreyan characters and mathematical notation, it's interesting to note the similarities between the two. Two names transfer directly – $\Theta\Sigma$ and $\omega$ (Theta Sigma and lowercase Omega) – and the writing on the Doctor's card and the Old High Gallifreyan in *The Five Doctors* contains both Greek and mathematical symbols. We should also mention $\delta^3\Sigma x^2$ and $\sqrt{x^2}-\pi$, respectively the Doctor and the Prosecutor, from a document appearing in the original edition of *The Making of Doctor Who*.

**The Skull:** In its simplest form, the skull is the symbol for danger. The iconography of poison bottles and pirate flags. When a skull appears, it is a warning of primal danger, of destruction of the self, basic and personal. In *Image of the Fendahl*, it was an indestructible skull that sucked "the soul, the life-force, whatever you want to call it"; it was death which fed on life. Pithier incidents of the skull as symbol occur in *Time-Flight*, where Nyssa, the only one whose mind was resisting the Master's illusion of Heathrow Airport, caught a terrifying glimpse of rotting bodies and grinning skulls that was reality; also, in *The Masque of Mandragora*, where Hieronymous gives the hypnotised Sarah a poisoned pin, the head of which was shaped as a skull, with which to strike the Doctor down. Also note the skull motif in the décor of *Terminus*.

**Swastika:** The Nazis are favourite villains in any series, and have been used in *Doctor Who* from the pseudo-Nazis of *Genesis of the Daleks* to the actual thing, in *Remembrance of the Daleks* and *Silver Nemesis*. The two Dalek stories here are no coincidence; one of the standard traits of the Dalek race is racial intolerance (again another issue being brought out strongly these days). The swastika, actually a good luck charm used by Hitler for his own purposes, is well known for representing hatred and intolerance.

**Spiders:** *Planet of the Spiders* may, at first glance, seem to have something to do with spiders. It doesn't. The spiders aren't spiders at all. They're symbols: a science-fiction monster in place of a demon, but a demon nonetheless. Cho-Je, the Tantrist monk who runs the Somerset lamasery that is the setting for the story, tells Mike Yates that meditation can be used to summon evil forces. Which is precisely what Lupton (initially conceived as the Master) and his gang do. They are motivated by greed or anger or ambition. Meditation doesn't bring them peace, but their own vices crystallised into a physical form.

And when the Doctor's old friend K'Anpo speaks of the Time Lord's greed, he says, "Not all spiders sit on the back." Demons aren't really creatures unto themselves, but represent our vices. And the spiders represent the greed and ambition of Lupton and company. Interestingly, the largest spider of all – The Great One – is reserved for another failing entirely: the Doctor's fear. He must return the blue crystal to her despite his fear. Her destruction stands for his overcoming of that fear.

**666:** "The sixth child of the sixth generation of the sixth dynasty of Atrios. Born to be the sixth and final segment to the Key to Time" – and so said Princess Astra, and she was right, too. However, it's a bit of an unfortunate image, as it's the only time a hint of Satanism has been given to a sympathetic character during the series.

**The Gate...** is, of course, *Warriors' Gate*. Placed at the junction of universes – "according to co-ordinates we're at no where and no time". Heavily guarded, the greatest obstacle to crossing through is fear of the unknown. The answers to the dilemma can be reached by entering, but to do so requires trust in oneself and in the quest you are engaged in. An instant's pure belief. It is often the Doctor's role to take this step and by doing so redeem the society he is dealing with. He does it most blatantly in *Warriors' Gate*, but also in *Pyramids of Mars* and *Planet of Evil*. The destruction of the gate in *Timelash* was a most atypical act: a most atypical use of the symbol for *Doctor Who*, and one which resulted in a not-quite-satisfying narrative. The gateway is fear of answers, crossing it an affirmation!

**The Gallifreyan symbol...** is of modern-day Gallifrey, present on the formal regalia of the Time Lords. Whilst it is perhaps essentially meaningless as a design, it does incorporate the circle, a symbol for infinity, whereas the centre pattern suggests either an hour-glass, representing time, or the infinity sign on its side. Funnily enough, it is also the symbol of the Vogans from *Revenge of the Cybermen*.

**The Chalice:** The chalice is always offered, always brimming. The chalice is temptation, the presentation of your dark desires. In the movie *Excalibur*, in Percival's quest for the Holy Grail, he reaches the cavern of Morgan le Fey – "Drink, warrior. You must have travelled far, and through great hardship. Drink, and forget." This is the classic example, "There are many pleasures in this life, many cups from which to drink." With these connotations, it is hardly surprising that it appears seldom in *Doctor Who*. In *Vengeance on Varos*, the Doctor sees a hallucination of Peri offering him such a cup whilst in the death zone.

And a more subtle (well, sort of) use: In *Time and the Rani*, the wondrous alloy the Rani creates to explode strange matter, Loyhargil, is simply an anagram of Holy Grail.

It is no coincidence that poison is also associated with the chalice, for succumbing means destruction. The Doctor never succumbs; nonetheless, he becomes less cautious at times, dissuaded from his quest, as in *The Brain of Morbius*. "Drink, Doctor?" says Dr Solon.

**The Tarot:** The fortune teller in *The Greatest Show in the Galaxy* draws the card of the hanged man, foretelling one of the Doctor's more bizarre acts in the Dark Circus. In the actual pack, however, the card is a non-violent one representing the "letting go" or acceptance of fate. Similarly, the card in *Image of the Fendahl*, Death, foretold the nature of the Doctor's adversary, but the card is more synonymous with change or metamorphosis. Perhaps it was actually foretelling *Ghost Light*.

**The Smiley Face:** A rather strange symbol, it originally meant "Have a nice day", or the equivalent. These days, it has connotations with drugs, but is also being used in many other ways, usually in a fairly "twisted" fashion; for example, in *The Howling*, the smiley was used to indicate the presence of Eddie, the worst of the werewolves. In *Doctor Who*, a variation of the smiley is used by *The Happiness Patrol* to mark favourable citizens while Ace herself wears the *Watchmen* logo, from Alan Moore's mature-age comic: a smiley slashed with blood.

**Plant Life:** Plants are always the symbol of life, but it can be two types of life. The first is the symbol of the seed or flower, the promise of new life. In the novel *The Neverending Story*, Bastian turns a grain of sand – all that remained of the realm of Fantastica – into a seed, from which grew the Forest of Light. In *Revelation of the Daleks*, the Doctor presents the people of Necros with the flower that will save the galaxy from famine – a little grandiose, but this is frequently the Doctor's final act in the narrative, to point towards the future. In *Delta and the Bannerman*, not a plant but a child is used for this symbol.

The second is the symbol of the vine. This is life where it should not be; strange, alien and unnatural life. The vine becomes the tentacle. Monstrous vegetable / animal hybrids appear throughout science fiction, perhaps most famously in *Day of the Triffids*. And, of course, in *Terror of the Vervoids* and *The Seeds of Doom*. These are plants that transgress the boundaries of extreme, of normality, of the natural order which in *Doctor Who* is equated with the just and the good. The most symbolic use of the vine occurs in *Planet of Evil* (and similarly in *The Keys of Marinus*, *The Chase* and several others), where the entire jungle manifests a weird and threatening presence. The basic fear of order being over-turned and this life destroyed. Devoured.

**Burnt Toast:** A symbol for chaos and social disorder. In the conventional English tradition of a dignified breakfast, and the American motif of a neat table with the wife dutifully pouring tea / coffee for her husband, burnt toast is an unwelcome reminder of things that disrupt our cosy view of the world, things that are never quite under our control.

*With thanks to Larissa Hunter, Peter Griffiths, Fiona Simms and Matthew Milner.*

# 31 Things I Wouldn't Know if I Didn't Watch Doctor Who

**by Mike Morris**

*From The Doctor Who Ratings Guide, June 2000.*

1. The Mona Lisa is a fake, as a simple X-ray would prove beyond all doubt.

2. All green lifeforms are evil.

3. Anyone dressed in black is evil, but charismatic.

4. Anyone dressed in white is nice, but dull.

5. Arrogant, dictatorial leaders with a short temper will always go insane under stressful conditions.

6. Aim for the eyepiece.

7. French people are all surly, don't talk to each other, understand English but don't speak it, and have a curious predilection for watching English news in cafes.

8. Contrary to medical opinion, keeping feverish patients warm is essential.

9. Life on Earth began 400 million years ago, not 3.5 billion years ago as is commonly claimed.

10. Alien life forms are every bit as civilised as we are, and you can't simply assume them to be hostile. However, they will nearly always try to take over Earth sooner or later.

11. The eyepiece. The stalk at the top of the dome.

12. All forms of intelligent plant life will try to kill everything and should be destroyed immediately.

13. All that stuff about them not being able to go up stairs is just wishful thinking.

14. Shooting at alien lifeforms with a conventional handgun is a pointless exercise; just run.

15. If an alien is chasing you, it doesn't matter how slow they appear to be moving, they'll catch you sooner or later.

16. You can twist your ankle anywhere, even on completely smooth and untreacherous surfaces.

17. Spanners can do more damage than you think.

18. Purple horses with yellow spots are excellent interplanetary ambassadors.

19. Giving your child a name that is anagrammatical of "master" is an unwise temptation of fate.

20. Anyone / anything whose body has been cybernetically enhanced is evil.

21. Plastic is evil.

22. I said, AIM FOR THE EYEPIECE!!!

23. Tea-trays are far stronger than is commonly imagined.

24. For some people, small, beautiful events are what life is all about.

25. Continental drift is a completely bogus theory; the continents looked just the same sixty-five million years ago.

26. Laying on a jeep / some coffee is a complex military exercise, and not in the least bit risqué.

27. Anyone who invents a machine that is decades ahead of its time is either a) evil or b) being used as an unwitting pawn by an alien menace.

28. All-powerful evil aliens since the dawn of time are easily detained by board games and can be trapped in an old bottle without undue difficulty.

29. About 90% of colony ships crash and most will lose all their technology in the process.

30. If you thought the O.J. Simpson trial was dull, far too long, totally incomprehensible unless you were following it from day one, and had all sorts of questions left unresolved at its resolution, trust me; it's like that on other planets too.

31. Alien menaces have made man into a technologically advanced species, and without them we'd still be a bunch of Neanderthals living in caves. So, on the whole, they've been rather good to us, haven't they?

# The Rule of Four

**by Simon Kinnear**

*From Shockeye's Kitchen #17, Spring 2006*

It's one of the cornerstones of classic *Doctor Who*. The Doctor is trapped by his enemy, all looks lost... and then that piercing scream bleeds into the end credits and we have to wait a week to find out what's happened. For all its claims towards terror, there's something refreshingly safe about the *Doctor Who* cliffhanger. Maybe it's nostalgia. Or, perhaps, it's the subconscious knowledge that you know where in a story you are from what episode it is.

The classic structure of a *Doctor Who* story is remarkably consistent, utilising the same 4x25-minute format throughout the series' original run. It accounts for a whopping 88 of the televised stories and, if you adjust the double- and feature-length episodes (and break up *The Trial of a Time Lord* into four stories) that number rises to 99 out of 160 stories: over 60%.

The four-parter as seen throughout *Doctor Who* is a discrete block of narrative, obeying its own, relatively fixed, logic. While it has roots in classical dramatic structure as defined by Aristotle, via the three-act structure of the feature film (ask Robert McKee), *Who*'s serial format gives its narratives a distinctive flavour all of their own – which, incidentally, is why feature-length omnibuses of *Who* can be such gruelling experiences: they weren't designed to be watched that way.

In *Doctor Who*, each of Aristotle's tenets of structure – exposition, development, complication, climax and denouement – are formalised into a set timescale: twenty-five minutes each (apart from the denouement, which in *Who* terms refers to the TARDIS dematerialising to the bafflement of whoever is watching). The function of episode one is to hook viewers into coming back the next week, gathering momentum as it builds towards its cliffhanger. Episode two maintains the pace, and is typically where the bulk of the plot resides. Episode three is less complication than a stall, relaxing the pace after the revelations of the previous week but marshalling events in time for... episode four, which is obviously where things get sorted out.

Think about it: the Doctor arrives, meets up with some folk who tell him about nasty goings-on, which he then witnesses. *[Cliffhanger]* He survives, meets the people doing it, tries to stop them but is captured. *[Cliffhanger]* The enemy's plans near completion as the Doctor languishes behind bars, but he manages to escape. Despite nearly getting killed in the process *[Cliffhanger]* he's worked out a counter-plan and puts it into action, defeating the bad guys and saving the day.

*Doctor Who* plots generally run along the same well-oiled tramlines, because the four-parter is such an effective application of narrative logic. It has seen off the threat of epic twelve episode serials, budget-friendly six-parters, double-length episodes and condensed three-parters to become the key building block for any good *Who* writer. And yet, here we are in 2006 and a silent revolution has occurred, consigning the 25-minute format to history.

These days, we're lucky to get a mid-story cliffhanger three times a year, and the dominant mode of storytelling is the one-off 45-minute episode. Mary Whitehouse and Michael Grade couldn't bury the Rule of Four, and yet Russell T Davies – the programme's saviour – has done it with one impatient look at his watch. "Nah, too long, let's get the story over with tonight!"

But has *Doctor Who*'s storytelling changed so radically? When I think of *Doctor Who*, I still think of it in terms of the traditional four-parter as described above. However, in the early days, the series was conceived as a serial along the lines of the 1930s *Flash Gordon* adventures; the fact that the self-contained story wasn't formalised in the title until *The Savages* says it all. The stories of Terry Nation, in particular, carried the conspicuous air of "make it up as you go along" momentum, reaching some kind of pinnacle in *The Daleks' Master Plan*, a story whose structure was fluid enough to incorporate a stand-alone prologue, a Christmas special and even a quasi-sequel to *The Time Meddler*.

Yet, in reality, the four-part story existed from the beginning. If *An Unearthly Child* is the hook to story and series alike, then the adventure in prehistoric Earth establishes the conventions of the remaining episodes from the off. "The Cave of Skulls" is the progression ("where the hell are we? What are we going to do?"); "The Forest of Fear" is the stall (it consists entirely of a thwarted escape, a staple convention right through the classic series) and "The Firemaker" is the climax, as they finally get out.

As the series developed throughout the 60s and into the early 70s, the four-parter remained a reliable template, albeit locked in permanent battle with its more bloated sibling, the six-parter. There was the occasional epic to gatecrash the party, but this duopoly held sway for a long time. Yet, gradually, the four-parter asserted its supremacy as the six-parter's limitations became apparent.

In a serial format, a story's turning points generally need to coincide with the cliffhanger – and unless you have a story with a surplus of revelations (*The War Games*, say), the only way to do that is to drag out or recycle the pattern of development and complication. Whilst this suits the claustrophobic slow burn of a Troughton-era base-under-siege narrative, with its escalating series of minor victories and greater threats, by the Pertwee era the six-parter had become an ungainly mix of overextended four-parter and serial travelogue. The worst offender is *Frontier in Space*, which has the feel of a postmodern critique of *Who* storytelling, such is its predilection for locking up the Doctor.

In contrast, the Pertwee four-parters seem much fresher, faster and balanced – and it's no surprise that many of them were written by Robert Holmes. It was Holmes, in my opinion, who perfected the template circa *Spearhead from Space*, and by the time he grabbed the structural baton from Terrance Dicks, he banished longer stories more or less forever and made the four-parter the series' natural idiom.

Tellingly, it's during Holmes' tenure as script editor that we see the purest example of the Rule of Four in *Doctor Who*. Perhaps surprisingly, it's *The Deadly Assassin*, a story often regarded as radical in content but which, in structural terms, couldn't be more typical. Every episode is pared down to near-abstraction: the first episode is one long cliffhanger, foreshadowed in the opening minute; episode two is ablaze with progression, possibly the most densely plotted 25 minutes in the show's history. The Matrix-bound episode three is about as extreme a stall as you can find. And, just for luck, episode four climaxes in a threat to the existence of the entire universe.

The formal perfection of the Rule of Four is such that you can see its stamp in longer stories, where writers have recognised its benefit in ordering the *Doctor Who* narrative. It especially suits seven-parters. The first four episodes of *The Daleks* is textbook stuff (in fact, it borrows so heavily from its predecessor's capture-and-escape plotline that Anthony Coburn could sue), yet the twist at the end of episode four ("The Ambush") sets up, effectively, a whole new story. Everything we've seen so far becomes the expanded first episode of a new four-parter: in mathematical notation, (1234) 234. *Inferno* goes one better. At its heart, this is a compact four-parter about a scientific experiment going awry, but, where most stories would faff about for an episode, Don Houghton deepens and enriches the material by introducing the parallel universe. It's a four-parter inside a four-parter – 12(1234)4 – and, if you look closely, you'll see that it obeys the rules of the format beautifully.

As Holmes' influence came to dominate, he overhauled the six-parter in a similar way by injecting a canny switch of perspective at the point of climax (or, in the case of *The Seeds of Doom*, before the hook). The 4+2 or 2+4 structure enables a fascinating dynamic in terms of drama – both *The Talons of Weng-Chiang* and *The Invasion of Time*, for example, kill off major villains in episode four to allow the real threat to take centre-stage.

If the Holmes era has a flaw, it's that – ironically – Holmes loved this format so much he brought it into the traditional four-parter, pioneering an unfortunate trend towards the overstated climax. Against the formal perfection of *The Ark in Space* or *The Robots of Death*, we have *Terror of the Zygons*, *Pyramids of Mars* and *The Hand of Fear*, all of which all relocate in their closing stages in an attempt to punctuate the drama. The result is a sense of disappointment – all that carefully wrought claustrophobia is allowed to dissipate. At its best, the issue is that what comes before is simply too good to support the ending. At its worst, it's lazy writing.

The Rule of Four could survive such minor discretions, but it was severely damaged by Christopher Bidmead's storytelling revolution: out with the capture-and-escape plotlines, in with elliptical, cerebral sci-fi. Ironically, Season Eighteen is the only season in *Doctor Who* history composed entirely of four-parters, but its involved, one-note narratives lack the sine wave patterns of the best *Who* stories, despite brilliant cliffhangers giving the stories the semblance of structural integrity. The Bidmead influence persists into the Davison era, most pervasive in *Kinda* (whose originality is hampered by convention; it's *Who*'s equivalent of a round peg being forced into a square hole), but apparent generally in the number of stories that don't seem to go anywhere. It's arguable that the decision to shove *Who* from its traditional slot into a twice-weekly schedule was determined less by ITV's Saturday night dominance than the realisation that these stories had to be told quickly if they were to survive.

In this light, Season Twenty-Two's 45-minute episodes should have been the natural solution but – with exquisite bad timing – the show's creative driving force was Eric Saward, a notable disciple of the four-parter. In the 25-minute format, Saward gave us *Earthshock*, which is one of the great examples of how to do a four-parter. In the 45-minute format, he offered *Attack of the Cybermen*, which isn't. The problem with Season

Twenty-Two is that the writers are still thinking in terms of trying to match turning points to cliffhangers, with the result that stories either start too late (through over-extended hooks) or end too early (caused by misjudged climaxes). Saward only ever solved the problem, in *Revelation of the Daleks*, by doing away a conventional *Who* plot entirely (where's the Doctor? Or, for that matter, the Daleks?), but that wasn't much of a long-term strategy.

The result, after the interregnum, was a return to 25 minutes but the emergence of the shorter three-part format. And, to prove that his earlier mistakes were no flukes, JN-T hired the wrong man for the job again. As the story length shortens, so Andrew Cartmel's ambitions are getting larger, and something had to give. That something was coherence. The McCoy three-parters are faster than anything previous, but they're too fast; removing the breathing space of the episode three stall means that there's simply too much going on. Not that Cartmel could deal with four-parters, either: if there's a great four-parter inside *Ghost Light* struggling to get out, there's a positively brilliant five-parter in *The Curse of Fenric*.

If the 1980s had a lesson, it was that the storytelling couldn't change until the format changed. The Rule of Four is a marvellous thing, but its parameters need to be respected. Robert Holmes isn't the most original of storytellers, but he understood the format implicitly. So too did David Whitaker, Terrance Dicks and (schooled in the similar demands of serial radio) Douglas Adams. It didn't matter that Chris Bidmead and Andrew Cartmel brought astonishing, daring ideas into the mix, because those ideas didn't suit the particular needs of *Doctor Who*.

Which brings us to *The TV Movie*, whose failure you can pinpoint to a bizarre inversion of the shortcomings of 1980s *Who*. Where that decade suffered from neglecting the Rule of Four, *The TV Movie* slavishly follows it when it doesn't need to. A feature film has the luxury of shifting the emphases of its turning points to create its own rhythm (something which *The Five Doctors* got right, as anyone who has ever tried to watch the episodic version will know). Yet, *The TV Movie* stops and starts like a *Doctor Who* story, with the would-be cliffhangers all too apparent.

Ironically, had a full series been commissioned in 1996, we probably would have seen a format similar to the one we have now. But, by refusing to shake off the Rule of Four, *The TV Movie* made *Doctor Who* look old-fashioned.

When the new series was announced in 2003, one of the first questions asked was, "will there be cliffhangers?" Fandom knew deep down that the 4x25 format was deader than dead, but it's hard to shake off that tribal allegiance. Russell T Davies had no such hang-ups; if you want to show a twenty-first century audience what this series can do, you only get one shot. So you'd better do it fast.

At first glance, *Rose*'s breakneck pace and brush-strokes exposition go against every one of *Doctor Who*'s storytelling conventions, yet it's worth bearing in mind that, from the Doctor's point of view, the story begins in situ. He's already arrived on Earth, become aware of the Auton threat and is very much on the case. Effectively, we're watching the second half of a classic *Who* story and, judged this way, it obeys the Rule of Four beautifully: what else is Rose's interruption of the Doctor's plans but a classic episode three stall?

It's not until *The End of the World* that we truly get a taste of how radical the new format is going to be. There is a classic *Who* plotline lurking under the FX (think *The Robots of Death*), but it's rattled through at such a blistering pace that there's barely time for any progression, let alone a stall. For years, fandom has regarded the two-parter as the weak, ineffectual cousin to the mighty four-parters and, in its barest outline on paper, *The End of the World* is Exhibit A for the prosecution. And yet, watch it not through structural eyes but with the wide-eyed wonder of a child new to *Who*. The big stories here are Rose's acclimatisation to time / space travel and the tantalising hints of the Doctor's past, and these stories are only just beginning come the end credits. *The End of the World* is no truncated four-parter, but the beginning of a much longer journey.

The influence of American drama cannot be understated. Since the early 90s, American drama has been in thrall to the arc, the all-encompassing narrative thread that binds the individual episodes together. The beauty of the arc is that it can be as dominant or as loose as you want to make it. *Star Trek: The Next Generation* had ongoing plotlines (the one about Klingon politics, for example) that it could dip into and out of; *Babylon 5* had an intentionally novelistic structure that demanded committed viewing. The middle ground was staked out by *The X-Files* and *Buffy*: predominantly episode-of-the-week, but with strategically placed "marquee" episodes it was vital to watch to understand the longer story.

Nowadays, the dominant form is a hybrid, where an individual episode's plotline combines both episode-of-the-week and arc in unpredictable ways. The most daring of these is *Lost*, which formally brackets its sections by use of flashbacks (past = story of the week; present = arc). Even *24* seems to have given up on the sustained storytelling of its early seasons; the speed with which it devours narrative has effectively turned the series into "story of the hour".

In other words, RTD has a lot to play with and the 2005 season is notable for the finesse with which it weaves the competing demands of arc and "on the night" closure. Cleverly, he chose to centre the overall theme around the changing character of the Doctor himself; something tangible to regulars, but accessible to casual viewers. You don't need to be up to speed with the vagaries of Centauri politics to understand what's going on week by week, and I'd argue that there are only a few critical stories by which we need to gauge the Doctor's progress from fatalistic survivor to spiritual rebirth (*The End of the World, Dalek, The Doctor Dances, The Parting of the Ways*).

This A-plot is echoed by Rose's own voyage of discovery, which is mapped out in the gaps between the episodes noted above. *Rose, Aliens of London, Father's Day* and *The Parting of the Ways* all use Rose's relationship with her family as a yardstick by which we can measure her progress. Note that, with the exception of the all-important season finale, RTD keeps the "Doctor" and "Rose" episodes apart so that nothing too vital is invested in a single episode.

The remaining episodes, whilst not critical to the arc, nonetheless play an important role. Both *The Unquiet Dead* and *The Long Game* act as the control to the big story arcs, the former by showing the Doctor trying to be "Doctorish" before he's ready, the latter by detailing the misadventures of Rose's alter-ego, Adam. And *Boom Town*, placed before the finale, is an eloquent summation of how far our heroes have come... and how far they still have left to go.

The arc has undoubtedly changed things for *Doctor Who*. The 2005 season isn't the first time *Doctor Who* has used an overarching theme, but neither Seasons Sixteen nor Twenty-Three really changed the structure. The umbrella changed the emphasis of the season but it continued to operate in discrete four-week blocks, with only a two-part coda in each (the final two episodes of *The Armageddon Factor; The Ultimate Foe*) really giving the game away that anything bigger is at stake.

In contrast, the 2005 season trusts a lot more to its arc. Crucial details of characterisation or narrative (most obviously, "Bad Wolf") are developed throughout the season, taking the weight off individual episodes to allow them more freedom than *Doctor Who* normally allows. Critics of RTD's scripts have complained that he has an aversion to closure, frustratingly leaving his i's undotted and t's uncrossed. That is a just criticism of the traditional self-contained *Doctor Who* adventure, but in an arc the individual episode by definition remains incomplete to leave room for the invisible scaffolding provided by later episodes.

I'd argue that the traditional *Who* equation of turning points with episode endings continues in Series One. What's different is that, instead of hokey old "jeopardy" situations, RTD's endings are far subtler – a gentle stroll down a mountain path as opposed to hanging off the cliff. *Rose* and *World War Three* end with significant decisions for Rose, whilst *Dalek* and *The Doctor Dances* see a more relaxed Doctor return to the TARDIS.

What these innovations mean is that the traditional arrive-liberate-leave *Who* adventure has been freed from its reliance on the self-conscious turning point of the cliffhanger, permitting a huge amount of narrative compression. Note: that's compression, not revolution. The essential building blocks remain exposition, development, complication and climax, and – to be honest – it doesn't take a huge leap of imagination to remake these stories as classic four-parters.

Take *Dalek*, for example. Joe McKee pointed out in the last *Shockeye's Kitchen* that, by the time the Dalek is revealed, you've watched "Two episodes worth of story, with a couple of chases, incarcerations and escapes thrown in to pad the thing out. Here, it's the first ten minutes." Although I'd argue that the Dalek reveal is the end of episode one, not episode two, I think he's spot on. All that's changed structurally is the length. Just compare *Dalek*'s climax to *Robot* episode four, and you'll see how this story might work in the classic 4x25 format.

The extent to which the Rule of Four survives, and also how much it has changed, is clearest by looking at the 2005 season's surrogate four-parters. Proponents of the classic series format can point to *The Empty Child / The Doctor Dances* as proof of its durability, for Steven Moffat's story is pretty much required reading for anybody interested in how a *Doctor Who* four-parter should work

Russell T Davies' own two-parters, however, use the formula in more intriguing ways. *Aliens of London* ticks all the boxes; in fact, the first half of *World War Three* consists almost entirely of corridor-chases: a classic "episode three" gambit. But what's different is the fluidity that compressing four parts into two gives RTD. He squeezes the hook (spaceship crashing into Thames) and climax (Downing Street blows up) of the *Who*-ish plotline in a bit, yielding the space for a whole different story about Rose coming home, that simply wouldn't be possible if the set-up and resolution were three weeks apart instead of one.

By the end of the series, the "neo four-parter" had become even more unpredictable. *Bad Wolf* and *The Parting of the Ways* are, nominally, one story, but the two episodes are so completely different in scope and style that the Rule of Four breaks down. In fact, I'd go as far as declaring them the modern heir to the joined-at-the-hip *Frontier in Space* and *Planet of the Daleks*. Sure enough, *The Parting of the Ways* actually reboots its narrative to "hook" (the opening stand-off aboard the Dalek mothership), before racing through "progression" (Rose sent home), "stall" (the defence of Satellite 5) and "climax" (Rose's return). It's certainly not your common-or-garden four-parter.

A year on from *Rose*, and with the 2006 season about to air, it's obvious that Russell T Davies is far from the structural dilettante he's often portrayed as. The man definitely understands traditional *Who* storytelling (there's the Rule of Four again, almost back to full-length, in *The Christmas Invasion*) but, after over a decade and a half's experience in TV drama, he's worked out that *Doctor Who* no longer needs to be in thrall to it. Like an architect, he's studied the blueprints, determined the foundations, digested the forward-thinking concepts of other movements, and forged his own style. If *Doctor Who* in the twentieth century was all too often monolithic and pre-fabricated, Davies has brought the more iconoclastic eye of a Norman Foster or Daniel Liebskind.

I imagine we'll be seeing some striking some designs being raised in the 2006 season. Some of them will be toweringly grandiose, some quirky and intimate – and many are bound to be controversial. But, whatever the style, take a moment to dig deeper. More often than not, I bet you'll find the foundations of a classic *Who* four-parter and hear the periodic echo of that end credit "sting".

# 10 Silly Story Titles (and What They Should Have Been Called)

**by Mike Morris**
*From The Doctor Who Ratings Guide, July 1999.*

1. *Doctor Who and the Silurians.* Obviously. Although, given that Malcolm Hulke's working title was the even worse "Doctor Who and the Monsters", perhaps we got off lightly. "The Silurians" would have been fine. Or how about this: "Dawn of the Eocenes"?

2. *The Deadly Assassin.* As opposed to all those non-deadly assassins you see hanging around, presumably. Apparently, the working title was "The Dangerous Assassin", which is simply ludicrous and leads me to believe that Bob Holmes was taking the piss. "Eye of Harmony" would have been snappy, although it might have given the plot away a bit. "Assassin" would have been good too. Or better still, what about "This is specifically written to piss off the president of the DWAS"?

3. *The Massacre of St. Bartholomew's Eve.* Now that's snappy and dramatic, isn't it? Actually this is a kind of a compound entry for all those other Hartnell stories which have been given silly titles like "100,000 BC", "Dalek Cutaway" and the like. It's time to stop this insanity now and call them by their proper names, dammit!

4. *Kinda.* Not bad in itself, but until I saw the thing I thought it was pronounced as in "I feel kinda funny" – you know, the American abbreviation of "kind of"... then again, changing it would require changing the name of the tribe, so I suppose we'd better leave it as it is.

5. *The Two Doctors.* Look, *The Three Doctors* and *The Five Doctors* were anniversary stories and hence forgivable. There's no excuse for *The Two Doctors*, which is just silly. What kind of response would they have got if the next story was called "One Doctor and a large-breasted companion on an unconvincing plastic planet"? A quick dig among the working titles reveals some cracking names as well; "The Androgum Inheritance", "The Seventh Augmentment" and, best of all, "Parallax".

6. *The Invisible Enemy.* Actually, I could see it perfectly well (more's the pity). What was wrong with "The Enemy Within"? And, if they'd used it then, they wouldn't be able to use it as a title (sort of) for the Telemovie, which doesn't make any sense at all. Enemy within what, exactly?

7. *Time and the Rani.* Well, it is largely concerned with the Rani, so I suppose half of it's appropriate. Thing is, the story's so rubbish that I can't be bothered coming up with anything better. By the way, have you noticed that 90% of stories with "Time" in the title aren't up to much? Wonder why?

8. *Revenge of the Cybermen.* Isn't there a contradiction in terms here? This is one of three stories which had the working title "Return of the Cybermen", which isn't up to much, but I half-think it deserves to be there for sheer persistence. Alternatively you could call it "Pursuit", after the whole Pursuit of Voga thing, or just plain old "Planet of Gold".

9. *Delta and the Bannermen.* Which is just silly. "Flight of the Chimeron" will do fine.

10. *City of Death.* A bit too vague for my liking. And, given that only a few people die during the story, it's a bit inappropriate too. I mean, come on, if there's anywhere on earth which deserves to be called the City of Death, it's London, where a guy can't go to the shops without being gunned down by an Auton / killed by a lethal plague / menaced by a dinosaur then evacuated, etc. I reckon this should be called "Quest of the Jagaroth" or "A Gamble with Time" (as originally intended).

# Horror

**by David Carroll**

*From Burnt Toast #1, February 1990.*

*"Fear is with all of us and always will be..."*

—the Doctor

*Doctor Who* was not conceived as a horror program, just as the Doctor was not conceived as a Time Lord. It just happened that way. And, of course, actually calling it a horror program detracts from the overall variety that goes into its production. *Doctor Who* is a comedy, a drama, a satire, a space opera and an action / adventure show, among others, and in many of these aspects it excels. But, despite all this, it is the horror that holds a special significance for many people. Indeed, the two greatest periods of the show's history (in my humble opinion anyway), that of Seasons Thirteen to Fourteen and Seasons Twenty-Five to Twenty-Six, both achieved their successes through formats intended to scare. The other era of the *Doctor Who* horror story, Seasons Four and Five, holds a similar fascination to those who have actually seen it. Time and again, the show has proven it can send shivers up the spine, often with exhilarating results.

I suppose the first question is: what is horror? Particularly, what is that wonderful subgenre called Gothic Horror? Well, at first glance, the dictionary doesn't help much. According to *Chamber's Twentieth Century*, horror is *"n. (obs.) shagginess, raggedness: a shuddering: intense repugnance"* whereas gothic is defined as *"adj, of the Goths or their language: barbarous: romantic"*. While the first definition probably explains the appeal of *The Abominable Snowmen*, it is the second that is more important. The Gothic genre is both barbaric and romantic, an essential contradiction. It is neither the gratuitous blood-letting of the splatter-movie nor the more realistic approach to horror as typified by Stephen King. The Gothic story depends on shadows and implied violence, a feeling that something is very wrong coupled with a deep familiarity. It need not be intended to scare – *The Addams Family* is supremely gothic – but when called upon to do so certainly can. It is often very traditional, relying a great deal on mythology and legend, but uses modern twists; it can be uplifting or fatalistic, tragedy or comedy, surreal, but relevant.

And that, more or less, is my definition of Gothic Horror, which probably explains why I've never worked as a dictionary compiler. Long-winded as it is, however, we can start to see the attractions of the genre, why it is so popular. But perhaps more importantly is why anybody would bother in the first place; why do people enjoy scaring themselves? Fear is a negative emotion, so is horror a form of masochism, should we all be locked up? As can probably be expected, this question has been examined many times, particularly in relation to Stephen King, who is really the first modern author to introduce horror to a mass market. Writing to inspire terror, horror and repulsion, in order of preference, he sees his profession as an alternative to the analyst's couch and many people would agree. In this rather chaotic mess we call society, horror is a release valve and, as in any times of disorder, the genre is currently flourishing.

In America during the Great Depression, many people were turning to pulp fiction and comics such as the Shadow, and later Batman, to forget their empty stomachs, whilst the vampire tale which had just emigrated from England was there to stay. This was the era of H.P. Lovecraft and Algernon Blackwood, and of course many others who haven't passed the test of time so well.

Other examples aren't hard to find, either. Victorian England, the background of many horror tales itself – *The Talons of Weng-Chiang* and *Ghost Light* among them – was the creator of many horrific stories. With the sharp contrasts between the "deeply conservative morality and intense nationalism" of the time and the often-appalling fate of many of its lower castes, it again provides the contradictions inherent in the gothic form. The "penny dreadfuls", cheap and lurid fiction published weekly, were a prime example, and the most famous of them, *Varney the Vampire*, made its titular villain as known then as Dracula is today. Forming a huge serialised novel, the story ran for over two hundred chapters published from 1845-1847 before Varney threw himself into a volcano in a fit of remorse. Varney wasn't an isolated fancy. Apart from his work on that most famous of detectives, Arthur Conan Doyle often wrote ghost stories. Three of the major influences on modern horror and science fiction span the nineteenth century: Frankenstein, Doctor Jekyll and Mister Hyde, and Dracula.

And what about our favourite television show? As I've said, it is a show of great variety, an anthology of stories that seems to shift its whole emphasis every three years or so (it's still too early to tell if the shorter seasons will protract this). Certainly, at the moment, it is in a period where gothic horror plays a major part, and there is no doubt *Doctor Who* does it very, very well. It seems strange that a show which – although not a children's program – has children as a significant part of its audience can achieve this. But, like its content, the maturity of the intended audience fluctuates, often quite rapidly. A friend of mine once commented that *The Greatest Show in the Galaxy* was so creepy and occasionally shocking, not because it was as graphic as any of the current horror movies, but because it was a *Doctor Who* story, something we have grown up with. The production team has long realised the effect of using familiar objects, from daffodils to clowns, to inspire fear, and this may be reflected in our own attitude to the show itself. And since the program never can be (or should be) a slasher movie, it uses shadows, the implied and the unknown to great effect. The occasional use of shock tactics, such as Mags' transformation and some of the more repulsive puns from *Ghost Light*, certainly doesn't hurt either.

The roots of the current trend can be found in *Paradise Towers*, a story which successfully combined the general silliness of Season Twenty-Four with much darker overtones. Then, suddenly, the show became deadly serious. In contrast to the hard sci-fi of much of *Remembrance of the Daleks*, the strange girl, played so beautifully by Jasmine Breaks, was the first example of what came to dominate the season (children with power can often be an incredibly strong motif in print, but rarely does it work so well on screen). Then came *The Greatest Show in the Galaxy*, *The Happiness Patrol* (not true gothic, but a very close relation, mock-gothic, as we've come to call it), and a year later the superb *Ghost Light*, the even better *The Curse of Fenric*, and *Survival* (almost mock-gothic itself) in Season Twenty-Six. Shows like *Battlefield* and, to a lesser extent, *Silver Nemesis* were also very dark, reflecting the overall maturity of the seasons. This maturity has other benefits as well. Because they are horror stories, the opportunity is there to use other scenes that, whilst not necessarily scary, have a similar emotional impact. Ace's "distraction" of a guard being the prime example from *Curse*. (This point can be extrapolated to show one of the great uses of horror in a literary sense. It can be used to demonstrate some of the more unpleasant aspects of human nature with sometimes surprising honesty and insight.) With all this, it's easy to see why we've had a wonderful two seasons' worth of entertainment.

Whether all this will last is uncertain, not helped by the uncertainty of the show's actual future. Looking at the past, we saw the first horror era turn into the short-lived science fiction of Season Six and then the action / adventure of Jon Pertwee's reign, whilst the second era was more or less forced into the silliness of latter Tom Baker by the growing "public concern" over the show's often-violent content. What happens now is anybody's guess, depending largely on who receives the rights to make it. Call me a stick-in-the-mud traditionalist, but to say I'm hoping that Sylvester and Sophie will remain with the program and current themes similarly stay a while would be an understatement. As always, time will tell, it usually does.

# INTERLUDE

## The Key to a Time Lord - 2
by Scott Clarke
*From Enlightenment #121, April / May 2004*

### Episode Two: Characterisation
*"More of a tennis player than a cricketer."*

Well-written characters help us believe in *Doctor Who*. They bring focus and coherence to dreams. But what makes crunchy old Amelia Rumford, blustery Henry Gordon Jago, or the tragically unhinged Sharaz Jek so essential and memorable? When I think of *Doctor Who* characters (villains or otherwise), I think of larger-than-life, iconic figures like Davros, Leela and the Chief Clown. Or well-drawn and complex characters like Lawrence Scarman, Borusa and Ace. Perhaps it's the perfect marriage of pantomime (vivid, fascinating, entertaining characters that grab you immediately) and acclaimed BBC drama (with its multilayered characterisation).

*The Caves of Androzani* is all about characterisation. Episode two shines in this regard. It's a near-flawless example of how character drives plot and generates mood.

Having just escaped Chellak's firing squad, Peri and the Doctor are led to Sharaz Jek. The fifth Doctor, in true fashion, extends his hand to greet the recluse, only to be rebuffed in favour of Peri. What follows is a fascinating "dance" between the three characters, as Jek attempts to make clear his intentions towards Peri, while the Doctor diffuses and intercedes at every opportunity. Witness the look of alarm on the Doctor's face when Jek places his hand on Peri's shoulder; he knows what he has to do. By the next scene, as Jek moves towards his "exquisite child", the Doctor springs up and literally injects himself into the scene. The Time Lord wants to keep Peri safe and calm; that's his motivation. He fires off a steady stream of flippant remarks, keeping a jocular tone to disarm the situation. And Jek knows what the Doctor is doing – "your eyes tell a different story" – but he's trying to keep Peri happy. Peri is equal parts fear and disorientation, and Nicola Bryant expertly conveys the dread factor.

View the episode and you'll be stunned by how seamlessly plot is conveyed within the internal reality of the characters. The Doctor manipulates Jek's ego to discover his plans. A moment later, Jek's hatred releases the tale of Morgus' betrayal like a litany he's recited a thousand times. Jek's obsessiveness dispenses the plot. Brilliant!

But nowhere is character-driven plot more evident than through fellow captive Salateen. At a structural level, his role as info-dump donkey is clear, but he's much more than that.

"He doesn't say why he blames Morgus," Peri asks.

Salateen responds, "I've heard the story fifty times."

Of course he has, and it's driving him round the bend; he's been cooped up in close quarters with this nutbar for months! By finishing the story, he reveals his own pent-up frustration, resignation and cynicism. And when he explains the consequences of touching raw spectrox, it's done with irony, cynicism and a certain glee. He can't wait to share it with the Doctor and Peri; he wants vindication.

Similar strategies are employed in other *Doctor Who* stories. *The Stones of Blood* takes the need to bring casual viewers on board with plot exposition by layering this plot necessity with small character revelations. The Doctor's sense of fair play makes him confide in Romana about the Key; it's also a lovely little acknowledgement of his growing affection for her.

The mood of the piece is also bred through characterisation. Holmes has fashioned Sharaz Jek as an iconic *Phantom of the Opera* persona; his tight-fitting jumpsuit and abstract mask induce both mystery and allure. But it's also the complexity of the character that strikes the viewer. He's an emotional cripple, stuck in his vengeance and his lust for the life he's lost. All of his scenes resonate with the same trapped feeling. He's as much a prisoner as the Doctor and Peri.

Similarly, as Morgus' greed leads to his fall from grace, we go from the breezy opulence of his office to the desperate fugitive wandering the cramped caves of Androzani Minor. The desperation of the characters infuses the mood of the story. It could be argued that the character of the first Doctor sets the mood for the entire program. His secretive nature and unpredictability juxtaposed with his benign, grandfatherly appearance immediately keep us intrigued and off-kilter.

Characterisation also facilitated the structural realities of the program. Companions were created as audience identification, helping to ask questions, aiding in the dissemination of vital plot information, sorting through all the technobabble. Writers were consistently challenged to make these roles interesting. Companions brought out different qualities in each successive Doctor: Ian and Barbara, with their "fish out of water" perspective, served to accentuate the first Doctor's alien qualities while

Jamie was the perfect cohort for the second Doctor's playfulness. The format of the show, plopping the TARDIS down in a new location of time and space every few weeks, necessitated the steady introduction of new characters and they needed to immediately capture the imagination/attention of the audience. Imagine if Sharaz Jek had been a typical bumpy-headed alien from *Star Trek: TNG*. I seriously doubt he'd have remained in our consciousness the way he did. Amelia Rumford in *The Stones of Blood*, with her police truncheon and sausage sandwiches, was an eccentric that viewers would find both familiar and amusing.

And, of course, because of the limitations of character development for the regular TARDIS crew (the Doctor needing to remain an enigma, the companions needing to be identifiable to the audience), guest characters were an opportunity to explore human (or alien) nature a little deeper. As entertaining as it might have been, you'd never have seen Sarah Jane take off on a bloody rampage of vengeance (although we were headed that way with Ace). To this day, I am struck by the tragic sadness of Lawrence Scarman in *Pyramids of Mars*, who refuses to give up on the memory of his beloved brother to the point that it results in his own death.

It's a curious, but stirring, alchemy between script and thespians that create these larger-than-life figures. Scriptwriters for *Doctor Who* were extremely inventive in their ability to overcome the built-in limitations of the format, as well as exploit its strengths. Actors such as Maurice Colbourne (*Attack of the Cybermen*), Geoffrey Bayldon (*The Creature from the Pit*) and Angela Bruce (*Battlefield*) were able to overcome the challenges of poor scriptwriting to enhance otherwise lacklustre productions.

It seems somewhat assured that, as *Doctor Who* moves through its re-birthing process, character will continue to be front and centre, if the past work of Russell T Davies is any indication, most likely reflecting the needs and expectations of contemporary audiences. With a 45-minute episode format, there will certainly be more opportunity in terms of structure to include more character emphasis. And the casting of an actor of Christopher Eccleston's calibre is heartening indeed. New icons, for a new generation, will continue to inhabit our dreams and mirror back to us the rich complexity of human experience.

# I CROSS THE VOID
# BEYOND THE MIND

It's hard to believe, but there once was an age when people actively hated Jon Pertwee's *Doctor Who*.

It was back in the 1990s. The classic series had ended its run and many of the fan cognoscenti of that era, who were writing in genre magazines and the New Adventures novels published during that time, expressed little but contempt for the Pertwee era. One popular New Adventures author – we will preserve his anonymity here – said on a convention panel that he had ranked every Pertwee story zero out of ten in a then-recent fan survey... including *Inferno*, which the popular author had elsewhere praised as the greatest *Doctor Who* story ever written.

It's not hard to understand how this happened. Some of it was a reaction to the nostalgia of the *not we* – non-fans in their 20s whose affection of *Doctor Who* began and ended with the memory of watching Pertwee on shag carpeting. Part of it was also a reaction to the prevalence of Jon Pertwee himself as a professional raconteur on the convention circuit at the time. And some of it is a tendency of *Doctor Who* fans to "detourn" (as Amanda Murray put it in her essay on Pertwee in *Licence Denied*) things that had once been popular.

Dave Owen's essay, "Jonny Come Home", expresses vividly the frustration of a Pertwee fan living in that era and brilliantly excoriates the smug conceits of the anti-Pertwee movement while at the same time pointing out a central truth: the Jon Pertwee era of *Doctor Who* was populist entertainment of the best kind. And there's nothing wrong with that at all.

Pertwee's mix of high fashion, high dudgeon, fast living and Venusian karate still finds its attractors (as Scott Clarke attests) and detractors (as Mike Morris lists). And while some feel that the move to a more populist approach after Jon Pertwee's first season let down the promise of more complex, morally ambiguous stories, others would argue that more complex, morally ambiguous stories can be still be found at its most populist distillation: a season opener featuring the Daleks. That the Pertwee era sparks such a range of commentary speaks well of it and its capacity to tell stories that set opinions, and imaginations, on fire.

Jon Pertwee's tenure as the Doctor no longer sparks the negative reaction it once did. In fact, for the most part fandom has mellowed toward the Pertwee era. The author who once gave him zero out of ten now praises his stories regularly. Fan fashion has moved on to detourning Christopher H Bidmead's stories and the Sylvester McCoy era these days; future popular authors reading this collection in 2022 will doubtless be giving every David Tennant story zero out of ten.

We look forward to that. But first, let's put on the velvet jacket and fire up the Whomobile...

# Jonny Come Home

**by Dave Owen**
*From Bog Off One Hundred, November 1993*

Try walking into a gathering of British *Doctor Who* fans, introducing yourself, and saying that your favourite part of *Doctor Who* history is the Jon Pertwee stories, and you are likely to be laughed out of court. A recent questionnaire of UK fans asked "Which of the Pertwee stories would you most like to see go missing from the BBC archives?" A still-more-recent gathering of fans featured a recreational event known as "Pertwee Hurling"; contestants would clutch a pre-recorded video tape of the recently restored *The Daemons*, run up to the line yelling an apposite Pertwee line of dialogue (for example, "You ham-fisted bun-vendor!" or "If you have a tool, it's stupid not to use it"), and attempt to project said video cassette as far as possible.

It's the latter incident that best summarises the chattering contingent of UK fandom's attitude to the third incumbent of *Doctor Who*'s title role: an utter disregard for the preservation of the video tape, combined with an encyclopaedic knowledge of its contents. Tat Wood summed it up perfectly in his *DWB* article in that magazine's recent Pertwee special. He loved the Pertwee stories, but he does not actually like them.

That said, Tat is a bit of a clever-dick – as are all the Pertweehaters (that's an ugly expression, how about "dandiphobes", or "harlepaths"?). I suspect it would be not too far from the truth to say that, as the message in most Barry Letts stories is hammered home as subtly as a Venusian Aikido blow to the neck of some innocent guard, there is less scope for intellectual analysis than other parts of the programme's history offer. So perhaps the widespread over-familiarity (which, of course, breeds contempt) with the *Doctor Who* of the first half of the seventies tells us more about the state of fandom than it does about the stories.

If I'm going to have a quiet night in, then I might spend it by myself watching *Kinda* or listening to *The Massacre*. If, alternatively, I return from the pub with a contingent of lager-crazed psychotics desperate for a good time, then we'll flick on UK Gold (the BBC's answer to American television: all repeats and commercials) and, chances are, experience something of the calibre of *The Time Monster* or *Colony in Space*. This ritual will be interspersed with urgent whispers of "Hang on – you can see her knickers in the next scene", and "Look out for the totally unnaturalistic way he's holding that sonic screwdriver", and, of course, whenever Nicholas Courtney appears, roars of "LIBERTY HALL, DOCTOR TYLER, LIBERTY HALL!"

The fact of the matter is that everyone has seen all the Pertwee stories so many times that we have completely run out of clever things to say about them. Certain participants are now hailed as heroes – when Courtney appeared on a stage at a convention in Exeter, the entire audience were wearing eye-patches, a la Brigade Leader Lethbridge-Stewart in *Inferno* – and every self-respecting gay male fan can itemise Jo Grant's wardrobe and quote her monologue from the prison-ship scene in *Frontier in Space* verbatim. On the other hand, fandom's whipping-boy of the moment has to be none other than Jon Pertwee himself.

I suppose it's inevitable that Pertwee and the character he played in *Doctor Who* should irritate those who edit and contribute to *Doctor Who* fanzines. He is a pillar of the establishment, used to being the centre of attention and utterly aloof, either as the Time Lord trapped on a planet with humans who are so beneath him intellectually, or as the elderly actor, spending his weekends entertaining halls full of young fans with anecdote and hyperbole. Neither is a bad person, but the angry young socialists who spend their weekends labouring over a typewriter and under the misapprehension that *Doctor Who* is worth complaining about need something to rebel against, and he fits the bill.

Yes, I did say "socialist" then. There's a bit of an assumption of left-wing superiority in UK fandom at the moment. I suppose it stems from twenty years of watching a crypto-socialist darting around the galaxy ensuring that even if all men were not created equal, then they damn well will be by the end of episode four. Pertwee's Doctor – and, to an extent, the man himself – comes with all the trappings of the bourgeoisie: the port, stilton and smoking jackets. Whilst his deeds are pretty much identical to those of his predecessors – siding with the military, being on first-name terms with presidents and rebels alike, lecturing on morals – the fact that they fit into present-day Earth make those discontented with our present status quo see him as one of "them": our oppressors.

So, maybe the reason that so many UK fans shy away from saying "I like Jon Pertwee, the Doctor he played, and the stories he appeared in" is that they're afraid of saying "I endorse, nay, heartily approve of the antics of this pompous dandy." Which is a bit daft, really. I enjoy the *Carry On* films, but I don't go around acting like Sid James (usually). I suppose that the *Carry On* films are a good comparison to the Pertwee stories: we've all seen them too many times, but nonetheless love slumping in front of them with a crate of cold beers on a bank holiday.

# Wine, Cheese and Moralising
by Scott Clarke
*From Enlightenment #99, July / August 2000*

The Pertwee era has always been like comfort food for me; when I'm sick, tired or just plain worn down by the world, it serves as the best possible tonic. The quintessential image I have of the third Doctor is from *Day of the Daleks*, sashaying into Sir Reginald Styles' drawing room with a vintage red wine and a tray of Gorgonzola cheese. The only thing missing was an Ogron at his feet to fetch his slippers.

Later on in that same story, the Doctor would be seen tasting a little "twenty-second century hospitality" as he imbibed and nibbled with that misguided Dalek-collaborator, the Controller. Even with bone-headed Ogrons and screeching Daleks at every corner, there was always time for some civilised fare.

Certainly, there was plenty of wine and soya-cheese to go around at the Nuthutch in *The Green Death*. Even amidst a group of earnest tree-huggers, the Doctor managed to add an element of "joie de vie". And then there was that highly suspicious line he uttered at the beginning of *Carnival of Monsters*, as the Doctor and Jo stepped into the hold of an Edwardian cargo ship, "Ah, the air is like wine!"

This man wasn't going to let galactic domination or ten-foot-tall, bug-eyed monsters get in the way of the finer things in life.

The Pertwee Doctor was the epitome of the upper-middle-class, English intellectual. A kind of Henry Higgins (as portrayed by Rex Harrison in *My Fair Lady*) for the fourth dimension. Arrogant, rude, impeccably dressed and constantly moralising to anyone within earshot.

"Why can't the English learn to speak?" railed Henry Higgins.

"The power was within you all along. All you needed was a little encouragement from me," assured the Doctor.

Higgins believed that social class was basically a fraud and that even a flower girl could be trained to appear and behave as a duchess given the proper training and environment. He had absolutely no tolerance for façade or pretence, and yet look at the way he ran his household, conducted his affairs and treated poor Eliza Doolittle.

Pertwee's Doctor loved his smoking jackets, frilly shirts, and antique cars, but he always had a mouthful of insults to inflict on the various civil servants and authority figures he encountered ("You, sir, are an idiot"). And yet, look at the "authority" he commanded himself. When the Doctor and Jo showed up on Peladon, he was immediately mistaken for the Earth Chairman delegate. Nobody dared question it. And he was certainly up to the challenge.

Quite simply, the man had all the answers – or at least all of Barry Letts' answers – and he didn't suffer fools gladly. ("Did you fail Latin too, Jo?") If only we'd rid ourselves of our desire for material possessions (crushed velvet and dematerialisation circuits notwithstanding), clean up our filthy little planet and learn to live in peace with the Sea Devils, we'd all be a lot better off.

But what makes the third Doctor so irresistible, even today, is that he was very much a product of his times: the early seventies. Things were settling down a little bit after the turbulent sixties and the "me" generation was just starting to gear up. Wine and cheese parties were all the rage in suburbia, but people still talked about making the world a better place. One could pamper oneself, but still feel that one was making a difference. The id, the ego and the super ego living in, er, harmony.

I have no doubt that when the Doctor was exiled to Earth, he took a long hard look at his 500-year-old existence and said, "Might as well live the good life." When you're restricted to one planet and one time, suddenly clothes matter.

And so he tinkered with the TARDIS console as if it were an errant eight-track tape player, engaged his passions for gadgets and chase-utility vehicles, and set out to transform Jo into an elegant, upper-middle class, intellectual consort (or scientist, so he said). She was certainly pulling it off by the time *The Curse of Peladon* was transmitted.

The third Doctor became the "cultural laureate" of our little UNIT family. That little bit of class that raised Sgt. Benton and Mike Yates beyond their corned beef sandwich / "football match on the tube" lives.

Juxtaposed against the debonair Doctor were the Brigadier and the Master. In the earlier stories, the Brigadier served as the Doctor's back-up, heightening the Time Lord's sense of authority. He was Colonel Pickering to the Doctor's Henry Higgins. Sturdy and reliable, he always asked the practical questions (later, of course, he took on the equally necessary, but somewhat misplaced role of buffoonish authority figure to be mocked).

The Master, by comparison, was the gentleman's genteel nemesis. His elaborate master plans and traps always allowed the Doctor to come across as clever and suave. With a villain like that, one never had to worry about mud on the waistcoat. Here was an arch-enemy you could sit down with over drinks before engaging in lethal battle. By comparison, the Daleks, Cybermen and Ice Warriors were positively proletariat.

Alas, the champagne toast at the end of *The Green Death* would be the last of its kind. Season Eleven brought independent Sarah Jane Smith and her sensible shoes. Suddenly the old Doc looked over-dressed for the occasion.

Short of a little drinky with Edward of Wessex in *The Time Warrior*, the party was over. Come to think of it, there wasn't quite the same reception upon his second trip to Peladon either. And Mike Yates in *Invasion of the Dinosaurs* proved what the product of too much moralising could be.

Metebelis 3 finally saw the unravelling for our dandy friend. The first time he showed up, his fancy threads were (symbolically?) left in tatters. The return trip finished him off. Or did the times just change? I guess by that point we'd polished off the bottle of Chardonnay, licked the cheese from our finger tips (and gotten it all over our crushed velvet jackets). We were ready to face a world that was just a little bit unpredictable.

Jon Pertwee wasn't my favourite Doctor. His stories rarely inflamed my imagination. But when the rain starts pouring down or work starts getting too stressful, it's nice to know he's there.

# Everything Old is New Again

**by Robert Smith?**
*From Enlightenment #111, August / September 2002*

*"The series the BBC chose to replace* Doctor Who *in the Saturday tea-time slot was, famously,* The Exile *starring Jon Pertwee as an alien stranded on Earth who's forced to assist the UN in investigations of unearthly phenomena. Those few* Doctor Who *fans still around often argue that the new series was little more than a blatant copy of their favourite, and that some elementary rewrites of 'Spearhead',* The Exile's *debut story, would have made it an ideal opener for a revamped and reformatted seventh season of* Doctor Who. *It's true that many of the cast and crew of 'Spearhead' had previously worked on* Doctor Who, *including writer Robert Holmes, but the two series were fundamentally different in many ways, and this script could never have succeeded as an instalment of the B&W series."*

—Andrew Wixon,
reviewing *Spearhead from Space*, at *The Doctor Who Ratings Guide*.

Any long-running series must change, as *Doctor Who* has proved over and over again. And it's not as though the series hadn't changed before; the most obvious is the change in lead actor after three seasons, but the whole style of the program had undergone massive restructuring, previously. The Hartnell era has one base-under-siege story; the Troughton era is chock full of them. Hartnell's historicals were dropped as soon as Troughton took over. The only "sideways" story – so prevalent in the Hartnell era – that appeared during the second Doctor's run is *The Mind Robber*. The state of play by the time of Season Six is almost wholly different to that of Season One.

Possibly because it's commonplace now, but the change in tone considered the most fundamental to the series isn't the first regeneration, it's the second. The difference between Season Six and Seven is the single biggest change the series ever experienced. Which is quite a feat for anyone watching *Survival* and *The TV Movie* back to back (which nevertheless had the same Doctor at the beginning, a cameo by the Daleks and a Master with Cheetah-like eyes in the opening montage). Even Season Eighteen, the other quantum leap of this magnitude, takes several stories to phase out its incumbent crew.

That said, events flow reasonably smoothly from episode ten of *The War Games* through to the conclusion of *Spearhead from Space* episode four, providing a great deal of justification for the changes on display and taking great care to reintroduce the brand new concept that *Doctor Who* has suddenly become. Despite the fact that he's in the opening title, we don't actually see Jon Pertwee's face for over half of episode one (the first "shoes" scene is carefully played to avoid showing us the new Doctor directly). Season Eighteen does something similar in this regard, except that it uses a slow panning scene lasting almost two minutes and then it's on with (brand new) business as usual, without a word of explanation.

Season Seven strips away almost everything the series had been up until this point. Instead of a mysterious alien travelling through space and time, bumbling his way through bases under siege with his young friends in tow, we now have an action-hero Time Lord trapped on Earth. Not only that, he's also a member of a regular paramilitary support structure and he spends time with a professional scientist who never even enters his TARDIS. By the time we discover they've replaced the TARDIS interior with just the console (whose sickly green hue probably had the richer viewers regretting their decision to invest in this newfangled colour television), it's almost as though they were trying too hard to reinvent the series.

Even the comedy is gone after *Spearhead from Space*. It's a pity that Jon

Pertwee abandoned his natural talents in favour of becoming the most serious Doctor of all. *Spearhead* proves he's a gifted comedian at the height of his powers and the rest of his era shows that he wasn't nearly as adept at serious drama. A more comic Pertwee era would have dated far less obviously, I think. After all, the Graham Williams era might look tacky and full of seventies kitsch, but we're prepared to forgive that entirely, simply because it's so funny.

Not counting the TARDIS exterior and console prop (and Benton, though he was just a glorified extra), there's exactly one link to the past, but it's a pretty tenuous one. If you'd sat Patrick Troughton down at the end of *The War Games* and asked him to guess the only element of his era that would be used in the next incarnation of the series... well, he'd probably tell you to bugger off and leave him alone, you sad fanboy. However, I'd bet any odds that to name a minor supporting character who appeared in two stories would be an awfully long way down any list you forced him to make.

And yet, instead of floundering and defining itself in terms of what it isn't, Season Seven positively relishes its new format. The Brigadier's reintroduction of the concept to Liz is exactly the sort of thing that would have been in the pilot episode of most other shows (and repeated as a *Prisoner*-esque voiceover in the opening credits forever after). Season Seven also establishes Robert Holmes as the master craftsman of *Doctor Who*, hungry to be part of the new blood redefining the show. After more years than most successful shows get in their entire lifetime, this is anything but a tired old series.

Of course, Season Seven was a dismal failure, as far as the viewing public was concerned.

*Spearhead from Space*'s respectable ratings of 8 million viewers had fallen to 5.5 million by the time of *Inferno* and Barry Letts was even instructed to develop a possible replacement series. (A lot of things suddenly make a disturbing amount of sense when you realise that his vision of a replacement for *Doctor Who* consisted of a white-haired Australian cowboy who is comically out of place in London.) Season Eight's format was hastily rejigged for less gritty action and moral ambiguity, in favour of family oriented teatime fare and a dimwitted companion. And it worked too, with the remainder of the Pertwee era enjoying high ratings and a popularity second only to the Tom Baker era.

Season Seven was mostly forgotten about until the post-cancellation revisionism of the nineties rediscovered the third Doctor's most ignored season (the last three Pertwee stories to be novelised were *Inferno*, the Season Seven-esque *The Mind of Evil* and *The Ambassadors of Death*) and simultaneously tore down the remainder of the Pertwee era. These days, it's hard to find a fan who doesn't number at least two of Season Seven's stories among their top Pertwees – and invariably all four. *The Ambassadors of Death* has often come under fire for its perceived weaknesses, but it's a great story that actually deals with the consequences of the previous story in a remarkably subtle way, with the Doctor and the Brigadier's antagonism being slowly eroded over the course of its seven episodes. Personally I rate it above *Inferno* – although when you consider that my least favourite story of the season is *Inferno*, it's clear we're dealing with something quite special.

*Doctor Who and the Silurians* is a towering masterpiece of moral complexity and epic storytelling that never once drags. By the time actual innocent people start dying on screen in the middle of London, it's clear that we're not in the black and white era any more, Toto. Malcolm Hulke creates the Pertwee era's greatest triumph by taking his frustration at the inherent limitations of the Earthbound setting and turning it into a work of genius that pits humans and Silurians against each other. Both sides are simultaneously the monsters and the victims, where there are no easy answers and where good people (and Silurians) do bad things for noble intentions.

It also has one of the best endings of any *Doctor Who* story... that proves to be unsustainable in a long-running series. Which is a pity, because if the Doctor had gone up against his UNIT friends in the following stories we might not have had an enduring format on our hands, but it would have been unmissable viewing.

All the monsters of Season Seven are at least partially homegrown – and those that aren't are barely glimpsed. The Nestenes are behind the invasion, yes, but it's the Autons and Channing who carry the bulk of the story and they're all created in a very Earthly plastics factory. Thankfully, we only glimpse a single rubber tentacle desperately trying to prevent Jon Pertwee's mouth from gurning its way into pantomime. The aliens of *Ambassadors* are barely seen... and not only do they spend most of the story within very human-looking spacesuits, it is Carrington's xenophobia that's the real monster of the story.

*Inferno* is sadly stuck with the Primords, who are a sort of poor-man's Season Seven monster, created from the rage of the Earth – or something – for no readily apparent reason, except that it's the house style by now. There's a laughable scene where the Doctor and the Brigadier climb the catwalk of silence to have a minor conversation and then climb down again that undercuts the seriousness of the story. Thankfully, the parallel universe plot soon gets underway, turning a potentially drab story into a fascinating one.

The parallel bits of *Inferno* actually show what the series would have been like if the ending of *Silurians* had been taken to its logical conclusion. In some ways, it's a pity that that wasn't used as the point of divergence (thus explaining why it's suddenly popped up as well) to show us how things might have gone. The Doctor going up against the Brigade Leader is fabulous drama and a great way to end the season.

With Season Eight, all this changed. There's a consolidation of ideas: Munro and Hawkins are replaced by new regular, Mike Yates; one-off villains like Channing are replaced by the Master; and Sergeant Benton actually gets some characterisation instead of being just another soldier. Of course, Liz gets replaced by Jo, Pertwee the actor gets replaced by Pertwee playing himself, the Brigadier by a caricature and the sense of unstable, gritty drama by cosy teatime viewing with lashings of CSO.

Some of Season Seven's ideas and villains came back, but always in diminished form. The Sea Devils are the Silurians minus the moral complexity (the Doctor blows up the Sea Devils' base in exactly the way he criticised the Brigadier for two years previously) and the Autons take a back seat to the Master in their second appearance. General Finch (*Invasion of the Dinosaurs*) is a less sympathetic version of General Carrington. *The Mind of Evil* has some of the grittiness of Season Seven, but it also features a machine that suddenly starts teleporting for no adequately explained reason and is afraid of the purity of men's souls, or something.

If the series came back as different from what we know as Season Seven was from the Troughton era, there would probably be an outcry today, with fans deserting the show much the same way the public did back in 1970. Season Seven works (critically, at least) precisely because it's so uncompromising in what it's trying to do: re-establish the most versatile television series ever as something entirely new.

Of course, if a new series were even half as good as Season Seven, we'd be very fortunate indeed.

# 10 Official Writer's Guidelines for the Pertwee Era

by **Mike Morris**
*From The Doctor Who Ratings Guide, November 2001*

TOP SECRET documents have come to light. In 1969, Pertwee was in place, backed by cutting-edge stories crafted by the previous production team. But fear not, this would change. Between 1970 and 1974, Terry and Baz had a plan. They knew what their stories should be like. And they had rules. Recently discovered in an old public toilet in Tooting Bec, beneath the carcass of a decaying Yeti who couldn't get out because the door was too small, researchers have found the official guidelines for Pertwee-era *Who* stories. They also found the master tapes of episode four of *The Tenth Planet*, but mistakenly taped over it with a celebrity edition of *Stars in Their Eyes*. Oh well.

And, for the first time in history, here they are.

1. The Doctor has a time machine and can go anywhere or "anywhen" in the universe. Please bear in mind, however, that most alien planets look like a quarry or a single, unfurnished room, so he tends to stay on twentieth century Earth quite a bit.

2. As you will be aware, the Doctor is a Time Lord and thus far more intelligent than mere humans. This may suggest that you make him unusually clever, but we would prefer it if instead you make everyone else unusually stupid.

3. We are currently in negotiations with the BBC to reduce the duration of the episodes from twenty-five minutes to fifteen minutes, as Terrance's missus is complaining that his dinner keeps getting cold and Barry's Buddhist Centre closes at seven o'clock. While this has not yet come into effect, it may happen at any moment, so please include ten minutes worth of irrelevant material that could be removed from the story without affecting the plot in EVERY EPISODE. We suggest a good, long car chase.

4. A recent survey has revealed our audience demographic; 63% are children. We feel that this is not a lucrative market, and would prefer the show to be watched chiefly by yokels, and in particular poachers. Please include a poacher or yokel at some stage wherever possible to woo this untapped audience.

5. It is written into the contract of Jonny Bignose – sorry, we mean Mr Pertwee – that he must have a twelve-minute fight scene and a moralistic speech included in every story. However, we are trying to piss him off by making the fight scenes desperately unconvincing and the speeches incredibly boring and pompous, so please oblige us in this small detail. We've a bet on that he'll quit within five years and blame it on the breakup of the "family". Yeah, right.

6. Further to this point, we feel it would be an interesting direction to counterpoint the Doctor's natural charisma (so brilliantly established by Bignose during his first season) from time to time by making him pompous, opinionated, right-wing and patronising.

7. Please allow the Doctor to drop the name of at least one historical figure in every episode, as this reinforces the mystery of the character. Obviously there are limits; we would prefer it if the Doctor did not mention meeting Jesus Christ! Stick to tasteful characters that the Doctor might conceivably form a friendship with, such as Genghis Khan, Hitler, Napoleon and Mao Tse-Tung.

8. A note on the treatment of UNIT. We feel that the military are all too often portrayed in a stereotypical fashion. We would like to avoid this. We visualise UNIT as having an old warehouse as their HQ and about five soldiers to spare. Also, their leader was originally portrayed as a warrior of poise, stature and judgement. This was valid, but we see the Brigadier in a different light; a buffoon who blows things up all the time is a more interesting characterisation, and this is the direction we wish to take.

9. We have, in our spare time (such as it is!), been thinking about the future of mankind, and have come to the conclusion that rural living is unsustainable. The future for mankind lies in the city and in urbanity. Scenes such as those in *Spearhead from Space* spread an irresponsible anti-urban message. Please avoid this. Set stories in rural villages, wherever possible, thus implying that the countryside is incredibly dangerous. Portray all rural people as stupid and stereotypical, to suggest that your neighbours will be smelly inbreds if you move out of London. These steps may seem curious, but the future of the human race hangs in the balance and these measures might just save the world.

10. Could you put the Master in it somewhere? Anywhere will do. Don't worry about logic or motivation, we'll, er, work that out later. Honest.

Signed, Baz and Tel. Oh, and if you know of any vacant positions going for a producer or script editor, please let us know. Please. Anything will do. Anything at all.

# You Did It Yourselves!

**by Daniel Clarke**

*From The Doctor Who Ratings Guide, July 2003*

Let me get one thing straight; I'm none too fond of the Tom Baker serial *Terror of the Zygons*. This may seem a bizarre thing to say at the beginning of a review of *Day of the Daleks*. Nevertheless, I believe it to be a comment of vital importance because how I view the two stories heavily affects how I interpret the oft-used phrase "adult television".

The former serial is pure B-movie stuff. It's a simple, bog-standard alien invasion in which a comic-book, one-dimensional alien race attempt to wrest the planet Earth from one-dimensional, stereotypical Scotsmen. Everything is portrayed in black and white with, of course, the one-dimensional, stereotypical Scotsmen being firmly in the white. To make matters worse, the cast does not take the (admittedly laughable) situation seriously. Tom Baker's Doctor, in particular, takes the mickey out of the paucity of Zygon invaders. The cast's lack of conviction is such that the audience cannot be expected to take the situation seriously either and the result is a story without a credible threat. Despite the story's obvious shortcomings, fandom labels *Zygons* as a "classic" and even more inexplicably as "adult television". If "adult" connotes the presence of blood and guts then, sure, this story is "adult". If "adult" denotes references to drugs and prostitution then, sure, the Hinchcliffe era as a whole is "adult".

Yet, in my opinion, "adult television" is nothing to do with gratuitous violence. Indeed, given *Doctor Who*'s large child audience, it could be argued the inclusion of such violence by Hinchcliffe was nothing short of irresponsible. Instead, I am of the opinion that "adult television" is television which explores complex human characters and their reactions to events in a mature (yet entertaining) way, possibly giving the audience food for thought in the process. Against such criteria, *Day of the Daleks* is an astonishingly adult piece of television, which, thirty years on, is as compelling and (given the present international climate) as relevant as it has always been.

Time travel is such a key element of *Doctor Who*. It is therefore rather lamentable that so few stories from our favourite series deal with the consequences of voyaging through the fourth dimension. Fortunately, on the two occasions where the series explored the subject (here and in *Mawdryn Undead*), two brilliant pieces of television were made. In this case, in a twist which (along with that in the film *The Sixth Sense*) remains one of the finest that I have ever witnessed, it is revealed that a group of terrorists, in attempting to change the past, are caught in a temporal paradox. In short, they created the terrible future which they were attempting to avert. There can be little argument that the aforementioned revelation is exciting, original and, on first viewing, totally unexpected. The power of Pertwee's performance and the brilliance of Louis Marks' writing combine to make the "you did it yourselves" scene truly special. Even Dudley Simpson's incidental music contributes in a positive way! Despite the greatness of this scene and the revelation contained therein, a good twist does not alone create classic television. A quick look at *The Sixth Sense* demonstrates this well. Although the twist in that film is outstanding, the film does not (in my opinion) bear repeated viewing because, once you know the truth, there is very little to look out for. The whole film is geared towards surprising the viewer and no one can be surprised by a revelation on more than one occasion. Where *Day of the Daleks* succeeds is that it does far more than surprise the viewer. It sets up a situation which is in itself genuinely interesting (and frightening) and, as all good "adult television" does, shows us the reactions of diverse, complex characters to that situation...

In *Day of the Daleks*, the audience is confronted with the terrifying situation of a Dalek-occupied Earth, an Earth in which, as the Doctor puts it, "Human beings are only fit to live the life of a dog." The Daleks regard the human race as little more than an expendable workforce, whose only value is to dig for the minerals that they need to service their ever-expanding empire. No one disputes the undesirability of the Dalek occupation. What is disputed is the way of making the lives of the downtrodden and subjugated human populace better; Louis Marks presents us with two polar-opposite "solutions", that of the "quisling" controller and that of the "terrorist" guerrillas. The actions of both parties are entirely understandable and sympathetic. The latter think the correct response is to fight and defeat the Daleks (through the murder of another human being) so their children can grow up without the need to live through the terrors that they themselves have experienced. The Controller, in contrast, believing that it is impossible to defeat the Daleks, sets about working with them so he can negotiate a better lot for his people.

Both reactions are, as I have said, sympathetic, but, importantly, both provide no solution to the undisputed problem of the Dalek occupation. The terrorists, in trying to defeat the Daleks, actually create the situation which they are trying to avert and the weak-willed Controller, driven by the selfish (yet understandable) desire to protect the life of himself and his family, fails to extract any significant concessions from the Daleks. Instead, he accepts the demands of the Daleks for inhumane increases in factory production and uses Dalek-like tactics to get the factory owners to comply with those demands. Far from aiding humanity, the Controller, to the benefit of the Daleks, moulds his human subjects into an efficient working force. The key point is that in the twenty-second century, there are no good guys and bad guys. Nothing is black and white. Instead, there are several groups of misguided, but well-meaning individuals who all lack the correct answer to their problem.

In short, Louis Marks creates a believable situation...

This is not mere serendipity. There are several indications in the script that the writer was keen to get across, as a theme, that in this world there are no black and white solutions to complex problems. The contrasting characters of the Doctor and Jo are interesting in this regard. Jo represents the simple-minded citizen who blindly accepts the situation as it is presented to her. Significantly, she believes that the situation in which she is plunged is black and white. She calls the terrorists "thugs" and states that at the root of the problem in the twenty-second century is the "criminal guerrilla organisation". As she sees it, the Controller is whiter than white and is doing his best for humanity. The Doctor, in contrast, considers the situation to be complex one and throughout the four episodes is keen to point this out...

> The Doctor: *"Fanatics, not thugs, Jo."*
> Jo: *"You don't know the situation."*
> The Doctor: *"Neither do you Jo, neither do you."*

He castigates first the Controller, then the terrorists for the blindness of their actions: "You, sir, are a traitor, a quisling", "You're still asking me to perform murder." By showing us the natural interaction of the Doctor and Jo, Louis Marks manages to emphasise his theme about things not being black and white without forcing the message down our throats. Significantly, he doesn't even come down on the side of either the Controller or the terrorists (both parties allow the Doctor to travel back to the twentieth century at the story's denouement when they realise he has a chance of defeating the Daleks). Instead, the author merely gives the audience food for thought – which, of course, is what all adult television should do.

In a story so dedicated to portraying a complex world, the presence of the "evil" Daleks themselves, the ultimate black and white race, may seem somewhat perplexing. I, nevertheless, believe that their appearance in the story is both effective and necessary. The presence of the Daleks, who are motivated by genuine feeling of xenophobia and hatred for the unlike, in no way undermines the complex world created by Louis Marks. More importantly still, if the occupiers had in any way sympathetic motives, the entire dynamic of the story would change. What makes the story work so well is that the undesirability of the occupation is undisputed; the Controller and the terrorists both want to improve the lot of the human race but have different methods of trying to achieve that aim. If we had any sympathy with the occupiers, then Louis Marks would have had to construct a horrendously complicated and in turn less effective story.

Indeed, if we had any doubt about the "evilness" of the occupiers, the use of a suicide bomb by Shura at the story's finale and the Doctor's positive response to it would have been, I submit, utterly unacceptable. In this light, the use of the Daleks was quite intelligent. Why create a substandard, undeveloped and (given *Doctor Who's* budget) lousy-looking fascist alien race, who are no more than poor relations of the Daleks, when you can use the Daleks themselves? Finally, fans often criticise this story for failing to use the Daleks enough. I respectfully contend that such critics miss the point. The Daleks are meant to be the power behind the throne who, as all occupiers do, use a misguided member of the occupied race (here, the Controller) to rule said race according to their will. The Controller is such an effective character precisely because in trying to help humanity he actually helps the Daleks.

All of Louis Marks' work would, however, have been for nothing if his script had not been played out with conviction by the members of the cast. Fortunately, the actors all give charged performances in a production which really does the talent of the writer justice. From the excellent performance of Aubrey Woods (as the Controller) to the wonderful portrayal of the Doctor by Jon Pertwee, there is barely a duff performance to be seen. Even the minor characters play their parts with utmost seriousness. The factory owner, for example, only appears in one scene but in his short amount of screen time manages to put such intensity into his acting that his performance is genuinely memorable. The performances, for which in truth one cannot find enough superlatives, are nicely complemented by the stylish production. The sets and costumes, in contrast to those in *The Dalek Invasion of Earth*, really make the audience believe that they are viewing events in the twenty-second century. Every time I watch this serial, I cannot help but find myself being drawn into the world on screen. So determined are the production team to make this serial work that they even decide to create a fabulous-looking new monster in the Ogrons, possibly the best monster ever designed in the series. Finally, Dudley Simpson, not wanting to be left out, creates a quality score which – given some of his work in Season Eight – is not something that director Paul Bernard could have taken for granted. Put simply, the entire production gels so fantastically that only the cynical could fail to be convinced by the situation presented to them.

Earth of the twenty-second century is so superbly realised that it is easy to forget the sheer tension of those scenes set in the present day. This tension is partially created through the innovative technique of having the worsening international situation reported to us through the media. Both newspaper articles and UNIT radio broadcasts are used to pass on to us the required information. More originally, an actual television reporter gives a live news report of the events which are unfolding at Auderly House. Although the above methods are used to cut costs, they are nevertheless effective because in real life most people don't see international conflicts first hand; they help the viewer believe in the unfolding situation on screen because such reportage is so familiar.

The tension in the twentieth century scenes is augmented further by the convincing acting of the guest cast, with the portrayals of the Brigadier and Sir Reginald Styles being particularly noteworthy. Sir Reginald is shown throughout to be so committed to the cause of peace that he will not let "minor" issues, such as an assassination attempt, sway him off course. From his angry response to the Brigadier's offer of protection to his exasperation at having to hurriedly leave Auderly House during the Dalek assault, we get the portrait of man genuinely terrified at the prospect of a third world war. Significantly, the portrayal of Sir Reginald makes the audience believe that there is a genuine, credible threat facing humanity. Equally charged is the performance of Nicholas Courtney, who gives one of his finest performances in a UNIT uniform. The Brigadier is shown throughout to be both short tempered and committed to his responsibilities; this helps to bring home the impending threat in a truly chilling way. Unusually, the Brigadier is shown not to suffer fools gladly – including the Doctor. "This particular squabble may end up in a third world war," he barks. The man means business.

As I see it, the three most successful *Doctor Who* adventures of all time are *Inferno*, *Day of the Daleks* and *Pyramids of Mars*. All three have something in common: namely, that we are shown what will happen if the Doctor fails. In the former, we are shown the destruction of the planet Earth through volcanic explosions and in the latter we are presented with the famous 1980 scene. Similarly, in *Day of the Daleks*, the principal source of tension lies in our knowledge of what will face humanity if Sir Reginald and his peace conference fails: the horror of Dalek invasion and occupation. Thus, in contrast to *Terror of the Zygons* (where the audience never truly believes that six Zygons will take over the Earth), in this serial we are presented with a credible threat which seems frighteningly real.

Finally, I will turn to the two common criticisms of this serial, the most famous of which is that "Only three Daleks actually attack Aulderly House." My response to this criticism can be shortly stated. When I first saw *Day of the Daleks*, I never noticed the dearth of Daleks. When I saw *Day of the Daleks* for a second time, I never noticed the dearth of Daleks. Indeed, I never realised the truth until I was told about it by various fans. Paul Bernard directed the sequence with such style that even knowing of this "fault", I cannot help but be excited by it. The continual shouting of the Doctor, Brigadier, Benton and Styles only adds to the tension and the shot in which Bernard zooms out from the Brigadier-Styles argument to reveal Captain Yates barking orders on his walkie-talkie is a particular favourite of mine. In contrast, the presence of the bloody awful Magma creature in *The Caves of Androzani* is painfully obvious on first viewing. To those fans who continually say that *Caves* is a classic in spite of the Magma creature but that *Day* is ruined by the "three Daleks sequence", the phrase "double standard" comes to mind.

A second criticism of this serial is that after beautifully constructing a time paradox, Louis Marks undermines his own premise by allowing the Doctor to go back in time and change history. Such a criticism is fatally flawed in the following respect. Whilst the Doctor does avert the murder of the delegates by evacuating Aulderly House, we are not given any evidence that he actually succeeds in averting a third world war. Instead, we are left with the very real prospect that the peace conference will fail. In the present unstable international climate, the idea that the cost of failing to bring peace is all-out war is very sobering one. How very sad that, thirty years on, Louis Marks' serial is as relevant as ever.

*Day of the Daleks* is an astonishingly powerful and grown-up piece of television that should, in my view, be regarded as one of the true classics of *Doctor Who*. It may not have sex and nudity. It may not have gratuitous violence and excessive swearing. But it does make you think – and that's the mark of all true "adult television".

# Love, TARDIS-style...

**by Terrence Keenan**
*From The Doctor Who Ratings Guide, February 2004.*

Love in the TARDIS has been a well-explored topic in the long run of *Who* books, with companions hooking up with each other (Roz and Cwej, Fitz and a temporal variant of Sam), companions having crushes on the Doctor (Sam again) and even once a companion starting a booty call with our hero (read *The Dying Days* to find out about that little tidbit). The books are aimed at an older audience than the TV series, so you could get away with showing the love stories that fanboys dreamed of happening in the serials.

Leaving out *The TV Movie* (for obvious reasons), any sort of *Who* couplings and romances have been smuggled in through the back door. After all, *Who* is a children's / family show, and snogging and shagging would have corrupted minds already teetering on the edge due to ultra violence.

Mention love in the serials and the usual suspects pop up: The first Doctor pitching the woo and getting engaged to Cameca in *The Aztecs* (the most overt love story involving the Doctor), Ian and Barbara, Ben and Polly, Sarah and Harry, the fourth Doctor and Romana II, the fifth Doctor and Tegan, and the fifth Doctor and Peri. Most of these can be explained through fan wish-fulfilment and, in the case of one, behind-the-scenes romance.

But, there is one true love story in the long history of *Who*. It might have popped up by accident, hovered in the background, and then became as overt as would be allowed in *Who* by the end. That it ended on a downbeat note makes it all the more poignant. It culminates in a powerful exit scene that transcends a less-than-stellar era.

*L'affair de Josephine Grant et le troiseme Docteur.*

It's something I've noticed before. However, it really comes together when you watch Seasons Eight through Ten in order. You have to wonder if it was something that Barry Letts and Terrance Dicks had planned all along, or discovered it by accident and decided it would be a nice way to sum up our little Jo.

On the surface, the first meeting between the Doctor and Jo is to show that Miss Grant is not the Mighty Liz Shaw, capable smart scientist of Season Seven. However, it's also how boy meets girl in many a screwball comedy. If this were Hollywood in the Thirties, then Jo would be played by Carole Lombard and the Doctor by Cary Grant. Our bubbly Jo introduces herself to the Doctor and wrecks his project with a fire extinguisher. The Doctor insults Jo. Jo apologises with those big brown eyes of hers and manages to ingratiate herself with the Doctor. The Doctor softens a bit, lets her tag along.

From there, the Doctor and Jo get in and out of trouble, rescue each other and, by the time *Terror of the Autons* ends, Jo is in love with the Doctor – and not in a daughterly way, either. And the Doctor might be in love with Jo, but if he is, he much better at hiding his feelings than Jo. (Then again, he is a Time Lord and not a human, so that comes with the territory.)

So, over the rest of Season Eight, we see this dynamic duo get into and out of dangerous situations, swap the occasional insult and life story, and be ready to die for each other, highlighted by the finale of *The Dæmons*, where Jo is willing to die in place of the love of her life, the Doctor. Alas, the Doctor is still unwilling to admit his feelings.

In Season Nine, Jo is still hung up on the velvet-wearing frilled dandy with the mighty nose, but the Doctor by now is pretty oblivious to this. He does care for Jo, but still isn't willing to admit his feelings (or is unable to). However, by *The Time Monster*, the Doctor tells Jo the "daisiest daisy" story, which is the first overt chink in his love-proof armour. Again, the season ends with Jo willing to sacrifice herself in the name of love, and does so, only to be saved by the Chronovore.

Business picks up in Season Ten. In *The Three Doctors*, Jo wants to stay at the Doctor's side through all the strange events that occur, even wanting to share his exile in Omega's anti-matter universe. The Doctor might be touched by Jo's wish to remain with him, but he's still unwilling to admit his feelings. In *Carnival of Monsters*, the next big crack in the love barrier appears in the Doctor. He's determined to return to the Miniscope to rescue Jo, because it's starting to dawn on the old boy that he's in love.

While on the Master's police ship during *Frontier in Space*, there's a scene where the Doctor and Jo tell their life stories up to that point. On the surface, it's supposed to distract the Master while the Doctor tries another daring escape, but it sounds more like a couple reminiscing about how they first met and their first impressions of each other. Also, when Jo thinks the Doctor is drifting out to space, she tries to put on a brave front, but breaks down into tears, because she's afraid she's lost her true love.

In *Planet of the Daleks*, the Doctor is furious and also deeply sad when he thinks the Daleks have blown up Jo along with the Thal ship on Spiridon. Another sign of love pops up and says hello. Their reunion is far more affectionate than you'd see between friends. Jo has a flirtation with Latep and, at the end, Latep offers to take Jo to Skaro, after asking permission from the Doctor. The Doctor gives his blessing, but you can tell he hopes Jo will say no, which she does, because Jo is hoping old Big Nose will get the hint.

*The Green Death* brings the love story out into the open. It begins with the Doctor and Jo having a cute argument over where they're going. It gets more serious when the Doctor finally comes out and admits his love by proposing to her. "I'm offering you the universe and all time." But Jo is fed up and decides to meet another "Doctor": one Professor Clifford Jones, whom she describes as "a younger you" (she might have well added "shaggable"). The Doc says, to himself, "The fledgling flies the coop," which is his way of saying, "I love you, you flibbertigibbet, and I'm too late." Jo and Cliff meet in a cute way, just like the Doctor and Jo in *Terror of the Autons*. Sparks fly, and it's obvious that love is in the air between Jo and Cliff. Even the Doctor sees it.

What does the Doc do? He acts like a jealous old twat in episode three where he barges in on Jo and Cliff pre-snog and drags Cliff off to do boy's stuff. There's a moment of tension when it's hinted that the Doctor's jealousy might be behind his choice to kill the maggots first before saving Cliff's life. By going back and curing Cliff, the Doc shows he's ready to give Jo away. In the final scene, Cliff proposes to Jo, and she accepts. Jo gives Cliff a gift by calling her influential uncle and getting him to back the Nuthutch. Cliff takes Jo on a honeymoon up the Amazon, a land just as strange as Inter Minor or the Ogron planet or Spiridon. Cliff then tells the Doc he'll take care of Jo, a blatant way of showing that even old Cliff knew Big Nose's feelings toward Miss Grant. The Doctor puts on the love-proof armour for a moment when he presents her with the crystal and asks for a slice of wedding cake. But, by this time, the holes are obvious and the Doc drives off into the setting sun, after one last glance back at the Nuthutch.

You know, just as I finished writing this, I think I answered my own question about whether or not the Jo / Doctor romance was planned. I think it was. Once Barry Letts and Terrance Dicks decided to switch companions, they decided to smuggle in the love story. And, once smuggled in, they allowed it to surface and hide when needed, before bringing it out for all to see for Jo's finale.

So, there it is, the one great love story, TARDIS-style.

# EARTH SHOCK

Tom Baker astutely noted in his remarks in *Doctor Who: A Celebration*, "[*Doctor Who*] is like a hovercraft – on a fine line all the time. You don't dare touch the ground... There's so much nastiness in the world, so much violence and horror, I want to keep away from it, bury myself in make-believe." He's absolutely right. It's *Doctor Who*'s ability to never quite touch the ground, to never strive for "realism" in any way, shape or form, that makes it so enduring.

However, while *Doctor Who* may not exactly touch the ground, it certainly passes over it. More importantly, while *Who* may not necessarily reflect the reality from where and when it was made, it almost certainly refracts it: it isn't a program that sets out to make a grim and gritty recounting of economic oppression, it's a program that sets out to make *The Sun Makers* instead.

There are many people who think that *Doctor Who*'s casual relationship with real world concerns almost give it a pass from criticism, particularly when it comes to gender or race. Fortunately, fan writers are willing to question that sometimes-prevalent attitude. They are also interested in noting where *Doctor Who* is ahead of the curve, such as how the series can be so queer positive.

In many respects, the genius of *Doctor Who*'s politics is that it has none, except those which occur in the context of a particular story. The Doctor can be both anarchist and apparatchik of the state; pacifist and warmonger; leftist, centrist and neocon (*Doctor Who* was all about big-tent politics long before Ronald Reagan). And that, frankly, is part of the fun.

No one will ever mistake *Doctor Who* for the social realism of a Ken Loach film or the hard-won-and-lost political realities of *Battlestar Galactica*. Nor should they. *Doctor Who* is a larger-than-life melodrama; a product of the imagination of a particular time and place. And yet, like the box that transports its central character, it's much bigger on the inside.

# The Talons of Stereotyping
by **Graeme Burk**
*From Enlightenment #113, December 2002*

*"TVOntario has cancelled six installments of the science fiction series Dr Who because a Chinese Canadian group found them 'dangerous, offensive, racist stereotyping of people of Chinese origin'... The six cancelled shows were called The Talons of Weng-Chian (sic) and the (Chinese Canadian Council For Equality) said they 'Associate the Chinese with everything fearful and despicable.'"*

—*The Toronto Star*, November 6, 1980

*"The story does have one fault, however, and that is the poor realisation of the giant rat used by Greel to keep people away from his lair beneath the Palace Theatre."*

—David J Howe and Stephen James Walker,
*Doctor Who: The Television Companion*, 1998

Twenty-five years ago, *The Talons of Weng-Chiang* aired on British television. It was voted the best story of Season Fourteen by the members of DWAS at the time. In 1993, it topped the charts in DWB's 30th Anniversary survey and in 1998 it was ranked by readers of *Doctor Who Magazine* as No. 2 among the best *Doctor Who* stories of all time.

*Doctor Who* fans – and I wholeheartedly include myself in this collective group – clearly love *The Talons of Weng-Chiang*. And yet, we seem to be collectively blind to its flaws. As the exchange of quotes shows, TVOntario, the Canadian public television station, felt in 1980 that there was the potential to offend the Chinese community when they refused to broadcast it. It's true the complaints of the Canadian Council for Equality were the result of a pre-emptive strike on the part of TVO – who referred the story to them – and that no one from the public complained per se. However, "dangerous, offensive, racist stereotyping" seems to indicate the Chinese community wasn't exactly pleased when they were apprised of it.

But here's the $64,000 question: if it was known as far back as three years after broadcast that aspects of *Talons* were... let's say "problematic" for the moment, how is it that two decades later the "one fault" in *The Television Companion*'s assessment is the giant rat?

**"He's a Chinese, if you hadn't noticed."**
But before we get into this, perhaps we should look at some history.

Back in the late-nineteenth century, Chinese immigration across the Pacific Ocean to the North American west was in profound flux. These so-called "coolies" provided cheap – and quite often disposable – labour to a continent that was expanding westward. But such expansion – an estimated 48,000 Chinese immigrants came to the US in the 1850s – was eventually treated with a baseless (and racist) contempt and suspicion that this cheap labour force would steal jobs and possibly threaten homeland security. In 1882, the US passed the Chinese Exclusion Act, which banned Chinese immigration.

In the midst of this anti-Chinese sentiment came a fictional genre of The Yellow Peril. This genre of pulp fiction was characterised by intelligent, evil – and invariably "oriental" – masterminds intent on destroying the West. These are hardly realistic portrayals; rather, they trade in stereotypes of long-dead Mongol warlords and submissive coolies. Although associated with the Victorian period, the first examples of it did not appear until the 1890s, and the most popular example of it, Fu Manchu, was not created until 1913, well into the Edwardian era.

In interviews, Robert Holmes acknowledged his debt in *Talons* to the creation of Arthur Sarsfield Ward, better known by his pen-name "Sax Rohmer". *Talons* is set in a fantasy London overrun with the secret Chinese Tongs and opium dens that Ward created. And yet, it is a London that never existed at all. While the Yellow Peril genre came out of reactionary hysteria to Chinese immigration to the US, by 1891 there were a scant 582 people of Chinese origins on the Census rolls in Britain. The Tongs were barely more than fraternal organisations. And while there were clampdowns on "opium dens" in Limehouse at roughly the same time as Ward first published *The Mystery of Fu Manchu*, it needs to be pointed out that opium was still an over-the-counter item available from the local chemist.

Robert Holmes himself admitted that such a world never existed. "I am a fan of that fictitious Victorian period with fog, gas lamps, hansom cabs and music halls," he stated in an interview in *DWM* #100. "We look back on it and say that's what it was like, although of course it wasn't – people were slaving in dark, satanic mills and starving in London gutters."

And that seems to satisfy many. Alan Barnes' essay on *Talons* when it was awarded the No. 2 spot in *DWM*'s 1998 survey neatly sidesteps all the problems about race by reiterating that it is a "fantasy" and "pure theatre". Which of course it is; no one would ever call *Talons* a historical. The problem is, it's a fantasy where a race in our real world is portrayed as villains based on a genre of fiction born of ignorance that uses derogatory racial stereotypes.

**"I understand we all look the same."**
**"Are you Chinese?"**
Given the degree of stereotyping in the script, would it have necessarily improved the production to have an Chinese actor playing the part of Li H'sen Chang? It's hard to judge this, but certainly the decision made by Maloney and Hinchcliffe – ironically, a more difficult choice, given the need for the creation and application of prosthetics – exacerbates the existing problem of how race is portrayed in *Talons*.

*The Talons of Weng-Chiang* would never have been made in the US in 1977 in the way it was in Britain. If an episode of *Charlie's Angels* – hardly the most sensitive of television shows – featured a Chinese villain in 1977, an Asian actor would play the role. Hollywood doesn't exactly have an honourable history with Asians – Charlie Chan was played by a Swede, after all – but, by the 70s, the notion of putting an Caucasian actor in "slant eye" makeup to portray someone who is Chinese was considered a racist practice akin to blackface.

So why was it done here? Part of it is an idea that cuts to the heart of British dramatic casting generally. There is a mindset in Britain that sees portraying another ethnic group as, essentially, a form of "dressing up". Thus, you have John Bennett playing Li H'sen Chang, Jonathan Pryce playing the Vietnamese character "The Engineer" in *Miss Saigon*, or The League of Gentlemen playing a south Asian family of newsagents. In the British cultural context, assuming another ethnicity in a role is no different than a bloke playing Widow Twankey in panto or a Scotsman putting on an accent to play a French detective. And that's good enough for some; according to Howe and Walker in *The Television Companion*, "[John Bennett's] performance and make-up are so convincing that it is difficult to believe he is not actually Chinese." Which may be perhaps the most facile comment ever made in *Doctor Who*-related criticism, ever. John Bennett is filling out a caricature of how a Caucasian views an Asian, albeit a multi-layered one. There's nothing necessarily wrong with that; Apu in *The Simpsons* does much the same thing, but Apu is a character in a cartoon. Li H'sen Chang is not.

I don't think that director David Maloney or producer Philip Hinchcliffe had any sinister motives in casting John Bennett to play Li H'sen Chang. In fact, I think if they were questioned they probably would say that the reason they didn't cast an Asian to play the role was that none were to be found to play that part at the time. Which is, of course, false, but it identifies a more systemic discrimination at the heart of British television in the 1970s: there were no roles for minorities, and no minorities could allegedly portray such a role anyway. As Gary Gillatt points out in *Doctor Who: From A to Z*, it's a subtle form of racism that just about every minority has experienced at one time or another in the entertainment industry. Instead, we have the next best thing: an actor slanting his eyes under an inch of latex, talking in pithy aphorisms in a suitably ethnic voice.

**"Some slavering gangrenous vampire comes out of the sewers and stalks the city at night; he's a blackguard."**

But we, as *Doctor Who* fans, don't ask that question, or indeed any questions about race or racism in the *Talons of Weng-Chiang*. We write it off as "fantasy" or as "genre pastiche", or we just ignore it and pretend the only problem is the fluffy rat. None of the major episode guides or resources on the series has addressed it. *The Fourth Doctor Handbook* is not much better than *The Television Companion*. Even the progressive-leaning *Discontinuity Guide*, which criticises the stereotyping of Silverstein in *The Web of Fear*, draws a veil over any similar aspects in *Talons*. (The lone voice in the wilderness has been Gary Gillatt, who made mention of it throughout his tenure as editor of *DWM* and in *From A to Z*.) Many old-timers in fandom consider TVO's cancellation of *Talons* a 1980 version of political correctness gone amuck.

In fact, fandom has gone the exact opposite route, hailing *Talons* as a classic, placing it the top ten of most of the major polls of the past twenty years. Three thousand *DWM* readers can't be wrong. Why then do *Doctor Who* fans love *The Talons of Weng-Chiang* so damn much?

The answer is simple: we love it, because it's good. Really good.

Believe me, I love it too. The hype is true about *Talons*. Everything people say is great about it is actually great: the witty dialogue, the sublime Holmesian characters, the scary situations. The fully realised faux-Victorian world.

In fact, I would go so far as to say *The Talons of Weng-Chiang* is how we really want *Doctor Who* to be. We want *Doctor Who* to have night shooting, great production values, lots of film and outside broadcast, intelligent, witty scripting, exquisite direction and a Sherlockian Doctor. We want *Doctor Who* to combine historical costume drama with science fiction and add suspense, horror, comedy and the grotesque alongside genre-filching with gleeful abandon, and the best writing and direction.

If you asked me right now how I would want any new *Doctor Who* film or TV series to look, I would say without any hesitation, "Like *Talons*." I remember as a teenager rewinding my VCR to watch the initial TARDIS materialisation in episode one again and again. Watching the police box light a fog-laden Victorian street at night on film, I wished all *Doctor Who* could look like that. I don't think I was the only one wearing out video-cassettes either; just about everyone praises *Talons* similarly.

But here's the problem. Fans have found the Holy Grail of *Doctor Who* with *Talons*... but it's a poisoned chalice. Everything else is totally, absolutely and utterly perfect about this story and in so many ways it completely and totally exemplifies better than anything else what *Doctor Who* can and should be. The problem is, it just uses completely derogatory stereotypes as part of its genre-filched setting.

Is it any wonder that, for twenty-five years, fans have taken the high road?

**"The Cabinet of Weng-Chiang in the house of an infidel. We will recover it."**

*Talons* is hardly the first *Doctor Who* story to rely on convenient stereotypes; it's a tradition that extends from El Akir in *The Crusade* and Jamaica in *The Smugglers* to Toberman in *The Tomb of the Cybermen*. It would be simplistic to completely write off *Talons* for racial stereotyping and short-sighted casting. Robert Holmes' script is cleverer than either such thing. There is much that can be recovered and viewed as subverting the status quo.

Chief among them is Holmes' inversion of Yellow Peril stories. It's clear that Dr Joseph Wong, the president of the Chinese Canadian Council for Equality, probably didn't get past episode one of *Talons* (though, in fairness, why should he?) when he castigates the production for its "evil Fu Manchu character". Li H'sen Chang certainly looks the part at first, but the truth is much more complex. *Talons* isn't about an educated Chinese megalomaniac destroying the West – the mission of most Yellow Peril villains – but about a time-travelling monster who manipulates a Chinese peasant to do his bidding. And, in tragic fashion, the peasant is elevated above his lot and then cast down by that monster. In his eagerness to please a god that can never be pleased, Li H'sen Chang becomes a character we have sympathy for, and, by episode five, when Chang is disgraced and pathetic, we even feel sorry for him – which speaks as much about the pathos imbued in John Bennett's performance as the pathos imbued in the characterisation.

However, this doesn't let Robert Holmes off the hook. Li H'sen Chang might not be Fu Manchu but it can be argued that he is merely a cut above being a "submissive coolie", and however many nuances you add to a stereotype you only make a more nuanced racial stereotype. There is much more to recover from the story's views on race that are positive (the Doctor, for example, either ignores or derides the attitudes of others towards the Chinese and Litefoot is much more enlightened than his peers), but there are still lingering questions.

### "He's left us a Chinese puzzle"

Is *The Talons of Weng-Chiang* racist? I don't think it is. But I don't think it's a particularly flattering moment for the series or for British drama either. I know of Asian *Doctor Who* fans who have never seemed particularly fussed by this story. At the same time, while I rank *Talons* among my favourite and best *Whos*, I don't think I could show it to my ten-year-old goddaughter who loves *Doctor Who*.

Whatever the case, it's time we started addressing the questions it raises about the portrayal and casting of ethnic groups, rather than pretending they're not there. I don't think this needs to be a bad thing. Fans of other media sit with these uncomfortable tensions about how race is portrayed. So many things in the past of our popular culture are now detourned due to their unfortunate use of stereotypes, from *The Lone Ranger* to Will Eisner's otherwise groundbreaking comic, *The Spirit*. It is still possible to enjoy these things; it requires honesty and a willingness to discern the good and bad of what is being viewed. And, in struggling with these things, we can see where they were complacent with stereotyping, and where they cunningly subverted it as well.

We don't need to ban *The Talons of Weng-Chiang*. But we should be debating and engaging it a good deal more, and not turning a blind eye to what others outside our fan culture can see clearly. *Talons* is a brilliant, ground-breaking series that defines *Doctor Who*. But it also portrays Chinese people at best as gullible and servile, and at worst willing conspirators for evil.

It's time we started to admit that there is one overriding flaw to *The Talons of Weng-Chiang*. And it has nothing to do with the fluffy rat.

*Historical Note: In 2009,* Doctor Who Magazine *rolled out the sequel to its 1998 series-spanning survey, this time including all 200 or so stories in both the classic and new series. The Talons of Weng-Chiang is still in the top ten, and while it has a lower ranking (dropping from No. 2 to No. 4), it scored a higher approval rating than the 1998 poll, scoring 91.45%, up from 89.95% eleven years previous. It's clear that the hold The Talons of Weng-Chiang has over the imagination of Doctor Who fandom isn't going away, if that wasn't already obvious from the number of new series stories featuring an abundance of night shooting, fog and sumptous period sets.*

*In the latest accompanying essay about* Talons, *written this time by Philip MacDonald, there is the first explicit commentary ever on the thorny racial dynamics. MacDonald writes, "Slightly harder to ignore is the fact that every passing year makes it tricker it turn a blind eye to the portrayal of Chinese characters." He goes on to praise how the Doctor underimines the casual racism of the age, and then concludes, "Only an idiot would accuse* Talons *of being actively racist, but the spectacle of a (very fine) white actor in slanty-eyed make-up fronting a bunch of Oriental extras is something that plonks the production firmly in a bygone age."*

*As my 2002 essay reprinted above indicated, I think there are a lot more issues at stake than MacDonald or DWM has credited. Nonetheless, the fact that the very casting of John Bennett and the portrayal of Chinese in the story has gone from being ignored with some minor handwaving to being written off as dated is progress, I suppose. I'm just not sure where it's progressing... –GB*

# Queer as Who

**by Scott Clarke**
*From Enlightenment #114, February / March 2002*

A blue box materialises in your bedroom, whisks you away on wild, campy adventures with a travelling eccentric; you defeat screeching pepperpots that tell you there is only one way to be in the universe; you trade quips with smart, haughty ice queens donning fabulous wardrobes and then, when you're finally ready to call it a day, you're delivered to a planet where you really fit in.

It's a queer geek's nirvana.

Being queer often equals being the outsider or the "other". Whether it is the bombardment of male / female coupling imagery in the media, predetermined norms around who you take to the prom or parental rejection, the queer experience is often a sense of being on the outside looking in. The sudden appearance of the TARDIS, ready to whisk us away from this reality, is a potent fantasy. It's an escape; a portable "island of misfits". Companions such as Vicki, Steven, Adric, Turlough, Peri and Ace have been rescued from unpleasant realities to become part of a "chosen family" in the TARDIS. In many ways, this is akin to the popularity (verging on cliché) of *The Wizard of Oz* within gay male culture.

Look at the character of Adric for a moment. Whatever else one might think of young Mr Waterhouse's talents as a thespian, the actual character probably generated a significant sense of identification with young gay males. Alienated, even amongst outcasts, Adric never quite fit in. He was always looking for something to believe in (see *State of Decay* or *Four to Doomsday*), a place where he could belong. In retrospect, it's a pity that Adric's character wasn't written more consistently (and less cloyingly), as it might have been a rich opportunity for the writers to explore his "outsider" aspects.

Ace is probably a more successful example of a character that queer youth could identify with. A misfit who is taken under the Doctor's wing, accepted for who she is, but also guided (some would say manipulated) to begin to realise her full potential. Am I suggesting that Ace was a lesbian? I don't think it really matters; it's more the emotional impact that her circumstances convey.

And, like finding Oz somewhere over the rainbow, an equally compelling aspect of travelling in the TARDIS is the sense that it could transport you to your own special place in the universe. Susan finds her place on twenty-second century Earth shacking up with David Campbell; Romana heads up the Tharil Liberation Front in E-Space; and Nyssa embraces her destiny as a pharmacist on Terminus. That feeling of being ultimately delivered to where you really belonged all along resonates with everyone who has felt different or like an outsider.

Is *Doctor Who* inherently gay? The series has never had an openly gay character (I am speaking of course about the television show only). Oh sure, there were strong intimations that old Vivien and Amelia shared more than just sausage sandwiches, and one has to wonder about a couple of those Moroks in *The Space Museum*. But, even as one experiences the larger themes present in *Doctor Who*, there often seems to be something else going on under the surface.

Camp offers another layer of appeal for many queer fans (in particular, gay male fans). While the highly "affected" or exaggerated style of *Who* certainly appeals to children, there can be no denying that it holds a special place in the hearts of its bent admirers. I've always felt that *Doctor Who* speaks more to the bent side of my nature than say *Star Trek* or the testosterone-induced *Buck Rogers in the 25th Century*. When *Star Trek* wanted to address homosexuality, they merely trotted out some funny-foreheaded aliens for a "very special *Star Trek: The Next Generation...*" and the powers-that-be patted themselves collectively on the head, and moved onto to the next issue of the week.

It's probably the very fact that so much wit, colour and eroticism are so cleverly embedded in a host of stories that speaks so delightfully to the queer aesthetic; it's almost subversive in its slyness. With "its" high-pitched, preening voice and suggestive shape, that hermaphroditic curiosity, Alpha Centauri, was certainly an inspired creation in the great annals of camp. On the one hand, a silly creature for kids to adore; on another level, a walking, talking phallus. Alternatively, there is the gender bending of Eldrad in *The Hand of Fear*, the delightful gay male / fag-hag relationship between Count Grendel and Madame Lamia, and the sham marriage between Julian Glover's deliciously over-enunciated Count Scarlioni and the deluded, doomed Countess.

And what of the Doctor's implied asexuality? With the exception of the Fox TV movie, there is nary a hint of which way the Doctor "swung" throughout the series' history (and no, I do not accept – or except – the "he has a granddaughter" defence). Watching *Star Trek* or *Buck Rogers*, there was no question that Kirk, Picard or Buck were explicit examples of heterosexual virility (despite Buck's propensity for spandex). Janeway had her share of dalliances (holographic or otherwise) as well. 'Twas never a worry with the good Doctor. For me, he could easily be a gay man; I could claim him for the team if I so desired. As it was, the good Time Lord's asexuality just made it a non-issue. As a queer kid, I could relax, go for the ride and identify with the hero without any troublesome subliminal conditioning.

The tyranny of homogeneity in mainstream culture is frequently addressed in *Doctor Who*. Monsters like the Cybermen and the Daleks, with their credos of "we are the supreme beings" and "you will be like us", represent monolithic perspectives on the world. The pressure for queer people to conform to a heterosexist worldview is often over-whelming. In the workplace, at family gatherings, or in representations in the media, it's unavoidable. The Doctor, however, is always on the side of tolerance, debunking the idea of one perfect state (Enlightenment is the choice after all) and upholding diversity.

Central to challenging this homogeneity for queer people is the experience of coming out. Stories like *The Pirate Planet* and *The Mutants* offer us interesting subtext on coming out. In the former, the psychic gestalt on Zanak, the Mentiads, offer us a curious comparison to a queer culture. In this case, they are a group of men who have been labelled social pariahs by the mainstream for their misunderstood psychic abilities. It's quite interesting how the crimes of the greater society (destroying inhabited planets and raping them for their mineral resources) are directly tied to the "coming out" of a new Mentiad. In our own society, many queer people decide to come out in order to stand up to injustice and intolerance, rather than remain silent.

Although *The Mutants* is traditionally seen as a "British colonial" allegory, some interesting parallels can also be drawn to the coming-out process. The Solonians are oppressed and marginalised by the mainstream (represented by Earth's Empire) and once they begin the process of metamorphosis into Mutts they are hunted down as hideous monsters, because their natural evolutionary change isn't fully understood. I clearly remember watching this story, wondering how I would hide my scales once they started to appear, and thinking it was worth being a monster for a while, in order to evolve into the beautiful being Ky.

Some might argue that I'm grasping at queer straws (those would be pixie stix), but I would be quick to point out that all art is subjective, and that, while intent on the artist's part can be a powerful political statement, the receiving impact / perspective of said art is just as critical.

Where I sit, there is definitely something more than a little bit queer about an eccentric "doctor" who travels around the universe in a police box, subverting the natural order of every society he comes in contact with, and giving himself a makeover every hundred years or so.

I'm funny that way.

# Is Who Afraid
# of Virginia Woolf?

by Dave Rolinson
From Circus #9, Spring 2002 (revised Spring 2009)

Janet Fielding, actress behind everyone's favourite stroppy Australian air-stewardess-cum-post-punk New Romantic, challenged fandom by criticising the outdated sexist features of Doctor Who's format. This attack on a fundamental part of the series should have provoked fans into re-evaluating Doctor Who and their responses to it, but for the most part it prompted defensive arguments about individual companions, or, worse, anti-feminist feeling that is characteristic of fandom's anti-theoretical, anti-intellectual or even anti-analytical bias. Fielding refused to appear on a documentary to defend her points, sensing she'd become a scapegoat, but surely her comments were fascinating to anyone interested in how the series works? It's hard to stereotype feminism – given the way it melds with other theories, and how key feminists have disagreed with each other over its scope – but that hasn't stopped fandom.

Long-running texts are always fascinating barometers of changing approaches to given subjects. I'm not interested in just criticising the rubbish companions (the Peri essay can wait), and can't do justice here to the entirety of feminist theory. But thinking about companions on screen, and the reasoning of production teams off screen, means we can think about gender and the representation of women through ideas of '"patriarchy" or male dominance.

Early feminism looked at the exclusion of women from important positions, and critiqued how men represented women, which was valuable but queried by later feminists; for instance, Elaine Showalter argued that "we are not learning what women have felt and experienced, but only what men have thought women should be". Of course, if I only wrote about the *Doctor Who* stories made by women, this essay would be much shorter. The wider meaning of "patriarchal" male dominance is at the heart of this essay: how patriarchy is revealed through media forms and culture. *Doctor Who* coincided with "second wave" feminism in the late 1960s and 1970s, and although this was superficially addressed through the "Women's Lib" statements given to Sarah Jane Smith in her early stories, the fact that she settles into the less independent role required by the format is a more interesting, unconscious, echo of "second wave" feminism's concerns with how these problems are manifested in the culture.

**Attack of the Cyberpersons**

From the early feminist viewpoint of looking at "patriarchal authority" via cultures that excluded women, the BBC during *Doctor Who*'s lifespan is an obvious candidate. *Doctor Who* is notable for the male bias in its producers, writers and directors, and the wariness of lead actors towards input from actresses playing companions. Many of its fans were male, and I've often wondered whether these facts are all connected. To serve the format overseen by male production teams, female companions are often under-developed characters who get into situations for reasons of plot expediency regardless of how stupidly they have to behave to get into those situations, and those characters become hard for female viewers to identify with (the role of the companion, as Elisabeth Sladen saw it). As Janet Fielding pointed out, nobody can identify with a woman who tries to climb a rock in high heels.

So this is more complicated than simply saying that the dominance of male staff inevitably led to women being prevented from expressing themselves. Arguably, the programme's most important producer, Verity Lambert, could hardly hire lots of women writers and directors when so few were coming through the system or when women were less interested in what has been called a male genre (although it should be noted that Lambert's *Doctor Who* was not exclusively science fiction but achieved huge audience figures as a family drama – a lesson learned by the post-2005 series – rooted around a family set-up). And female directors were subsumed within the format too. There's a shot in the first part of *Horror of Fang Rock*, with the Doctor and Leela talking at a table, during which the camera zooms in to a medium close-up, leaving us with a typically *Doctor Who* composition: the Doctor looms large in the foreground, while Leela is adrift in the background, looking the Doctor's way (they're both facing front) asking questions, "feeding" the star. Given that this was directed by a woman (Paddy Russell), there's more to this sexism-in-*Who* lark than blaming the attitudes of individuals.

Interestingly, Fielding argued that this sexism was the fault of the programme's narrative structure. Somebody had to be (metaphorically) tied to the railway lines to be rescued, and this didn't happen to the Doctor (other than, literally, in *The Deadly Assassin*, when there was no companion). Also, companions had to scream to tell the audience when to be scared, a device still used in supposedly "ironic" horror movies like *Scream*. However, aren't these excuses for bad writing? The Doctor didn't have to scream. He was able to channel his fear into intellectual consideration and brave one-liners. Male production teams could not let companions find an expressive escape from fear; too often, they collapse into hysteria. Even in the most structurally *Who*-like episodes of *The X-Files*, when Mulder saved Scully from that metaphorical 7:23 from Darlington, Scully was allowed to be (to paraphrase Jo Grant) slightly more intelligent than a whelk. We can accept that companions got into trouble because that was their narrative function, but we need to look more closely at the nature of that trouble, which sometimes borders on misogyny. Do fans get their kicks from watching women in danger? How many of the most-revered "classics" depend on women in danger, particularly suffering violence, and how often is that element of "threat" listed as part of the reason that that story is a classic? Take *The Robots of Death*, in which male robots on a male-run ship stalk and strangle women in some of the most voyeuristic sequences in the programme's history, or *Genesis of the Daleks* (and other stories) in which Sarah Jane is being brutalised. The fact that Sarah Jane, the character who most openly talks about the independence of women, is then so often brutalised, perversely echoes Molly Haskell's *From Reverence to Rape*, which observes how women on screen are most viciously dealt with at times when women off screen argue for more independence.

**Women and the Future**

Janet Fielding rightly identified weaknesses in the format, but they're not necessarily weaknesses in the genre; the companion need not be subservient. The lack of what John Nathan-Turner called "hanky panky" in the TARDIS meant that *Doctor Who* did at least avoid the traditional narrative drive (what theorists might call the "Oedipal trajectory") in which the girl is the object of male desire until he gets her and settles down. The programme is not sexless: the Doctor doesn't lust after companions, but plenty of other characters do, and the publicity made capital of their attributes (the anti-hanky-panky JN-T made sure Nicola Bryant wore tight tops). Laura Mulvey, in her hugely influential 1970s essay "Visual Pleasure and Narrative Cinema", talked about how the camera embodies the "male gaze", which makes women sexual objects to be looked at, and how that gaze is tied in with power and ownership (an example of feminism tying in with psychoanalysis and ideology). Choosing the lascivious shot of Peri's bikini-clad body in *Planet of Fire* would oversimplify Mulvey's theory, but it's striking for its pointlessness: it isn't anyone's point-of-view, it isn't helping the story. If I enjoy that shot (and, as a heterosexual male, I do) I can't deny that it is a sexualising gaze, regardless of the post-2005 fan standpoint that the programme wasn't previously sexualising because the Doctor wasn't trying to snog the assistant.

It's less helpful to note examples of casual sexism, although there are many. Favourites include the Doctor in *The Moonbase* asking Polly to make everyone some coffee while he thinks of something, or Zoe, whose continuing baffling combination of being attractive *and* clever is most memorably described in *The Invasion*, when soldiers ask "Can't we keep her, sir? She's much prettier than a computer", rendering her a non-independent possession.

Instead, we should note that science fiction need not necessarily give women roles that are subservient or even domestic. Why should Polly put the kettle on? Companions are taken out of society, taken away from normative family roles and the expectations of women held by our society at the time. Fictional societies in space in the distant future should not treat women in the same way as 1960s Earth, even if they're being made on 1960s Earth (mind you, the Swinging Polly epitomises the decade's questioning of those sorts of roles anyway, until she steps out of the decade and into the format). To take an extreme viewpoint, part of Shulasmith Firestone's argument in *The Dialectic of Sex: The Case for Feminist Revolution* is that women can be free only by escaping childbearing and child-rearing... through technology. Surely, on those terms, *Doctor Who* companions can get a level of freedom through technology; I don't remember any getting maternity leave. Of course, normative family relationships appear in individual stories, and also several "TARDIS crews" weren't "crews" but family units, from Grandfather / Ian / Barbara / Susan to Tegan / Nyssa / Adric. TARDIS male-female relationships were still split along the lines set out by Nancy Chodorow in *The Reproduction of Mothering*, with women in the domestic space and the Doctor taking the public role and getting cross when they venture out without him or his permission.

I'm not being wise in hindsight: many of *Doctor Who*'s clichéd representations of women were clichés at the time or even before the show started. Although futuristic settings and genres don't need to contain sexist roles for women, *Doctor Who* is not attempting to be adult science fiction with layers of complexity akin to literary SF, and so reverts to stereotypes. In an article on *Quatermass* and *A for Andromeda*, Joy Leman found that male characters used reason but women responded emotionally and had "women's intuition". Quatermass himself is the benevolent patriarch, women "still have to focus the 'love interest' and serve the brilliance of the Professor, even though academically well equipped themselves". The times were an influence: in *A for Andromeda*, "Andromeda can be read as the portrayal of the 1960s new professional woman – a woman who put intellect first and had to be taught, by a man, to express femininity and to respond to emotions." *Doctor Who* not only continued these attitudes, but the clichés of pulp SF. We can all think of *Doctor Who* equivalents to Lisa Tuttle's list of gender stereotypes in Clute and Nicholls' *Encyclopaedia of Science Fiction*: The Timorous Virgin ("good for being rescued, and for having things explained to her"); the Amazon Queen ("sexually desirable and terrifying at the same time, usually set up to be tamed"); the Frustrated Spinster Scientist ("an object lesson to girl readers that career success equals feminine failure"), and the Tomboy Kid Sister ("who has a semblance of autonomy only until male appreciation of her burgeoning sexuality transforms her into Virgin or Wife"). Tuttle adds material for detractors of post-1989 *Who*: "[More recent] women's characters exist only to validate the male protagonist as acceptably masculine – that is, heterosexual."

## The TARDIS Effect

In *Doctor Who*, men have the answers, and women defer to their interpretations of events. "What's happening, Doctor?" is snappier than "Tell me how to interpret this new planet, because I am unable to unless you filter my experience for me," but the meaning is the same. As Simone de Beauvoir argued in *The Second Sex*, gender is constructed by society ("One is not born, but rather becomes, a woman"), and since the Doctor chooses and explains the societies they visit, he dictates this understanding. Look at their ability to understand foreign languages, the translation convention explained to the delight of continuity lepers as the "Time Lord gift I allow you to share": companions' understanding and expression are being controlled by the Doctor.

TARDIS travel erodes or abuses feminine strength. Women who get into the TARDIS with a serious career (scientist, journalist, teacher) soon find themselves halfway up a cliff in impractical heels. Women with intelligence have something feminine missing (Zoe and Romana I), and lookers can't have brains (in *Spearhead from Space*, we are told that Liz Shaw is "not just a pretty face"). Many Doctor-companion relationships are built upon him teaching the inferior woman. Then, they are often given to men in unconvincing romances. Leela enters the TARDIS as a proud warrior and leaves in *The Invasion of Time*, on some drip's arm: tamed and taken home to meet the relations. In *The Green Death*, Jo leaves with a younger Doctor figure...

The Doctor calls the TARDIS "girl", but it's a more masculine environment (I'll stop before a phallic reading of those ionic columns, the rising and falling Time Rotor and the door control). The exterior provides a box to put women in, and is highly symbolic: the police box's historical context gives it connotations of patriarchal reassurance (or, for the Target novelisation of that sentence, police box = police = police man, as in *An Unearthly Child*, *The War Machines* or *Logopolis*). The Doctor patrols his galactic beat with young girls who can't keep up with his brilliance but give moral support by making tea and wearing tight clothes. Women trying to make more of a contribution are punished, and told they would have been fine if they'd done what the Doctor said. Paternalistic in all incarnations, he is a strict parent, warning his charges to not leave his sight, and initially reacting aggressively to Ian and Barbara's substitute parenting of Susan. Her departure in *The Dalek Invasion of Earth* is a transition from familial male-ownership to the male-ownership of marriage.

Mary Tamm and Janet Fielding were right to grumble about their characters. Romana I was a genius Time Lady, but everyone except Douglas Adams forgot. As script editor, Adams spearheaded Lalla Ward's assault on the Best Companion trophy (can anyone be a strong character when designated merely "companion"?) by giving Romana II intelligence, wit and (sometimes) autonomy. Stephen Gallagher then wrote *Warriors' Gate*, for most of which she is that tabloid-myth Female Doctor. In one scene, she passes the Doctor's orders down the line to Adric in a format-baiting (possibly Waterhouse-baiting) rejection of *Doctor Who*'s sexist orthodoxy. After stating her qualifications (to fix K9), she is central to the action, knows the science, gets the best lines and then realises her self-sufficiency and leaves the Doctor. When Ward left, Romana could have regenerated, but the production team told us that the Time Lord team was too powerful. The show "needed" weaker companions or ones more deferential to the format, like Sarah Jane Smith, whose deference to male authority was unspoilt by that tokenistic "Women's Lib" tag. She acquiesces to programme-maker and fan beliefs that female characters need to have the science-fiction elements explained to them, and the underlying belief that female viewers need to have the science-fiction elements explained to them.

By the 1980s, the show's sexism was both a symptom and a cause of the programme's outdatedness. JN-T put the sex into the programme's sexism, understanding pre-*Baywatch* teenage boys (or those dodgy Dads said to "hang around with a hobnob"), with skirts being raised or, in Nyssa's case in *Terminus*, dropped. Some companions' impractical and / or revealing costumes were their only characteristics. The high heels (the kind Germaine Greer might call "fuck-me shoes") worn by Tegan were a revealing symbol of *Doctor Who*'s attitudes towards women. The impracticality of their outfits aids capture (in some cultures, women's feet are painfully bound to restrict freedom of movement) and provides rescuing opportunities.

The Davison era put its lead characters into uniforms, both literally and metaphorically. Each companion had their role spelled out: scientist, mathematician (because in a crisis situation you can never have enough mathematicians), navigator. Nyssa was developed with more care than some previous companions, and so more intriguingly revealed the male production team's attitudes. The importance given to absence in feminist and psychoanalytic theory (relating to the absent penis) in depictions of female inadequacy makes Nyssa's characterisation interesting, because she is defined by absences: the gaps in her scientific knowledge (not even that jackanapes the Master exploited her dearth of telebiogenesis qualifications), the loss of her family, the loss of Traken. When we meet her in *The Keeper of Traken*, we saw her homeworld as a place where women defer to men and where Kassia's rejection of this system is, in *Doctor Who* tradition, a move to evil. Tegan, meanwhile, is Adric and Nyssa's mother figure, and the Doctor's nagging wife. The Davison era's often boring TARDIS scenes are so rooted in domesticity (as Andrew Cartmel put it, "*Neighbours* with roundels") that gaps between seasons may involve the Doctor being nagged to put up some shelves he's never got around to.

Women had strong jobs in the Davison era – scientists, soldiers, spaceship captains – but were they women? The script editor protested that only six-foot-tall men could be ships' captains, so it should be positive that women were often cast in male-written parts, although it's also reflective of the superficiality of characterisation in that era. However, the era has strong points. In *The Caves of Androzani*, the only female characters – Peri and Timmin – are the only survivors of a masculine bloodbath, as even the Doctor "dies". Admittedly, Peri spends the whole story staring into the headlights of that metaphorical 8:41 from Crewe, and Timmin is sidelined until late on, but it is still a powerful factor. Equally interesting is Tegan's divorce, er, departure, in *Resurrection of the Daleks*, after a dull macho story. In these two stories, the governing ideologies of masculinity collapse, though the companion is still running around after the hero, complaining.

The tendency of companions to complain in the 1980s may seem to be a shift away from deference, but (a) it never altered their narrative function and (b) it risked defining female independence as format-obstructive whinging rather than anything positive. If Sarah Jane was the programme's outdated attempt to reflect "second-wave" feminism, Peri's whingeing was out of step with feminist criticism that examined "pleasure" for female viewers in popular texts. Replacing her with Bonnie Langford's Mel, a less-than-one-dimensional character but one with boundless enthusiasm, opens the door for a reading of Mel as in touch with feminist theory – a door which, in the interests of common sense, I hereby nail shut.

### Battle for the Planets of the Women

In *Kinda*, women pass archetypal wisdom down the maternal line, as revealed in Panna's reincarnation into Karuna: "We are One." The restrictive vision of mirrors and TV monitors does not work here because women have their own voice without a male filter, often reproducing and subverting the male voice (fittingly, in what is after all a male-authored text). The Mara is male when it penetrates Tegan, and makes her hold out her hand as in marriage. Todd is the only woman present when the box is first opened, and the only one who screams, because she understands the force of what may be unleashed. It is another box trying to hold a female force, just as Nyssa spends the whole story in a box: confined to the TARDIS (noting that this isolation was aided by the male production team not being able to find enough for the companions to do need not ruin the theory). Hindle goes over the edge because the male thrust of colonisation is revealed to be ineffective. As Elaine Showalter wrote about Joseph Conrad's *Heart of Darkness* (a massive influence on this script), *Kinda* "pursues the penetration of a female wilderness". Though Showalter attacks Conrad's story as "an allegory of male bonding and the flight from women", *Kinda* reworks its themes. As Cassandra May argued in *Matrix*, "on Deva Loka Freud's masculine forces are disempowered": "Hindle – having, appropriately, been threatened with the return of 'Daddy' by an exasperated Todd – sees Sanders coming through the jungle and collapses, clinging to his chair and calling 'Mummy!'... Aris undergoes the Oedipal trauma of separation from his mother's body and finds himself confronted with a woman who offers her body to him as a sexual, rather than a maternal, object." Femininity is the solution to the institutionalised rape of colonialism. However, Tegan's "escape" is from feminine awakening. She finds a different voice (Fielding's excellent "low" voice) but it is taken from her by men: Aris and the Doctor, to whose box she returns, in uniform, to follow her old role.

*Vengeance on Varos* questions the portrayal of women, and its effects on how women view themselves, in the conversion of Peri and Areta. After acknowledging their role in *Doctor Who* ("anything could happen to us, just for their amusement"; they could almost be watching *The Robots of*

*Death*), they almost become "birds". They are then snatched from a scene of potential character exploration and made helpless, as the Doctor and Jondar rescue the girls-in-peril. As the Doctor notes the need of "reimprinting their identities", it feels as though the format has done precisely that.

Ace has been praised as a change from the norm, but that only goes so far, despite the Nitro-9 bomb-throwing gimmick (a cheap way to circumvent the Doctor's pacifism, and all the more troubling for lacking a lasting, morally defining "no more janus thorns" stand-off) and a lack of boob tubes. Her adolescent angst is still a plot device to start adventures, more rewarding in tone but similar in spirit to Mel's desire to go swimming in *Paradise Towers*. More effort was made with characterisation because by now *Doctor Who* writers were drawn from dull soap operas. Ace mixed out-of-touch attempts to portray youth culture with the soap device of giving her baggage (as the set-up for a later reveal, in the tradition of soap, or what we now wearily call an "arc").

But Ace's role as a companion is often disturbing. *The Happiness Patrol* draws from the same cliché used by *The Two Ronnies* and the unmade *Doctor Who* "comedy" *The Prison in Space*: the planet ruled by women. Meaning, of course, the planet ruled badly by women to prove how well-run our male world is. I'm being unfair to the programme's anti-Thatcherite message, but even those intelligent political subtexts can't quite hide the fact that Ace helps the men to bring down Helen A's government and restore benevolent patriarchy.

In *The Curse of Fenric*, Ace dips into the waters of the unsubtly named Maiden's Point and emerges as a woman. But, like her flirtation with a soldier, the Doctor uses her sexual development, virtually prostituting her. As Steve Grace wrote in *Infinite Dreams*, vampirism is "a broader metaphor for the awakening of sexuality... biting symbolising the deflowering of those young maids; they become vampires too because, now they have tasted of that fruit, they are considered unclean... Ace is now an adult." Ace opens herself up to the Doctor more than any other companion, and while the others just wanted to know what was going on in the plot, Ace is enslaved to his interpretation not just of the plot but of her own emotional development and her identity as a woman. Although he had previously left Susan to grow up for herself, he now constructs Ace's womanhood around his own point of view (her "faith" in him), cleansing her of maternal influence (as Audrey is symbolically washed away). Whereas women in *Kinda* draw strength from timeless femininity, *The Curse of Fenric* portrays time as a weight around Ace's neck. The sources of power passed down from her mother are "pure evil since the dawn of time", and need to be redirected by a man.

*Survival* repeats this idea, as the Doctor and the Master fight to abuse her power (her ability to escape from the Cheetah Planet). But the writer of *Survival* is a woman, Rona Munro, making it an interesting story to study. Munro allows Ace to enjoy and exploit her power, an archetypal power constructed by society (the planet). Following inbred instincts, the boys fight each other, but the women draw wisdom and love – for each other. Subtexts in the script were lost, as Munro explained in Jonathan Bignell's *Writing for Cinema*: "I wanted to have these Cheetah people be basically incredibly wild, and very very sensual and very very sexual, and very outgoing... And this was quite a female thing, so Ace really had a relationship with this Cheetah woman as a kind of lesbian subtext... [but] nowhere did that appear on screen." Again, "emotional truth" was undermined by a male production team (placing what I'm doing nearer to "feminist critique" than the "gynocriticism" that looks at women as controllers of meaning, regardless of the fact that a woman wrote the story). This process is paralleled in the script, as the men win. Karra is killed by the Master, and Ace suppresses and denies her power, instead calling the TARDIS "home". Like *Fenric*, there are hints of the female Oedipal complex and penis envy, with Ace redirected from desire for her mother (baby Audrey and Perivale) and father (Fenric in the guise of Sorin) by fumblings with Jean, Phyllis and Karra, and by a fascinating triangle with the (eternal father figure) Doctor and the Master.

There is a depth of companion characterisation in these stories which makes them open to interpretation. Finding interesting – negative – ideas seems unfair, when so many *Doctor Who* stories lack this depth and so can be, by comparison, almost dismissed from this kind of interpretation. The seriousness (especially in *Survival*, a nuanced script obscured, as so often in *Doctor Who*, by drab realisation) invites readings of the companion's role. By critiquing that role, I'm not saying the series should go back to not caring, just showing the depths (even paradoxes) that are suddenly open to us. For instance, other companions joined the Doctor for adventures, to the extent that Polly apparently never told anyone her surname, but Ace essentially gives him her womanhood.

So, deciding whether a companion is a sexist portrayal or not is more complex than noting whether she shows a bit of leg. Companions' characters are prone to the fluctuations of different production teams, writers, directors and other variables that were more likely in the days before tone meetings. But the actresses concerned share one interesting complaint: that the characters revert to stereotype after a few stories. Are one-off companions, as characters rather than format-servers, the answer? Take the 1996 TV movie: Grace Holloway doesn't scream, doesn't twist her ankle, is given intelligent dialogue and a key role in the story. The

Doctor is often innocent and she is often his teacher. Could a new companion per week work, with women educating the Doctor about their society? There is scope for new discussions of the impact of the romantic tenor of the 1996 TV movie on the sexuality asserting relationships at the core of the post-2005 series (to re-use a joke from the 2002 version of this essay, "This contraceptive device – it fits perfectly!").

Perhaps companions should have been abolished in the early 1970s, when technology made the need for a large cast less vital. By regularly placing women in inferior roles, *Doctor Who* reinforced the patriarchy. Viewed as characters rather than format-servers, every single character in the history of *Doctor Who* was fundamentally flawed... apart from Romana II. Because I fancy her.

# Anarchy In Who, UK

**by Ian Farrington**
*From Shockeye's Kitchen #8, November 2000*

The first thing seen in *Doctor Who* was a policeman, the ultimate example of British justice: a uniformed Bobby reassuringly checking the dark and misty night looking for danger and protecting us from crime.

However, authoritative establishment figures would seldom be presented in any sort of positive way throughout *Doctor Who*'s history. Nestling somewhere between the chalk 'n' cheese of Federations of *Star Trek* and *Blake's 7*, authorities would often be presented as suspicious and the programme would take a decidedly left-of-centre approach to establishments and power.

**"It would be wrong to describe *Doctor Who* as revolutionary... "**
Really? What about *The Happiness Patrol, The Space Museum, The Macra Terror, The Trial of a Time Lord* (parts one to four), *The Reign of Terror* and many more where the Doctor and / or his companions assist an (often armed) uprising?

**"Well, yes, but these are all about people fighting against totalitarianism or military aggression. It's not the other extreme either; there's no 'Yessir' subservience."**
Very rarely. The programme never felt a need to toe a middle-class line. *Doctor Who* has never had a Prime Directive, a legislative excuse to stand back and do nothing.

**"The series works on judging each situation independently."**
Yes, so when the third Doctor is exiled to Earth he may complain about the insular attitudes and bureaucracy of the British establishment, but he never feels the need to go off and join the Socialist Workers Party.

**"That raises an interesting point: is the Doctor, or the programme as a whole, politically biased?"**
It's certainly political. The number of political stories are far too numerous to list (you could argue there's no such thing as an apolitical story). But is the programme, for example, left wing? You could argue that *The Happiness Patrol* is a satire of Thatcher. *The Sun Makers* attacks the tax system. *The Green Death* promotes "food for all" over big business (as well as, twenty years early, commenting on pit closures). Virtually all of Malcolm Hulke's stories both ridicule the class system and, by using Silurians / Sea Devils / Draconians in an allegorical way, point out the evils of racism (Hulke, by the way, was a committed Marxist).

**"There must be (small c) conservative stories."**
Well, stories that use right-wing myths often use them in order to debunk them. See the survival-of-the-fittest theory in *Survival*, racial purity / segregation in *Genesis of the Daleks* and the get-what-you-want / want-what-you-get discussions that lie within *Vengeance on Varos*.

**"Are you saying *Doctor Who* is socialist?"**
No, just that its format promotes liberal metaphor... Oh, all right, yes – it's more left wing than right. For example, the Daleks' stories all condemn fascism, while Season Twenty-Five overflows with attacks on right-wing attitudes: every story except *The Greatest Show in the Galaxy*.

**"The programme only became political when Barry Letts took over as producer in 1970."**
Really? So, the sixties were devoid of political comment or anti-establishment thought? What about *Planet of Giants'* green messages, or *Galaxy Four's* gender role metaphors, or *The Ice Warriors'* over reliance on computers? 1960s *Doctor Who* rarely challenges authority, but that's not to say it didn't promote anti-conservative ideals.

**"*Doctor Who* makes a distinction between authority gained by democratic means..."**
But the third Doctor was still a shameless royalist, claiming in *Inferno* that the Windsors were a "charming family" and bowing to hereditary power in *The Curse of Peladon*.

**"... and illegal control."**
Didn't stop production teams using democracy to scare the bejesus out of us.

**"How so?"**
In both *Terror of the Autons* and *Resurrection of the Daleks*, what appear to be policemen are in fact part of an evil alien regime.

**"Funny how most aliens are necessarily evil."**
Except in Malcolm Hulke's stories. He knew that really convincing aliens had characters and viewpoints, and that a single race couldn't be generalised into one, any more than humanity could.

**"But, getting back to the point, they're not real policemen."**
No, but when we get the real deal, do they inspire confidence? They're either bungling idiots (see *Ghost Light*, *The Talons of Weng-Chiang* or *Black Orchid*) or non-existent (where are the police during *The Awakening*, for example?).

**"Come to think of it, didn't the show's first producer, Verity Lambert, describe the Doctor as anti-establishment?"**
She wasn't wrong. Hartnell refused to kow-tow to Kublai Khan and Nero, Pertwee swatted aside numerous government officials and often ignored UNIT's plans ("I sometimes think that military intelligence is a contradiction in terms!") and by Tom Baker's time it was expected that the Doctor would disagree with authority. Perhaps that's the real reason behind Mary Whitehouse's fury: a children's hero who attacked the status quo. It is a relishable irony that the Doctor travels in a TARDIS that looks like a police box.

**"So, authorities are a bad thing...?"**
They certainly mess things up a lot. The army commit genocide in *Doctor Who and the Silurians*, a civil servant orders an attack on the Sea Devils in their eponymous story, just as the Doctor is negotiating a peace (both these stories were written by Hulke) and, in *The Curse of Fenric*, the army plot to poison Moscow with chemical weapons.

**"The army generally do the right thing in *The War Machines*, *The Seeds of Doom* and *Remembrance of the Daleks*..."**
True. They're a useful plot device. But look at how power affects people: Sir George Hutchinson in *The Awakening*, Chessene in *The Two Doctors*, Harrison Chase in *The Seeds of Doom*... they all go bonkers!

**"So, power corrupts and absolute power corrupts absolutely?"**
Most of the time. We see a lot of good-natured rulers (such as Marco in *The Masque of Mandragora*, the Governor in *Vengeance on Varos* and the King in *The Curse of Peladon*), but they all have rogues or systems usurping their power. And, who are the most corrupt lot? As the Doctor says in *The Trial of a Time Lord*, the Daleks, Cybermen and Sontarans don't have a thing on the Time Lords, whose ten million years of absolute power has turned them into the meddling, paranoid and arrogant race they have become.

**"What does the programme say to its audience?"**
It tells us to question things, be sceptical, make our own judgements and not look upon arbitrary decisions and situations as necessary facts.

**"OK, so we don't trust authority."**
That's right... but who am I to tell you that?

# Is the Doctor a Pacifist?
by Gian-Luca Di Rocco

There are many things that I was surprised to learn when I joined the greater world of *Doctor Who* fandom. One was that Adric was an unpopular companion. Another was that *Colony in Space* is generally considered a dud. And a third was that the Doctor is a pacifist hero. Or at least, that's what fans kept telling me for the past two decades since I joined fandom: in person, in articles and reviews published in magazines and fanzines, in books written by fans, and online in chat rooms and discussion boards.

This particular perception of the Doctor is alive and well today. "Nearly everyone agrees that the Doctor should always be a pacifist... not using weapons," claimed one poster to *The Doctor Who Forum* in April 2009. Another poster confirmed, saying, "The Doctor brandishing the pistol [in *The Seeds of Doom*] seemed like a pragmatic move at the time, and since he wasn't going to use it anyway it [carrying a gun] doesn't go against his pacifism."

"Well, there's pacifism and pacifism, isn't there?" A third forum member replied. "The Doc certainly enjoyed his punch-up in *The Romans*, but I can't see him then casually stabbing the guy through the heart afterwards... The Doc isn't a Thal Pacifist, but he is an optimistic pacifist."

These quotes suggest several typical fan notions about the Doctor. One is that he has always been a pacifist, and should always be. Another is the idea that the Doctor should not be carrying or using weapons – and if he does, as long as he only threatens and never actually uses the gun, he can retain his pacifist principles. Finally, there is the suggestion that the concept of pacifism is something the Doctor ideally subscribes to but quite often isn't able to put into practice.

While fan chatter on a discussion board may not qualify as an epidemic of discourse, it does serve to demonstrate that the view is still alive and well in fandom. This perhaps isn't surprising, especially as these posts come not too long after *Doctor Who* itself arguably attempted to identify the Doctor as a "pacifist" for the first time, in the 2008 season episode *The Doctor's Daughter*. Indeed, the broadcast of this episode resulted in a flurry of story reviews (some of which published online at such websites as Den of Geek, "The House Next Door" blog, Behind the Sofa, Pop Vultures and even good old rec.arts.drwho) which attributed pacifism as being a defining trait of the Doctor's.

The Doctor doesn't actually state that he is a pacifist in *The Doctor's Daughter*, but the script essentially labels him as one through guilt by association. General Cobb lumps Jenny in with the Doctor and Donna because "she comes from pacifist stock" (i.e. the Doctor). Not only does the Doctor not argue the point, but moments earlier he had identified himself as coming from the Eastern Zone which Cobb had just finished saying was a place where "an outbreak of pacifism" had recently occurred. The end of the story sees the Doctor, in the most unsubtle way possible, declare himself to be "a man who never would". Some fans have taken this to mean "a man who never would kill out of anger or revenge" since the Doctor is speaking to someone who had just shot his new-born daughter, but given the pacifist / war dichotomy presented throughout the story it's not too difficult to view the statement as simply meaning "a man who never would kill".

There is only one problem with defining the Doctor as a pacifist: the fact that it isn't true.

Often, when fans discuss a scene where the Doctor is obviously violent or is forced to kill, the scene is dismissed as an exception to the rule or idea that the Doctor is a pacifist who never kills. Looking back closely at the history of *Doctor Who*, however, it becomes readily apparent that "exception to the rule" hasn't happened once, but literally dozens upon dozens of times. In fact, rather than being the exception to the rule, it is probably more accurate to say that it is the rule. Whether it is sending an entire fleet of Ice Warriors into the heart of the sun, gunning down Ogrons, blowing up a whole colony of Sea Devils, trapping a bunch of Zygons in their spaceship and blowing them into smithereens, or de-mat gunning a Sontaran into sweet nothingness, the Doctor's history is littered with examples of him being a killer. In fact, it could indeed be the case that, were it not for the Master being responsible for wiping out a good chunk of the universe in *Logopolis*, the Doctor is actually responsible for more on-screen deaths than any other single character in the history of the show (counting the Daleks as separate from their creator). Yet, as we've seen, the idea that the Doctor is a pacifist persists to this day. Why is this?

The problem perhaps stems from people's definition of "pacifism" and what it means to be a "pacifist". What exactly do the fans mean when they use this term? Are they stating that the Doctor believes in achieving peace through non-violent solutions? Do they mean that he resolves conflicts without using a gun or a weapon? Or is it perhaps a merely symbolic gesture: is the fact he doesn't carry a gun and travels in a weaponless ship a symbol of his peaceful nature and intentions?

It might be helpful to define what "pacifism" means, since there appears to be more than one school of thought on its precise definition. Perhaps the most commonly understood meaning defines "pacifism" as the refusal to use force or strength to defend one's self against an aggressor – even in cases of self-defence. In *Doctor Who*, this concept is seen in its most extreme form in *The Daleks* and *The Dominators*, where two societies (the Thals and Dulcians respectively) refuse to fight or defend themselves against an aggressive, hostile force (the preferred choice being to flee from the aggressors). In *The Dominators*, the Doctor describes the Dulcians as a society that has adopted a philosophy of "total pacifism" – but this definition perhaps isn't very helpful as it doesn't really give a definition of what "less than total" pacifism would constitute. The suggestion is presumably that it would constitute a society that is pacifist in theory or ideally, but not when actually confronted by an aggressor. That would render the definition of pacifism as being fairly worthless though; it would be a pretty meaningless "ism" if the concept isn't actually applied when one is forced to put it to the test.

It's unlikely that any fans view the Doctor as someone who would qualify under this particular definition of a pacifist. The Doctor is not a character who believes that "violence, even in self-defence, is unjustifiable under any conditions" (as one dictionary has defines the term); he has violently killed too many times to mention. Nor is he someone who believes "surrender or migration should be used to resolve disputes" (which is another dictionary definition). Given that the Doctor isn't someone who is naturally involved in many of the conflicts he encounters but in fact interferes and intervenes in the affairs of others, the definition is especially inappropriate. He doesn't arrive on Earth (or anywhere else) and say "well you're about to be invaded, but it's not my planet, not my 'dispute' and therefore not my problem". He makes a point of getting involved and fighting evil. As the Doctor once said, "There are some corners of the universe which have bred the most terrible things, things which act against everything we believe in. They must be fought!" Not exactly the words one expects to find coming from a pacifist.

Perhaps what fans really mean when they describe the Doctor as a pacifist is more in line with the other, less-rigid definition of "pacifism": an opposition to war and violence as a means of resolving disputes. This definition is much closer to the Doctor's character, particularly in a story like *Doctor Who and the Silurians*, but it still isn't a great fit. For one, it ignores all those times when the Doctor does encourage or approve of war or violence for a race of beings in order to save themselves, such as when he encourages the Thals and Dulcians to fight against their aggressors. It also ignores the many occasions where he uses violence himself to defeat the enemy. The definition is also problematic for the Doctor with regards to the notion that pacifism is about settling or resolving "disputes". That might be an accurate way to describe a conflict between two nations or a civil war, or even a legal matter – but "dispute" doesn't really do justice to a situation where an all-powerful race of aliens is hell-bent on invading, enslaving or wiping out another race and their planet.

What about the fan notion that the Doctor's "pacifism" is more symbolic in nature? This view would hold that the Doctor is a pacifist in the sense that he does not carry a gun or travel in a craft that contains weapons, exemplifying a pacifist outlook and speaking to his peaceful intentions (an "optimistic pacifism"). This is an accurate description of the Doctor's intentions, but does return us to the problem that there doesn't seem to be much use in having a philosophy which only exists as something purely theoretical but is never applied (and is in fact contradicted) in actual practice. It suggests again that perhaps a more accurate term to describe the Doctor's character would be more constructive rather than to put qualifiers on the term "pacifism" in order to justify its usage.

Moreover, the fact that the Doctor doesn't carry a gun or weapon may symbolise peaceful intentions, but peaceful intentions and pacifism are not quite the same thing. The latter is a non-violent philosophy put into practice in an attempt to achieve the former. If it is argued that not carrying a gun symbolises a pacifist outlook, the difficulty becomes reconciling this outlook with what the Doctor actually does to achieve peace.

The truth of the matter – articulated by Davros in *Journey's End* – is that the Doctor might not carry a weapon but he is quite often assisted by those who do, or by those he "fashions into weapons". The latter is more a feature of the new series (all of the companions in *Journey's End* are perfect examples), whereas the original series saw the Doctor regularly working with the military and travelling with many companions who were not above a good punch-up where necessary. This included all the male companions in the 60s, UNIT, Leela, K9 and Ace. Many of whom carried weapons.

As for the idea that the Doctor can retain pacifist principles if he picks up a gun, threatens someone with it, but doesn't actually use it (which happens in such stories as *The Seeds of Doom, Warriors of the Deep, The Mark of the Rani, The Parting of the Ways* and even *The Gunfighters*), this is, quite bluntly, a false notion. The act of threatening with a gun is in fact "using" it, and this usage certainly doesn't signal a peaceful intention in any way. Indeed, it's a tactic the Doctor will only use if he thinks that his opponent will believe that he actually will use the weapon in question and feel threatened. It's tantamount to saying that a bank robber could be considered a pacifist if he never actually intended to fire the gun he threatened the bank teller with.

In the end, the peaceful symbolism which stems from the Doctor not carrying a gun is a superb character trait, one that is essential to how the show defines itself and definitely should be continued for as long as the show is made. However, practically speaking, this symbolism doesn't amount to much with respect to pacifist actions or solutions. Perhaps it is more accurate to state that what his non-weapon carrying really symbolises is that the Doctor is "non-aggressive" or "non-hostile": he doesn't mean anyone any harm. Or, as Terrance Dicks once said, "He is never cruel or cowardly. Although caught up in violent situations, he is a man of peace."

Why not then simply bring meaning to the symbolism and make the Doctor explicitly a pacifist? It could be argued that, since the Doctor is ideologically in favour of peace, he should be solving problems using peaceful means rather than violent ones.

The problem with writing the Doctor as a pacifist is two-fold. The first is the problem neatly encapsulated in *The Dominators*: when faced with an aggressive, hostile powerful threat that is interested in either destroying and / or enslaving, there are typically three options a society faces: flee, submit or fight. The Doctor could flee in just about every story – except for when he is exiled to Earth of course – but this would make for a very boring, repetitive and somewhat cowardly series. It would make for a very short series if the Doctor simply surrenders. Of course, because it's not the Doctor's planet that is usually under threat, for the Doctor there is a fourth option – which would be that he could simply mind his own business and not get involved in the affairs of others. This of course is the polar opposite of what the show is about: the Doctor is someone who deliberately gets involved in the affairs of others and fights their aggressors on their behalf. The format of the show essentially mandates that the Doctor is a fighter rather than a pacifist.

Some may argue in response that it is not the fact that the Doctor fights evil that makes him a pacifist but rather the means by which he does so. Leaving aside the issue as to whether one can truly be a "fighting pacifist", this leads us to the second problem. Once the writers create a thoroughly evil, all-powerful race or villain for the Doctor to stop, there is the thorny question of what he has to do in order to defeat them. There are generally three options: reform, imprisonment and execution. If the monsters are either mindless killers or thoroughly evil (as they so often are in *Doctor Who*), then reform isn't going to be an option as it just isn't realistic – and often there isn't time to do it before the baddies put their dastardly plans into action. Imprisonment isn't normally an option either – the "all-powerful" bit (or even just "very powerful") means that it is usually tough to keep them imprisoned, and there is also the issue of what happens when the sentence is over. Imprisonment in time or for eternity does happen every now and then, but that can only be used so often without getting repetitive. That leaves us with the third option, one that gets used quite frequently: the killing option. This is why the show's format (and its choice of adversaries in particular) pretty much necessitates that not only is the Doctor not a pacifist, he is also a killer to boot. Sometimes directly, sometimes vicariously, but a killer nonetheless. This, in turn, means that, despite his peaceful intentions signalled by not carrying a weapon, the Doctor is quite often forced to be violent in some way (albeit not always physically so) to protect the lives of others.

Is there an argument to be made that one who only kills as an absolute last resort in self-defence or in defence of another could still be considered a pacifist? If there is, it is a difficult argument to make for a show like *Doctor Who* with a sci-fi / fantasy premise, simply because it is difficult to argue that the Doctor has only killed as the absolute last resort. Many times, the deaths are arguably unnecessary (in the strictest sense) and even for those that were, it would not be too difficult to think up other options that were or could have been available, particularly since *Doctor Who* doesn't often portray events with the gritty realism of a Vietnam flick.

The trend of the Doctor being a killer has continued well into the new series, despite the occasional attempt to make a strong statement that the Doctor is not a "killer" (most notoriously in *The Parting of the Ways* and *The Doctor's Daughter*). The Doctor gets Mickey to wipe out the Slitheen (and anyone else who didn't manage to get out of 10 Downing Street in time) in *Aliens of London*. He kills the Sycorax leader without even turning to face him, and kills the spawn of the Racnoss the following Christmas. *School Reunion* sees Finch make a comment that the Time Lords were peaceful to the point of indolence while the Doctor is something much different – which the Doctor doesn't deny. The Doctor also seems to tacitly approve of the Ood murdering their former captors and potential slave purchasers.

The Doctor is not a pacifist, historically never has been, and has frequently killed or used other forms of violence in order to achieve peace and a resolution to the imminent evil threat. If that's the case, why do we bother with the Doctor not carrying a weapon or a gun to symbolise peace? After all, he could have a concealed gun or weapon in his coat and it would, from outward appearance, be signalling his peaceful intentions to others. Is the value only to signal non-aggression?

I wouldn't say "only". In my view, the best thing about the Doctor not carrying a weapon or a gun is not that it is a symbol of a philosophy that gets thrown away whenever convenient, but rather that it forces the Doctor (and the writers) to come up with solutions to defeating the enemy using wit and intelligence. Something that I worry can be forgotten in this era of heavy sonic screwdriver use and magical characters to save the day. The Doctor using his wits and intelligence makes him an interesting and unique action hero, and it also helps to make the stories more interesting when you can see how the Doctor was able to come up with an intelligent solution based on all the clues and materials that were made available. If you rely purely on violence (or de facto magic), too often there is the danger that the show will become repetitive, boring and lose a good deal of its uniqueness. Although, it should be noted that, just because the Doctor uses his wits, it doesn't necessarily preclude him from also using violence at the same time. The two concepts are not polar opposites. For example, he outwits Shockeye and Davros in *The Two Doctors* and *Remembrance of the Daleks* respectively, but few would argue that he doesn't also use violent methods in the process. This is in sharp contrast to the endings of *The Seeds of Doom* or *Planet of the Dead*, where the alien menace in the end has its guts blown out of it by the military without any type of cunning plan involved. These endings are fine every now and then (and there are some thirty-three years in between those two stories) but is the sort of thing the series should try to avoid doing too much.

It is important and proper that the character champions peace, doesn't carry a gun or weapon, only kills reluctantly and as a last (if frequently used) resort. Just because the Doctor needs to be a fighter and occasionally a violent killer, it doesn't mean that we want the character to regenerate into Rambo either. But as fans of the show (including the fans who write for it), it is perhaps time we use more accurate terminology or engage in more discussions as to what the correct terminology should be, and perhaps should not be so concerned or outraged if in future the Doctor continues not to adhere to anyone's doctrine of pacifism. Because, despite what might be suggested in *The Doctor's Daughter,* when it comes to fighting the enemy and killing when necessary, the Doctor is a man who has, and who would.

# INTERLUDE

## The Key to a Time Lord - 3
**by Scott Clarke**
*From Enlightenment #122, June / July 2004*

**Episode Three: Horror**
*"Leave the Ark, Vira."*

Horror can be distilled to the vulnerability of being human in a hostile universe and our insatiable desire to witness its results. In this respect, *The Ark in Space* episode three nails it.

The last remnants of humanity lie dormant on an orbiting space station, completely dependent on their technology; enter the Wirrn, giant insects not bent on invading the freshly habitable Earth below, but the human body itself. They don't need air; they can "infect" you with a bit of slime to the back of the hand. Those poor freeze-dried buggers might as well be week-old babies lying in their cribs with a dingo at the door. Human accomplishment is undercut by the vulnerability of the human body itself.

Episode three begins with Noah pulling his hand from his pocket to reveal a nasty case of bubble-wrap-itis. The horror on his face says everything. Overhead, we hear the sure voice of the long-dead High Minister, extolling the virtues of the indomitable human race. In tragic fashion, Noah struggles to warn his comrade and intended mate, Vira, of the doom they all face. It's a classic horror scenario, reminiscent of the werewolf who is all too aware of his/her fate, or Frankenstein's monster, who battles with the internal impulses of destruction and tenderness. Not only is Noah changing physically, but the Wirrn is also taking control of his mind, forcing him to act against everything he holds dear.

Losing ourselves, our identity, is a very powerful fear for human beings, exploited in many stories, from vampire myths to the Borg. In *The Ark in Space*, loss of identity takes on tragic proportions because it's really all these humans have left, the very thing they've tried so desperately to preserve. For Vira, this takes on special significance. After Noah confronts the Doctor and Vira in the corridor, tries to warn them and then flees, Vira reveals that she and Noah were "pair-bonded for the new life". In this perfectly balanced utopia, created millennia before, fate deals a cruel hand to Vira. The only man she can possibly have a future with is turning into a creature that wants to destroy her.

The Ark, like Frankenstein's monster, or the "Company" in *Alien*, represents humanity's smug belief that technology can raise itself beyond the clutches of nature. Witness the reactions of each human who is revived (with the exception of "stitch-up" Rogin): none of them can initially conceive of the fact that their technology has let them down. Not only that, but the Wirrn are literally absorbing that technical know-how from their bodies and using it against them.

There is also a sickening sense of inevitability built into the structure of all good horror stories. Each time Noah is encountered, his transformation has progressed at an alarming rate, illustrating the imminent danger to everyone on the Ark. We've seen the end result of this transformation (the Wirrn in the closet) and we've seen the wriggling grub stage. Our morbid curiosity forces us to see the cycle completed, which occurs very effectively by the end of the episode, as the last hints of Noah's human face vanish into that of the bug-eyed creature. We achieve a simple, yet effective, catharsis.

We recognise the part that is like us and mourn its loss, while being repulsed by the alien side. As a kid, part of me wanted Noah to be recovered, while part of me wanted to see how far it would go. I was fascinated by how yukky he would get.

Kids in particular tend to be intrigued by the gross-out factors related to the human body (farts, vomiting, blood and guts, and messing around in the muck). These are things that fall outside of the "clean" rules of the adult world (don't burp at the dinner table, don't squirt ketchup on the dog). Kids want to see what's under those fancy clothes and, by extension, what's under that smooth skin. In this way, body horror in *Doctor Who* is wonderfully subversive. Never mind that it breaks all the rules of Sydney Newman's original vision for the programme, or that Mary Whitehouse built a crusade out of trying to suppress it.

On one level, Vira and Noah represent pompous authority figures, with neat tunics and stern expressions. When Noah is first slimed, one wonders if he is rather more concerned that his manicured hands have been messed up than whether his DNA is about to be re-sequenced. On a purely base level, it's gratifying to see such a character come unwound, even as we're terrified by the loss.

If Hinchcliffe and Holmes cut their teeth with horror on *The Ark in Space*, by the advent of Seasons Thirteen and Fourteen they would be virtually chewing off the legs of unsuspecting viewers. The writers became highly adept at the twisting of human anatomy and spirit. *Planet of Evil*'s Professor Sorenson, aping Dr Jekyll and Mr Hyde, tampered with forces beyond his understanding, leading to anti-matter infection, grunting interjections and rampant bed-head. Another professor, Solon, played slice and dice with alien extremities in *The Brain of Morbius*, resulting in squishy brains all over the floor. Who could forget those terrifying scenes of a blind Sarah Jane, stumbling around the stormy cliffs of Karn, menaced by a mentally challenged, hook-enhanced henchman? And my personal favourite, *The Thing from Outer Space* homage *The Seeds of Doom*. Keeler's slow transformation in a Krynoid, like Noah's fate, is both tragic and horrific.

But horror can be traced further back in the series' history to stories like *The Tomb of the Cybermen*, *Spearhead from Space* and *Inferno*. The Cyber mantra, "you will be like us", is yet another expression of body horror and possession/loss of identity. *Spearhead* delighted in the Stephen King hallmark of taking familiar, comfortable objects and imbuing them with danger and terror. Much has been written over the years about the effects of storefront mannequins coming to life and mowing down unsuspecting street patrons; indelible images for a generation of English school children.

It seems very fitting to me that even in its 26th (and seemingly last) season, *Doctor Who* returned to the horror well yet again. *The Curse of Fenric* engaged us with vampire mythos, evil since the dawn of time, creepy Viking curses, church catacombs and plenty of good old-fashioned possession. Scenes that stay with me include the sight of Haemovorised Jean and Phyllis inviting the soldier into the misty waters, and Dr Judson rising from his wheelchair, his eyes a piercing green.

While no one could ever claim that *Doctor Who* was explicitly a horror programme, it always lent itself well to the genre. Monsters became a hallmark early on and the production team could always unleash its creativity through the cheapest of means (bubble wrap, foam, fake blood, etc). The show was at its most popular and memorable during the seasons that were heavy on horror. Kids (of all ages) connected with the concept of being scared behind the sofa and grossed out of their evening tea. Russell T Davies and his creative team are well aware of these facts and have named it as a key ingredient of the new series. And I, for one, wish them well in that effort.

# THE TWO TOM BAKERS

For many years, *Doctor Who* fans could define Tom Baker's career as the Doctor as the period when he wore a cravat and the period when he didn't. Tom with a cravat equals solid production values, no more than one dodgy effect per story and Robert Holmes' script editing. The cravat-less years saw humour pushed to its event horizon and beyond, ideas so dizzying they threatened to invite a parasitic race of bull-like dancers to your front door via a black hole, and a budget of 14 pounds and thruppence per story.

You can blame it on the necktie, you can blame it on the producers, you can even blame it on Mary Whitehouse. Whatever the case, there seem to be two distinct periods of Tom Baker's career as Doctor Who – and indeed there seem to be two different Tom Bakers fronting it. One is Tom Baker the unknown actor, making an impression in the biggest part of his career; the other is Tom Baker the larger-than-life personality making every gesture bigger and grander every time.

Of course, all this ignores a third Tom Baker: the desultory one going through the motions during his final year. It scarcely bears thinking about.

Such analogies ignore the subtleties and nuances of everyday life: the transition between the gothic-horror Doctor to the comedy-science-fiction Doctor is almost imperceptible; the former prefigures the latter, while the latter freely borrows from the former. All the talk about send-up, intertextuality and comedy in the Graham Williams era ignores that it was a time in *Doctor Who*'s history that featured some of the most solid science-fiction stories the series has ever shown. And let's not forget that the whole concept of creating "eras" by producers of *Doctor Who* is an exercise in pure artifice.

But then, the whole notion of Two Tom Bakers is pure artifice which has its origins, in part, in 1983. When John Tulloch and Manuel Alvarado's *The Unfolding Text* was published – the first scholarly analysis of *Doctor Who* to ever appear in bookstores – it turned this dichotomy of Tom Bakers into a veritable bloodsport to further its discussion of authorship. As this history was being written by the winners (in this case, John Nathan-Turner), they heaped scorn on Graham Williams' version. Which is a shame, because it ignored the simple fact that it was ultimately very entertaining. As was Philip Hinchcliffe's version.

Whether there was one, two or a multiplicity of Tom Bakers quietly telling us what horror lays ahead, offering us jelly babies, screaming "What!?" with increasing intensity and talking about reality at a 45-degree angle to everyone else, we can't deny one thing. It was seven years of television no one will ever forget.

With or without the cravat.

# Williams' Lib

**by Robert Smith?**
*From Enlightenment #99, July / August 2000*

Undervalued and underappreciated for fifteen years, the Graham Williams' era underwent something of a brief renaissance beginning shortly after the producer's untimely death. It's still an era remembered primarily for its over-the-top humour, some dodgy acting and even dodgier special effects. Fans dismiss it easily as cheap and disappointing after the magnificence of the Hinchcliffe era.

Yet, when they wanted to do a gothic Hinchcliffe-horror story, the production team were just as up to the task as their predecessors. *Image of the Fendahl*, *Horror of Fang Rock* and *The Stones of Blood* all display characteristic Hinchcliffe traits, at least in part, and they're all superb stories.

The special effects might be dodgy in places and risible in others, but they demonstrate a production team trying to push the series forward. In the wake of *Star Wars*, the series turned increasingly to space operas and intergalactic battles on a budget the series could barely afford. Stories like *City of Death* demonstrate that, had the production team stuck to what the BBC was good at – historical costume dramas and eloquent actors performing a literate and intelligent script in three rooms of a mansion – then the era could be just as visually convincing as any other.

Instead, the production team, and Graham Williams in particular, was keen to push the stories ever forward. *Underworld* is perhaps the most extreme example, with the director feeling confident he could pull off an entire underground civilisation, a luxurious spaceship set and an astonishing number of extras with a CSO backdrop. The budget meetings must have recalled the preliminary outline for *Invasion of the Dinosaurs* ("London gets invaded by dinosaurs, you say? Yes, I think we could pull that off convincingly...").

*The Power of Kroll* was written specifically to include the largest monster ever seen in the show. Surely any sensible producer on Williams' budget should never have come up with such an idea? Even Robert Holmes, renowned for overestimating production teams' ability to render convincing monsters – everything from the giant rat to the Magma beast show up this rare flaw – was dubious. The fact that it's a barely passable effect is probably fortunate in the extreme. Yet the series never stopped pushing itself under Williams, Read and Adams. Williams has even gone on record saying that you could change 15% of the series per year (in the sense that the audience could accommodate 15% adjustment to established fact). These are not the words of someone trying to get a formulaic runaround in the can by 10:00pm.

*

*Star Wars*, of course, wasn't the only influence on the era. Williams and Adams would constantly journey to the local bookstores to see what the science-fiction-reading public was into. That's a fairly literate attitude to the series and one that might have made for more of a niche show – but the ratings don't bear that out at all. It's an interesting approach to a period that was dismissed as "too silly" by Christopher Bidmead.

For better or worse, the era simply wasn't interested in retreading the glories of the past. Aside from *Destiny of the Daleks*, the Sontarans and the rumoured appearance of the Zygons in *Shada*, it's almost completely devoid of returning villains. (Or friends, for that matter. Borusa is the only returning non-villain to show up and even then a different actor plays him.) Season Sixteen features none at all and also has only a single Earthbound adventure. In fact, there are only five Earthbound adventures in the three years, including *Shada*.

It's interesting to note that both *Destiny of the Daleks* and *The Invasion of Time* featured surprise villains (in Davros and the Sontarans). That's not a million miles away from the shock appearance of the Master in *The Deadly Assassin*... which worked precisely because there were so few other returning villains surrounding him. That's a lesson JN-T never learnt (but that's the subject for another article).

On the other hand, the Williams' era was rather fond of the Time Lords. Perhaps buoyed by the success of *The Deadly Assassin*, they not only wrote a continuity-heavy sequel to it (obtaining special permission from Robert Holmes as a last-minute filler to replace a story involving 15,000 killer cats filling Wembley stadium; you can't accuse the era of underambition), they seemed to pop up all the time – and not in the Time-Lord-missions manner of the Letts or JN-T eras. Instead, the Time Lords' influence is felt all over the galaxy, in decidedly non-typical ways.

Perhaps it's not so surprising, given that the Doctor's people finally had a mission statement in *The Deadly Assassin*, with their corruption allowing them to interfere (or interfere retroactively) all over the place. Every story in Season Fifteen contains some mention of Gallifrey or the Time Lords. *Horror of Fang Rock* has the Doctor reminiscing about Gallifreyan lighthouses, *The Invisible Enemy* tells of a never-before-mentioned Time Lord superbrain, the Fendahl were supposedly destroyed by the Time Lords on the fifth planet and the Ursurians have a file on Gallifrey. *Underworld* has its Time Lord mythology in spades, defining more about them than perhaps any other non-Gallifrey story.

The Guardians are jumped-up Time Lords (Romana even believes she's sent on the quest by the president, until midway through the season, when the Doctor gets to do some clever mid-season exposition for the viewers who missed *The Ribos Operation*) and *Shada* is dripping with Time Lord mythology. Even *State of Decay*, a leftover script from this era, has the Doctor finding a hitherto unmentioned directive about the great war with the Vampires and his duty as a Time Lord to destroy them. The Time Lords we do run into are definitely non-traditional ones, like Drax and Chronotis (and not a single evil renegade in sight). It's a bit of a sideways step for the show, but it helps establish the Doctor's race as one with its fingers in pies all through time.

*

There's another way in which the era took its own approach. The role of women in the series, never something the *Doctor Who* could be particularly proud of, got greater, and more careful, attention then ever before.

A large part of this was the companions, of course. Graham Williams knew how fortunate he was to inherit Louise Jameson as companion – so much so that he point-blank refused to believe she was leaving the series until the very end of *The Invasion of Time*, explaining the clunky leaving scene. Despite being clad in a leather miniskirt, she was a companion who demonstrated her intelligence and assertiveness in equal measure and was played by an extremely capable actress. What's more, for the first time ever, we had a companion who didn't scream (*Talons* aside), which was quite a step forward for the series (and one that wouldn't be seen again until the tail-end of the series with Ace).

Both actresses who played Romana were also quite a find – surprisingly, perhaps, in an era noted for actors going over the top. However, the nature of Romana succeeded where that of Liz Shaw had failed; Romana was an intelligent companion, often the equal or better of the Doctor. She proves, if proof be needed, that Barry Letts was flat-out wrong in his assessment that you couldn't do *Doctor Who* without a ditzy screamer constantly baffled by the simplest of challenges.

With the lead actor getting ever more out of control, it often fell to the companion to carry the day, meaning that Romana got more of the limelight and had ample opportunity to demonstrate that the Doctor-figure didn't need to be male at all. Romana's schoolgirl outfit has been mentioned as inspiring lechery among the dads, but Lalla Ward intended it to show schoolgirls that they too could be just as capable and successful as Romana. That's quite a stunning assessment of the character on the actress' part. I can't imagine Katy Manning having the same thought.

The supporting characters also improve over the era. From the confident and able Marn and the con-trick of the true villain in *The Pirate Planet* to Lady Adastra and Karela, there is a growing trend of actresses playing their meatier roles with a professionalism that their male counterparts increasingly ignored. It's a trend that regressed for a while under Eric Saward's macho and violent editorship and only fully returned with Andrew Cartmel.

*The Invasion of Time* sees the first female Gallifreyan – and quite a delight she is too. *Underworld*, for all its faults, sees the series' only on-screen female regeneration. *The Creature from the Pit* features both Adastra ruling the planet and Romana menacing her male captives with nothing more than sheer bravado.

On the subject of David Fisher stories, *The Stones of Blood* is an interesting hybrid. On the surface it looks like a gothic horror tale, with mansions and sacrifices and moving stones. Yet the obvious villain of the tale is but a pawn and the main contribution the Doctor has over the first two episodes is to realise that de Vries is very scared indeed. He even gets tied up and almost sacrificed and has to be rescued by Amelia Rumford.

Both Vivien Fay and Amelia are superb characters. There's a lesbian undercurrent to the story that appears vital to the Megara plot... except that all the stuff about citric acid proves useless to the Doctor's case, so it was characterisation in disguise all along. Romana completes the triumvirate of capable female characters very nicely. The Doctor seems out of place in the opening episodes and gets used as the villain to trap Romana on the cliff. Vivien even calls him a "typical male".

One of JN-T's first decisions was to get rid of Romana and K9, feeling that the leads had become too knowledgeable and capable. His reasons are understandable, but it seems like the series was regressing into formula, with Jo Grant replacing Liz Shaw all over again. Seasons Sixteen and Seventeen prove beyond all doubt that an intelligent and resourceful companion could be a match for the Doctor and more, with no loss in storytelling or enjoyability.

All good things come to an end though. On screen, the Williams' era ends with *The Horns of Nimon*, containing an out-of-control Doctor, some of the funniest jokes, over-the-top acting and worst special effects the series ever had, a surprisingly complex plot involving a parasitic race building black holes on the doorsteps of civilisations in decline – and a Romana who plays it straight and cool, inventing a better sonic screwdriver and talking Soldeed into submission in a blast of righteous fury. If it weren't so postmodern, it would be quintessential *Doctor Who*.

# A Year in the Life

by **Graeme Burk**
*From Enlightenment #142, November 2007*

*Doctor Who* fans are naturally suspicious of naming any period in the series' history as a "golden age". Fans are taught from an early age – or at least from the first time they watched *Invasion of the Dinosaurs* – that there's no such thing as a golden age. And they're probably right about that. Most bygone ages are as ordinary and mundane as right now. Bestowing an extraordinary status like "a golden age" imbues that time with an almost supernatural status, as though it should be rendered bulletproof from criticism.

Nevertheless – and I'm sure you saw this coming – I would like to say that if I was the type of person that called a period in *Doctor Who*'s illustrious history a golden age, I would almost without hesitation say it was 1977.

Think about it: Leela sent out beyond the barrier. The Doctor's face carved in a mountain. "You're the evil one." The Doctor explaining relative dimensions to a savage. The sandminer's being stalked and people murdered by elegant-looking and pleasant-sounding robots. Bumblebees. Robophobia. A blackguard emerging from the shadowy Victorian fog. Beware the eye of the scorpion. "I'd have propelled him onto the pavement with a punt up the posterior." Trapped in a lighthouse with no escape. "Of the three men's fate we found no trace." "Contact has been made." An adorable robot dog. A miniature Doctor and a miniature Leela inside the Doctor's brain. Mother Tyler's second sight. The glowing skull in Fetch Priory. Corridors named after Inland Revenue Forms. "Perhaps everyone runs from the Tax Man."

A year full of moments like these. Brilliant shining moments that will forever be etched in my brain. When I close my eyes and think of *Doctor Who*, I think of 1977.

1977. Not Season Fourteen or Season Fifteen. In spite of the year being bifurcated between producer Philip Hinchcliffe's last three stories and

Graham Williams' first four, in spite of the almost (but not really) radical shift in tone between seasons, even in spite of the budget cuts that left the first part of the year vastly more affluent than the second half, I still think of 1977 as a single, unbroken stretch of *Who*: seven stories comprising 30 half-hour episodes that show *Doctor Who* at its most imaginative, compelling and entertaining.

The series came into 1977 having made two of its most important breaks with the past: two months before, the Doctor and Sarah Jane – by that time one of the Doctor's longest serving and best-loved companions – parted amicably. This was not only a break with an assistant who will always be most associated with Tom Baker's Doctor, but the severing of the last tie with the previous regime's version of *Doctor Who*. The following story, viewers finally saw the Doctor's home planet up close and personal for the first time. By the end of 1976, *Doctor Who* had effectively closed one chapter and opened another.

Appropriately, the first episode of *Doctor Who* in 1977 was broadcast New Year's Day. What was the new world that greeted *Doctor Who*? In many ways, it wasn't very different. The Doctor was battling the creeping unknown that lurked in the dark corners of existence. On paper, the first story of 1977, *The Face of Evil*, sounds like a shopping list of every science-fiction trope of the seventies: planet inhabited by now-savage descendents of space travellers, worshipping their ancestors' technology as a god.

But it's so much more than that. The Doctor seeing his own face in the rock that contained their evil one immediately takes those tropes and changes them radically. Suddenly, everything looks different – full of mystery and perplexity and real possibility. And then there are the characters: not the usual ignorant savages, but guileful characters who are manipulative and cynical and driven by competing motives. Their greatest hero is a woman who, in spite of being trained as a warrior, chooses to question the very basis of her society.

And that's not even mentioning the huge excitement factor of the story, where jeopardy exists at every turn and just as one threat is taken care of, there's a bigger one to come, piled on like a thinking person's Bond film on a BBC budget.

In short, *The Face of Evil* is awesome; a vastly underrated story. But it's emblematic, for me, of what's so great about the state of *Doctor Who* in 1977. It's *Doctor Who* like we've always known it but done extraordinarily well. The scale of imagination is bigger, the wit is sharper, the jokes are funnier and the suspense is greater.

*The Robots of Death* continues this with a story that looks at the implications of a robot-dependent society – and it looks gorgeous as well.

*Horror of Fang Rock* has a similarly besieged setting but throws in the most entertaining cannon fodder in *Doctor Who*'s history as the embodiment of the Edwardian class struggle gets picked off one by one. *The Sun Makers* does a full-scale satirical assault on the politics of taxation and yet it is also one of the most suspenseful stories that year.

Even the failures have something worth watching. For all the deficiencies of design and direction, *The Invisible Enemy* is staggering in the scope of its ambition and ideas, which include a sentient virus and clones of the lead characters that are shrunk to microscopic size in order to explore the inner workings of the Doctor's brain. If anything, the lesser stories serve to demonstrate the turbulent conditions they were made in. Outgoing producer Hinchcliffe's move toward more adult fare led to his dismissal when Mary Whitehouse complained about a violent cliffhanger in *The Deadly Assassin*. His replacement, Williams, came in with not only an edict from the powers-that-be to tone down the violence and horror but to do so with virtually half the budget. That Graham Williams was able to keep everything going at all is incredible; that *Horror of Fang Rock*, *Image of the Fendahl* and *The Sun Makers* are just as good as Hinchcliffe's last three serials is nothing short of awe-inspiring.

(And when the money was there, it was gorgeous. Fans will probably always hearken back to the days when sets were all lacquered wood and there was night shooting.)

They're very different visions of *Doctor Who*. Compare the first story of the year to the last one: both are fast-paced adventure serials that deliver great thrills, but *The Face of Evil* is a ghost-train ride of the highest order with horror and high-minded ideas, while *The Sun Makers* is an outright comedy, full of high camp, satire and brilliantly realised cartoonish characters.

Both share the same DNA, though. Much of that comes from script editor Robert Holmes, who edited virtually every story this year. 1977 was Holmes' last year and it's a testament to his skill as a writer and an editor that he was able to shape the scripts to vastly differing production needs and yet keep the quality of the scripts at an all-time high.

Perhaps the biggest asset, though, is Tom Baker, who reaches the zenith of his tenure as the Doctor in 1977: larger than life but never quite crossing the line into complete outlandishness. Baker's Doctor becomes wittier and sillier from the get-go: the opening minutes of *The Face of Evil*, where the Doctor eccentrically talks to the himself (and the viewer), almost seems like a New Year's Manifesto on how things would develop over the coming year. It's almost as though Baker, Hinchcliffe and script editor Robert Holmes realised that without Lis Sladen as Sarah, Tom would need to bring more of the Doctor to bear in the stories. Williams clearly saw this as a strength of the show during the first half of 1977 as he chose to enhance it greatly over his own serials. Whatever the backroom politics, on screen the Doctor was bolder and madder than ever, whether he was befriending Leela, running circles around Gatherer Hade or staring down the Rutan. *The Talons of Weng-Chiang* might be the finest two hours of Tom Baker's tenure as the Doctor, as he gets to act Sherlock Holmesian and yet show bemusement and flippancy toward the Victorian world he finds himself in. His charisma is absolutely magnetic.

Mixing up the companion also helped considerably: 1977 is virtually the Year of Leela – she only has another ten episodes to go in 1978 – and what a year it was. There has never been that sharp a contrast between companions. Whereas Sarah was virtually the second half of a double act with the Doctor, sharing a friendship and a rapport that's unique, Leela's relationship with the Doctor is a mentoring one. With Sarah, the Doctor was a gateway to alien worlds, but with Leela everything is alien. It puts an interesting slant on the stories, as even the familiar and commonplace – like Victorian London, or the TARDIS being bigger on the inside than the outside – gets looked at from a fresh perspective. This is helped by Louise Jameson's superb portrayal. Jameson doesn't so much portray Leela as embody the part. It's a performance that's full of nuance: even when she's not the focus of the scene, it's fascinating to watch what Jameson is doing. Leela and the Doctor will never have the rapport of Sarah and the Doctor, and yet it's made the Doctor / companion dynamic fresh and interesting.

Indeed, if there's one thing that can be said for the year 1977 in *Doctor Who*'s history, it's that the series demonstrated its total flexibility in the face of massive change: a shake up in the production team, a shift in the tone of the show, even a change in the emphasis of the lead characters; none of these things fazed the series in any serious way. The series continued being the intellectually fascinating, totally exciting, completely riveting and always entertaining series it had been, only better.

One day in the future from 1977, the BBC were dumb enough to cancel the show. Eventually, the BBC brought back *Doctor Who*. And when they brought it back they looked back to a time when the show had brilliant production values, and imaginative, witty and funny scripts, and a supremely charismatic lead character played by an actor at the height of his powers. They looked to the glossy, gorgeous stuff but also to the less-polished but still brilliant material. And they used this as the template for new *Doctor Who*.

1977 will live on forever in *Doctor Who*. Because it's a golden age.

# Was There a Hinchcliffe era?

by **Matthew Kilburn**

*From Faze #14, September 1998*

I'm going to open this article by breaking all the rules and giving a short answer to the question that I've set myself. Of course there was a Hinchcliffe era. We know this because it's been written about and commented on exhaustively since at least Jan Vincent-Rudzki's notorious review of *The Deadly Assassin* in *TARDIS* early in 1977. Fandom perceives it, and so in that sense it exists. In this article, I'm going to try to see how well the "Hinchcliffe era" can be defined and look at what this tells us about fan perceptions and about *Doctor Who* itself.

It's long been commonplace to divide the history of *Doctor Who* into "eras" for ease of reference and analysis. These divisions are usually marked by changes of actor or producer, and this can reveal a lot about the attitudes of the person making the decision. I remember at one meeting of my university *Doctor Who* society, the membership were polled on which stories should be shown the next term. One committee member wrote a list of all the available stories on a blackboard in the society's meeting room. The titles were divided up into William Hartnell tales (line), Patrick Troughton adventures (line), Jon Pertwee escapades (line), and then the serials with Tom Baker as the Doctor up to and including *Shada* (double line). After this, the heading "JN-T Stories" was introduced above *The Leisure Hive*, taking in everything shown up to *Survival*, and, by setting them aside, impugning the legitimacy as "real" *Doctor Who* anything produced by John Nathan-Turner.

"Eras" can thus be assigned priority and arranged in hierarchies, people choosing their favourites as they do their stories. However, by choosing groups of seasons associated with a particular creative person, they are endorsing what they perceive as that person's approach to *Doctor Who*, celebrating them as the auteur who at that particular moment made the programme what it was. It would be easy to argue against this approach to the series, were it not that the professionals indulge in it themselves. Messrs Letts and Dicks have made jocular reference to their period as the "golden years" of *Doctor Who*, but others have taken the issue more seriously. Graham Williams, for one, used to acknowledge that his stories were different from those which had gone before because of his superiors' reactions to *The Deadly Assassin* and their resulting orders to him to reduce the level of violence in the series. Williams always seemed semi-apologetic on this subject in interviews, as if he was accepting the constraints placed upon his work by the noisier fan critics of the late 1970s and early 1980s. John Nathan-Turner was far more bull-ish, boasting of the number of changes he was making to the series when he took over and (somewhat unprofessionally) frequently criticising the policies of his predecessor in several interviews during his first few years on the programme.

At first, Philip Hinchcliffe might not seem very different from this pat-tern. In interviews he has differentiated between the *Doctor Who* that he inherited and the *Doctor Who* that he wanted it to become; a little more dangerous, less tied to Earth, a programme that adults would want to watch on its own terms instead of condescending to it as part of their children's viewing. There is a crucial difference, however, between Hinchcliffe's attitude and those of his two successors. Williams had reac-tion against the perceived excesses of Hinchcliffe forced upon him; Nathan-Turner, seeking direction, positively embraced the anti-Williams cause. Hinchcliffe has expressed his priorities, chiefly in terms of build-ing up the programme's audience from its base in 1974, which was already higher than might have been expected from an early evening Saturday series commissioned by executives who expected its audience to be primarily made up of children. The emphasis was on continuity, rather than change.

The essence of the "Hinchcliffe era", then, lies not in its self-conscious attempt to break with the past, but with its drive to fulfil the latent poten-tial that existed in the already successful Barry-Letts-produced *Doctor Who* of the early 1970s to become something better. Hinchcliffe inherited the process from Barry Letts; it was already under way in Season Eleven, a season fashionably dismissed as the tired product of a moribund team. Letts had commissioned a dramatic new title sequence from Bernard Lodge that to my mind remains the best-realised in the programme's his-tory, its imagery encapsulating so much of what is good about *Doctor Who*. Of more consequence in terms of the narrative, there was a new companion, even if the latter's "independent" characterisation was let down by uncertainty as to how far Sarah Jane Smith's status as "women's libber" was to lead her away from the submissive and sup-portive role of Jo Grant and how far it would serve to confirm it. Sarah Jane's arrival does mark a season where its makers were trying to break new ground. *Invasion of the Dinosaurs* attempted an effects-led story beyond anything that had been tried in previous years. The plague-rid-den storyline of *Death to the Daleks* may be a hoary Nation device, but robbing the Daleks of their trademark extermination rays did the Daleks a dramatic service that they would never enjoy again once they were rel-egated to satellites of Davros. The necessity of establishing the vulnera-bility and eventual mortality of the then-most-enduring Doctor coloured the last two stories of the eleventh season; although flawed in their execution, both *The Monster of Peladon* and *Planet of the Spiders* began with praiseworthy intentions. *Monster* tries to be a more sophisticated story than *The Curse of Peladon* and where it fails, it does so because it doesn't know what to do with all the genies that have been released from the Peladonian bottle. *Planet of the Spiders* sets itself the task of expanding the "daisiest daisy" speech from *The Time Monster* into a full story while entertaining the viewer and indulging Jon Pertwee at the same time. It ends up as a pastiche and so for many epitomises not what was best about the Letts-Dicks-Pertwee period but the failure of the imagination with which the eleventh season is commonly charged.

That being said, the initial agenda of the eleventh season, if we can speak of such a thing, is not far removed from that of the twelfth. The dismantling of the "UNIT family" begun in *The Green Death* is accelerated in *Invasion of the Dinosaurs*, a UNIT story in which the Doctor is suddenly a visitor rather than a member of the Brigadier's team for the first time since *Spearhead from Space*. From this standpoint, it has more in common with *Terror of the Zygons* than with any other third Doctor UNIT story. The resurrection of the UNIT lab in *Planet of the Spiders* and *Robot* is a mark of homage to the past and an expression of Letts' caution, because UNIT HQ is not really the Doctor's base any more. When the TARDIS dematerialises from the lab set at the end of *Robot*, an expectation that it will return is generated, but it is unsurprising when the expectation proves false because the ties that bound the Doctor to Earth and UNIT were already becoming threadbare. *Invasion of the Dinosaurs*, in its portrayal of a London turned into alien territory, wholly undermines the cosiness of *Doctor Who*'s UK as depicted just two stories before in *The Green Death*. Separating the Doctor from the TARDIS and forcing him for most of Season Twelve to hitch lifts with time rings and transmat beams takes this desire – or need – to put the sacred cows out to pasture one step further. The Doctor was already becoming detached from whichever "establishment" he met in Season Eleven, and his transformation from patrician to bohemian enabled this process to become more accentuated; it did not actually start it.

The presence of Robert Holmes, of course, could not help but be of significance. Holmes was a highly professional writer and script editor who knew how to realise the demands of his producer. He also enjoyed a lengthy handover period with Terrance Dicks and began the process of setting up Season Twelve with Barry Letts, completing it with Philip Hinchcliffe. Robert Holmes had more experience of writing *Doctor Who* than any of his predecessors or successors and complemented Philip Hinchcliffe's enthusiastic ambition and desire to make his mark with personal experience of the directions the programme had taken in previous years. The continuity that Holmes provided manifests itself in surprising ways. I have a theory that certain of the properties of the Wirrn were inspired from Holmes watching *The Green Death* and seeing unrealised potential in the larvae and the "green death" they transmitted; some of the biobabble used to explain the deaths of the miners and Noah's transformation is very similar.

A mark of continuity which had wider implications was the encouragement Holmes and Hinchcliffe gave to the accentuation of an already-well-established vein in *Doctor Who* storytelling. Seasons Thirteen and Fourteen are accurately remembered for one story after another that exploited the theme of possession, sometimes extending to physical transformation, often in a period or pseudo-period setting. Fan critics have waxed lyrical about the debts owed to Hammer films, and some revisionists have argued the case for the stronger influence of the earlier Universal horror features. The influence of the literary ghost story of the late-nineteenth and early-twentieth centuries is probably just as great an influence. All were sources for plot and (as regards the films) design elements in mid-1970s *Doctor Who*; but the possession and transformation themes were firmly ingrained within the *Doctor Who* that Hinchcliffe inherited from Barry Letts. *Planet of the Spiders*, at Hinchcliffe's advent, is an obvious example of a story that played with possession, while *Inferno* and *The Mutants* terrified their audiences with the fear that someone apparently human might change without warning into a grotesque and hostile creature. Much has been made in recent fan writing of the limited possibilities that the Master offered, but his strength was that he, too, could turn the seemingly friendly colleague into the eyes, ears and instruments of his commanding, malevolent intelligence. The Auton stories offered comparable thrills, and reaching back into the 1960s we have the Great Intelligence and the Yeti. The poltergeists of physical and spiritual transformation and resulting corruption already haunted the *Doctor Who* mansion in the early 1970s; the regime of Philip Hinchcliffe simply released to them more corridors down which to travel, with a little more crockery to hurl about.

In the mid-1970s, *Doctor Who* was already a cottage industry and the ancillary products generated by the various licensees heavily influenced, as well as reflected, the way in which the programme was perceived. In the 1980s, John Nathan-Turner could be described as the high priest of the *Who* cult in the *Radio Times Twentieth Anniversary Special*; before him, one of the reasons Graham Williams gave for his resignation was that he was finding it impossible to keep up with the amount of merchandise surrounding the programme. Hinchcliffe wasn't disinterested in merchandise, but he knew that it wasn't his central activity and didn't let it dominate. If there was a high priest of *Doctor Who* during the Hinchcliffe producership, it was Terrance Dicks. Throughout the 1975-77 period, Terrance Dicks was the co-ordinator of the Target range of adaptations, balancing novelisations of the new Tom Baker stories with older stories from Jon Pertwee's Doctorhood. The policy that only the current Doctor should be featured on the cover illustrations didn't take effect until *Doctor Who and the Mutants* came out in September 1977, so the face of Jon Pertwee remained a prominent background detail on the children's bookshelves, with readers (admittedly a small fraction of the audience) soaking up stories based around a format that was already disappearing when Philip Hinchcliffe took over the producership. Meanwhile, *TV Comic* was publishing the comic strip, which often seems to have been based on *Doctor Who* as it might have been produced by ITC, somewhere between *Jason King* and *Space: 1999*. Other merchandise heavily promoted the star image of Tom Baker as the scarf-wearing fourth Doctor, usually based on photographs from *Robot*, but with occasional flashes of other influences, such as those transfers which superimposed the fourth Doctor onto the set of *Daleks: Invasion Earth 2150 AD*. This was not Nathan-Turnerist pluralism, promoting *Doctor Who* on the basis of its history, but the sometimes-unthinking eclecticism of those who see a profitable media property but can only exploit it to their best advantage by adding the ingredients that allow them to market it.

Another potential defining feature of a *Doctor Who* era is its supposed sense of concept. The Jon Pertwee Doctor is inextricably connected with UNIT in the minds of fandom and probably also with the general public. When Graham Williams moved into the *Doctor Who* office in early 1977 he attempted to give *Doctor Who* a unified cosmology, writing a document (printed in *Doctor Who – The Seventies*) that introduced the Guardians and the Key to Time, with powers beyond those of the Time Lords. This attempt to give *Doctor Who* a codified "high concept" would not be seen again until Philip Segal and John Leekley's "Bible" for Amblin in the mid-1990s. As both Williams and Segal learned, *Doctor Who* resists what are, in effect, fetters on its freedom to tell stories. The Hinchcliffe producership is marked by a rejection of preconceptions and preconditions and the most basic elements of what passes for the programme's format are strengthened. Much of this is due to the performances of Tom Baker and Elisabeth Sladen, whose characters principally serve to involve the viewer in the adventure, act on their behalf in solving the problem, and then take the viewer out of the situation with them. When Elisabeth Sladen left, one of the consequences was that Hinchcliffe had to find a strong enough companion character that compensated for the loss of Sladen's performance, given that as an actress she was irreplaceable; hence, Robert Holmes greeted Chris Boucher's Leela with open arms. The "high concept" in *Doctor Who* is found not so much in the format, which is little more than a storytelling device to link otherwise unconnected serials, but in the characters who enable that device to operate. At other periods in the programme's history, the Doctor and companions were reduced to the iconic, with little consistency in motivation from story to story, despite the attempts of the production team to give them character-stretching things to do which only showed their weaknesses.

Fandom esteems the Philip Hinchcliffe era partly because many of its latter-day opinion formers were at an impressionable age between 1975 and 1977. However, whereas several in the previous generation ended up loudly rejecting the Barry-Letts-produced Jon Pertwee stories of their childhoods, fan critics largely continue to hold the first three Tom Baker seasons in respect. While the critics of *Doctor Who* as broadcast between 1970 and 1974 have lashed out at the very features they once admired, such as the UNIT regulars, the cosiness of the Earthbound settings and the paternalist third Doctor himself, Philip Hinchcliffe's three seasons lack such tangible characteristics and so have to be discussed in terms of more subtle motifs than were provided by the UNIT setup. It's curious that the repetition of the possession / transformation plot has received so little criticism, but perhaps that is because it was usually one feature among many in the Hinchcliffe productions and it was a device already established as one of the most powerful in *Doctor Who*'s repertoire. There wasn't very much originality in the ingredients of Hinchcliffe's *Doctor Who* either, but his team can at least be credited with serving up refined versions of well-loved recipes. The principal defining characteristic of the Hinchcliffe era is that its producer, perhaps because he had one of the series' most experienced writers as his script editor, didn't let other considerations detract from putting storytelling first, not just through scripting, but through acting, design and overall execution. A thin consideration perhaps, but earlier and subsequent makers of *Doctor Who* were sometimes too distracted by the margins to grasp its importance.

**Afterword**

The intervening years between the first publication of this article and the second have seen a little more information emerge about the production of *Doctor Who* in 1973/74, which supports the argument that Season Eleven was intended to make changes in the way that *Doctor Who* told stories and the shape of the stories that were told. The DVD release of *The Time Warrior* saw Jeremy Bulloch remembering being sounded out about joining the Doctor and Sarah in the TARDIS at the end of the story: the gap of three months between the end of recording on *The Time Warrior* and the start of work on *Invasion of the Dinosaurs* left plenty of time to incorporate Hal into the remaining stories in the season. Though superficially similar, Hal could not have been a Jamie figure; Pertwee's Doctor had no need of such a foil and his character was integrated into the institutional setting of stories much more comfortably than was the Troughton Doctor. Hal would probably have been an outsider, a rogue element running among the looters in evacuated London, pally with the Exilons, and advising the miners on Peladon on insurgency tactics. With Sarah already envisaged as being outside the regular UNIT setup, though, a Hal on these lines was already largely redundant; Letts and Dicks would have wanted to pay more attention to Hal's mediaeval worldview, while Jamie's eighteenth century origins were largely forgotten after a few stories. Incorporating Hal would doubtless have been difficult in the context of keeping Pertwee happy, establishing Sarah and (in the case of Letts and Dicks) making *Moonbase 3* and keeping a keen eye on post-*Who* opportunities. It's perhaps more important that the idea was dismissed, if it was entertained in the first place; but if Bulloch's reminiscence is correct, Barry Letts was still willing to ask more radical questions of the format than might be apparent from the broadcast season. Those of us who discovered the series after Season Eleven were as good as introduced to Mike Yates as a traitor and never knew how much of a shock his betrayal must have been to viewers in 1974.

Reviewing Season Eleven now, other points strike me which did not in 1998. Not only does *Invasion of the Dinosaurs*, with its phantom space fleet, return more obviously to the "near future" setting of the UNIT stories than any story since Season Seven, it presents us with a notional spaceship (and even more notionally, a fleet of them) containing human beings in suspended animation in preparation for the rebuilding of humanity, an idea incoming script editor Robert Holmes clearly thought deserved further exploitation after being almost incidental to Malcolm Hulke's teleplay. Visually, there is a pronounced change in the colour palette. If the previous four seasons were coloured red and green, following the dominant colours in the title sequence, Season Eleven is likewise blue and green, making the series a little less lurid but more brooding and perhaps also more natural, as opposed to artificial, anticipating the shift to the Gothic.

While *Doctor Who*'s original central theme of displacement from the seemingly rational and ordinary is part of the Gothic, if the Hinchcliffe-Holmes era is the programme's most Gothic phase, then a good case can be made for including Season Eleven too. Linx's appearance is reminiscent of the troll in one of the major late-eighteenth century Gothic paintings, Henry Fuseli's *The Nightmare; The Time Warrior* itself begins the visits to imagined history which become a regular part of *Doctor Who*'s storyscape in the mid-1970s. Sarah Jane Smith never gains Jo Grant's resistance to hypnotism and begins a career of questionable worth as a subject of possession. *Death to the Daleks* wants to be more interested in a society which has rejected technology for superstitious ritual than it is in the Daleks themselves. Fetishisation of technology in *Doctor Who* had ended and fascination with more literary and artistic roots had taken hold. Perhaps Season Eleven asked questions where the three following seasons were better at finding answers which worked on screen and held an audience – but that last Pertwee season still provides at least a rough template for what followed it.

# Heart of Darkness

**by Rob Matthews**
*From The Doctor Who Ratings Guide, October 2002*

Situated more or less at the heart of the show's run on screen, and as the culmination of the extraordinarily effective Holmes / Hinchcliffe partnership, Season Fourteen really is one of those turning-point seasons of *Doctor Who*. It features not a single bad script; has three stories that are now considered "classics"; has solid production values; and introduces the Robert Holmes version of Gallifrey, the Time Lords and the Master. I'm not surprised that so many fans would nominate the season as their favourite. And yet, it's also derivative and violent and self-consciously baroque. Plus, it marks the first time the show got in serious trouble with that gang of busybody biddies who set themselves up as that nation's guardian angels, the National Viewers and Listeners Association, leaving the show with a taint it never entirely shook off and which – arguably – finally killed it.

I suspect its popularity is partly attributable to simple texture: dark, baroque scripts and dark, baroque sets, right down to the TARDIS console room used for this season – built only because the original had become warped, but it's telling that Hinchcliffe decided to go with a more gothic design instead of a straightforward replica of what had come before. It suited the Doctor's personality more, and in that sense could be seen as the prototype to the set built for the later McGann Telemovie. The scripts often allude to gothic literature and, in terms of production, the stories all have more of Old Dark House than Shiny New Spaceship to them: Renaissance Italy, Victorian England, a Halloweeny

Gallifrey that's all ghoulish green and shadows, the twenties art-deco look of the sandminer and its crew in *The Robots of Death*. Only *The Hand of Fear* has a particularly "modern" look and it's arguably the least successful story of the season (while still no failure). And there are several highly effective horror moments and set pieces – not least the Voc robots, the Peking homunculus and the remarkably original third episode of *The Deadly Assassin*. It's *Doctor Who*'s House of Horrible, full of "Do you remember the one where..." material.

Not that I'm suggesting it's all style over substance. Rather, it's a successful coordination of the two. Great production isn't used to gloss over shoddy scripts, but rather to render them as effectively as possible on screen. I know it seems obvious that's the way the show should have been made all the time, but we all know it didn't always work out like that; there were a number of production mistakes made in the Davison era in particular (*Kinda* and *Warriors of the Deep* were too brightly lit, and with *Arc of Infinity* you'd think they'd filmed a few actors running around Amsterdam and then tried to write a script around it). In Season Fourteen, only *The Talons of Weng-Chiang* can really be accused of style over substance (and I'm sure there's hardcore Holmes-Hinchcliffites who won't even concede that that's true).

But I think what I like best about this season is its portrayal of the Doctor. Baker's at probably his very best here, with more of an edge to him than before, and fewer excursions into the land of scenery-chewing than later. Not that I don't love the scenery-chewing Baker too, mind you, but that's a matter for another review.

The fourth Doctor of this season is angry, cynical and alone. Not always noticeably so; in fact, not often noticeably so, but Baker's characterisation is very much suited to these scripts, most particularly those by Holmes and Boucher. What really strikes me about this season is that the Doctor is most in his element when he's battling against dogma, be it superstitious or societal / political.

Consider the opening story, *The Masque of Mandragora*. An almost comically decorous title, and some evident cribbing from Poe, but it's not simply gothic pastiche or a collection of mere effects. It's actually about something. It's not regarded as highly as, say, *Spearhead from Space* or even *Terror of the Zygons*, yet it has more substance than either of those stories (both of which are highly flawed in plot terms and have no thematic depth to speak of). It's set at the dawn of the Enlightenment, and the Doctor's mission here is to ensure that history stays on track, that mankind makes the difficult leap from an age of superstition to "the dawn of a new reason". His speech about Mandragora turning humanity into "sheep, useless sheep" is very telling, as is the effectively disgusted way he spits out that word. This is a Doctor who champions ambition and rationalism, and has no use at all for the world of oppressive superstitions. His disdain for "that old fraud, Hieronymous" echoes throughout the season, in his contempt for "religious gobbledygook" in *The Face of Evil*, in his dismissal to Leela of the "superstitious rubbish" of the Black Scorpion cult in *The Talons of Weng-Chiang* – and in his quiet but clear disgust at Borusa's adjustment of the truth in *The Deadly Assassin*.

"The very powerful and the very stupid have one thing in common," he says to Leela in *The Face of Evil*, "They don't alter their views to fit the facts. They alter the facts to fit their views. Which can be uncomfortable if you happen to be one of the facts that need altering." A more succinct summation of the more unpleasant aspects of organised religion and secular politics I have yet to hear. It's one of my favourite lines in all *Doctor Who*, simply for its absolute refusal to tolerate bullshit. Admittedly, I have my own personal reasons for admiring this: I'm gay and homosexuality's a fact of the type mentioned above, abominated by people who can accept the word of millennia-old propaganda texts about magical men who rise from the dead, but not the idea that some people might be attracted to members of their own sex.

Okay, my anger's showing. But there's a point to be made here. Anyone who's read Tom Baker's excellent autobiography knows that Baker had even more reason to be angry at this sort of nonsense. And perhaps some of his childhood anger was stirred up by these scripts: because for my money he's always at his best when angrily relieving people of their prejudices or assumptions.

Incidentally, in its opening story of this season, the show demonstrates some commendable open-mindedness: not least in making the Doctor's two rationalist allies in this story, the Prince Giuliano and Marco, obviously homosexual. Not that I'm trying to make some silly and simple argument that "gay equals good" or something. I'm just impressed that a seventies children's show would feature such progressive elements – this is after all the decade that gave us *Love Thy Neighbour* – and that the terrible Whitehouse didn't pick up on it.

The Doctor of Season Fourteen is a permanently dissatisfied, mercurial wanderer, who prizes curiosity and open-mindedness above easy answers and establishment fictions. And, with the Time Lords revealed not as a bunch of eternally benevolent wizards, but rather a group of fusty public schoolboys with no concern for the truth, this Doctor is also more of a lone figure than ever before. That's a very important development. Lurking in the background too is a sense that he actually wants to be alone. He rather too willingly ditches Sarah to go to Gallifrey – even though he's genuinely pained to let her go – and doesn't ask Leela to join him aboard the TARDIS, despite having formed a friendship with her. Rather, she just jumps in.

Depth, anger, a bit of a dark side. There's some character development here, albeit on the quiet. But I think that's what really makes this the most effective of the Holmes / Hinchcliffe seasons. Baker is well and truly established. He's the heart of the show.

# 10 Things I Want to Say About the Graham Williams Era (Taking in "Why Various Other Shows are Rubbish" on the Way)

by **Mike Morris**
*From The Doctor Who Ratings Guide, August 2000*

**1: Clarity is the soul of knowing what the other chap's going to do...**

I should warn everyone from the kick-off that this is going to be a bit of a rant. And it always seems fair to start off a rant with a bit of a "well, this is where I stand" spiel, so here goes.

I'm loathe to pick a particular era as my favourite. I'm loathe to say that old line "*Doctor Who* is all about..." and then use it to align myself with a particular era. You see, my acquaintance with the show is primarily through the magic of the video. As such, I didn't grow up with Pertwee or Tom or Peter, but watched them all together. And liked them all, because they were all the Doctor, and all I really wanted from the show was the character of the Doctor, on account of how great he was. Whoever he was.

So comparing eras of the show seems odd, to me. The eras of Pertwee, Hinchcliffe, Williams, Davison, etc, are just too difficult to compare. How can you say that *Ghost Light* is better / worse than *The Androids of Tara*? How can you compare the social, passionate allegory of the McCoy years with the camp horror of Hinchcliffe? They simply aren't in the same world. You like them or you don't. But the arguments of one being better than the other seems odd, because the emphasis is so vastly different.

With that in my mind, I'm now going to say why I like the Williams era so much and what makes it so great. Why, although I have oh-so-much time for *Caves* or *Fenric*, nothing quite reduces me to gleeful childhood like *The Androids of Tara*. And why the Williams era, more than any other, is simply beyond comparison – not only with other eras of *Doctor Who*, but with any piece of television in history.

## 2: You must have something in mind...

Plotting. It's said a lot that the strength of *Doctor Who* is in its logical plotting and concise, simple storytelling. Hmm. This, of course, wipes out an awful lot of mid-eighties *Who* immediately, which is often the point of the statement. I'm not sure of the truth of that statement, but it's probably true that there's nothing quite as annoying to a *Doctor Who* fan as a plot vacuum.

What is strange is that the Williams era is frequently held up as an example of perfect storytelling... more because of the change of emphasis that followed it than anything else. Which is what I mean about comparisons: sure, the Williams era places emphasis on plotting if it's compared with Season Eighteen, but in comparison with earlier eras it's not such a big factor. In fact, the Williams era moved away from simple plot-based stories, towards something much more fun.

The real heyday of the logical, well-thought-out plot was probably under Barry Letts. Seasons Seven to Eleven barely have a plot vacuum between them. But the Williams era frequently didn't bother with plotting. Perhaps the best examples are the rickety "two invasions" structure of *The Invasion of Time* and *The Stones of Blood*, which happily glosses over every question raised in the first two episodes.

And there's more. The leading lights of the era aren't examples of plotting in the strictest sense of the term. *Horror of Fang Rock* doesn't really have a plot at all. *The Ribos Operation* gets the main plot out of the way in the first two episodes, and then takes flight. *The Pirate Planet* isn't so much a plot as a series of ideas. *The Androids of Tara* has a plot, sort of, but it's really just an excuse for a bit of swashbuckling.

*Terror of the Autons* is the perfect plot-based story. And, as such, it's pretty unsatisfying. During the Williams era, the show realised that, although plots are all very well and good, they're not wildly exciting. The Williams era magic came from elsewhere.

## 3. Good looks are no substitute for a sound character...

It's the characters, innit?

Well, it is. Quite how much influence Graham Williams had on the show during his tenure as producer is, well, uncertain; it wasn't nick-named The Tom Baker Show for nothing. But what Williams did do was insist on good humanoid villains on "an equal footing" with the Doctor, rather than the madmen and B-movie monsters of the Hinchcliffe years. The hallmark of Seasons Fifteen to Seventeen is the memorable characters with strong, logical motivation. There's no need for a figure like the Master to give a human face to something nasty, green and impervious to bullets. Most Williams-era scripts aren't monster-based at all, especially when you discount the early portion of Season Fifteen. All the main protagonists have their motives discussed; not only do we know what Scaroth or the Pirate Captain or the Graf Vynda K are up to, we understand why they're doing it. Which leads to a genuine empathy with the "bad" guys, instead of the standard "cor, he's a nutter" response.

In spite of unconvincing accents and dodgy spaghetti-masks, all four of the characters I mentioned above achieve some sort of desperate, twisted nobility. This is because they aren't evil, they aren't mad, and they aren't power-hungry maniacs. The only thoroughly evil villain of the Williams era is the Shadow, and has there ever been a worse (and more out of place) bad guy?

For those three years, *Doctor Who* became a genuine human drama. It got called "silly", but that's because it stopped hiding behind the clichés of ranting madmen and papier mache masks. It created proper characters, and began to experiment with wit and tragedy and humour. It exposed the inherent silliness of the program as a whole, but still had an underlying quality... which is why *Doctor Who* fans who dismiss the Williams era seem to be missing the point of being *Doctor Who* fans at all.

### 4: Now that's an idea...

"Silly" is a word which I'm guilty of bandying around a lot, and I use it in a positive rather than negative sense. Which is wrong of me. Because, although I frequently say that *Doctor Who* is a daft kids' show I just happen to like, that's only half-true. If you only look hard enough, deep enough at the Williams era, you begin understand that it's not silly at all. Not really.

The Williams era is full of ideas, you see. Which should be the staple of an escapist fantasy, but sometimes isn't. And escapism by definition is ludicrous. But it implies imagination, and imagination is something I like. It's also something which doesn't date. It's a quality that is deeply, deeply silly and pointless, but it's still the most wonderfully liberating thing in the world.

Williams-era stories create worlds. I don't mean planets, I mean worlds. Hollow worlds that jump through space, or labyrinthine worlds that work like printed circuits, or subterranean worlds ruled by jumped-up computers. They're wonderful worlds where anything's possible; inertia can be neutralised, time can be dammed or looped, magnifactoids can be eccentricolometed. And when someone tells me that's just stupid, I generally grin smugly in the knowledge that it's not.

I don't have to justify it by saying it's allegory, or serious drama. I don't pretend there's a point to it. It simply taps in to the part of me that doodled walking trees in my schoolbooks when I should have been paying attention, that made up crazy fantasy-games with my friends, or played football in my back garden and imagined I was in Old Trafford and I'd set up Mark Hughes' last-minute winner.

The Williams era presents ludicrous situations as if they were the most natural thing in the world, it "makes the impossible possible" by using badly painted cardboard boxes and dodgy sets, and it never loses sight of itself by taking itself too seriously. It doesn't bother with myriad appendices dealing with the history of Middle Earth. Neither do we get unending politics with "The Federation" and "Cardassia" and neutral zones and treaties with Bajor, because that really is interminably, clunkingly, boringly daft. Certainly, it's far dafter than seaweed taxmen, robot parrots and animals made of an addictive drug.

The era glorifies a pair of layabout dreamers who gad about being witty, intelligent, brave, happy, badly-dressed, well-dressed and who always retain the ability to laugh at themselves. It villainises self-interested yuppy types (Scaroth), humourless arrogant royalty who think they own the universe (the Graf Vynda-K), and fanatics who take their own little worlds too seriously and lose sight of what's important (Tryst). People with no imagination. No ideas. The Williams era does have a moral message; it's that dreaming is the most wonderful thing of all, as long as you don't forget you're actually dreaming.

### 5: I'm just having fun...

The other night, after a pint or eight, I brought some mates home... but I'd forgotten to carefully hide my *Doctor Who* videos away. "What's that?" one of them said and, before I knew it, they were demanding to watch a *Doctor Who* video. Which is when I felt as though I was in an aeroplane with one wing missing and a merrily burning engine.

It could have been worse. I gauged the mood of the crowd, I thought about it carefully, and I gave them *The Pirate Planet*. They laughed at all the right bits, they hooted at K-9's battle with the Polyphase Avatron, and they stayed up until half-four in the morning watching all four episodes. But I was still defensive. Because, although I'll happily tell most people that the Williams era was a bit of a laugh, I suddenly wasn't happy with people laughing at my show. Somehow, I felt that they'd missed the point.

The Williams era wasn't a bit of a laugh. Well, it was, but... only sometimes. Both Tom Baker and Graham Williams took the show desperately seriously, even if some other influences didn't (hello, Douglas Adams). And, for all the stand-up comedy of Seasons Sixteen and Seventeen, the show is still serious when it matters. On the occasions that the balance goes wrong, the result is the trashy "I can say something funny with every line" extravaganza of smart-arsery that is *The Creature from the Pit*. Most of the time, the laughs are never inappropriate.

And so we got a lot of laughs while running around Paris, or wondering where a dull icy planet has got to, or seeing a balding bloke from Somerset doing a terrible impersonation of a guard. But when confronted with the notion of planets being crushed to the size of a football, suddenly the laughs stopped. That's not funny, because people died.

My mates laughed. Planets being crushed to the size of footballs is as daft as it gets. And that was when I knew that they didn't get it, not really. People dying – even in the most ludicrous way imaginable – is hardly something to laugh at.

The era is seen as *Doctor Who*'s light, funny phase, but that's only half true. It also encompasses some of *Doctor Who*'s best-ever moral scenes, starting as early as the Doctor-Rutan confrontation in *Horror of Fang Rock*. But even when you leave those Hinchcliffe-era hangovers behind, they're there. There's the Graf's final soliloquy in *The Ribos Operation*, the aforementioned Doctor-Captain scene *The Pirate Planet*, and the magnificent finale of *Nightmare of Eden*.

So the belief that the era's great because it was only light-hearted family fun is only half true. The series glorified humour, and it spent a lot of its time being superbly flippant. But that flippancy was taken incredibly seriously. As seriously as it should be.

**6: If you'd been down there with me, you wouldn't find it so amusing...**
In the "great moral scenes" I listed above, I missed one out. It's in *City of Death*, and it's a little overlooked. It's probably my favourite of the lot.

The Doctor strolls into Scarlioni's cellar, where Romana's been busy making a "field interface stabiliser" for Scarlioni. He takes in the scene at a glance, tells her to stop, and informs the Count that he's going to stop him. The Count laughs, and with a wonderful villain line tries to blackmail the Doctor into helping him. ("If you don't, it'll be so much the worse for you, for this young lady, and for thousands of other people I could mention if I happened to have the Paris telephone directory on my person.") The Doctor refuses.

Why's that so great? Because it's one of those moments when the Doctor throws off his witty exterior, revealing his inner presence as a world-saving hero. And yet, there's more. In his refusal to trade witticisms with the Count, he illuminates the difference between them. The Doctor is witty. But he knows when to stop. The Count is smarmy and cynical, and wrong.

We all know how witty the Williams-era dialogue was. But witty dialogue is ten-a-penny, there's thousands of shows that manage that. Even writers of poor-to-average sitcoms manage a bit of wit.

*Buffy the Vampire Slayer* is witty. It might well be the wittiest show on television. But I just don't find it funny, really, because it laughs at the wrong things. Where the Williams era is written from the perspective of a couple of layabouts, *Buffy* is written from the perspective of shiny, happy, middle-class, genetically modified, fashion-obsessed, white, bitchy teenagers with perfect teeth. The Williams era villainises people with no sense of humour; *Buffy* villainises pale, antisocial people who wear biker jackets and don't interact with the society of the pretty people. Dropouts. The Doctor and Romana, essentially. Although the Giles-Buffy relationship is more or less a Doctor-companion one (eerily, the stuffy bookworm / pretty teenager combination is everything the sixth Doctor-Peri relationship could have been with better writing), it somehow accentuates the difference between the two shows. *Buffy the Vampire Slayer* is Count Scarlioni; clever, mocking, intelligent. And smarmy, hollow, trashy, mean-spirited. And, ultimately, I just don't like it.

### 7: Bafflegab, my dear...

My earlier mention of a field interface stabiliser leads me on to one of the most wonderful attributes of the Williams era. Technobabble. No era has better technobabble than this. What on earth is an ambicyclic photon bridge? A dimensional osmosis damper? Most wonderful of all, a magnifactoid eccentricolometer?

Technobabble's normally a bad thing, but not here. This isn't a science-fiction era. The technobabble's just thrown in to remind us that we're in space, and therefore anything's possible. They're just words thrown together to sound all cool and space-agey and yet at the same time ridiculous. And they do, they do. So here's to the technobabble of the Williams era; the pinnacle of the art of spouting nonsense.

### 8: He's the one you should be talking to...

What's *Doctor Who* about, anyway?

The Doctor.

It's not surprising the way the show follows the character of the incumbent Doctor. The Pertwee era is gentlemanly, civilised. The Davison era is fast-paced, not quite as eccentric as what went before, and looks pretty, but is still surprisingly thoughtful. The McCoy era has its moments of cuteness, but there's always an underlying menace.

The Doctor of the Williams era is magnificent. That's maybe the most obvious statement in the world. But he is, he just is. He runs around, he confronts the baddies, he's witty, he reads books like Peter Rabbit, he's silly, he has a higher self-opinion than one might think, he's deceptively stupid but really incredibly intelligent, he throws us all off guard with his silliness and then in a flash he produces something amazing. He doesn't care how he looks, because he knows that the only people who really matter won't care either. He's at once daft, playful, thoughtful and heroic. And he won't change himself because he knows he's right. In short, the Doctor is the Williams era.

And maybe that's why a lot of the era feels so right. Because the show follows the Doctor's character, and the two are so perfectly in sync. There's no moments that don't feel right (as per Davison and Colin Baker), and no moments when we wonder what he's up to and who he is (McCoy). Crucially, he's never even dislikeable, as Pertwee's Doctor could be from time to time; *The Daemons* being a good example.

So the criticism of the show at the time, when it became known as The Tom Baker Show, at once missed the point and was unerringly accurate. It was the Doctor's show, it was a show dominated by the Doctor. It abandoned reality for a series of crazy worlds that could only exist in the Doctor's mind, and made him a central feature. The series' early tenet (realistic and well-thought-out environments, be they future worlds or historical) was totally abandoned. The Tom Baker Show indeed.

But the Williams-era universe – with its surfeit of pleasantly middle-class characters, its vaguely silly Guardians and its killer gorse-bush thingies – never seemed anything other than real, mainly because it was so perfectly in keeping with the Doctor himself. And a world that was based largely on a character as great as the Doctor is, quite simply, the best world possible.

### 9: I read a lot...

There's a lot that's been said about the show's postmodern cleverness during this era, the intertextual referencing, all that stuff. I'm not entirely sure what it all means, but it's something about the show recognising its own limitations and revelling in its own clichés. I think.

Well, yeah, it does sometimes. But I'm yet to be convinced that it's a major part of the magic, with the exception of the odd one-liner. That kind of stuff never grabbed me as all that clever. I didn't like *Scream*, for example. It was just a crappy horror movie, and just because it acknowledged all its sources (more crappy horror movies) wasn't enough to make it any good. *Scream* was a film where self-referencing was the main feature. The main features of the Williams era were ideas and characters, both of which were conspicuous by their absence there.

There is the odd bit of self-referential humour in the Williams era, such as the Doctor's wondering at why people "always ask you to go alone when you're walking into a trap". But these really aren't anything more than incidental touches; they certainly aren't the main feature. Okay, so maybe the Complex in *The Horns of Nimon* – with its array of corridors that all look the same – was a clever acknowledgement of *Doctor Who*'s visual limitations. And, when the Doctor starts sticking paper stars on the walls, maybe it's part of the same joke. But it works much better on the level of a sci-fi realisation of the minotaur myth, and as for paper stars... well, they're just funny objects, those weird little things that only teachers carry suddenly being seen in the middle of a science-fiction story. The notion of a benevolent alien hero carrying paper stars about is much funnier than any amount of self-referential humour. Similarly, the one overt allegory of the era (*The Sun Makers*) works much better as a drama than as a satire.

What's great about the Williams era is its lack of obvious precedents. If you want knowing nods to other bits of film and television, go watch Seasons Twelve to Fourteen. That was the real era of intertextuality, when every B-movie horror under the sun was adapted, rewritten and parodied. And yes, there was self-referential humour too, as in the Doctor's "won't it be a bit large for the six of you?" comment in *Terror of the Zygons*.

By contrast, *Nightmare of Eden* comes straight from Bob Baker's imagination. And, when the Williams era does borrow, it borrows from myths and fables – which gives the stories something of a mythic quality themselves. Talk of postmodern tongue-in-cheek humour, whatever that is, detracts from the era for me. Williams-era *Doctor Who* was unlike anything else on television, and the more influences and acknowledgements that are spotted, the less magical it becomes. So this isn't an area I like to stress, because I don't think it's what made the stories great.

### 10: And you don't know where we're going!

And so I finally wobble to my conclusion. Such as it is.

The Williams era stands alone. It wasn't science fiction; it wasn't even television, in fact. It was escapism. It was the creation of another world. Yeah, that's what it was; the creation of another world, or even another universe. A wonderful universe. A universe where a character like the Doctor was completely plausible, and where he could do just about anything, and where he always won.

And, basically, that world made no apologies for itself. You can either like it or lump it. But, as far as I'm concerned, it was infinitely better than the real one. And – for me – that world, and the way it was created, sums up everything that's great about *Doctor Who*.

It's the definitive era. And I love it to pieces.

# LOVE AND/OR MONSTERS

Classic *Doctor Who* fandom is defined as being very male. It's an image that it hasn't really tried to shake; in the nineties, Virgin published *Doctor Who: The Companions*, a book whose sole purpose was to provide men with... ogling material (we say politely). Even today, in this post-2005 fangirl renaissance, we still have *Doctor Who* DVD extras called "Girls! Girls! Girls! The 1960s".

It's not that there haven't been female fans of the classic series. In fact, during *Who*'s peak in North America in the early 1980s, there was anecdotal evidence to suggest that the girls, in fact, often outnumbered the boys. It's just that, somewhere along the line, the product began to be defined as something demographically for the lads. A geekier subset of the *Top Gear* generation, perhaps.

The fan product reflected that. While TV fandom in the 90s became more interested in female-dominated sports involving words like "shipping" and "squee", *Doctor Who* stuck, more or less, with what it did best: metatextual analyses of *Ghost Light*, love letters to the Troughton and Hinchcliffe eras, and excoriations of Jon Pertwee. That the holy relic (and sacred cow) of the Doctor's asexuality remained untoppled until Russell T Davies came along (no matter how hard Philip Segal tried) probably helped this. Regardless, you would never see a volume like our Mad Norwegian Press stablemate, *Chicks Dig Time Lords*, until after 2005, no matter how many signatories there were to the Paul McGann Estrogen Brigade in 1996.

And yet, we would argue that the energy that might have gone into discussing a codified relationship between, say, the Doctor and Melanie Bush probably went into other things – and not just discussions of *Ghost Light*, Hinchcliffe and Pertwee. Just as the stereotype portrays a man as someone who can't talk about their feelings but can talk rapturously about the engine underneath the new Ferrari, so too were there things that the fanboys might, well, squee about.

The companions, for one. While there isn't much discourse about shipping the classic series characters (though we have one in Section 3, "I Cross The Void..." and we commissioned one here), people are happy to talk about their feelings and thoughts about a companion, and what attracted them to the viewer. This is hardly surprising, given the crushes many fans have (including both of your editors, who these days would prefer to forget their encounter with Sophie Aldred at a convention in Chicago in 1995). At the same time, the subtle alchemy between writers, producers and actor in creating what must be one of the most thankless roles on television merits such attention.

And then there are the monsters. Fanboys love monsters. They love to analyse what makes creatures of fibreglass and clunky metal scare people so. They love to mock them relentlessly. And they love to create stats and consistent histories and overarching narratives about them. And sometimes, they'll analyse, mock and discern statistics all at the same time.

"Love" isn't spoken about very much in classic *Who*. Curiously, two of the most explicit uses of the word "love" were in a speech before an execution and as a codeword to release nerve gas in the heart of the Kremlin. Nevertheless, *Doctor Who* fans love a lot of things passionately. These are some of them.

# Classic Shipping
## by Deborah Stanish

If you're new to the world of *Doctor Who* and are female, you're going to bang up against a common fandom trope: the girls are only in it for the pretty. And hey, I'm shallow enough to give some credence to that theory. David Tennant is pretty. Very pretty. Even straight up, backslapping straight men think he's pretty. And Chris Eccleston? A panther of a man who oozes sex appeal. So, yes, there is a bit of eye candy involved in the new series. But does that mean the new kids are fans of *Doctor Who* or merely fans of the pretty Doctor and his hot assistants? Are they interested in the stories or just the romantic relationship that the new series has pushed?

When I first fell into *Doctor Who* fandom, I reacted as anyone with a new passion is wont to do: I ran in with arms wide open, declaring love and puppies for everything. Did I appreciate the tensions between Old School fans and us new folk, clodding about and leaving our unmentionables like "shipping" and "sexual tension" all over fandom? Absolutely not! Did I understand the grumblings about how the show was being sexed up for the new audiences? Not a bit. Didn't everyone see the blazing chemistry between the Doctor and Rose that created a hot lava flow of bad fanfic that oozed throughout the internet, burning everything in its wake?

Apparently not. There were holdouts, the die-hard asexualists, "The

Doctor doesn't think of his companions like that" crowd, who had not time or patience for the squeeing horde of fangirls who were in their base stealing their fandom. As time went by, I learned to appreciate those differing opinions. But the question lingered: was it possible to apply a new viewer's eyes – with their tendency to give priority to emotional arcs over good ol' fashioned sci-fi, their supposed reliance on superior CGI and annoying habit of seeing sexual tension everywhere – to classic *Who* episodes?

For me, the first exposure to classic *Who* didn't help matters. Being a rather linear person, I just started counting backwards and ended up falling into the cracked-out universe of the eighth Doctor. Throughout the Eighth Doctor Adventures and Big Finish audios, you barely need to break a sweat to build a case for the more intimate Doctor / companion relationship. But, let's face it, the eighth Doctor oeuvre, particularly the Big Finish output, is very New *Who* in its sensibilities.

So I stepped back a bit further and picked up the thread with the third Doctor. I'd been told that Katy Manning as Jo Grant had some fantastic chemistry with Jon Pertwee so I jumped in with both feet... and immediately fell into a bog. To this point, I'd only lifted my head briefly from the EDAs and the audios to peek at a few classic episodes, so this was my first go at old school *Who* in its multi-episodic glory and, at first, it was a bit of a trudge. I could actually feel my fandom cred slipping away every time I raised my eyes to check my watch and realised chunks of time had passed and nothing much had actually happened, or whenever I groaned at the model clay monsters. Even the adorable Jo wasn't able to lift me from the morass. The truth was, gentle readers, I wasn't loving it.

Then, it happened. That moment in any show that tips you from casual viewer to full-out fan: Pertwee's Doctor slapped Jo on the arse in *Terror of the Autons*. They were lying in the field after escaping the Autons and, as he scrambled to his feet, he slapped her on the *arse*. Did he say "Hey! Let's go!" or give her a hand up? No! He gave her bum a slap and then they were off. Now my ears were perked and my eyes were open. The little chucks on the chin, the fond smiles, the Doctor's inability to fire her as she stared at him wide-eyed, with a sense of false naïvety; this could definitely add up to something.

I was completely gone when, in the very opening scene of *The Curse of Peladon*, we learn that the Doctor effectively cockblocked Mike Yates from a night of dancing with Jo by dangling a joyride in the TARDIS in front of her. Then he makes her a Princess of TARDIS, which sounds a lot like the Time Lord equivalent of first base. And, while Jo is momentarily distracted by the pretty boy prince, there's never any doubt who is the real star as soon as the Doctor enters the room.

Of course I'm being flip, but the truth of the matter is, there is a depth of feeling between these two characters. They care for each other, put themselves in danger for each other and turn to each other when the chips are down. The feelings they share can very easily be read as something more than what we are seeing on screen. Nowhere is this more evident than in Jo's final story, *The Green Death*. By this time, I'm no longer fazed by plastic monsters, so giant maggots are handwaved away without a thought and the sometimes-tedious secondary characters are like the appetiser you nibble on while waiting for the main course – which is, of course, the Doctor and Jo.

Feeling confident, I decided to randomly sample a few more Doctors, starting with classic *Who*'s prettiest, Peter Davison. Season Twenty was the year of Turlough, Tegan and Nyssa, five Doctors, and a bunch of immortal space pirates. The TARDIS was crowded with short skirts, pegged pants and amazing shoulder pads. So, what happens when you mix, let's be honest, a hot Doctor with all that exposed flesh, makeup and eyeliner? Surprisingly, not much.

I've said it before and it bears repeating: a shipper ships. We just can't help it. We look for those personal connections in between the cracks of the story and wonder how they'd play outside of the confines of the thirty minutes to sixty minutes allotted. Sometimes it's a spiritual connections and sometimes, well... it's clothing optional, if you know what I mean. And I think you do.

But what should have been a perfect storm of hot shipping action, Season Twenty was a bit of a cold fish. There were flashes here and there: Tegan and Turlough played just shy of *Moonlight*-style banter; Nyssa's parting scene in *Terminus* was touching for both Tegan and the Doctor's reactions, plus added spark to the femslasher's playground; and the Doctor and Turlough had some interesting interaction in *Enlightenment* that, with a bit of stretch, could give the slashers something to play with. So why wasn't the TARDIS a sordid hotbed of love and lust?

I'm going with the outside-the-narrative theory that producer John Nathan-Turner steered the fifth Doctor toward a very specific characterisation. The Doctor was boyish and young; reactionary, rather than proactive. His characterisation deliberately lacked the raw sensuality that great power and intellect, however packaged, delivers.

I've been told by friends who were in the trenches at the time that Davison's casting caused a bit of flailing. Here was a young, very pretty, very blond actor coming straight off his role as the roguish Tristan in *All Creatures Great and Small*. Not only was he a marked contrast with Tom Baker's curly mopped Doctor, but his obvious sex appeal was something new to deal with. And the choice appears to have been "stamp it out, tamp it down and for god's sake, keep your hands to yourself!"

Davison stayed true to the party line, wearing his heart on his sleeve but keeping everything else firmly tucked in. I admire his ability to play it totally straight. It's often tempting for an actor to break character slightly, to push those bounds and Davison managed to project an aura of charm and concern without crossing that line. Unlike David Tennant's tenth Doctor, whose eyebrows deserve their own billing and who managed to pull off one of the filthiest moments in New *Who* history: his slight smirk and raised eyebrow during Donna's "And I got the best part" speech in *Journey's End* clearly implies that there are much better parts that she was missing out on. With one expression, the Doctor out-Jacks Captain Jack Harkness.

Compared to the easy sensuality of the new series and the flirtatiousness of the third Doctor, Season Twenty is practically puritanical. Does this mean all was lost in the effort to apply the New *Who* sensibility of tarting up the TARDIS? Not even a little bit. It just means, from a shipping perspective, we have to get all subversive-like. Practically alternate universe, if you will.

It was a challenge, but not impossible. Any wayward glance or slight grin is enough to keep a shipper fat and happy for an entire season and, despite having to work a little harder in Season Twenty, it wasn't that difficult a task. The Doctor's frustration with Tegan has potential, as does his easy reliance on Nyssa. As I previously mentioned, Tegan and Turlough showed a few sparks that could easily be fanned into flames. After all, they were stuck under those floorboards in *Terminus* for an awfully long time. Even Tegan and Nyssa's relationship had a hurt / comfort appeal, particularly after *Snakedance*, that can be irresistible to shippers.

In contrast, the seventh Doctor, particularly in his interactions with Ace, brought that connection to the series on a silver platter. This relationship is a bit trickier, since it was clearly designed to be a teacher / pupil, mentor / student sort of thing and that's exactly how it comes across. Usually. Sylvester McCoy was only forty-four years old when he filmed his first season but he was clearly pegged as the old duffer travelling with a bright young thing, in this case Sophie Aldred who was actually twenty-five when she first appeared in the series. While the viewers were meant to see a huge age difference, compare that to Christopher Eccleston's portrayal of the ninth Doctor at forty years of age to Billie Piper's twenty-two years. Puts a different spin on things, doesn't it?

For the most part, they played it straight. The seventh Doctor is a cipher, the voice of reason to Ace's rash behaviour – except when he's egging her on, of course. He hides his true intentions and vaguely manipulative ways behind a sardonic grin and whimsical appearance, but with a single word can flip your interpretation of their relationship on its head.

From the beginning, there was a sense of fond exasperation on both sides but, again, there was that underlying tenderness that is the trademark of a solid Doctor / companion partnership. At times, the Doctor is indulgent but he doesn't coddle, knowing full well that Ace is more than prepared to take care of herself. He is clearly delighted with her and they have no problem invading each other's personal space while at the same time respecting that line in the sand that the new series, with its rampant hugs and cuddles, jumped over without a backward glance.

I'm not going to rehash the mess with both the production team and the BBC that encapsulated the McCoy years, yet, despite the off-screen tensions and crossed wires, the seventh Doctor and Ace stories resonate, transcending some of the frankly ridiculous material with their portrayals. Even as the Doctor becomes more mysterious and Machiavellian, Ace never loses faith and neither do the viewers. Can the viewer tip those emotions into a full-on new series reading of overwhelming subtext? Oh, yeah. Just listen to McCoy purr "Wicked" to Ace in *Ghost Light* and you have no problem making the leap.

Feeling smug with my analysis, I took on my biggest challenge: the Baker years. No, not Colin Baker, Tom Baker.

I'm going to be a heretic and admit that the fourth Doctor was never a favourite. Back when I was taking my classic *Who* babysteps, I underwent the new fan right-of-passage of watching *The Key to Time*. I enjoyed the story, but Tom Baker left me a little cold. My initial impression was of excess: too much hair, too many teeth, too much scarf and too many Romanas. I didn't feel or see the depth I'd appreciated in the other Doctors. There were some bang-up stories in this era but I didn't feel the same emotional pull as I'd had with other incarnations. Even the ridiculously shippy *City of Death* played more the on-screen story of Tom Baker and Lalla Ward than the Doctor and Romana.

Irrational? Absolutely. I also realised at that point that I'd hit the wall that all *Doctor Who* fans eventually run into: the Doctor you're just not that into. Still, I soldiered on, cherry picking episodes and enjoying the stories, arcs and villains. I was starting to fill out my membership card for the asexualist club when I stumbled onto *The Deadly Assassin*.

Well, hello there, Tom Baker. The overblown political intrigue felt a bit trite and had me seriously wondering if George Lucas was a fan (I'm looking at you, *Attack of the Clones*), but, once the Doctor shed the coat and scarf and entered the Matrix, I had that headtilt moment once again.

Without his props, he was laid bare, no scarf to hide behind and no companion to act as a narration device. It was up to Baker alone to bring emotion and depth to his battle with the assassin. I'm sure there's a deeper essay in here somewhere about how the Doctor in a companionless story brings more sensuality to the role than he does when surrounded by comely young women. But for now let's just say I've got a new appreciation for the fourth Doctor that has absolutely nothing to do with seeing him come over all Colin-Firth-as-Darcy, standing in the water in only his breeches and wet piratey shirt. Ahem.

Obviously, the question of whether the new viewer is going to pick up the same signals from the classic episodes as from the new series is a resounding "yes". They may pick up on and expand the Doctor's relationship with his companion, be intrigued by the Doctor's sense of pathos or barely constrained power. They may, however shallow it sounds, be inspired by how the Doctor looks dripping wet in the middle of a bog. Whether they walk the path of the shipper or choose to read more into the emotional story than what is presented on screen, it is barely a stretch to apply a modern viewer sensibility to the classic series.

This brief trip into the Whoniverse archives proved my hypotheses and had the unexpected result of creating a feeling of solidarity with some of the disgruntled classic *Who* fans. There's no denying the new series has been "sexed up" for the new millennium and (although this may result in my being forced to hand in my shipper card to the central office) I don't always think that's the best approach. As a friend said when comparing the classic series to the new, the classic episodes pushed science and the mystery as the main story while the personal story filled in the blanks, in the new series it's all personal story while the science and mystery plays as the backdrop. After comparing the delightful subtext of past Doctors with their companions and the current-series Doctor, who spends a good bit of time mooning over something or other when not dodging advances from admiring females, I wouldn't mind a bit less text. Shippers need little more than a lingering glance, a piece of string and a bit of chewing gum to construct entire universes. The new series doesn't have to try quite so hard to help us connect the dots. We're already there.

# 10 Possible Girlfriends from Doctor Who

**by Mike Morris**

*From The Doctor Who Ratings Guide, July 2004*

We all know the pressures on the single man / woman in society to find a partner, even though when I was a kid no one wanted to get married, free love was still in vogue, and couples didn't sigh sympathetically when you said you were happily single. I blame *Ally McBeal* for this pesky change in attitude; to make it worse, looking for one of those girlfriend-things (or boyfriend-things, depending on your gender / orientation) seems to involve lots of going out, meeting people, making small talk, trying to be civil to strangers, obeying complex rules about when you can call somebody and generally wasting valuable time that could be spent lying on the couch watching *Invasion of the Dinosaurs*. More trouble than it's worth, I reckon, so I long ago opted for a different system; this involves becoming a socially inept hermit, immersing oneself in a fantasy world and considering the merits of hypothetical relationships with fictional characters. It's far more satisfying, you know.

Anyway, the world of *Doctor Who* has thrown up a few characters over the years who I thought I had a good chance of going out with, if they weren't, you know, fictional (they *are* fictional, aren't they?). So this is a variation on those good-looking companions list; ten potential girlfriends from the wacky world of *Doctor Who*. And no, Peri's not in it; there are some far more interesting candidates out there...

**10. The Nemesis Statue (*Silver Nemesis*).** Shiny, sentient weapon made from the living metal Validium. Okay, so one wouldn't really expect to have much in common with this artefact and conversation could conceivably become a bit laboured at times. She tends to go away for long periods too. Still, Ace said she was beautiful, and no one would dare bully the kids or anything like that. Not when her orbit was near Earth, anyway.

*Top moment:* How many women do you know who've destroyed a Cyber Fleet?

*Drawback:* Long distance relationships are tricky. And let's face it; a statue that started both world wars and killed JFK would really piss the neighbours off.

*Potential:* Sadly, 0/10.

**9. The mother from** *Dragonfire*. She's not bad looking and she seems very rich, which in my more cynical moods seems more than enough. Besides, her daughter's a dote and I reckon she needs a responsible parent.

*Top moment:* None, really. Okay, to be honest I've only included her because she looks a bit like this girl I used to have a crush on.

*Drawback:* The fact that she didn't notice a gigantic and bloody massacre happening on Iceworld indicates that she might be a touch self-centred.

*Potential:* Not good. 2/10.

**8. The Rani (***The Mark of the Rani, Time and the Rani***).** A sort of a cross between Doctor Frankenstein and Suzi Quattro. A bit into that whole science thing and, let's face it, she'd be the one wearing the trousers in any sort of relationship. Still, she's terribly attractive and she gets to take the piss out of the Doctor and the Master all in one go. Just so long as she doesn't turn anyone into a tree, I reckon she'd be great fun.

*Top Moment:* All together now: "Leave the girl..." Kudos for kneeing the Master in the bollocks too.

*Drawback:* Apparently, sociopathic scientists are difficult people to form a relationship with. Although maybe that's just because no one's tried hard enough.

*Potential:* Might be a fun fling, but I can't see it happening in the long run. 4/10.

**7. Enlightenment (***Four to Doomsday***).** A bit of an ice queen, admittedly. And her natural form's a touch green and flaky for my liking. Still, when she turns into a human she's gorgeous and, what with her being an android and all, she'd stay that way forever. Plus, if she moaned about you watching football or something, you could just unplug her for a bit and rearrange her limbs into amusing poses.

*Top moment:* Her definition of love as "the exchange of two fantasies."

*Drawback:* It's a bit of a silly name. And she's not exactly a barrel of laughs.

*Potential:* Obvious difficulties, but I reckon it might be crazy enough to work. 5/10.

**6. Wrack (***Enlightenment***).** Okay, so she's terrifying. And amoral. And she seems to laugh a lot at killing people. Frankly, confront me with people like that and I turn into a quivering wreck that will do pretty much anything they say. Still, though, she's got a certain something...

*Top moment:* Her interrogation of Turlough.

*Drawback:* Well, the whole thing about her being evil, obviously. Bit of an age gap too.

*Potential:* Realistically, it would be difficult, but what the hell? I believe in a thing called... no, never mind. 6/10.

**5. Todd (*Kinda*).** She's smart, good-humoured, kind, sensitive and she flirts with the Doctor! Come on, what more could you want from anyone? I think she's just great.

*Top moment:* "So many questions, Doctor."

*Drawback:* She fancied a Time Lord and even got to hold hands with him. I can't compete with that.

*Potential:* Okay, my first five choices were probably a bit of a long shot, but now I think I'm being more realistic. Oh yes, I am. 7/10.

**4. Professor Rachel Jensen (*Remembrance of the Daleks*).** She's smart, she's sarcastic, and she's just wonderful. She just edges out Toos from *The Robots of Death*, who by an astonishing coincidence (known as the Michael Sheard Effect) is just like her, only younger and screams more. Okay, so Rachel seems a bit cynical, and her job would probably come first, but I'd be prepared to make that sacrifice.

*Top moment:* Not many people can be attractive while saying the words "do you think I'm enjoying finding out that the painstaking research to which I've devoted my life has been superseded by a bunch of tin-plated pepperpots?" But Rachel Jensen can.

*Drawback:* I don't like begonias. I'd also be a bit afraid of her.

*Potential:* Now we're really talking. 8/10.

**3. Ray (*Delta and the Bannermen*).** Lovely Welsh girl who wears silly big bows in her hair, says things like "He's been ionised!" and drives motorbikes, but for some reason is obsessed with a dull mechanic. God love her, she's as thick as two short planks too. But she's funny, and adorably naive, and aw, she's so cute. She'd always cheer you up, Ray would.

*Top moment:* Whenever she says "He's been ionised!" Bless.

*Drawback:* I lived in Wales for two long years. I'm not moving back there for anyone.

*Potential:* I would walk five hundred miles, and I would walk five hundred more (just not to Wales, that's all). She's lovely. 9/10.

**2. Anita (*The Two Doctors*).** Stunningly beautiful Spanish lady, who's kind and sensitive and loyal and resourceful and good-humoured and intelligent and, oh, marvellous. Quite what she sees in Oscar Botcherby is anyone's guess, but if she can fall for him, it makes me think I'd have an outside chance.

*Top moment:* The way she coaxes Oscar to look for the plane crash is hilarious.

*Drawback:* I can't really think of any, now that Oscar's out of the picture... I suppose it would be a bit of a chore learning Spanish. Although I do know all the lyrics to "La Bamba".

*Potential:* Such stuff as dreams are made of. 10/10.

**1. Susan Foreman.** Oh, lovely Susan Foreman. She always gets overlooked in these good-looking companion things, so maybe it's just my quirky tastes, but I think she's uniquely, outrageously beautiful. So she got a few crap scripts; so bloody what? She not only has the most compellingly gorgeous face, she's all playful and giggly and naïve and funny, and I find her energetic and uplifting and sod all you people who call her a useless screamer! She's fun! She's great! She's stunning! Oh, I'd marry her tomorrow.

*Top moment:* When she gets off with David Campbell by just tilting her head in that irresistible coquettish come-hither way. The lucky Scottish git.

*Drawback:* Curiously fragile ankles mean you'd want a pair of crutches on standby. One would also have to put up with over-bearing in-laws who whip her off to the Death Zone without so much as a by-your-leave. But these are mere trifles.

*Potential:* Some people tell me that I'm a fool to pin all my romantic hopes on a fictional character from a 40-year-old television programme suddenly becoming real and walking into my life. I call these people quitters. 11/10.

# Miss Wright
## by Graeme Burk

Once, a long time ago, I was talking with some fellow *Doctor Who* fans about companions. We were talking about who were the best and who were the ones we loved.

"I've always been a Sarah man," said Roger. "*Sarah.* Not Sarah Jane. She's smart. She's charismatic. She has wonderful chemistry with Tom Baker's Doctor. And she's gorgeous."

"I agree," Tommy enthused. "That scene when she's on the tranquilo-couch in *The Ark in Space* kept me... going for weeks as a teenager."

I shake my head. "That's... so much more information than I need."

"For me, it's always going to be Ace," Wendell piped in. "Sophie Aldred's a great actress and the character is both vulnerable and accessible at the same time. She's that wounded, wild girl you meet at a party. You want to protect her but you're also in awe of her at the same time."

"You really need a girlfriend." Roger noted while finishing his pint of Caffrey's.

Justin was next. "For me it's a choice between Leela and Tegan. Brilliant, different characters played by sensational actresses who give way better performances than their scripts often merited."

All eyes, look to me. "What about you, Graeme?"

I look down at my pint of Hoegaarden.

"Barbara," I say quietly.

"BARBARA!?" The table erupts.

Roger was first. "You're joking, right?"

"No."

Then came Justin, "That's just... *wrong.*"

"What's with you?" Tommy said with anger mixed with shame. "Do you have some kind of a mommy complex?"

"A thing for bouffant hairdos?" Wendell added.

"None of the above."

"Then what is it?" Roger asked.

"I think she's the most influential *Doctor Who* companion ever."

My friends all looked at me as though I've grown a second head. Fortunately I'm used to this. One of them is willing to take the bait. Justin eyes me coldly.

"Okay. So why is Babs the über-companion?"

"Can I just say," said Roger, "that I hate this British affectation of calling Barbara 'Babs'. Frankly, she's 'Miss Wright' to you and me. And you should never forget it."

We laugh at this. I piped in, "I have to agree. I've never been fond of this cosy, camp nonsense of making Barbara sound 'fab' when she's not. It smacks of ungraciousness."

"All right," Justin continued undeterred. "Why is Barbara so influential, then?"

"Because of her place in the story of the Doctor."

There is a howl of what I will politely term delight. "Okay, everyone brace themselves for impact." Wendell orders everyone. "Graeme's got a theory." Everyone grabs the table.

I glared back at them and continued. "I presume you're all familiar with a story called *An Unearthly Child*?"

"*100,000 BC,*" corrected Tommy. I gave him what Terrance Dicks termed "a warning look".

"In *An Unearthly Child* episode three, there's this moment when Ian, Barbara, Susan and the Doctor are trying to escape back to the Ship, only Za and Hur, who are following them, get attacked by a wild boar. Barbara refuses to listen and goes to help them. As Ian and Barbara tend to Za, the Doctor is disgusted by this show of compassion. And who gets in his face? Barbara. She tells him straight up, 'You treat everyone and everything as something less important than yourself.' It's an incredible scene. Then, two stories later, in *The Edge of Destruction* — "

Tommy can't help himself. "*Inside the Spaceship.*"

"Leave before I do something 'orrible to your ears. Anyway, in *The Edge of Destruction*, the Ship is heading into the Big Bang and instead of flashing an error message that reads 'You have misused the Fast Return Switch and are now headed to your doom', the TARDIS makes everyone re-enact a Harold Pinter play. Are you with me? The Doctor, now paranoid beyond belief, accuses the schoolteachers of sabotage. And who gets in the old man's face once again? That's right. Barbara. And it's one of the most incredible scenes. Jacqueline Hill gives it everything she's got. She tells him, 'How dare you! Do you realise, you stupid old man, that you'd have died in the Cave of Skulls if Ian hadn't made fire for you?' and she goes on to recount what they did for him with the Daleks after he tricked them into going into the city on Skaro. And then she says, 'Accuse us!? You ought to go down on your hands and knees and thank us! But gratitude's the last thing you'll ever have, or any sort of common sense either'."

"It is a good scene," murmured Roger as he took another sip of his next pint of Caffrey's.

"It's one of the *best* scenes," I retorted. "And, at the end of the story, you have the equally wonderful scene where the Doctor apologises to Barbara. Barbara says, 'What do you care what I think or feel?' and the Doctor replies, 'As we learn about each other so we learn about ourselves.' And now the two have this wonderful friendship. But, more than that, the Doctor is a better person."

"But isn't that just because Hartnell softened his performance?" asked Wendell.

"Well yes," I replied, "but I think it noticeably softens after this particular scene which I think justifies an in-story explanation. I think the Doctor's absolutely right. As he learns about Barbara, so he learns about himself. Barbara makes the Doctor human."

My friends pondered this for a moment.

Roger caught my implication first. "So you're saying forty-two years before Rose and Eccleston's Doctor did it, Barbara was teaching the Doctor empathy and making him more human as a result?"

"Yes."

"Okay. Anything else there that might prove that theory?"

"*The Aztecs.*"

"Wait." Tommy slammed his hand down in a solemn gesture that only succeeded in spilling what was left of his Rickard's Red all over the table. "If your theory is that Barbara humanises the Doctor, it doesn't work here because the Doctor's alien perspective is correct."

"Hold on..." said Justin, wiping up the spilled beer with a napkin. "It's the *Father's Day* of the Doctor/Barbara relationship. Think about it. Barbara gets the opportunity to change history and because she's human she does it and disaster follows. But both *The Aztecs* and *Father's Day* have scenes where the Doctor is disappointed but understands why the companion does what they do."

"Just as important as that," I added, "is that the two understand each other better as a result. Hartnell's Doctor even generously points out to Barbara that while she couldn't save the Aztecs, she did save Autloc even if she betrayed him. That's a far cry from the man who told her she was wrong for calling him inhuman. I think the Hartnell Doctor and Barbara are like the Eccelston Doctor and Rose in that both pairings become better people as a result of their interaction."

"Good God," Wendell gasped, shaking his head. "Are you trying to... ship the Doctor and Barbara?"

Roger did a very good Hartnell impression. "Shipping on the Ship, eh, hmm?" We all laughed.

"No," I replied, "but it's clear that the Doctor values Barbara in a way that's different to Ian or Vicki. You watch the pair of them in the opening episode of *The Chase* and there's a real bond between them as they sit out in the sun together, mocking the other's singing. Barbara's the one who takes care of him. There's that wonderful scene in *The Rescue* where the Doctor absent-mindedly asks Susan to open the doors and Barbara steps in and suggests the Doctor show her how to do it now that Susan's gone. It's really sweet."

"It's interesting you mention that," Roger said thoughtfully. "When you mention Barbara, fans today immediately think of Ian. But most of that relationship is down to what David Whitaker put into *Doctor Who in an Exciting Adventure with the Daleks* in the relationship between Ian the rocket scientist and Barbara the secretary moonlighting as a tutor. We all assume they're a couple; yet, take *The Romans* out of the equation and they're just good friends. It's fan wish-fulfilment that puts them together."

"But you can't just ignore *The Romans*." Wendell said, holding up his empty pint glass and trying to make eye contact with our waitress.

"There's real intimacy there in her relationship with Ian. It's obvious they've shagged. They're positively post-coital. It's shocking how adult it is."

Justin nodded. "True, but Barbara has other romances. There's Leon Colbert in *The Reign of Terror* and there was also... what's the name of the Thal in *The Daleks*?"

"Ganatus?" I offered.

"Maybe."

"It's *The Mutants* by the way."

"Shut up Tommy," everyone said in unison.

"Whatever the case," Justin continued, "between them and Ian in *The Romans*, Barbara probably had more beaus on screen than Jo or Ace. And Barbara clearly didn't settle on Ian until late in the day. If she did at all."

"But isn't that just another facet of how much better written the original companions were?" I asked. "Honestly, Barbara is downright central to the actions of several of her stories. You can take Sarah out of *Pyramids of Mars* and little changes in terms of plot. You take Barbara out of *The Aztecs* or *The Keys of Marinus* or *The Web Planet* and the whole story collapses. You can say the same for Ian or even Steven. After Innes Lloyd changes the show to make the Doctor the hero, the companion almost becomes perfunctory. The female companion even less than that."

"I don't agree." Roger leaned back in the booth. "I think you lose something by reducing characters purely to their plot importance. Sarah does nothing for *Pyramids of Mars'* plot, but her relationship with the Doctor makes it utterly enjoyable to watch."

"True," I conceded. "But what makes Barbara so integral is that she has so many facets and roles. Barbara's remit isn't to be an 'assistant'. Her role is to be the female lead. It's why she gets to be the hero so much more."

Roger remained unconvinced. "Maybe. But I still don't buy it."

"Neither do I." Wendell agreed. "A companion is more than what's on paper. There's how the actress fleshes out the part. Watching Jacqueline Hill is like watching my Mom."

Justin dryly commented, "I'm not touching that last remark."

"Neither am I," I said, "but I think part of what you say betrays a very typical attitude that the best actresses to play a companion are the ones that are girlish and in their early 20s. Jacqueline Hill broke that mould long before Catherine Tate did."

"But Catherine Tate is funny and a great actress," said Wendell.

"So is Jacqueline Hill. Have you watched *The Romans* lately? The woman is a genius at both farce and situational comedy. She has a wonderful range as an actress from quiet intimate scenes like the one with

Vicki in *The Rescue* to full-on outrage in *The Aztecs*. And when she's terrified – like in *An Unearthly Child* or *The Daleks* – there's nothing mannered about it, it's close-to-the-knuckle terror. She's a superb actress."

Justin jumped in, ready to take up the cause. "And not just as Barbara. Lexa in *Meglos* would be a stock religious nutter if anyone else played it. But Jacqueline Hill is fantastic in those scenes with Edward Underdown which reveal hidden tenderness between Lexa and Zastor. Another actress might have ignored that in favour of something more vitriolic."

"Exactly." I felt a flush of excitement. "I don't think Jacqueline Hill, or Barbara as a character, gets nearly the credit she deserves. All the things you say about Sarah, Tegan, Ace, Rose... they're all true. But I think Barbara did a lot of those things that made them great first. Barbara and the Doctor didn't just love each other, they respected each other. I don't think you can say that of other companions. The Doctor might have had affection for them, the companion might have had awe for the Doctor but the Doctor and Barbara had unwavering, hard-earned respect. The only companions the Doctor ever argued with about leaving were Ian, Barbara and Tegan – and with Tegan it was mostly about the circumstances. That's a sign of real friendship to me. And if you want to go inside the story, you could argue that, without Barbara, the Doctor would still be an antiheroical bastard."

It was at this point we noticed our beers had been completely drained. We started looking for our waitress. There was a long pause.

Then Wendell said, "Are you going to defend the bouffant?"

"*Mad Men* shows it's pretty good hair by early 1960s standards." I replied.

"No, *Susan's* hair is pretty good hair by early 1960s standards." Justin retorted.

It was going to be a long night...

# Real

**by Mike Morris**

*From The Doctor Who Ratings Guide, April 2001*

In 1963, a couple of teachers wandered into the TARDIS and *Doctor Who* was born. It's interesting that unlike, say, *The TV Movie*, *An Unearthly Child* is told from the point of view of two ordinary people. Ian and Barbara are there to be normal and then to be astonished, and in that way astonish the viewers.

In 1981, Tegan Jovanka did more or less the same thing.

Of course, the parallels aren't wildly strong. By that stage, we all knew what the TARDIS was; we weren't so easily shocked by the thing being bigger on the inside than on the outside, and Tegan made sense of it all a bit quicker than Ian and Barbara did. But, as Tegan wanders into an empty control room, nervously says her name into the communicator, and then gets lost in a maze of corridors, the TARDIS became something it hadn't been since that first story: hostile. Tegan is scared. She sees a police box appear from nowhere (again, we're used to that) and she's terrified. By the time she blunders back to the console room and demands to speak to whoever's in charge, Tegan is a wreck who just about keeps her composure. And the viewer empathises with her.

In those first couple of episodes of *Logopolis*, Tegan is happy, sarcastic, brash, angry, scared, tired, frustrated, excited and funny. And, in that short time, she became something that *Doctor Who* had rarely seen before: a completely believable human being. I'll go further; she was the most convincing character ever to appear in *Doctor Who*. Because of that, she was also the most interesting. And, combining those two factors, the conclusion is inescapable; Tegan Jovanka was the best, the greatest, the most fascinating companion ever to grace our little TV show. But, although she's generally popular, I haven't seen enough scribblings celebrating the sheer wonderfulness of Tegan. I'm not sure why. After all, in a run comparable to Jamie's or Sarah Jane's, she was around for almost all of the Davison era. She got some wonderful scenes, and Janet Fielding played them brilliantly. Tegan's leaving scene is frequently acknowledged as one of the best.

Anyway, I'm in a mood for redressing balances today. So, if I may, I would like to rave about how great Tegan was for a bit. And I won't even mention Janet Fielding's legs... oh, except I just did.

Too often, she's oversimplified as being "feisty" (horrible word) or "ballsy" (biologically tricky, I'd have thought). Well, she is, of course, but then again she isn't. *Doctor Who* has had many other feisty companions, Ace being the most prominent of them. But Ace's grinning with delight at every monster and endless pyromania can grow wearing after a while; while the Ace of Season Twenty-Six showed some depth, the early Ace is one-dimensional in her, er, ballsiness. Tegan's a different proposition. She won't show weakness if she can help it and likes to think of herself as independent, but most of the time she's actually scared, and that only makes her more believable. The best example of this is in *Earthshock*, when she insists on accompanying the troopers; she regrets her decision within minutes and admits that she's "just a mouth on legs". Later, she shows herself to be far more than that when she grabs a gun from a Cyberman and blows it to pieces. Later still, she tries the same thing and can't fire the gun properly. Tegan's got a loud mouth, and (brilliantly) she knows it; she knows she's not as tough as she likes to appear, but she's actually braver than she thinks she is; the fact that she's not wildly intelligent only makes her courage more admirable. Come on, could *you* figure out how to work a Cyber-gun in that situation?

Tegan is impressive when she's trying to look tough because we know she's not, really; we know because every now and then we see her other side. Tegan's friendship with Nyssa and her friendship with the Doctor show us a fiercely loyal woman who tied Season Nineteen's disjointed TARDIS team together; a factor specifically mentioned in *Castrovalva*, when the Doctor assigns her the role as the "coordinator". It's great to see Tegan pretending that she can cope, desperately not trying to let the Doctor know that the TARDIS is crashing, or that Adric is missing. In the early scenes of *Castrovalva*, Tegan always seems on the point of collapse, a moment away from running off into the TARDIS corridors shouting "I can't do this!" I think it's her presence that gives the early, TARDIS-based episodes their mettle.

Tegan, of course, didn't like people. She didn't like Turlough, of course, and she didn't like Adric very much. It's hard to blame her, but that gave the TARDIS an interesting edge. I'm one of the few people who love that bit in *Kinda* where Tegan and Adric trade insults; her scenes with Turlough in *Terminus* are a treat, particularly because Turlough gets the upper hand.

Somehow, though, Turlough and Adric were Tegan's friends nonetheless, as we saw when Adric died (how tragic) in *Earthshock*. Tegan steals that scene as she demands an explanation off the Doctor, and then when none comes she collapses into Nyssa's arms.

That happened again in *Terminus* when Nyssa left. The Nyssa-Tegan friendship is a wonderful part of the Davison era, and Nyssa's leaving scene is more about the breaking of that friendship than her leaving the Doctor (who accepts Nyssa's decision as the right one). It's also as much about Tegan as it is about Nyssa. When Nyssa says "like you, I'm indestructible", Tegan proves her wrong by breaking down in tears; it's unbelievably poignant and makes that scene the second-best companion departure ever.

The best, of course, is Tegan's. Yes, I've seen Sarah's and Jo's and Susan's, but this was so simple, so abrupt, that it pushes all of those off the scale. It takes the marvellous friendship that the Doctor and Tegan had built up (particularly after Nyssa left) and ends it all in a few moments of pain. Tegan's leaving hurt the Doctor in a way no one else's did, because this was a companion who'd been with him since the start, so the effect of her storming out is to make him decide to change his ways. It's a great scene; great because of Tegan's refusal to blame her friend; great because, although apparently simple ("it's stopped being fun"), there's a lot more to it than that. Surely it stopped being fun when Adric died? And, while *Resurrection of the Daleks* was a particularly bloody adventure, Tegan had seen plenty of death before. Tegan's reasons are more complex, surely: the fact that the way out of this life was so easy, that she had seen a side of the Doctor that she didn't like, that realities of life with him finally hit home to her... or, maybe... well...

The Doctor's relationship with Tegan is an interesting one, and it deserves a lot more analysis than I can give it here, but I think the reality of Tegan's leaving lies in her feelings about the Doctor. They're friends; but maybe more than that, at least on her side. They look more or less the same age, they get on well, and surely there's only so many times a guy can save your life before you become a bit interested. As for the Doctor, well, he admits that sometimes Tegan takes his breath away... something to think about, that. A love affair, or at least a bit of a crush, would explain a lot: Tegan left because the nice man whom she was developing feelings for suddenly became Davros' executioner, and flippantly destroyed the Daleks by releasing a virus, to the point that she found it all too much to take. It also explains why the Doctor ran after her with a jilted cry of "don't leave, not like this", and why Tegan came back almost immediately and murmured "Doctor, I will miss you". Food for thought?

There are a lot of things about Tegan I can't go into in detail, or I'd be writing until next year. That's the beauty of her character. Tegan is a mass of contradictions; brave and frightened, determined and irresolute (in *Snakedance*, she refuses to confront the Mara in her mind, regressing to a six year old in her garden instead), brash and self-doubting, angry and tender... the list goes on.

But the key lies in her plausibility (which is why it's not unthinkable that she had a crush on the Doctor, because she wasn't just another companion). Of all the scenes I've mentioned, I've omitted a personal favourite; when Tegan tries to force open a filing cabinet in *Frontios*, and mutters "rabbits" under her breath. Now that, to me, is brilliantly real.

Most companions have been revisited at some point. We've met up with Harry, Sarah, Liz, Mel, Peri, Susan, Jo... pretty much everyone, really. Me, I'm more interested in what happened to Tegan when she ran out into London, alone and without anything in the world.

Then again, maybe some questions are better left unanswered.

# Monster's Ball

**by Scott Clarke**

*From Enlightenment #115, April / May 2002*

Monsters in *Doctor Who* are not scary – unless you're a complete tee-totalling wuss. The only reason I ever found myself behind the couch as a kid was to hunt for the damned *Programme Guide* I'd misplaced. Who's afraid of talking bubble wrap, foam rubber and freaking polystyrene!

Okay fanboys, close your mouths and wipe the spittle off your copy of this fanzine. It's time to take a serious look at this monster fixation.

They aren't frightening.

The Daleks were, of course, the original tin-plated meanies, designed to appear as inhuman as was humanly possible. With their robotic appearance, screeching metallic voices and unrelenting logic, the Daleks were supposed to represent cold Nazi uniformity and racial purity.

I don't think so. A couple of wobbly pepperpots scattered around Studio TC-3 of BBC Television Centre do not substitute for the icy terror of row upon row of precision, expressionless storm troopers. I repeat: they aren't frightening. Nix as well on sophistication. And yet, somehow they add something to the program, to its essential "*Who*-ishness".

The Daleks and their monster siblings, the Cybermen, Yeti, Ice Warriors and the Sea Devils, could never have been that naturalistic; the censors and the budget were never that accommodating. Let's face it, Mary Whitehouse was a heck of a lot scarier-looking than any Zygon or Primord. Where they do succeed is as a form of expressionism. This is most often characterised by heightened, symbolic colours and exaggerated imagery; not a bad description of your typical *Doctor Who* monster. What the hell is a Gel guard supposed to be anyway? It's a projection of Omega's mind, created from his context of an anti-matter universe. It merely needs to look bizarre and campy to fulfil our expectations.

The titular villains in *Planet of the Spiders* don't have to be realistic, creepy arachnids; there was no way on *Doctor Who*'s shoestring budget that the production team was ever going to convey that kind of sensuality. Instead, what we get is almost a "fetishistic fakeness". Because the spiders are so blatantly unreal, we actually feel affection for them. Rather like we feel close to the Michelin Man or the Jolly Green Giant. This may be one reason why we're so fixated on the multiple return visits of our favourite monsters.

My father used to joke that Cybermen had those "handles" on their heads for easy stacking, while a friend once asked me, "So, when an Ice Warrior takes a shower, which part comes off?" I think these ribbing comments expose a deeper truth about the heightened reality that surrounds *Who* monsters. The production limitations contribute to their appeal. Naturalism is thrown out the window in favour of creative expressions of reality.

What this gives us are unique storytelling opportunities, not only in a given story, but stretched throughout the series' history. In the 1960s, the viewer was left imagining how the Daleks made it up the stairs of the *Marie Celeste*. By the 1970s, viewers were laughing along with the fourth Doctor as he taunted his foes to follow him up a rope in *Destiny of the Daleks*. The 1980s brought us full circle with *Remembrance of the Daleks* and the thrill we felt at seeing a Dalek actually ascend a set of basement stairs.

Monsters also needed facelifts throughout the years and God knows the Cybermen were the biggest fashion victims this side of Gallifrey. Built-in light bulbs might have been all the rage in 1966 (or 1986 if you'll have it), but no self-respecting Cyberman would be caught dead in a pair of flared utility pants by the twenty-sixth century. Even the mind-controlled Yeti clued into Weight Watchers by 1967. (Or was that the early eighties? Dammit...) Why would monsters need to engage in makeovers? Whatever the reason, we love them all the more for it.

Many *Who* monsters were gross in the same way that plastic barf or one of those concoctions we made with our seventh-grade chemistry set and assorted leftovers from the fridge was. When Morbius' brain splatters onto the floor, we're not watching the visual stylings of a James Cameron or a Wes Craven, we're talking about something we cooked up in the garage with our odd friend Nigel. It appeals to that same instinct. In fact, I would go so far as to say we liked the monsters precisely because they were something we could envision making in our own garage.

So what makes a particularly effective monster in *Doctor Who*?

Terrance Dicks says they need to be green. Let's check our list here: the Krynoid was green, ditto on the Wirrn, and if you answered "Ice Warrior", help yourself to another glass of Scaroth's private stock. But alas, no, it isn't the colour green, my friends.

Simply put, it's the iconic nature of the damn things. By establishing all of the strengths and limitations of a given monster, all of its particular character quirks, the writers can begin to play with this "package of reality" to reveal all kinds of rich truths. Take, for instance, the recent Big Finish audio, *Jubilee*: it relies heavily on our iconic understanding of what a Dalek is. Our collective familiarity with the history of the Daleks is accessed and utilised to explore deeper themes. As the story unfolds, we're introduced to a variety of characters who each react to the very idea of a Dalek in ways that could almost be called a "meditation on a monster". Issues such as conformity, power and free will are cracked open with an immediacy that only the iconic nature of a Dalek could provide. It's like using Santa Claus to explore consumerism or Cinderella to talk about gender dynamics.

Hell, whenever I've watched *Doctor Who* lately with my best friend's goddaughter, she isn't digging her nails into me with abject fear, she's more likely exclaiming that something is gross, proclaiming it "so fake" or asking me why it can't move its neck. Nevertheless, the image of giant maggots is ingrained in her brain and she will be able to screech "exterminate" in her best Roy Skelton pitch.

So, let's hear it for foam rubber, bubble wrap and polystyrene; they're the building blocks of our childhood mythos.

Ain't that scary?

# Metaphor of the Daleks

by Nick May
*From Shockeye's Kitchen #3, Spring 1999*

I've never been much of a one for the Daleks. Maybe it's the story-by-numbers formula of storytelling; their shock appearance at the end of the first episode, the tunnels or the ugly-but-nice local help, but it just grates on me. In a recent article in *DWM*, writer Marcus Hearn says, of *The Evil of the Daleks*, "By episode seven, the Daleks had done everything that they were going to do in *Doctor Who*." Which is pretty much true. The first two Dalek stories are rightly regarded as classics, or, in another sense, they demonstrate the full range of the Daleks' abilities if they were to rigidly adhere to Terry Nation's guidelines. As a faceless collective of all-conquering menace, there wasn't much else they could do. *The Chase* is just a plotless runaround where the Daleks get to blow a few people away and *The Daleks' Master Plan* is a tiresome, three-month runaround where the Daleks get to blow a *lot* of people away.

In 1966, Terry Nation was dividing his time between working on ITC's *The Saint* and trying to sell a Dalek spinoff series called *The Destroyers* to the Americans. At the very same time, William Hartnell had quit *Doctor Who* and Innes Lloyd had had a very novel idea on how to change the lead actor. Question was: would people go for it? If they didn't, there needed to be something to fall back on to keep the people watching. And people liked nothing more than a good Dalek story. In came David Whitaker and a new lease of life for the Dalek story genre.

*The Power of the Daleks* sees the beginning of Whitaker's vision of the

Daleks. It raises the question of what the Daleks – power depleted, stranded and totally outnumbered – would do to survive. What they would really, truly do. One only has to look at Nation's later *Death to the Daleks* to see what his version of the creatures would do: shoot a few peasants and miraculously take over the planet in ten minutes flat. A total lack of strategy. Not exactly the hallmark of the most brilliant race in the universe, is it? What David Whitaker did was to give the Daleks that purported intelligence. Instead of nuking a couple of colonists and laying down the law, the Daleks take a look at the lie of the land and size up what to do from there. They play it meek, get access to the scientific equipment they need and build up an army. *Then* they start nuking colonists. There is even a trace of gallows humour as the Daleks kill Lesterson, their saviour. He pleads to be spared, fails to convince and is exterminated. "Yes, you gave us life," the Dalek grates as it fires. There's gratitude.

But, in both of his Dalek stories, Whitaker does something that Terry Nation would never have thought of: he takes the spotlight away from the Daleks. In *The Power of the Daleks*, the discovery of the Daleks means all sorts of things to all sorts of people. To Hensell, it means a potential work force that can bring all sorts of advantages to his colony and make him rich, to boot. Lesterson sees them as a scientific breakthrough. Bragen sees them as his chance to overthrow Hensell. What the Doctor is up against isn't the power of the Daleks per se. It's the powerful greed that their discovery has caused. What the would-be manipulators find out to their cost is the literal translation of the title.

It is a much more polished product that we get at the other end of Patrick Troughton's debut season. In *The Evil of the Daleks*, David Whitaker tackles the very nature of evil itself, using the backdrop of the Daleks' attempt to distill the Human Factor to make them more successful. What we get is an exploration of human nature, both its good and bad qualities. Along the way, we probe the psyches of man and Dalek alike – and even the Doctor, who is, possibly for the first time since the opening season, less than lily white in his actions. Evil is personified by Maxtible, whose greed is, in the grand order of things, fairly trivial. After all, he'll be able to turn lead into gold, but who'll be left alive to see it? We are led to conclusions about him and asked to draw comparisons between his evil and that of the creatures he is working for. Both are driven by desperation for conquest: Maxtible's conquest of the scientific world, the Daleks for more universal aims. The conclusion that is drawn is that, by seeing their separate aims, it is obvious that evil is a universal factor. From a man tempted by promises through to the philosophy that guides a race, we are shown the full spectrum of evil and told that it is a spirit that cannot be crushed.

The extent of the Daleks' evil only really hits home when we compare them with their humanised counterparts. A Dalek without the desire to kill isn't a Dalek. It is a playful, meandering mess. Their methods of dealing with the mistake they've made are equally extreme. One minute prepared to fill all Daleks with the Human Factor, the next to descend into civil war to preserve racial purity. Theirs is an all-pervading evil, one which only allows totally ruthless solutions to their usually self-created problems. Their final end is one of the most deserved comeuppances in the series history.

But it wasn't the "final end". There followed a return to traditional form, all exterminating in tunnels and one-track minds again. However, in 1975, the influence of another writer saw a return to the Whitaker method in more ways than one. Terry Nation's *Genesis of the Daleks*, co-written (unwillingly) to some extent by Robert Holmes, came at a time when America had lost the Vietnam War and, for some, it is an amazing anti-war classic. But, in the context of metaphorical analysis, it is much more than that. The Daleks, who hardly feature in the story at all, once more serve to highlight the greed and ambition of those around them. They serve to personify Davros' ambition. He struggles against the Kaled government to complete his life's work. Nothing matters but the completion of his dream. After all, this is a being who equates the theoretical death by virus of millions to where the Daleks will put him in history – and thinks nothing of it. Even the sacrifice of his own people is no matter. To them, the Daleks personified an unknown new world that was shaping up into something disturbing. They are his means to a brighter future and anyone who disagrees has to go. It is fittingly ironic that he pleads for pity before they kill him. Why? Because he wasn't one of them.

*Genesis* is also interesting as the second Dalek story to get into the psyche of the Doctor himself. Throughout their numerous confrontations, he has entombed them in molten ice, trapped them in exploding buildings and countless other deadly finales. Yet, when asked by the Time Lords to destroy the species at their conception, he cannot do it. It is the word "species" that puts it into perspective. Only the Daleks destroy entire species. We see that the Daleks have come to equate with those things that the Doctor cannot allow himself to be. He lets them live for his peace of mind. So now, turning the issue on its head, the Daleks have just become the Doctor's saving grace. An irony with severe implications for the future.

The Daleks were never this interesting again. Davros, through some cock-and-bull excuse, survives being blasted and returns. He doesn't even bear a grudge for being exterminated. It's only when Eric Saward takes over and introduces Davros' plan to start all over again – and the ensuing civil war – that things get interesting. Even then, he just uses them as tanks. The point that David Whitaker and Robert Holmes were trying to make with their contributions to the Dalek oeuvre is that the Daleks are an intelligent species whose ideology and mental processes operate differently to ours. They're not an all-conquering life form for nothing. They're intelligent and ruthless beyond some throwaway line to remind us. But, more than that, the true horror of what they do comes out in what they highlight in us. They are the evil in our shadow. We know they are evil, but can we, like the Doctor, say we are any better?

# Womb of the Cybermen

by Tom Beck
From *The Whostorian Quarterly #20, Winter 1995*

I begin this essay by asking an extremely important question: where are all the Cyberwomen?

Doesn't seem to be any, does there? I've seen every extant episode involving the silver warriors (including the six surviving parts of *The Invasion* plus snippets of *The Tenth Planet* and *The Wheel in Space*) and I've never noticed a single Cyberfemale. As far as I can tell, the Cyber race is strictly stag. The distaff side seems to be completely absent. Which is kind of strange, isn't it?

Am I the first to wonder about this? I'm single, which has perhaps made me a bit too sensitive about the subject, but I still think it's a topic meriting investigation. There have been a lot of recent breakthroughs in the scientific study of sex and gender, including their evolution and genetics. There are important implications for society in the presence or absence of sex. And besides, just because there's not supposed to be any hanky-panky in the TARDIS seems to me a poor reason to deprive the Cybermen of the joys, comforts and complexities of a little feminine companionship.

First, let's examine what we know about the tall, dominant Cybermen. They made their first appearance in *Doctor Who* in the 1966 story, *The Tenth Planet*, which was William Hartnell's valedictory episode. At this point, they were not yet the silver giants we have since come to know and love so well. As originally shown, they were lumbering, cloth-faced creatures, obviously humanoid actors under all that swathing. They looked more like mummies than monsters. They wore what appeared to be accordions on their chests along with funny headpieces with jughandles. They also had individual names.

Although I haven't seen all of *The Tenth Planet* (actually, I wasn't even aware of *Doctor Who* in 1966), I don't think the Cybermen could have had the same impact back then as people's first view of the Daleks in 1963. I doubt, for instance, that the day after *The Tenth Planet* aired there were legions of kids running around Britain pretending to be Cybermen. Still, their eventual popularity grew to rival that of the evil pepperpots.

Because what they have become since that rather inauspicious debut is hard to overestimate. From a variation on the classic mummy to a technophobe's wet dream of a nightmare, engendering at least as much myth as (if not more than) the Daleks, the Cybermen have arguably become the favourite monsters / villains of many, perhaps most, *Doctor Who* fans. If you include David Banks' brilliant book, *Doctor Who: Cybermen*, along with their many appearances on the show and in the novelisations thereof, the Cybermen have made a contribution to the *Doctor Who* mythos second to none.

What accounts for this extraordinary impact? Besides their dramatic visual appeal, endearing relentlessness, and the exceptional stories they have graced (*The Invasion* and *Earthshock* are just the best of their many tilts with Doctors and company), there is the ineluctable fascination with their entire ethos, their nature, their very being. Created by *Doctor Who* script editor Gerry Davis and his unpaid scientific advisor Dr Kit Pedler, the Cybermen derived from one of the finest traditions of science fiction: "If this goes on." Pedler, an eye surgeon, was interested in prosthetics, the replacement of organic body parts by artificial imitations. He wondered what would happen if, as the technology developed and improved, it were taken too far: i.e., at what point does a person with such replacement organs cease being human?

The Cybermen were his cautionary tale, his attempt to deal with the potential dark side of prosthetics and transplants. However they evolved, wherever they evolved (not conclusively dealt with in *Doctor Who*, or, rather, dealt with in several different ways), they were certainly the result of an attempt to achieve immortality through perpetual replacement. When one of the body parts wore out, it was replaced. Eventually, almost all of their bodies were cybernetic replacements. Over time, this led to the development of a new species of being, barren of emotion, driven instead by a will to conquer. Barren in others ways, too: the only way they could reproduce, ensure their survival as a species, was to capture and enslave organic beings and then convert them into new Cybermen.

Which doesn't answer my question: where are the broads? Don't the Cybermen ever convert organic females into Cyberbeings? And if not, why not?

Beyond the legal question (blatant discrimination on the basis of gender), there are also important psychosocial implications in this sexist pattern. For one thing, if there really are no Cyberwomen, then we have a very likely explanation as to why the Cybermen are always so nasty and unpleasant: sexual frustration, pure and simple! Unrelieved erotic urges. Unrelievable, in fact. Libido is an extremely deep-rooted drive in humans, almost impossible to eradicate. Just because you no longer have the right parts isn't going to stop you from wanting to perform the act. An amputee misses his lost limb; do you think a eunuch doesn't get horny?

I'm serious. The Cybermen have retained at least part of their organic brains. Doesn't that imply that they may also have retained at least some vestiges of humanity's instinctual drives? Hunger, friendship, anxiety, security, lust; they're in there somewhere, no doubt. Without the organic means to satisfy these drives, the Cybermen have had to sublimate their needs in a different direction: conquest and destruction, enslavement and conversion. With their towering, throbbing silver bodies striding forward unstoppably, their pulsating, tall, erect metal frames vibrating with passion, their ever-hard, rigid torsos glistening like they'd been rubbed with body oil, the Cybermen are a Freudian's dream come true (not to mention the ultimate male adolescent fantasy). Their overcompensation for their lack of fully functional male parts is so obvious that I can only wonder why no one has pointed it out before. Repression due to shame, perhaps?

And all because they have no women.

It's certainly a unique concept in science fiction: alien invaders who don't want to enslave our females. What happens to women on planets on the Cybermen's hit-list? Are they ignored? Fed into the synthesiser as fuel? Or – gulp – turned into Cyber-MEN? Not much of a choice, is it, ladies? Mashed or maled. Aren't the Cybermen missing a real opportunity? Mars needs women. Why not the Cybermen?

You can't even argue that they have no alternative role models to follow. *Doctor Who* has presented several groups with admirable affirmative-action policies. Look at the Movellans, for example. Plenty of women. (Probably. It's kind of hard to be absolutely sure, given what passes for the Movellans' hair, but some of them have to be female.)

No discrimination there. Plus you've got the invaders from Galaxy Four, the Sisterhood of Karn, the Rani, the terrible Zodin, Tegan Jovanka; plenty of equal opportunity for women or spirit. So the Cybermen can't even argue that allowing a few women into theirs ranks would dilute their aggressiveness!

It isn't always as clear with the rest of the *Doctor Who* monster brigade.

What about the Yeti? Some of those long-hairs might be women. On the other hand, they might all just be allergic to Nair. It's also impossible to tell about the Daleks, Mechonoids and Ice Warriors. The Sea Devils all dress in unisex costumes; no clues there, either. The Sontarans seem to have developed in a completely different direction, and with regard to the Rutans... well, I'd just as soon not find out about them. I can live without contemplating bowls of lime Jell-O making love.

But the Cybermen have no excuse for maintaining their policy of gender discrimination. Not only would recruiting a few Sarah Conner types, some Wonder Women, not hinder them in pursuing their long-range plans, it might even lead to a new day for the Cyber race. After all, they can't really point to an unbroken string of successes, can they? In fact, they can't even point to one! They've not yet conquered Earth after Rassilon knows how many attempts. They've never managed to change history. The Doctor still lives (only the first of his regenerations was even marginally their fault, and he got better pretty quick). One dead companion, that's all they've accomplished. One. Even the Daleks killed two!

So would women make a difference to the Cybermen? They couldn't hurt. Some new insights, a new slant on the problem, different experiences, added creativity... not to mention the joys of feminine companionship. It gets awfully cold at nights on Telos; wouldn't it be nice for the Cybermen to have women to snuggle up with?

Besides, women are supposed to be the repositories of new life, the engenderers of hope, renewal, revival. All of which the Cybermen need, desperately, in spades. A carefully supervised program of female-to-Cyberwomen conversions could lead to the rebirth of the Cyber race, the creation of a new race of fully realised Cyberpeople. Could there be any worthier goal for the "Human Potential Movement" than to spread its gospel among the Cybermen?

Not to mention the fact that their repugnant discrimination is no longer acceptable in our more enlightened age. Once, long ago, far away, it might have been just barely permissible to argue that in a wild-and-woolly frontier universe, the menfolk had to protect their wimmin (not that the Cybermen could have made this argument, even if they were inclined to). But no longer. Today's societies demand equality. The Cybermen are fighting a losing battle (so what else is new?). The time is coming when even they will be forced to change. Later if not sooner.

In fact, a group of Amazons on the planet Double X has filed a complaint against the Cybermen with the Intergalactic Equal Employment Opportunity Commission, charging them with unlawfully keeping qualified women out of open Cyber positions. Of course, the backlog of cases at Galactic Central (still bogged down in the most recent Census) means that this complaint probably won't come up for a hearing until at least 2995 (all the administrative judges are still involved in deciding the most recent disputed Gallifreyan election). On the other hand, all the bad publicity their policy of exclusion has caused the Cybermen might just lead them to seek an out-of-court settlement. We could be seeing Cyberwomen in action sooner than we think.

Mondas needs women!

# Occam's Dalek

**by Colin Wilson,**
**with additional contributions by Anthony Wilson**

It is a truth universally acknowledged that the history of the Daleks is broken beyond repair. In general, *Doctor Who* writers deliberately – and sometimes gleefully – ignored previous episodes in exchange for a good plot (or sometimes *just* a plot), so a coherent timeline has long seemed almost impossible to achieve. Indeed, after Cornell, Day and Topping in *The Discontinuity Guide* gave up on coherence altogether and suggested that *Genesis of the Daleks* wiped all previous episodes from history, that seemed like the only option and their double-timeline idea became widely accepted. In many ways, though, having that option has stopped us looking as hard as we used to. Because it turns out, by close analysis of the episodes (possibly to an unhealthy level, but when has that stopped us before?), it is possible to create a single timeline without resorting to wild conjecture or the *Genesis* reset button. Yes, it surprised us too. You do have to make some assumptions, but the result is surprisingly consistent.

The most logical approach is to use key indicators from the show as guide points around which a timeline can be constructed. These are: the date as given on screen; the nature of Dalek power sources; the state of Skaro; Dalek time-travel technology and their knowledge regarding the Doctor and the Time Lords. I have only used the TV series as it's quite complicated enough (and the audios are clearly following their own ideas of what happens when). I'm also only going into detail about the classic series as the post-Time-War timeline is surprisingly clear. Nitpickers may point out that *War of the Daleks* makes this effort entirely unnecessary as it already has a consistent timeline in which Skaro wasn't destroyed. There are two points against this. First, it's a book, so, for the purposes of this essay, it doesn't count. Second, and more importantly, it's a daft retcon, mostly written to remove *Remembrance* from history rather than fix any breach. Third, it's famously rubbish.

The dates given on screen form the framework around which the timeline must be hung. *The Dalek Invasion of Earth* comes first with a date of around 2165. *Frontier in Space / Planet of the Daleks* come next somewhere in the twenty-sixth century. *The Daleks' Master Plan* follows at 4000 and, astonishingly, that's it: only three dates are shown on screen. Neither *Day of the Daleks* (~2170) nor *Remembrance of the Daleks* (1963) matter, as the Daleks have time travelled so they could have come from anywhen.

These dates, and further information from *Planet*, lead to a slightly controversial conclusion. The Thals in that story are aware of the events of *The Daleks* and describe it as happening "generations" earlier. Although a generation is a difficult measure, it's implicit that *Planet* takes place no more than several hundred years after *The Daleks*. This is interesting because *The Dalek Invasion of Earth* is explicitly set around 400 years before *Planet*. Clearly *Dalek Invasion* and *The Daleks* occur around the same time (give or take a few centuries). Unfortunately, in *The Dalek Invasion of Earth* the Doctor claims that their current timeframe is "a million years" before *The Daleks*, but, as we've just demonstrated, he's clearly wrong. Wrong, wrong, wrong! A heroic and brilliant champion of life he may be, but as a purveyor of absolute fact, he leaves something to be desired. He also claims that Dalek development has been held up by "a thousand years" in *Genesis of the Daleks*. Really? Prove it! And was *The Evil of the Daleks* "the final end?" Clearly not, given the whole Time War thing, even if we were to assume that *Evil* post-dates any other Dalek story. And the corker from *Remembrance*: "You are trapped, a trillion miles and a thousand years from ... home". Wrong on both counts! A trillion miles would put Skaro practically inside the Solar System which can't be right, so the thousand years claim probably has as much veracity. In short, the Doctor's claims don't count as evidence as he's so clearly and obviously wrong on so many other occasions. Fortunately, this actually makes our life a lot easier.

Moving on, the Daleks are powered by static in *The Daleks*, *The Dalek Invasion of Earth* and *The Power of the Daleks*. In all other episodes, they need no external power. Oddly, this is equally true in *Genesis of the Daleks*, even though it must, by definition, come before those three stories. Extrapolating, this means that the Daleks must have lost the technology to power themselves independently at least once. Now, the Daleks may not be the brightest blobs on the block, but I reckon even they could only lose how to power themselves once. More than that seems like carelessness. Consequently, these three stories must take place after *Genesis* but before everything else. A reasonable theory would be that Davros built their original power sources but was killed before he could explain how they worked. When they began to run down, the Daleks had no idea how to replenish them and so were forced to use static as a backup.

The status of Skaro is probably the single biggest problem in Dalekology. The Daleks are clearly active on Skaro in *Genesis of the Daleks, The Daleks, The Daleks' Master Plan* (it's mentioned as being their home), *The Evil of the Daleks* and *Revelation of the Daleks* (mentioned as home again). The planet appears in *Destiny of the Daleks* but is explicitly mentioned as having been abandoned. It is also mentioned in *Planet*, but it is not at all clear that the Daleks are active there; in fact, the Thals strongly imply that they are not. Finally, it's blown up in *Remembrance of the Daleks*, which puts rather a hard limit on the order of its appearances.

Since *Planet of the Daleks* definitely comes between *The Daleks* and *The Daleks' Master Plan*, the only option is that there was a time when Daleks were not active on the planet between two other times when they were. It sounds convoluted, but is the only interpretation of the facts as presented. Equally, when written, *The Daleks* was clearly intended to be the end of the race on Skaro and there remains good reason to still take this as true. Presumably some Daleks had already left Skaro by the time of *The Daleks*, and it is these travellers who were the forerunners of the Daleks in *Power* and *Dalek Invasion*. This then allows the Thals to develop space travel before the Daleks return at a later date. Either way, we can (hopefully) be certain that the Thals are long gone from Skaro (either dead or driven out) by *Remembrance* because, if not, one would think that the seventh Doctor might have been a bit more reticent about blowing the place up.

Speaking of which... there are two reasons why this event has caused difficulty for us poor souls who want it all to make sense. First, if the Doctor's "thousand years" in *Remembrance of the Daleks* is right, Skaro is destroyed before it's mentioned in *The Daleks' Master Plan*. Fortunately, as I mentioned earlier, the Doctor's statement is clearly bunk, so this isn't really an issue. The second problem is that in *Destiny of the Daleks*, the Daleks dig up Davros on Skaro. These events then lead inexorably to its destruction in *Remembrance*, so *Destiny* et al should all take place after *Master Plan*. Unfortunately, this would mean that Davros would have been in his bunker for around 3,000 years. Now, call me cynical, but I can't help feeling that after that long both he and the chair he rode in on would be long rotted. This has led people to place the events of *Destiny* shortly after *Genesis* which then contradicts the dates and leads back to the dreaded two-timeline solution. There is a way out of this, but I won't get to it just yet. Suffice it to say, there is no reason that Skaro cannot be destroyed in *Remembrance* and any suggestions to the contrary involving it being rebuilt, founded somewhere else or the Doctor mistakenly blowing up the wrong planet are entirely unnecessary.

Before we go any further, I should discuss *The TV Movie*. Despite some complaints at the time, the presence of Skaro in the story is not a problem. There is nothing to stop the Master travelling to Skaro before its destruction and anyone who thinks otherwise clearly hasn't grasped one of the basic tenets of time travel. A much bigger question, one which the movie singularly fails to answer, is what he's doing there. Without this knowledge it's almost impossible to place this event into a timeline, although we can draw some limited conclusions. Given that the Daleks want to kill the Master, this must come after *Frontier in Space* (where they don't want to). And, since Skaro is not a pile of disintegrated rubble, it must come before *Remembrance of the Daleks*. One, rather attractive, possibility is that the Master is there at the behest of the High Council. They've used him before (*The Five Doctors*) and the agreement to pick up his remains seems rather odd unless he was working for the Time Lords. Perhaps they were trying to change the Dalek timeline again (having failed the first time) using an agent without the Doctor's moral qualms. They couldn't try to stop the creation again as they already had one agent there (*Genesis of the Daleks*), so instead they opt for another crucial point in the timeline: the return of Davros to Skaro after *Revelation of the Daleks*. Conveniently, this allows Davros and the renegades to learn of the Hand of Omega from the Master, nicely setting up the events of *Remembrance*. An even more insidious idea is that the Master was sent specifically to let that information fall into their hands, thus facilitating the destruction of Skaro. Such manipulation would not be out of character for the Time Lords. I freely admit there's no evidence for this, but it's an attractive possibility.

The state of Dalek time-travel technology can also define the order of episodes. Mostly, the Daleks use time-corridor technology (*The Evil of the Daleks, Resurrection of the Daleks, Remembrance of the Daleks*). It's not clear what they use in *Day of the Daleks*, but time travel is stated as having been a recent invention, so this story presumably comes before the others. Conversely, there is also the conspicuous appearance of a Dalek TARDIS in *The Chase* and *Master Plan*. This poses a problem, as the DARDIS (for want of a sensible name) is clearly more advanced than the time-corridor technology seen in later episodes (indeed, the Doctor describes time corridors as "crude and nasty" in *Remembrance*). Again, the implication is that *Remembrance* and the destruction of Skaro somehow happen before *The Daleks' Master Plan*. But there is a different possibility.

In *Remembrance of the Daleks*, the Doctor works quite hard to stop the Daleks getting transcendental time travel, which seems a touch pointless if he already knows they develop it later. Similarly, in *Army of Ghosts*, the tenth Doctor identifies the Genesis Ark as Time Lord technology because it is transcendental, strongly implying that the Daleks never developed such expertise, even during the Time War, which we absolutely know post-dates everything in the original series from the Daleks' point of view. Most importantly, if the Daleks had created the DARDIS, why don't we see more of them? It's not like they give a stuff about the immutability of time! They should be popping out of DARDISes from one end of history to the other. The simple answer to all these problems is that the Daleks never invented it at all: they stole it.

Let's assume that the Daleks nick a TARDIS. It is unlikely that they could penetrate enough of its technology to build any more, but they redecorate it in their usual Skaro-chic then keep it on hand for emergencies. When the Doctor steals the Taranium Core (a key piece of Dalek technology) in *Master Plan* and hops off in his time machine, they use it to follow him, with some success. Even so, he manages to wipe out their army, but, tellingly, we don't see what happens to the DARDIS itself which – one might assume by analogy with the TARDIS – is probably immune to the effects of the Time Destructor. We can therefore assume that, following *The Daleks' Master Plan*, non-Skarosian Daleks decide to use the machine to track the Doctor down earlier in his timeline and kill him before he can steal the Core. And that's *The Chase*. It's worth noting that most timelines put *The Chase* first, but seem to do this only because it was written first. There's no reason it couldn't come second and, if you accept that there was only ever one DARDIS, it has to. Certainly, when the Daleks talk of it in *Master Plan*, it sounds like there is only one. Equally, Ian and Barbara destroy it in *The Chase*, thus providing a nice explanation as to why the Daleks never built any more.

Back to those time corridors. Despite supposedly being the apocalyptic end of the Daleks (a claim undermined anyway by the Daleks' appearance in the Time War), the temporal technology shown in *The Evil of the Daleks* is pretty weak. In other serials, the Daleks can use time corridors to land them whenever and wherever they want. In *Evil*, they seem to need Maxtible's experiments to complete the link (although some short time hops seem possible without it). Now, they may be playing safe to avoid another *Day*-like predestination paradox but, even so, *Evil* must be fairly early in the development of time travel (since they get better at it and more blasé about it later on). Thus, *Evil* must pre-date the Davros cycle. Whether it pre-dates *The Daleks' Master Plan* is a more difficult call. We feel that it does, as this allows plenty of time for the civil war to take place, while the civil war itself provides a convenient explanation as to why the Daleks have been so quiet for 1000 years prior to *Master Plan* (as stated therein). It also explains why the Daleks (who are not known for playing well with others) feel the need for so many allies in *Master Plan*; they are still recovering from a devastating civil war. *Evil* may be difficult to pin down once you assume that it's not the final end, but these theories seem to make some sense.

Placing *The Evil of the Daleks* before the Davros cycle also opens the door on another nice little theory. From *Destiny of the Daleks* onwards, the Daleks are said to be emotionless despite the fact this had never been true before (one may suspect that either Terry Nation or script editor Douglas Adams were getting confused with the Cybermen). But *Evil* provides us with a rational explanation for this change. Presumably the victors of the civil war had all been exposed to the Dalek factor and thus were now über-Daleks. It's more than plausible that this could result in a greater dependence on logic and rationality.

And so we come to *Destiny of the Daleks* itself. As mentioned earlier, the timing of *Destiny* has caused some difficulties. How can the Daleks recover Davros so easily unless it takes place shortly after *Genesis of the Daleks*? And how does this square with everything else? Typically (although interestingly), the serial is not even consistent within itself: the Daleks are said to have been created "thousands of years ago" while Davros has slept for merely "centuries". Meanwhile, it certainly can't take place earlier than about 2200 as there is a mention of the "Earth Space Fleet". Fortunately, there is an oft-overlooked line from Romana which allows us to cut this Gordian Knot. When looking at the Movellan space craft, she says it has "time-warp capability". She's not forthcoming about what she means, of course, but the absolute implication – surely – is that the Movellans have time-travel capability. If so, and given that there's a Dalek-Movellan war, the Daleks must also have it at this point. Otherwise, said conflict would have been rather short. (Dalek: "We shall destroy the Movellan time capsules." Movellan: "Unless we cleverly nip back in time and stop you ever evolving." Dalek: "Bollocks.")

This allows the Dalek-Movellan war to take place after *The Daleks' Master Plan* because the Daleks (who have been around for "thousands of years") can travel back in time to recover Davros (who has been sleeping for "centuries"). Presumably, to avoid interfering with their own history, they travel back to the period when Skaro was abandoned after *The Daleks*. They also take human slaves from their own time zone (hence the mention of the Earth Space Fleet). The Movellans follow and the rest is history. Not only does this deal with the myriad inconsistencies of *Destiny of the Daleks*, it also removes any problem with the destruction of Skaro clashing with *Master Plan*. And we didn't even invoke anything not mentioned in the programme.

Last but not least, let us consider the Daleks' knowledge of the Doctor and the Time Lords. In *Day of the Daleks*, the Daleks know of the Doctor but do not recognise his third incarnation, so this must be the first time they have encountered him. Interestingly they don't recognise him again in *Frontier in Space*. Helpfully, the events of *Day* are removed from history, so it must come first. That way they can meet him for the first time twice. On another front, in *The Evil of the Daleks*, the Daleks regard the second Doctor as someone who has been made "more than human" by time travel, so they are clearly unaware of the Time Lords. This state of affairs seems to continue until *Resurrection of the Daleks*, where they suddenly and inexplicably know all about them, pointing to a missing adventure somewhere along the line, most likely between *Destiny* and *Resurrection*.

That covers the bulk of the reasoning, but there are a few, last facts that tell us some useful things. In *The Power of the Daleks*, the humans don't recognise the Daleks. We imagine that conquering the Earth made them reasonably recognisable, so this means *Power* must take place before *The Dalek Invasion of Earth*. In *The Rescue* (set in 2493), Vicki has only heard of the Daleks from the 2165 invasion; thus, there can be no Dalek activity between those times. In *Death to the Daleks*, Galloway claims that his grandfather fought in "the last Dalek war". So there had been more than one (or he would just say "the Dalek war"). Oh, and one other theory for story nerds among us: the drilling site in *The Dalek Invasion of Earth* was in Bedfordshire to make use of the shaft already part-created by Stahlman in *Inferno* and thus reduce the drilling effort. It doesn't help with the timeline, but we love the theory.

Phew! So there we are. Taken together, all the above can be synthesised into the following timeline. This is not the only possible version; some parts of it can be moved around without contradiction (particularly *Death*, *Evil* and *The TV Movie*), but, for much of it, this would seem to be the only logical order of events.

**Genesis of the Daleks** [Long before *The Dalek Invasion of Earth*] Daleks lose ability to power themselves without static electricity. Some Daleks leave Skaro.

**The Daleks** ["generations" before *Planet* (c.1800AD?)] The Daleks left on Skaro are wiped out. A Dalek taskforce from the far future lands on Skaro and resuscitates Davros (*Destiny of the Daleks*).

**The Power of the Daleks** [Before *The Dalek Invasion of Earth*, as humans don't recognise the Daleks (the script suggests 2020, but 2120 or thereabouts seems more likely)]

*The Dalek Invasion of Earth* [~2165]

*Day of the Daleks* [Daleks travel back to ~2170 from a time before *Frontier*, as they do not recognise the third Doctor] Due to weaknesses in their temporal technology, the Daleks create a predestination paradox which removes these events from history. As a result, Daleks temporarily abandon time-corridor technology as too dangerous.

*Frontier in Space* [Mid-twenty-sixth century]

*Planet of the Daleks* [Mid-twenty-sixth century]

*Death to the Daleks* [Post-2493, probably around 2600. Could go a few decades after any Dalek War other than 2165, but the Earth technology fits comfortably here and the Dalek War in question would be the *Frontier* one] The Daleks return to Skaro and begin to reinvestigate the possibility of time travel. They happen upon Maxtible's experiment in 1866.

*The Evil of the Daleks* [Daleks travel back to 1866. It's not clear when they come from, but I'm placing this after 3000 to allow for time corridor technology to be reinvestigated. The civil war then explains the Daleks' lack of activity for 1000 years. Towards the end of that time, they steal the DARDIS]

*The Daleks' Master Plan* (4000)

*The Chase* [Shortly after *Master Plan*, assuming there is only one DARDIS] The Movellan War begins shortly thereafter.

*Destiny of the Daleks* [c4500? Centuries after the Movellan War begins]

*Resurrection of the Daleks* [Ninety years after Davros was frozen; a rehearsal script dated this to 4590, which works rather well]

*Revelation of the Daleks* [Some time after *Resurrection*]

*The TV Movie* [Any time after *Frontier* and before *Remembrance*; here is as good as anywhere and fits with our surmise about the Master's purpose on Skaro]

*Remembrance of the Daleks* [The Daleks travel back to 1963 from a time post-*Revelation*]

**The Time War:** The Dalek timeline after the Time War is difficult to deal with in a linear fashion, because the Daleks are now completely severed from normal time. The result of this is that each of the three known groups of survivors is found at different points in history...

*Dalek* [2012] Fifty years have passed since the end of the War for the Dalek soldier.

*Bad Wolf* [100,100AD] Several hundred years have passed since the end of the War for the Dalek Emperor.

*Army of Ghosts* [~2007] The Daleks have been in the void since near the end of the War.

*Daleks in Manhattan / Evolution of the Daleks* [1930]

*The Stolen Earth / Journey's End* [~2009]

# Two-Four of the Daleks
by Richard Salter, Rod Mammitzsch, Scott Clarke, Graeme Burk, Mike Doran, Gian Luca Di Rocco and John Anderson
*From Enlightenment #109, April / May 2002*

*Two-Four:* Canadian slang for a package of twenty-four bottles of beer.
*Dalek:* A race of cyborgs from the British television series *Doctor Who*.
*Escape:* To get away (as by flight).
*Capture:* An act or instance of capturing: as an act of catching, winning or gaining control by force, stratagem or guile.
*The Two-Four Team:* Seven grown men who have elected to watch twelve episodes of captures, escapes and Daleks, consume a two-four of beer (and many other alcoholic beverages) and make smart-arse remarks all the while. It isn't pretty.

In order to prove that no era of *Doctor Who* can avoid the scrutiny and barbed comments of the Two-Four team, this time we decided on a Pertwee double-bill: the parking-lot-based *Frontier in Space* and the seemingly endless *Planet of the Daleks*. Will our heroes survive? Depends on how fast the pizza gets here.

**Frontiers of Sanity**
*Frontier in Space* episodes one to six

*The comments begin before the story has even started, when the usual VCR tracking advice message appears on screen.*
**Richard:** In the unlikely event of being entertained by this video...
**Rod:** Oh it's *Doctor Who* we're watching! I was told it would be *The Tripods*.
*The story opens with a ship in space.*
**Scott:** Is that the Canadarm on that ship?
**Graeme:** Wow, space shoulder pads.
**Richard:** Did they all have serious accidents?
**Mike:** They're all swollen up.
**Graeme:** "Isn't it the life being a SPACE PILOT? I love being a SPACE PILOT."
**Richard:** I think they wear so much padding to protect them from the seat belts.
**Graeme:** The costumes are a metaphor for the story itself.
**Rod:** I wonder if they wear padded codpieces.
*The space pilot describes a near collision with an object resembling a large box with a flashing light on top.*
**Luca:** It *is* a large box with a light on top.
*The Doctor and Jo arrive. Jo sees a another ship coming straight for them!*
**Graeme:** You know it's serious because they just did a crash zoom on Jo's face.
**Mike:** That zoom comes out of the special effects budget.
**Richard:** The padding in their costumes slows them down, so they use up more time. Therefore the padding creates padding.
*The bridge set includes a counter beneath the view screen.*
**Rod:** Is that an odometer?
**Richard:** It's how many minutes are left for this story.
**Rod:** Time to change the space oil!
**Richard:** Do you think the costumes come with built-in airbags?
*We move to Earth and meet the female president talking with a Draconian.*
**Graeme:** "You know, if you just let down your hair you could become a real woman."
**Luca:** Is that what she's saying to the Draconian?
**Graeme:** Look at her, she's pouting with sexual energy.
**Mike:** You don't get out much, do you Graeme?
*The Doctor and Jo are captured for the first of many times. We find out that the ship is carrying flour(!) and that the door to the space dock is 99% durilium.*
**Richard:** Unfortunately the other 1% is water.

Luca: "And the other cargo ship is carrying wheat!"

Richard: "Soon we will have all the ingredients we need for my birthday cake! Mwah ha ha!"

Scott: Listen to all the continuity references. This is a JN-T story!

Graeme: Good grief, it's the Ogrons. If the Master and the Daleks show up, I'm leaving.

*The Doctor and Jo are attempting to escape from this cell. Jo asks what the Doctor's gadget is for.*

Richard: "Jo, please undress and stand over there."

Graeme: That's the first escape.

Rod: And another capture!

Luca: That's the fastest escape and capture in *Doctor Who* history!

Graeme: Look, they're walking back into the cell.

Richard: They've captured themselves.

Graeme: It's getting too complicated to judge whether it's a capture or an escape, and it's only episode one.

John: [horrified] There's more than one episode?

*Episode two begins.*

Luca: A five-minute recap!

John: Oh no, not again.

Rod: They should have recapped from the part where the ship almost crashed into the TARDIS.

*Jo asks to see somebody in authority.*

Mike: "We want to see somebody with bigger shoulder pads."

Richard: "Would you like some flour?"

*They are taken to another cell.*

Richard: Does that count as another capture?

Graeme: No it doesn't.

Richard: It's a transfer then.

Rod: These people are all padded up because they keep bumping into things.

Luca: It's to protect the set.

Rod: It protects against inner ear infections

Luca: It's Front-ear in Space!

Graeme: My God, they really do have padded codpieces.

Richard: That's not padding.

Scott: That's appreciation for the president.

*The Draconian threatens to return to his embassy.*

Richard: His embassy is a small box.

Rod: They put them over their heads.

Richard: "I'm in my embassy!"

Scott: "I can't hear you!"

**Rod:** It's a very small empire.

**Richard:** What do you call a Draconian with a box over his head?

**John:** Ambassador.

*The multi-storey concrete parking lot makes its first of many appearances in a long scene of guards escorting the Doctor and Jo.*

**Graeme:** It's my university's parking lot.

**Richard:** All that was just to get back to their cell?

*Their guard is wearing a ridiculous amount of padding.*

**Rod:** "You're kind of short for a Stormtrooper."

*Episode three begins with the president receiving a massage from two other women.*

**Richard:** Threesome!

**Graeme:** Where's the porno music?

**Luca:** I can't wait for the uncut DVD.

*The president is told to think of her own position.*

**Luca:** What kind of position?

**Mike:** "I have a book!"

**Graeme:** "I think you'll find the Draconians have more positions than you."

*The mind probe is used on the Doctor. It's a small dish with a small red bead on it.*

**Rod:** It's a little roulette table!

**Richard:** I thought it was an Air Canada hors d'oeuvre.

**Mike:** Pertwee needs a T-shirt that says, "I am not a spy."

*The Doctor and Professor Dale attempt to escape from the moon base.*

**Richard:** How come their indoor suits have padding, and their space suits don't?

*Everyone cheers when Roger Delgado arrives. The Master's stolen ship uses exactly the same set as the cargo ship.*

**Luca:** The odometer's different.

**Rod:** They've spray painted it.

**Luca:** These ships are built to design, just like Cavaliers.

**Mike:** I don't think the Master drives a Cavalier.

**Luca:** Look, he's changing the co-ordinates.

**Rod:** They're episode numbers.

**Scott:** No! He's taking us back to episode one!

*Jo talks to herself while the Doctor escapes. The Master puts her on mute.*

**Graeme:** "I went through all this when I was dating her."

**Rod:** "That's why I dumped her."

*The Doctor takes a space walk.*

**Graeme:** Wow, they went to *no* expense.

**Mike:** If there's a corridor between the bridge and the cell, why is the

Doctor going outside to get there? I mean, if I want to go to the back room I don't climb out the window and go outside.

**Rod:** Well, it depends how much you've had to drink, Mike.

*The Draconians arrive to rescue the Doctor. Jo explains the plot to the Draconians.*

**Mike:** If it's so simple why does it take them five episodes to work it out?

*The Master and the Doctor are nearly sucked through an open airlock.*

**Richard:** How come the sheets on the bed aren't moving?

**Graeme:** Is this story ever going to end?

**Rod:** It's all ripped off from *Babylon 5*.

*The Master uses his device to show Jo her worst fears. They include a mutant, a sea devil...*

**Mike:** Richard Franklin...

*The Doctor goes on another space walk and finds a hatch on the side of the ship.*

**Rod:** "This is where I keep my stash."

**Richard:** The wires actually have shadows.

**John:** Call the restoration team!

**Graeme:** Get me Steve Roberts *now*!

**Richard:** To the CGImobile!

*Jo escapes from a cell with a spoon!*

**Mike:** It's Steve McQueen.

**Richard:** There's nothing Jo can't do with a spoon.

**Graeme:** Can I just say...

**Luca:** No.

**Graeme:** ...The director should be dragged in chains through the street.

*In the quarry, our heroes encounter a blink-and-you-miss-it monster.*

**Mike:** It's a Skroton!

*The Daleks arrive, but it's too late to save this story.*

**Mike:** Episode six is actually pretty good. The problem is episodes two through five...

## Plants of the Daleks
*Planet of the Daleks* episodes one to six

*This story carries on directly from the last.*

**Luca:** What happened to Jo's gun? She had it going into the TARDIS.

**Graeme:** It's the Zero bed!

**Scott:** By Ikea.

**Richard:** Why does the TARDIS have a *Blake's 7* teleporter?

*Jo records a helpful recap of what's going on while the jungle squirts unmen-*

*tionable fluids at her.*

**Richard:** Who's going to be listening to this recording? Says Big Finish as they go to work each morning.

**Graeme:** Why does the TARDIS need oxygen bottles?

**Luca:** Well that's Terry Nation for you, he doesn't know his arse from a hole in the ground.

*Prentis Hancock is qualified in space medicine!*

**Graeme:** If you have space syphilis, I can cure it.

**Rod:** I like the way their guns are attached like bank pens so nobody can steal them.

**Richard:** This ship is wobbling.

**Mike:** Well, you try making a spaceship out of balsa wood.

*The Doctor is rescued from the TARDIS, which is covered in gooey plant life, before he suffocates.*

**Luca:** It makes no sense. The TARDIS can fly through space without any air outside.

**Richard:** The Thals are wearing condoms!

**Graeme:** There's a lot of spurty things in this story.

**Rod:** Can we watch *Frontier* again?

**Graeme:** Ah, the surprise appearance of a Dalek at the end of the first episode.

**Mike:** In a story called *Planet of the Daleks*.

**Richard:** They spray painted the whole thing because they weren't sure it was a Dalek until they'd finished.

**Rod:** Did they open it up and spray inside too, just to be sure?

*A Spiridon pours chocolate sauce on Jo's infected hand.*

**Luca:** Rescued by Cadbury's!

**Graeme:** "I'm invisible so I talk in a whispery, raspy voice."

**Mike:** Their voices are invisible.

**Luca:** Those are mushrooms on her arms.

**Rod:** They're harvesting her. Jo's worth $40 on the street.

*More Thals arrive.*

**Luca:** It's a ship full of Thal women with big boobies!

**Rod:** I can watch this and still say that *Doctor Who* is my favourite TV show. How is that possible?

*Episode three is in black and white, which most of us agree is a vast improvement.*

**Mike:** The Daleks look more menacing in black and white.

**Graeme:** I think *The Chase* would disprove that assertion.

**John:** I think it's so perfect that the invisible aliens have to wear fur coats so that they can be seen.

**Mike:** How would the Daleks know if a Spiridon took off its coat?

*Inside the Dalek control room, Jo emerges from her hiding place in a bin.*
**Richard:** The Dalek in the corner was looking straight at her!
**Rod:** The clock on the wall only has four hours.
**Richard:** "When shall we meet?"
**Rod:** "At 3."
**Richard:** "Which 3?"
**Rod:** "The third one."
**Graeme:** Daleks are the masters of time.
**Rod:** Time flies when you only have four increments of it.
*The Daleks have a map. On paper.*
**Richard:** Somewhere there's a Dalek that can draw.
**Scott:** The Special Pencil Dalek.
**Rod:** It's almost a quarter past a quarter again.
**Richard:** How long do you think it will take them to cut through the door?
**Rod:** About a half of a third.
*Some Thals dress up as Spiridons to smuggle bombs.*
**John:** The bombs look like handbags.
**Luca:** The Thals are fur traders.
**Scott:** "These purses do not match our pashminas! My fashion is impaired."
*The Doctor tells us that the Daleks are vulnerable to extremely low temperatures.*
**Luca:** So are you!
**Graeme:** Isn't everything?
*A Dalek is pushed into the ice swamp.*
**Mike:** They have that nice ramp to take them straight into the ice.
*A Dalek tells a Spiridon that it has arrived late.*
**Richard:** "You were supposed to be here at half past a quarter. Where the hell were you?"
**Rod:** "We've been waiting for three quarters of a third."
**Luca:** "Go stand in the corner with the motionless Dalek."
*There is applause when we realise we've made it to the last episode.*
**Richard:** This is so lame.
**Rod:** Can we start *Frontier in Space* soon please?
*Latep tells Jo he fancies her, but she rejects him.*
**Mike:** "I wish you were Welsh."
*But the Daleks just won't give up. They insist they are never defeated.*
**Luca:** "Except for that one time..."
**Richard:** They're pretty crap when you think about it.
**Luca:** "We normally are defeated, actually."
*It's all over. Thankfully. There is a collective sigh of relief.*

**And So...**

**Rod:** So who can we blame this story on?

**Richard:** That was truly awful.

**Graeme:** That was bloody terrible.

**John:** I loved it. I expected I would enjoy *Frontier* more, but *Planet* was better. There was more running around and explosions, and it didn't make any sense.

**Rod:** Are you nuts?

**Luca:** The whole thing was supposed to be watched half an hour a week.

**Graeme:** I think both are dreadful.

**Mike:** The story that keeps you guessing is better than the story that repeats itself.

**Graeme:** How did *Planet* keep you guessing?

**Mike:** Did you know what was going on?

**Rod:** Is that the time? It's nearly a quarter to a third! I really must be going.

# Why Was the Master so Rubbish?

**by Paul Castle**

*From Shooty Dog Thing #2, Summer 2007*

Right from that first announcement of the return of the new series back in 2003, the most enthusiastically-wished-for returning villain has been the Master. Even now, as the new series is days away from airing, I'm still getting texts off friends with the latest rumours of a possible comeback. The name currently being banded about is John Simm, who guest stars as a character called "Mister Saxon" in this year's series finale. A couple of months ago, the character people were discussing was the old bloke from the double-bill *Torchwood* finale who could do the time-warp, and a couple of years ago it was the Bad Wolf who had gotten people all excited about all sorts of names (Davros, the Master, Fenric, you name it!).

What interests me is why the Master is such a popular character. Why do people so eagerly discuss his return every time *Doctor Who* comes back? He was regarded as the obvious choice for the 1996 TV Movie, and although I was too young in 1980 to have been aware of fandom's opinion regarding the arch-villain's resurrection in *The Keeper of Traken* (back when John-Nathan Turner was re-inventing the series for a brave new decade), I suspect that his return would have been longed for even back then. It almost makes you wish that Barry Letts and Terrance Dicks were able to bring closure to the character before the end of the Pertwee era, where the Doctor was supposedly going to lose an enemy but gain a brother; however, the tragic death of actor Roger Delgado simply made that impossible.

But, and please excuse me for being rude, the character of the Master was just so rubbish. He was supposed to be the Doctor's equal, a sort of Moriarty to the Doctor's Holmes, but a more apt comparison would be that he's a Captain Hook to the Doctor's Peter Pan (heh, with the *tick-tock-tick-tock* from inside the crocodile coming from his Grandfather clock TARDIS?) as his role is more to provide a dastardly plot that will fall apart spectacularly halfway through the last episode than actually be the Doctor's nemesis. How can a character with the wit and intelligence of the Master simply allow his plots to go disastrously wrong each and every time?

I think I have the answer. I propose that when the Master first showed up during the third Doctor's exile on Earth, rather than to actually be the Doctor's nemesis, he was merely playing the role of being the Doctor's nemesis. My reasoning follows...

**Before the Master**

In this little serving of fan-theory, I propose that the Time Lords we see in *The Three Doctors*, *The Deadly Assassin* and beyond are fundamentally a puppet government, present like Douglas Adams' President, Zaphod Beeblebrox, to deflect attention away from power rather than to actually wield it, and that they're too stupid to realise it. That's certainly the impression given in all the stories from *The Three Doctors* onwards, anyway. *The War Games* gives a different impression. These are more like the all-powerful, godlike beings you would expect the supreme power in the universe to be like and I doubt they would need a signal from the Doctor asking for assistance before they could track him down, not if the Elders from the first Doctor story *The Savages* were able to follow his travels through time with little difficulty. (Incidentally, the Elders were my favourite for the Enemy back at the big Time War in the eighth Doctor books back at the turn of the millennium.)

For want of a better title, I'll call *The War Games'* Time Lords the "Shadow Parliament". I hold that they could have picked him up at any time they liked, but it suited them to have the Doctor safely out of the way, because the one quality the Doctor never fails to exhibit is his ability to discover the truth. So, when the Doctor calls for help they've got no choice but to pick him up, as if the Time Lords have openly received a signal then it'd arouse suspicion to allow his liberty to continue unchecked. They hold a quick trial, which deplored his actions but placed him back on a planet where he'd have nothing but opportunity to continue to exhibit the characteristics which he was on trial for.

No, the whole thing is a façade to publicly slap the Doctor's wrists (as to the wider society on Gallifrey they want to discourage the Doctor's interventionalist policies) and get him off Gallifrey as soon as feasible to avoid any unfortunate events which would expose them; it's part of the Doctor's nature to investigate irregularities in the world-view of a people, and with him stuck on Gallifrey it'd not be long before he started poking his nose into affairs that they'd much rather didn't concern him. As a result, the Time Lords have the Doctor safely tucked away where they can keep an eye on him and they've cleansed his mind of any unfortunate memories of his involvement in the shadier side of Time Lord history, and all's well that's ended well.

**Distractions**

But that would have been far too easy, for the Doctor's the Doctor and he's too free-spirited to be content with exile on one planet in one time. He works day and night to repair his TARDIS, and even though he's had the all-important information about time travel blocked from his mind, they know that he's too ingenious to stay trapped for long. Not even placing him with UNIT keeps him distracted enough, as he continues to work on the TARDIS whenever possible; in *Inferno*, he even all but ignores the crisis in hand until work on his side project – the TARDIS console – shifts him sideways in time and inescapably into the heart of the adventure. (It's like a smart kid taking a book to school to read in the more boring lessons, only to be caught by the teacher and thus become actively involved in the lesson.) What's needed is a distraction and they know that, with his ego, providing a nemesis would not arouse the slightest suspicion.

So, in comes the Master, someone who the Doctor knows of old, to be a bit of a scallywag. The Master is employed by the Celestial Intervention Agency to keep the Doctor focussed on the here and now on Earth, and prevent his escape by simply keeping the Doctor too busy fighting alien incursions rather than working on his ship. And it's a role that the Master plays with relish. If you watch the episodes from this perspective you can see that the character simply doesn't care that he loses week in, week out, providing he can simply have fun bringing aliens to Earth for his old school chum to battle. His half-hearted attempts to kill the Doctor can be viewed along similar lines: of course he has no intention of ending the Doctor's life, not when the alternative is such fun – and if humans are to die, well, they're no loss. It's worth watching the Delgado stories with this theory in mind; he's so much more satisfying as a villain if you have a reason why his plans spectacularly fall apart each and every time.

The Doctor does manage to leave the planet during this time, but each and every time it's clear from the story he's been set up by the Time Lords (the shadowy ones, no doubt) to act on their behalf. It's only after the High Council (the puppet government) enlist his help to save Gallifrey from Omega and reward him with his freedom that the Doctor is truly free. His memory blocks are removed, but probably not in full until the seventh Doctor's time: who knows what happened in the Matrix at the end of *The Trial of a Time Lord* to erode the final barriers: a parting gift from the Valeyard? It's notable that the Doctor only meets the Delgado Master once (in *Frontier in Space*) after he's received his pardon. It's likely that the Master was already contracted for one more meeting (the shadow Time Lords not expecting the High Council to reward the Doctor's efforts so generously) so he was steered into those events. The Master's sudden loss of interest in the action halfway through *Frontier in Space* and *Planet of the Daleks* indicate that his services were no longer required, and he just left the Doctor and the Daleks to it.

### Payment – betrayal – insanity

In *The Deadly Assassin*, the story goes that Chancellor Goth found the hideously disfigured Master on the planet Tersurus, and brought him to Gallifrey after being overcome by the Master's abilities of mind-control. But is it a coincidence that the same actor who plays Chancellor Goth – Bernard Horsfall – also played one of the Time Lords who held the Doctor's trial in *The War Games*? It's not contradicted anywhere on screen that they're the same character, so let's assume that Goth was one of the tribunal who exiled the Doctor to Earth. Now, why then was he with the Master on Tersurus? If it's a coincidence, it's getting rather stretched.

What if the Master was meeting Chancellor Goth on Tersurus for a debriefing following his role in "Project Moriarty"? What if it was never the intention of the CIA to honour their side of the arrangement when they could easily eliminate the Master and save any messy business in the future? What if, rather than killing him, Goth's weapon caused the Master to half-regenerate into the skeletal nightmare he was in *The Deadly Assassin*? The Master's renowned for his incredible willpower; maybe when Goth was disposing of the charred body, it came back to life (now played by Peter Pratt) and slipped under the Chancellor's mental defences? Just as the whole of Season Eight arguably makes more sense with a Master out to distract the Doctor rather than kill him, *The Deadly Assassin* works better if the Master's been betrayed by his people. That gives him a motive for assassinating the President and setting the Doctor up for the blame. If the Master's mind has been severely affected by his failed execution and subsequent abortive regeneration, then that explains why the character now has nothing but a genuine desire to see the Doctor dead, even if Gallifrey itself be destroyed in the process. His mind would link the Doctor firmly with his ordeal, so that he would be as much to blame for his nightmare existence as Chancellor Goth and the Celestial Intervention Agency. If we regard the Peter Pratt and subsequent Masters as being brain-damaged by Goth's betrayal, that would go some way to explain why their schemes are so crazy; rather than an adversary out of the writings of Conan Doyle, he's now straight out of the pages of *Detective Comics*...

### The last of the Time Lords?

So, I dare you to watch *The War Games*, the whole of Season Eight, *The Deadly Assassin*, the New Beginnings boxed set, *Survival* and *The TV Movie* and write in with a better theory as to why the Master is so crap at being the villain... and yet so compelling an adversary that we so desperately want him to return in the new series of *Doctor Who*.

# Claustrophobia

**by Paul Masters**
*From Dark Circus #5, Autumn 1991*

*Historical Note: this article was written before* The Tomb of the Cybermen *was rediscovered.*

Telos, date unknown. Klieg has released the Cyber-controller and his army of frozen Cybermen from their tomb.
"You belong to us. You shall be like us..."

As these chilling words echoed around the frosty tomb at the end of episode two, claustrophobia gripped a generation of youngsters as it had never done before. Put simply, there was nowhere to run. Not only were the Doctor, Jamie and the Earth expeditionaries trapped by Kaftan, who had sealed them into the tombs but, even if they got out of there alive, they were still stuck on Telos, as their ship had been sabotaged.

This is, of course, the setting for the classic *The Tomb of the Cybermen* (1967), one of the most claustrophobic stories the series has ever produced. The idea of an isolated group of humans trapped by Cybermen is hardly an original one in *Doctor Who*, but in this story, it is turned on its head, with the Earth expedition actually setting out to find their captors. Not that there is anything wrong with the usual "isolated humans" plot; it had worked in both of the preceding Cyberstories (*The Tenth Planet* and

*The Moonbase*) and still works today, when it is used properly.

So why is it that this sort of story best suits the Cybermen, when they are so obviously designed for open-combat situations? It's no secret that your average *Doctor Who* fan enjoys being frightened or held in suspense. This is why stories such as *Earthshock* work so well, with people being picked off one by one within a series of dark, imposing silos, and with the Cybermen storming onto the bridge and commandeering the freighter, despite the Doctor's desperate efforts to keep them out. The tension in these scenes is derived from the fact that the characters are in a life-threatening situation, from which there is no possible escape. We see that their situation is inescapable and we feel for them. The same sort of situation occurs in *The Moonbase* and in *The Invasion*, such as the scene where Packer calls for Vaughn on his video screen, only to be greeted by the impassive stare of a Cyberman on its way up to destroy him.

As with any frightening piece of film or television, the claustrophobic Cyberstories often rely on the viewer's own imagination to build up the tension. This is certainly the case in *The Moonbase*, where the Doctor asks the base's commander whether the room in which they are standing has been checked for Cybermen. When he receives a negative reply, we instantly become fearful, hoping that the Doctor will run from the room in anticipation of what he will find. When he starts poking about and actually looking for them, we begin to question his sanity, then dive for the nearest sofa, knowing that at any moment a Cyberman will leap out and attack him.

This method of creating tension by having characters head into known danger is a favourite plot in Cyberstories. In *Earthshock*, several characters wander around the caves, unaware of the danger that they are in. The suspense in these circumstances is created by the fleeting shadows which we can see following them through the caverns, and thus our concern for them leads to a sense of apprehension. We hope that they will get out of there, but we know that, more than likely, they are doomed.

The tension in stories such as this can sometimes be so intense that, when the characters finally come to their grisly end, we feel more relieved than frightened. These are the moments that linger in a child's memory for years afterwards, as those of us who grew up with the show know only too well. As one friend of mine who is lucky enough to have seen Season Five recounts (regularly): "*The Tomb of the Cybermen* taught children the true meaning of fear."

When the Cybermen are presented in this way, they almost always manage to send a shiver up the spine, even with a messy script such as *Attack of the Cybermen*. The sewer scenes of that story managed to capture the atmosphere of some of the earlier stories: lurking shadows and a series of suspenseful appearances. It's a pity about the rest of the story, though.

There are also those stories where the Cybermen no longer seem frightening at all, such as *Silver Nemesis* and *The Five Doctors*. There is one simple reason: it is too easy to escape from them. All you have to do is run away! The most frightening thing that could happen to any character is that they are shot (which is unlikely, judging by their marksmanship in *Silver Nemesis*), but this is hardly the suspenseful, frightening stuff which we are accustomed to in a Cyberstory. Ace may have been frightened of them, but I don't think anyone else was.

It is quite a puzzle why the Cybermen work best in enclosed spaces. They may be designed for open warfare, but they were introduced to us as stealthy, fearful robots – and that's what we still expect of them today.

# Why I Love Ace
## by Sean Twist

It's not surprising that I would think about a girl from the stars while reading about the sun.

You see, that's one of the many things *Doctor Who* did to my brain: it rewired my neurons enough so that I have an insatiable appetite for all things scientifickity. Not that I understand half of what I read, but I'm like a lemming to a cliff: I've just got to know what's over that horizon.

So there I was, trying to muddle my way through the latest issue of *New Scientist*, reading about the Advanced Composition Explorer spacecraft. What this ship does is keep an eye on the sun, tracking the solar wind, because sometimes that stuff that blows off the sun can be bad. Now, there was lot more information there, but that's all I could take in before my brain shouted that geez, its back really hurt, please no more heavy lifting, sir, and did I notice that the short form for Advanced Composition Explorer was *ACE?*

I sat back.

Ace.

Dorothy Gale.

The last companion of the Doctor before the show went off the air in 1989.

The jacket with all the buttons.

Perivale. Nitro-9.

My aching crush for her, forgotten until just this moment.

*Wicked.*

Suddenly, I didn't want to think about boring old spaceships anymore.

*

Sometimes, a good thing comes at the wrong time. Ace was that good thing, and 1987 was that wrong time.

Making her appearance in *Dragonfire*, the last story in the already troubled Season Twenty-Four, Ace's arrival did not generate the usual "Oooh, it's a new companion!" excitement. In fact, my first reaction was more along the lines of "Now what?" A teenage kid, seemingly written for people who had heard of teenagers but hadn't met one firsthand. And she was blown to Iceworld by a "time storm"? Let me guess: that looks an awful lot like a tornado, right? And her name was Dorothy?

Come on. It was like being smashed in the head with a Judy Blume novel and the collected works of L. Frank Baum. If there was anything being inspired here, it wasn't confidence.

So, as we waited for Season Twenty-Five, we had time to ponder this new companion. Just what combination of old and new companion traits did we have? Was she a two-word character summation like Mel (eidetic memory! likes pink!) or was she the new Sarah Jane?

And so we sat, and added up just what information we had.

So... just what *did* Ace bring to the table?

1. **She's A Teenage Girl!** This had proven to be a rather successful trait in a companion on *Doctor Who:* Susan, Polly and Peri had all been popular with viewers for various reasons. Sure, the actress playing Ace, Sophie Aldred, was 25. Gotta let some things go. Besides, in a show about time travel, who acts their age anyway?

2. **That Jacket.** Ace wore a black bomber jacket, festooned with buttons and patches. It presented an odd mix of cultures, not all of them terribly endearing. Covering a jacket with band-related buttons was associated with both punk and new-wave fans; yet, by 1987, both of these musical movements were very much on the decline. Curious that a teenager in 1987 would dress that way, emulating a fashion that was four or five years out of date. As for the bomber jacket itself, it too was associated with the aforementioned punk movement, but was also more closely identified as the apparel of choice of skinheads, a racist group that preached racial non-tolerance. So, was Ace a retro punk girl? Was she culturally stuck in the early 80s, either due to stubbornness or obliviousness? Or was she a skinhead who hadn't got her brushcut yet?

**3. She Blows Stuff Up.** Well, at least this characteristic was unexpected. And she made her own explosives as well, giving them a Kurt Vonnegut-like name of "Nitro-9". Alliterative weaponry was a definite first for a *Doctor Who* companion. At least she didn't play the spoons.

So this was Ace: full of hormones, wearing (outdated) counter-cultural attire, and ready to lob homemade grenades if the situation called for it. Which, knowing *Doctor Who*, would be at least twice a week. No wallflower companion here, at least on paper: this girl was simply an assault. Or was she? We still really knew very little about this lost girl we'd met on a frozen world. It was up to Season Twenty-Five to break the ice. But would it break the character as well?

*

The four serials that made up Season Twenty-Five gave us a much clearer idea of who Ace was. In *Remembrance of the Daleks*, we see her wielding a Hand-of-Omega-powered bat like a street brawler, and even managing to blow up her very first Dalek with – you guessed it – her own Nitro-9. So she can handle herself in a fight, something we hadn't seen since the UNIT boys were around. Girl, as they say, got game.

So much for brawn, but how about brains? Well, in this same episode, Ace is smart enough to weigh whether her and the Doctor's actions against the Daleks actually did any good. This was refreshing, illuminating both who Ace was and the new tone to the series. So, while she's a definite player on Team *Who*, Ace isn't a mindless cheerleader. A bit like Tegan Jovanka, but without the bitchiness or ill-advised lingerie.

Yet there were still things that didn't feel right about Ace. As the stories progressed, the narrative reveals that were built upon the initial framework of her character seemed to fit; it was just the framework itself that was suspect.

First – and most glaring – was her chosen nickname: Ace. This isn't a term anyone in 1987 would willingly self-apply. If Ace was fond of irony, and chose a nickname most often associated with the sort of men who favour mirror glasses, hair gel and copious *Top Gun* references, well, okay. But Ace isn't that way at all. She's mercurial. She's excited one second, bored the next, very much a social animal who loves being surrounded by people; definitely not the outside personality who uses irony as a defence. In fact, Ace seems like someone who would be bored by irony, and irritated if she were asked to define it. She also seems to really like being called Ace and not just because it's a far cry better than

Dorothy. (Which, sadly, it is.)

Would a teenager from the late eighties really be that way? If they hated their first name so badly, wouldn't they just go with their last name? Calling Ace "McShane" actually fits her better, as future Big Finish audios would show. But it's clear that John Nathan-Turner's team felt "Ace" was the way to go. Which shows how in tune they were with the youth of the day. Which is to say, not.

Which again brings us to the jacket. As already pointed out, it was a fashion statement years out of date. But things became even more confusing when Ace's jacket buttons are examined – and not a single one is of a band. Instead, we have safe space-travel ephemera, Blue Peter badges and even a Rupert Bear badge. (Some photos show Ace wearing a *Watchmen* button, but rumours persist that JN-T asked her to remove it.) Anything vaguely political or antisocial – which is what teenage years are all about – is nonexistent. Is Ace being ironic? No, we've seen that she is anything but. Is this believable? Absolutely not.

What became clear is that Nathan-Turner's team wanted a "troubled adolescent companion", but not so troubled as to disturb the comfort zone of teatime telly. With her rough childhood, Ace's turning to the extremes of punk rock and making explosives would be understandable, if not worrying. But as a *Doctor Who* companion? She would be a tough sell to both the BBC and a field day to the Mary Whitehouses in the British media. So, instead, we have a companion with just a hint of danger, a whiff of rebellion and cordite, but not enough to alarm anyone. A cuddly Riot Grrl.

In short, Ace should be a complete failure.

But she isn't.

Which had nothing to do with the writers, and everything to do with Sophie Aldred.

*

Sometimes, a good thing comes too late. Sophie Aldred was that good thing, and by Season Twenty-Six, it was too late for *Doctor Who.*

The show had been in trouble for a while, with budgets being slashed and a growing sense of disinterest among the viewing public. With the previous two companions, two different approaches had been tried. With Peri, it was *Curvaceous Young Thing to Keep the Fathers Interested.* With Melanie Bush, we had *Mild British Celebrity to Hopefully Draw in Curious Viewers.* With Ace, with money getting tight and a sense the end was near, the production team decided to try *Unknown, but Affordable.*

Which was perfect for Ace, since there were no preconceptions before her appearance. Aldred's beauty was not of the pinup variety of Nicola

Bryant and there wasn't the feeling that she was playing in a pantomime. Aldred came across as real, a down-to-earth beauty who would catch your eye on the subway, with a smile that was genuine and surprisingly heartbreaking. Suddenly, there were crushes among viewers.

Like Susan, Ace was a way for viewers to connect back with the show. A teenage girl dealing with a mysterious old man seemed to have worked once before and Sophie Aldred made it work again.

*

With Season Twenty-Six, both the scope of *Doctor Who* in general and the character of Ace in particular did something unexpected: they both went for broke.

Ignoring the rather impossible budgets, the writers seemingly said "to hell with it" and set the narrative dial to *Cosmic Awesomeness.* Parallel dimensions, the Arthurian cycle, haunted houses with Neanderthals and angels, Second World War codebreaking (with vampires), and millennia-old plans for revenge (with wolves); oh, it was coming. It was as if the writers felt that not only should their reach exceed their budgetary grasp, it should be fifteen light years and six universes away.

And such tightrope daring also applied to Ace.

While we'd had companions with backstory before (most notably Turlough), Ace's backstory formed the backbone of three of the four final serials. Which had never been done to this extent before. Suddenly, the Doctor's companion wasn't there to be rescued or explained to; without her, the stories themselves wouldn't exist. Ace was now not so much a companion as she was a fellow traveller and, in many ways, an equal to the Doctor himself. They are truly Team *Who.*

Ace's past played a key role in *Ghost Light,* while *The Curse of Fenric* climbed up the narrative high board and dove even deeper into that past: during the Second World War, Ace comes to term with the mother she hated forty years hence and, in a nice bit of mindbending temporal jiggery pokery, actually helps create herself. (Note that I did not say "Timey wimey". Thank you.)

*Doctor Who* was being more daring and challenging its viewers more than it had done in years, so the role of the companion had changed from *Screaming Bystander* to *English Rose Heroine.* By the time we hit *Survival,* the flimsy character of Ace we met on Iceworld has been replaced by a much more realised, living character. While not perfect, Ace is far more vibrant and believable than any companion in years.

*Survival* was our last worthwhile televised visit with Ace, and it stands out not because of the rather stretched Cat People storyline, but because of how we see her hometown of Perivale. While *Curse* was undeniably Ace-centric, it overstepped the bounds by shovelling perhaps too much Bad Guy manipulation onto the character. (Making Ace a Wolf of Fenric, while coyly tying up narrative threads to the amusement of writers and fans, does her a disservice. Ace would have worked far better as a character to have only one *Weird Cosmic Thing* happen to her: the timestorm trip to Iceworld. Other than meeting a Time Lord, she doesn't need any more clever character buffing. Slapping the Wolf onto her slides deep into that valley we all know and love called Wankery.) Here, we see Ace's life pre-Doctor, and suddenly she starts to make sense.

The calm, empty streets of a Sunday in Perivale, with its rows of silent houses, depressed-looking stores and creepy gyms, with disaffected kids wandering around looking desperately for something to do, is one of the most horrifying things ever shown on *Doctor Who*. It screams Souldeath. And if viewers are digging their fingers into their chairs while watching, how could any one survive living there?

You'd have to wear lots of colour to escape the grey of the streets. Maybe something that could hold tonnes of shiny patches and badges. Like a bomber jacket, with all that puffy padding. And you'd have to make something, use your brain, or it will just drip out your ears like all those skinheads who go shouting hate at the Saturday football matches. Something to react against the monotone of this world, something with a little excitement, a little bang. And you'd need to reinvent yourself. Give yourself a name that won't tie you this world of polite and dusty living rooms, of yellowing copies of *The Sun* curling in overgrown back gardens, of teen pregnancy and living only for nights down the pub. Something theatrical. Something bold. Something... Ace.

Sometimes, we don't see the girl for the jacket and the shiny explosives. But sometimes, we really do, even twenty years on.

And that is totally wicked.

# INTERLUDE

## The Key to a Time Lord - 4

by Scott Clarke

*From Enlightenment #123, August / September 2004*

### Episode Four: Morality

Ace: *"We did good, didn't we?"*

The Doctor: *"Time will tell, it always does"*

*Doctor Who* is about good and evil. Sometimes it's as simple as "base under siege", other times it's as complex as touching two wires together...

In *Remembrance of the Daleks*, the Doctor allows the Hand of Omega to be nicked by the Daleks and taunts his old squash partner Davros into releasing his trigger-happy finger (or whatever protuberance he's got hidden under that tangle of wires). We subsequently learn that the Doctor has instructed the Hand to rendezvous with Skaro's sun, make it go supernova, take the planet with it, take out the Dalek mothership and then home for tea. Presumably this means curtains for the Daleks, and a pretty serious indictment of genocide for the Doctor. High stakes indeed.

But, as Ace explains earlier, one faction of "blobs" despises the other with such hatred that nothing short of total extermination will put the cat right. Is the extermination of an entire race acceptable, to allow others to exist in peace? Surely though, the Dalek faction that emerges from that showdown will reassert itself as the ultimate force for evil in the universe. What's a conscientious Time Lord to do?

Moral choices abound in episode four of *Remembrance of the Daleks*, as do consequences for choices made earlier. Mike Smith must accept the fact that his choice to follow Ratcliffe's "ideals" has destroyed his relationship with Ace, as well as his military career. It may also see the destruction of his home planet.

Mike is a very likable guy, an everyman in some ways: he's friendly, affable, loves his mum, rock and roll, bacon and eggs; hell, he's one of the good guys, isn't he? Well, that's the question isn't it? He could easily have uttered Ace's question to Mr Ratcliffe at the end of a very different story, "We did good, didn't we?" Well, of course not; he's working for a fascist organisation and he wants to protect Britain for Britons. But then again, that's my take on the proceedings.

And what of the Doctor himself, setting events in motion to wipe out his oldest foes. "Do I have the right?" his earlier incarnation might have queried. Earlier in *Remembrance of the Daleks*, as he sits chatting with the future butler of Bel Air, he reflects that "the heavier the decision, the larger the waves, the more uncertain the consequence".

I'm not here to argue ethics, but rather to talk about the tradition, influence and evolution of morality plays in *Doctor Who*. Back in the days of plague and infrequent bathing, a morality play was conceived as an allegory in dramatic form. It was intended to be understood on a number of levels, its main purpose as instructive or prescriptive and the characters as personified abstractions (charity and vice, death and youth, etc). Forerunners to the morality play can be found in medieval sermon literature, homilies, fables, parables and other works of moral or spiritual edification, as well as in the popular romances of medieval Europe.

Typically, the morality play is an externalised dramatisation of a psychological and spiritual conflict: the battle between the forces of good and evil in the human soul. Morality plays were an intermediate step in the transition from liturgical to professional secular drama, and combine elements of each. But their legacy lives on, particularly in the genre of science fiction, where allegory is frequently utilised.

From its earliest stories, *Doctor Who* used both its historical and science-fiction elements to recount allegorical stories and illustrate the beliefs of writers, producers or the wider society. Companions often fulfilled the role of "Everyman", grappling with issues of morality thrust upon them by virtue of the Doctor and the TARDIS.

In *The Aztecs*, Barbara Wright wants to apply modern twentieth century Western values to an ancient Aztec society she encounters. It is the alien and detached Doctor who reminds her that they cannot interfere. This is overtly because, according to the mandate of the series at that time, the past cannot be changed. And yet, there is also an undercurrent of moral stance as well, for what Barbara proposes to do the Aztec people in the name of justice and civility is murky, and bears some comparison to what the Spanish will ultimately do to them (even if Barbara's motives are more honourable).

Ironically, the coming of colour television signalled a change to a more black and white presentation of morality with the era of the upper-middle-class, liberal third Doctor. In stories like *The Green Death*, it's quite clear what the "right" choice should be. Sure, we have a few murmurs from the miners about jobs, but giant maggots wriggling across the bucolic Welsh countryside are clearly evil to be stomped out. So break out the elderberry wine and sautéed fungus and give peace a chance. It's also interesting to note that, in the story, the Brigadier is dressed down by the Prime Minister for his efforts. (UNIT continuity aside, there was a conservative government in power in 1973!)

*Genesis of the Daleks* introduces a lot more ambiguity into mix with its classic allegory of racial purity. Watch how the Kaled characters like Ravon and Ronson wrestle with their innate intolerance towards the Thals and the mutos, even as they slowly come to realise the folly of Davros' evil creations. *Genesis* is charged with several intensely dramatic and moral situations: Davros musing on whether he would release a deadly virus, or the classic "do I have the right" speech.

*Four to Doomsday* chastises Adric for his naïve belief in charismatic autocrats, while *Warriors of the Deep*, with the Doctor's epitaph of "there should have been another way", warns of the dangers of Cold War arms escalation. Notably, both of these stories are mediocre and not well regarded by fans. Perhaps it would be fair to say that *Doctor Who* as a morality play succeeds best when aided by solid drama and rich characterisation. We have to care about people who are grappling with larger moral questions or issues of the day. Modern audiences also demand a certain level of sophistication. Oddly enough, *The Caves of Androzani* probably resembles the morality plays of old most closely, with its representation of the Doctor as Friendship, and Peri as the Innocent, confronted by various characters representing Greed, Vice and Vanity.

*Remembrance of the Daleks* returns us to the same moral dilemma confronting the Doctor in *Genesis of the Daleks*. This time, though, he decides to proceed full throttle, concocting what appears to be an elaborate ruse to facilitate the Daleks' destruction. But the Doctor does wrestle with his conscience. In the coffee shop with John or when he cautions Ace about the effects of her boom box on the timelines, the Doctor is only too aware of the weight of his actions. Prescriptive morality doesn't sit well with our pluralistic society, but we do respond to individuals who grapple over difficult choices with integrity, aware of the ramifications of their actions. Ultimately, the Doctor's questions are as vital as his solutions.

Christopher Eccleston has hinted in interviews that the latest incarnation of *Doctor Who* will tackle contemporary issues, without necessarily hopping up on the soapbox. It seems assured that if future morality plays are woven seamlessly into good drama, the programme will once again provide relevant insights into what it means to be human, grappling with the larger questions of the universe. The battle between the forces of good and evil in the human soul, it seems, will continue next year. This time in widescreen.

# THE ONES WHO MADE US

Even today, *Doctor Who* opens with one of the most forceful statements in television: Title of Story *by* Name of Writer. The truth of that statement is actually much murkier (as David Agnew, Stephen Harris and Robin Bland prove), but the willingness to make such a statement is awesome. *Doctor Who* is a show that's *by* someone.

As a television program, *Doctor Who* has always been at home with its own artifice, with having its viewers well aware that it's a television program. From 1972's *The Making of Doctor Who* to *Doctor Who Confidential* today (with *The Programme Guide*, *The Making of a Television Series*, Peter Haining's and Howe / Stammers / Walker's books, and various versions of *Doctor Who Magazine* along the way), fans know *Doctor Who* is written, acted, directed, script edited, produced and created by artists, artisans, craftspeople and technicians. It's made by people doing a day's work.

It's a consciousness few other fandoms share. You don't have pages of fanzines and online forums devoted to, say, Marti Noxon's scripts on *Buffy the Vampire Slayer* or Michael Rymer's directorial vision of *Battlestar Galactica* (even though they should). Most television fans are interested in the characters and the world they live in (and maybe the actors who play them), not the people whose lives were spent creating those things.

That *Doctor Who* fans value the talent that make the show – that they are willing to look at their work (sometimes quite critically, sometimes quite lovingly) – makes *Doctor Who* fan writing as unique the people who made it. That we not only know David Tennant, but that we also know David Maloney and David Whitaker, is something in which we should take pride.

## The Sulphur Man
by **Dave Rolinson**
*From Fringeworld #2, November 2001*

It's difficult to argue in a *Doctor Who* fanzine that Robert Holmes is an underrated writer, given the number of eulogies aimed at the programme's most backlash-proof contributor. As writer and script editor, he established some of the series' most enduring ideas (the Autons, the

Master, the Sontarans, etc) and rewrote previously cherished continuity with lasting consequences. And yet, whilst we treasure his sparkling dialogue, subversive political themes and audacious concepts, doesn't he deserve wider recognition than the hack writer of episodic, formulaic drama series he painted himself to be? Although complicated by debates on television authorship (see my article on the JN-T years elsewhere in this book), it is fair to say that, despite working in a "formula" series, Holmes' writing stands out from the work of other writers, having its own dominant themes and style.

How to describe what Holmes brought to *Who* without saying "isomorphic controls" or "revisionist history of the Time Lords", or asking what he had against poachers? There's his witty dialogue, luxuriating in its own verbosity, crackling between characters in his (lazily, if not inaccurately, described as "Dickensian") propensity for double acts. It also conjures up a sense of place more efficiently than allegedly futuristic design. Like all great science-fiction writers, Holmes uses the future to comment on the present, playfully in *The Sun Makers* or with a sense of colonial discourses in *The Power of Kroll*. His is a very British science fiction and the nation is symbolised in his recurring use of once-great figures whose greed for power has resulted in grotesque decay, in the vegetable-envying Morbius, the putrefying Master of *The Deadly Assassin*, or Sharaz Jek. The same applies to his knowingly revisionist historical settings, from *The Time Warrior* to the story that sums up his intertextual (or, according to taste, plagiaristic, or even proto-steampunk) use of genre and myth, *The Talons of Weng-Chiang*. Common across these times is a concern for the nature of humanity, and how it is compromised by political and economic systems.

Consciousness, and its ideological struggle against groups threatening homogenisation, are the dominant discourses in Holmes' writing. Often this homogenisation is attempted through the use of the media, which Holmes configures in horror terms (a plot device that has aged well in these media-literate times). The Auton stories set their controlling evils around broadcast signals and satellites. In *Spearhead from Space*, a threat to the Doctor's life sneaks into hospital in the company of journalists. In *Terror of the Autons* (in which the Doctor is attacked by a phone), the evil threat is to be transmitted via radio signals. *The Caves of Androzani* is a tangled web of false messages broadcast by Sharaz Jek, Chellak and Morgus, around which people lose their identities, being replaced by replicas.

Holmes often sends up television: for instance, Runcible's witless political reporting in *The Deadly Assassin*. His ultimate metaphor for television is the Miniscope in *Carnival of Monsters*. A box in the corner of the room, it is distrusted by Inter Minor's grey-faced rulers (who are in favour of public service broadcasting), bringing colour and a ruthless commercial profit motive (as the bureaucrats predict, it also unleashes monstrous dangers on society). Prefiguring *Survivor*, it is the location into which our heroes are dropped and forced to survive. Like people in "reality TV", the Doctor and Jo are "livestock" to be exploited for commercial gain; as Jo puts it, "outside, there are creatures just looking at us for kicks?" The Doctor is appalled: "Roll up, roll up, roll up and see these funny little creatures in their native habitat! Poke 'em with a stick and make 'em jump!" There are many delightful TV in-jokes. In a sniggeringly simplistic portrayal of TV violence's corrupting effects, Vorg turns a dial to show that "the peaceful Tellurians can be made to behave in an amusingly violent way". This followed the controversy over *Terror of the Autons*, in which Holmes' wish to "frighten the little buggers" resulted in primetime asphyxiation. His overzealousness in the carnage department, particularly the blood and guts of *The Brain of Morbius* and the drowning sequence in *The Deadly Assassin*, excitingly pushed the limits but left the show open to "clean-up" TV campaigners, press criticism and an institutional crackdown. This is one of the few criticisms of Holmes to stand up, along with his apparent racism; take the "inscrutable Orientals" in his work on the treatment for the film *Invasion* and *The Talons of Weng-Chiang*.

*Carnival of Monsters* is also an entertaining examination of *Doctor Who*'s relationship with its audience. Vorg and Shirna arrive with a faulty machine just like the Doctor and Jo, and the fact that they appear on a production line might be a comment on the writing process. "Roll up, roll up and see the monster show!" Vorg announces, saying the Drashigs are "great favourites with the children". The crew of the SS *Bernice* are trapped in repetitive scenes shot slightly differently, which could be a statement on such formulaic drama as *Doctor Who*. Jo spends the story being captured, escaping and being re-captured; she acknowledges this pattern now ("here we go again!"), but by the next story has to accept it with a straight face. Jo points out that "they're saying exactly the same things as before", but is herself soon asking "What's happening, Doctor?" once again. The monster attacks on the SS *Bernice*, which the crew soon can't remember, may be an ironic comment on *Doctor Who*'s format, and its audience's response: an interruption to the mundane that is quickly forgotten.

In many of Holmes' scripts, the story turns on characters becoming self-aware, reasserting their ideology after noting the constructedness of the landscape around them. In *The Deadly Assassin*, the Doctor survives the Matrix by asserting that "I deny this reality". However, he cannot inspire this process in *Carnival of Monsters*, as none of the Miniscope's "exhibits" are ever fully aware of their fictionality. Often, the homogenisation threatened by monsters is an extension of the society they are attacking. In *The Ark in Space*, the Wirrn threaten a society that has homogenised itself. Man's "chosen" descendents have "eliminated" all "regressive transmitters" through ethnic cleansing. So, the sleepers (in their functional boxes) are in danger from "the infrastructure" (a social threat personified in the Wirrn). Noah, the humans' Prime Unit (whom Libri won't disobey), becomes the Wirrn's Swarm Leader (a term repeated from *Spearhead from Space*), and they too blindly follow him into space. As in *The Quatermass Experiment* (Holmes' debt to / borrowing from Nigel Kneale is too big a subject to tackle here), the human struggles against his takeover and ultimately sacrifices himself, motivated by "some vestige of human spirit". So, although Holmes' scripts call for self-awareness, Noah is just one of his characters to find it a painful process. In the Auton stories, those who escape the control of the Nestenes or the Master die. In *The Ribos Operation* and *The Mysterious Planet*, characters who seek outside knowledge are belittled. Most disturbingly, in *The Two Doctors*, when Chessene becomes self-aware and rejects Androgum augmentation, it is an act of bestial regression which leads her to lick up blood.

Often, individual consciousness is restricted by the state or by society, making Holmes *Doctor Who*'s most political writer. In *The Sun Makers*, the state engenders conformity, as much through the media's propagation of economic consensus as through the release of mind-numbing gas. The Doctor appropriates the means of communication, transmitting false messages to incite revolution among an oppressed factory proletariat. There's something sneakily subversive about *The Sun Makers*, the delicious idea of leftie revolutionary politics being transmitted to millions of young people during a primetime family action show. Ultimately, though, it's more a comedy about the tax system, as its misquote of Marx ("What've you got to lose?" / "Only your claims!") shows. Holmes is of course using the standard *Who* trope of overthrowing oppressors, but, as Philip MacDonald noted, when Terrance Dicks novelised the scene in which the Gatherer is gleefully murdered by cheering rebels, he toned it down so that the rebels "turned away in disgust" with the "feeling things had got out of hand, gone a bit too far". In fact, the conflict between capitalism and workers' rights is a common thread running through Holmes' work. Take *Spearhead from Space*, in which the menace comes from the automation of a factory, with the Autons uniformed drone servants, a workforce made passive (as General Scobie points out, you "don't get machines going out on strike"). Another android workforce appears in *The Caves of Androzani*, an explicitly political script with Thatcherism embodied in Morgus, using unemployment and (Falklands?) war as political tools, while asset-stripping industry. People are as much a commodity as the guns and spectrox. Throughout his scripts, power relations are defined by ownership and value, scarcity and plenty, but here he also topically challenges the allegiances of powerful multinational corporations.

Examine the essence of Holmes' work and you find the template for what fans see as "good" *Doctor Who*: pacey narrative, sharp one-liners, idiosyncratic characterisation, and the triumph of human individualism over the hive mentality. This is unsurprising, as Holmes set that template as script editor during its most successful period, establishing a restricted but hugely entertaining formula. But how to gauge the impact of Holmes' script-editorship? More than in many other dramas, the *Doctor Who* script editor could have a powerful influence on the programme's long-term development. Holmes wrote some of his best scripts to cover the failure of other writers to meet a deadline or provide workable scripts, but he also rewrote scripts by other writers to varying degrees (note, for instance, the relationship with other writers on *The Ark in Space*, *Pyramids of Mars* or *The Brain of Morbius*). To fully assess Holmes' contribution, it would be necessary to analyse the stories he script edited as fully as the ones he wrote, but it's clear that he left his mark not only on his entire period on the show but also in much of *Doctor Who* to come.

# On Being Cruel to an Electron in a Particle Accelerator

**by Robert Smith?**
*From Enlightenment #115, April / May 2002*

Douglas Adams was easily the most famous person associated with *Doctor Who*, in any capacity. His contribution to the show was contemporaneous with his period of greatest creative output; it's hard to picture the man we know as famous for missing deadlines working at a frenetic pace to salvage Season Seventeen dissolving around him while simultaneously writing and producing the *Hitchhiker's* radio plays and novels.

On paper, his contribution to the series isn't much greater than that of Donald Tosh or Peter Bryant. A brief script-editing stint and writing a couple of stories and then he was gone for good. Furthermore, both *City of Death* and *Shada* were co-written affairs that didn't feature his name (the latter not even being transmitted), while *The Pirate Planet* was heavily rewritten from its original six episode submission. Even for the

Season Seventeen lovers among us, it's clear that the only reason we give his contribution the level of respect we do is because of his later fame.

And yet, the brilliance is there if we look for it. *The Pirate Planet* is a case in point, taking the fairly mundane quest for the Key to Time and spinning it in an astonishingly outrageous way. A hollow planet that leapfrogs about the galaxy sucking the life out of other planets is a mind-boggling idea. Not one writer in a million could have come up with that. Yet it absolutely fits into the universe of *Doctor Who*, especially the universe that was the Tom Baker comedy science-fiction show. What's more, the story doesn't just hit us with one huge idea and leave it at that, it's positively overflowing with them. Time dams, the latent telepathy of the Mentiads, anti-inertia travel tubes, the segment being nothing less than an entire planet, it's all here and it's huge stuff.

Then there's the captain, possibly the cleverest supporting character ever created for the show. A shouting, ranting, blustering fool who is actually carrying out an extremely subtle and complex plan to defeat the true villain is sheer brilliance. All that stuff with Mr Fibuli being his friend was inserted by the script editor and you can tell. Bruce Purchase's overacting spoils the effect somewhat, but it's still a concept that shines through.

> **The Pirate Captain (Zanak):** A man who would not know what to do if he took over the universe, as he would only end up shouting at it. His great engineering feat was hollowing out the planet Zanak and filling it with engines so it could dematerialize throughout the universe and smother other planets for minerals, though this was actually a ruse for using the planetary gravitic fields to keep some time dams going to keep an old harpy alive for just another few seconds... Why he did this just goes to prove how mind-bogglingly stupid some people can be.

Mind you, the cliffhangers aren't much to write home about, suggesting that Adams didn't quite have the hang of the *Doctor Who* format. It's a pity episode two didn't end with the shock revelation of Zanak's true nature, instead of the more mundane double-danger cliffhanger. Episode three's cliffhanger is the best of the bunch, but mainly for the fact that it ends with the villains' laughter rather than the Doctor's fall (although the resolution is delicious). The technobabble ending almost works, but "almost" isn't good enough after what we've seen thus far. The real problem is the fact that Zanak's next victim is (boringly) Earth, which drags the story down to the level of lesser *Who* writers.

It's even more of a pity we didn't get the comedy cliffhangers of *The*

*Hitchhiker's Guide to the Galaxy*, although it's probably fair to say that Adams cut his teeth on the science-fiction cliffhanger format with *Doctor Who*. The character of Ford Prefect was a deliberate reaction to the fourth Doctor, being the type of guy who, when faced with saving the universe or going to a party, would go to the party every time. (Although you can't help but wonder if Ford was based in part on Tom Baker.)

Only two script editors were chosen by their producers after a single story submission. It remains one of the eternal mysteries of life that John Nathan-Turner chose Eric Saward over, say, Christopher Bailey, but it surprises no one that Douglas Adams was chosen based on his single script.

Even so, the first half of Season Seventeen was a production night-mare, with planned scripts falling through and a hastily reshuffled film-ing schedule, which led to Adams having direct involvement in the fin-ished product of a number of stories. Adams' fingerprints are all over Terry Nation's script of *Destiny of the Daleks*, which is a combination you'd have thought would never have worked. Oddly, this Terry Nation / Douglas Adams script is actually the third least likely hybridisation of all time. I've seen Gary Russell's rewrite of *Shada*'s opening scenes and it's not pretty. And the existence of *Slipback* shows that if you want to be Douglas Adams, the secret is not to be Eric Saward.

Many people have speculated that if we knew exactly why the three least likely hybrid stories of all time involve Douglas Adams, then we should know a lot more about the universe than we do now.

*City of Death* is, of course, the jewel in Adams' *Doctor Who* crown. It's the one story that even Season Seventeen haters like. It's the only Season Seventeen story that catered to the traditional strengths of *Doctor Who* production, with lovingly detailed period sets, a present-day setting, a monster convincingly realised as an actor in a mask and only two scenes of model work (although it still went to Paris!). You can almost see Williams and Adams writing the script with one eye on the budget... and this detracts from it not in the slightest, allowing the wit and the ideas to shine through.

The story is best remembered for Tom Baker at his funniest, but it's also astonishingly clever. Scarlioni threatening the Doctor via the Parisian telephone book is suave, funny and entirely believable. The art theme is one of the best integrated themes in any *Doctor Who* story, ever. Then there's the sublime way the story conflates beautifully into a single punch at the end. The plot has that mix of outrageous Adams ideas and wry comments on life: there might be seven Mona Lisas, twelve Scaroths splintered throughout time and the creation of all life as we know it, but Scarlioni's complex and sophisticated time-travelling plan is limited by the fact that he doesn't quite have the budget for it all. That's hilarious... and a telling comment on the series into the bargain.

**Scaroth (Last of the Jagaroth):** Last survivor of a warrior race, with the ability to splinter himself across the timeline when his ship exploded on a lifeless planet. Which is, when you think about it, a rather nifty ability to have at parties, or when you can't afford to settle the bill at a particularly expensive restaurant.

The remainder of Season Seventeen camps itself up further and further until it ends in triumph with *The Horns of Nimon*. The one featuring a race of giant bulls constructing black holes to leapfrog across the galaxy while conning lesser races with promises of glory if only they can pay for it all. The one that has some of the wittiest jokes in the entire series.

Yep, *Horns* was script-edited by Douglas Adams all right.

Then there's *Shada*, shortly to be seen with extra fanwank and unconvincing graphics in an online broadcast near you. Never transmitted and never officially novelised, it was nonetheless accidentally released on video thanks to JN-T's audacity (like Radar on *M\*A\*S\*H*, JN-T apparently handed Adams a whole bunch of otherwise unremarkable things to sign and slipped the *Shada* video release in among them). It too features the trademark Adams ideas, on this occasion tackling Time Lords as university dons, invisible spaceships and a book with time running backwards over it. Plus, there are witty lines like the universe being worthless as a piece of real estate and jokes about undergraduates.

**Salyavin (AKA Professor Chronotis, Cambridge):** Escaped criminal who spent centuries living as a university don, disguising his time machine as a college room and being very confused about how many sugars people took in their tea. He had the ability to project his own mind onto others and take them over, which could be rather useful in a tight spot, such as convincing the airline hostess to bring you extra peanuts on an especially long flight.

With the end of Season Seventeen, Adams was off to pursue fame, fortune and glory as *The Hitchhiker's Guide to the Galaxy* took off in earnest. His success saw the end of his involvement with *Doctor Who*, and his time on the show relegated to his author biographies, alongside his stints as a chicken-shed cleaner and bodyguard. And then he became even more famous and stopped listing any of them. His three stories remain unnovelised to this day (not counting the first *Dirk Gently* book), although a novelisation of his unmade film *Dr Who and the Krikkitmen* appears in the form of the third *Hitchhiker's* novel, with Slartibartfast taking the Doctor's role and Arthur Dent as the companion.

*Doctor Who* was a pretty minor stepping stone for Douglas Adams, but his style was almost perfectly suited to the era of the show he script-edited. He gave us stories that were bigger, smarter and funnier than anything else around them and showed us that *Doctor Who* really was only limited by the imagination. Douglas Adams was a rare genius in our time and we were extremely fortunate to have had his presence light up our series and show us that it could be better than we could possibly imagine. Even if only for a little while.

# Dave's 7

**by Nick May**
*From Shockeye's Kitchen #13, October 2002*

After a while, the seasoned *Doctor Who* viewer will be able to tell you that the moment someone mentions peaceful coexistence, you're watching a story penned by Malcolm Hulke. Similarly, you can tick off Eric Saward or Terry Nation's staple narrative ingredients as you go along once you've picked up the knack, regardless of which era they're writing for. Even the venerable Robert Holmes' twin fixations of horror and humour permeate all he writes. In all these cases, these men have written classics for more than one era of *Doctor Who* without altering their personal agendas.

What to say then of David Whitaker, writer of some of the show's earliest classics? Whitaker was the series' first-ever script editor and wrote seven stories that span a range of styles throughout the show's first seven years. What Whitaker had was an uncanny knack for evoking the feel of whichever era he was writing for. One only has to look at the disjointed, surreal *The Edge of Destruction* not as the fifty minute, nonsensical false start that it could be construed as, but as a pseudo-allegory on the uncertain direction of *Doctor Who* as a series back in the early days. It doesn't seem to go anywhere but still manages to go off on every tangent possible. Hardly surprising, for the purely educational history and science series of nine weeks previous was suddenly faced with the fact that everything that it was never supposed to be had just made it famous. If *The Edge of Destruction* was a bit of a mish mash on screen, it was almost certainly as disjointed at the production meetings that led up to it.

*The Rescue* is nowhere near as allegorical or inventive; it is pretty much episodes seven and eight of *The Dalek Invasion of Earth*, allowing for a happy upbeat ending as the Doctor gets a substitute for granddaughter, Susan. But the same cannot be said of David's next effort. In 1965's *The Crusade*, Whitaker uses one of the lynchpins of the show's output (the historical story) to subvert one of its other lynchpins (the overuse of moral absolutes). The good Thals against the evil Daleks, Marco Polo being an all-round top bloke because he's the key historical figure. Whitaker turns this on its head. Both sides have exponents of reason (Saladin, Joanna) and aggression (El Akir, the Earl of Leicester). Both sides want to end the war and motives vary from person to person, so whose side does the viewer settle on? "Show me a conflict throughout history," the Doctor says at the end of the novelisation, "where neither side believes that they are, in their own right, completely justified." Thus we have, for the first time in *Doctor Who*, the issue of across-the-board, ideological struggles being fought, and not just two homogenous factions duking it out until the Doctor sorts it out.

Paving the way for writers like Malcolm Hulke and Barbara Clegg in future series, David Whitaker used his stories and situations to highlight mankind's folly at the height of its excess. There are no two better examples of this than his two Dalek stories for Patrick Troughton's first season. In *The Power of the Daleks*, he takes Terry Nation's one-dimensional creations and not only gives them a bit more savvy than zapping a couple of natives and becoming default leaders of the planet, he turns them into the tokens that destroy an entire colony. Not in their usual manner, but by exposing the greed of several of the colony's key players, who pay with their lives for their ambition when the Daleks have everything they needed.

Similarly, *The Evil of the Daleks* shows the depths that humans (and the Doctor) will go to, willingly or otherwise, in order to survive and, in some cases, prosper, using the series' most evil race as a yardstick. Or a mirror. But what is more important is that, as the series moved along, so David Whitaker's style progressed with it. Once the Troughton era got into full swing, a radically different series emerged. The history and the often-fairytale science fiction had been superseded by thrillers and Hammer Horror. But, like *The Crusade*, Whitaker's next effort would stand out from the rest of that season like a sore thumb. Quite a cool sore thumb, mind...

Falling between *The Ice Warriors* and *The Web of Fear*, *The Enemy of the World* is notable for more reasons than just a lack of monsters. Once again, the "us against them" ideology of a lot of then-contemporary *Who* is turned on its head. The duplicity of politicians and the lengths people in power will go to stay on top are all dealt with through the Doctor's struggle with Salamander. Salamander's struggle with a convincing South American accent can wait until another time, but the story does take up the gauntlet where *The Crusade* left off, reminding us that our supposed public guardians are just more discreet. In one way, it's repetition, in another it just shows that things never really change. In the millennium between the two stories, human nature hasn't really altered. The man who secretly agrees to marry his sister to his enemy's brother to cement his position has evolved into the man who keeps a secret society in slavery to maintain his power over the world at large. As long as lies and duplicity seem the better option, there will always be people ready to take up the challenge of the power game.

*The Wheel in Space* is an underrated piece of monster-era *Who*. As well as an allegory on blind devotion to schedules and logic, this is David Whitaker's finest attempt at "going native" in an era's production scheme. The allegory takes, if not second place, then level-pegging with some fantastic horror set pieces: the "birth" of the Cybermen on the *Silver Carrier*, the blank-eyed Cybermats swarming to attack a terrified crewman. Whitaker tackles with aplomb the staple elements of the Troughton era: possessed crewmen, implacable monsters and a desperate team of stranded humans. For once, there is no alternative to the moral absolute, no allegory. The Cybermen are bad news and if the crew won't listen to the Doctor they've had it. Simple, but effective.

It would be interesting to see the original scripts for *The Ambassadors of Death*, David Whitaker's swansong. Dealing as it did with the possibility of peaceful coexistence, but not as Derrick Sherwin saw it, *Ambassadors* was re-written by peaceful coexistence guru and script editor's friend, Malcolm Hulke. Some of Whitaker's staple ideas remained. The ideological split within the accepted factions and the "alien menace" as a metaphor for human ambition are pure Whitaker. The scripts and his unfinished novelisation of *The Enemy of the World* (there's no Victoria and Salamander survives to stand trial at the end) would be interesting curios for what would have been next for *Doctor Who*'s most overlooked exponent of classic stories.

# The Rise, Fall and Decline of John Nathan-Turner

**by Graeme Burk**

*From Enlightenment #110, June / July 2002*

John Nathan-Turner was probably the most photographed producer of *Doctor Who*, ever. After the Doctors and companions, he is arguably the most recognisable face of the series even though his only appearance in the series itself was a fleeting cameo behind a telephone kiosk in *Arc of Infinity*.

His visibility is partly due to the fact that he was incumbent producer just as *Doctor Who*'s fortunes were in ascendance in the early-to-mid-1980s. But I think there's more to it than that. Even with a brighter spotlight, that much exposure requires a conscious effort. Traditionally, when interviews were required for the breakfast news or when there was a bit of publicity to do for the tabloids, or when a US convention came calling, producers would often send their stars to act as spokespeople for the series. JN-T would send his stars, but he would send himself as well.

*Doctor Who* in the 1980s was all about John Nathan-Turner. More than the Doctors, he was the star of the programme. That was his blessing and his curse.

### Rise

*The Leisure Hive* episode one is one of the most stunning changes to the series since it switched to colour. The agenda is set from the first second of the program. A new version of the theme song. Completely new title graphics. A new logo for the programme. And then fade into a slow, artful, pan along Brighton Beach, lasting precisely one minute and thirty-eight seconds, to the strains of music that sound a bit like Philip Glass. And then there's a new TARDIS prop. And the Doctor now wears a new burgundy costume. And K9 blows up!

JN-T's predecessor, Graham Williams, was fond of talking about the "15% solution", which meant that viewers were prepared to accommodate changes of up to 15% every season over what was done before. With *The Leisure Hive*, John Nathan-Turner worked out an 80% solution. By the end of his first season, with the last of the scripts by writers of the old guard and a new Doctor, he would achieve a 100% solution.

All of a sudden, *Doctor Who* looks glossy, even stylish. There are sets with ceilings and cunning use of effects (the TARDIS materialises on Argolis during a tracking shot). There's a muted Tom Baker and Lalla Ward still bantering, but this time about the actual plot. And there's an episode ending that seems cinematic, in every sense of the word. Even the question marks on the Doctor's collar seem oddly appropriate.

Watching *The Leisure Hive* is watching a younger man (John Nathan-Turner was only 32 at the time!) who was desperate to make a mark on the series and to make a name for himself. Six years prior, Hinchcliffe and Holmes totally changed *Doctor Who*, but they changed it from within using the writers, directors and cast chosen by the previous regime to enable their agenda. John Nathan-Turner eschewed that completely, jettisoning everything that went before. There is no safe and conservative "15% solution"; that's a game played by older men, more established in their profession.

In less than 20 minutes, John Nathan-Turner had established himself. And his future looked bright.

**Fall**

*The Two Doctors* episode two rests at the midway point of the story made midway through production of the season midway through John Nathan-Turner's tenure on *Doctor Who*. And, by the midway point of that episode, we have references to past incarnations, past companions, Sontarans, Rutans, Gallifreyan respiratory bypass abilities and the Time Lords.

A year or so later, there would be a particularly dire – and, until 1999, unseen – sketch by French and Saunders made on the set of *The Trial of a Time Lord*. In it, a *Doctor Who*-like show is being taped, and Dawn and Jennifer are playing "Silurian" extras. They spend a lot the time holding an unfunny discussion not about the wobbly sets or even the (extremely) silly costumes, but instead about the gibberish past continuity. Says Jennifer: "I think the Questioner is a Silurian as well but she doesn't have any gills." Replies Dawn: "No she's a Theron. You see, they take human form once they pass through the Matrix... I think."

Part of me thinks they got the idea for this from watching *The Two Doctors*. Certainly, I kept thinking about their sketch while watching the Doctor and Dastari argue about the symbiotic nuclei within a Time Lord cell structure.

There are still the hallmarks from five years before: the production gloss (although there are no gorgeous directorial flourishes), the music, and the question-mark collars. The innovative style that shone in *The Leisure Hive* has faded into a house style, reflecting a producer locked in a daily grind. What innovations that do exist – like the increased humour and the 45-minute episodes – seem half-hearted at best.

One of the few innovations during the period that was not half-hearted was the casting and characterisation of Colin Baker's Doctor.

JN-T was particularly keen on casting Colin Baker in the role. Peter Davison once described the casting of Colin Baker as a "Truffaut-esque" choice on the part of Nathan-Turner. It's a fascinating remark that deserves unpacking. François Truffaut, a director from the "New Wave" of French cinema in the 1960s and 1970s, often created films featuring characters that stood in as alter egos for himself. Additionally, while he would occasionally cast himself in his films, often he would cast others with a similar physical type and acting style to play the roles Truffaut himself wanted to play.

Suddenly, the casting of Colin Baker makes perfect sense. We have the producer of *Doctor Who*, known for being narcissistic and cutthroat to some and loyal and caring to others, who displayed a flamboyant persona in public (and dressed for the part accordingly in Hawaiian shirts), casting a flamboyant actor to play a Doctor who can be narcissistic, cutthroat and caring (dressed, on the producer's instructions, in "totally tasteless" garb).

The sixth Doctor was, in many respects, John Nathan-Turner's own attempt at playing the Doctor.

*The Two Doctors* is the third annual jaunt to a location abroad (this time Seville). JN-T had been doing this to get the series out of rock quarries and get a publicity photo or two in the tabloids. *Doctor Who* was a soap opera under his producership, not just in terms of the increased internal continuity ("I'm a great believer in continuity – not just for fans, but also for the general viewer") but in terms of the publicity the series received. *Doctor Who* vied for column inches in the tabloids the same way *Coronation Street* did: arranging for photocalls, providing leaks to reporters, even coming up with false rumours ("The part has not been offered to anyone yet, but we shall be considering either sex").

Meanwhile, the series itself was reaching the black heart of an increasing trend towards grim, violent material that had been brewing ever since Season Nineteen. Episode two of *The Two Doctors* finds Shockeye hunting for Peri in order to prepare her for supper. There's some sadism thrown in for good measure as well. Shockeye killing and eating a rat on-camera in a pre-watershed timeslot is perhaps the nadir of this trend.

In retrospect, you can see the vultures circling around. Season Twenty-Two started off with 8.9 million viewers for *Attack of the Cybermen*. Episode two of *The Two Doctors* had 6 million. Three days after *The Two Doctors* episode two aired, it was announced that *Doctor Who* was being taken off the schedule for eighteen months.

It took a publicity campaign secretly organised by JN-T to ensure that the BBC would publicly guarantee its return. But it went disastrously wrong. The series did return, but in a diminished form. After John

Nathan-Turner was ordered to fire his alter-ego, Colin Baker, the BBC rescinded their promise to let Nathan-Turner move on to another pro-gramme. During the hiatus, Terence Dudley offered to produce the series and was turned down by the BBC. It seems the BBC was not willing to forgive *Doctor Who...* or John Nathan-Turner.

**Decline**

Knowing that this was the last episode of the last *Doctor Who* story pro-duced by John Nathan-Turner, and the last time the series was recorded as an ongoing series by the BBC, does not diminish the impact of *Ghost Light* episode three. Watching it is like viewing a totally different series to either *The Leisure Hive* or *The Two Doctors*. The Doctor's character is darker and has a completely different relationship to the other characters (and the audience). The story is more like a puzzle where the pieces fall together artfully, without any need for a melodramatic moment of reve-lation.

Curiously, the past continuity seems to have scaled back to be about the ongoing saga. In particular, *Ghost Light* is concerned with developing Ace's character and her backstory. This was odd, because JN-T had pre-viously objected to elaborate character development of companions, dis-liking the "soap opera flavour".

Many have suggested that by this point John Nathan-Turner's role in the series had devolved to mere custodial work, leaving the actual series development to script editor Andrew Cartmel. Indeed, one almost pic-tures JN-T as David Bowie's alien in *The Man Who Fell to Earth*, forcibly confined to *Doctor Who*, suffering the tortures of hostile timeslots, and reduced episodes and resources from a banal but polite BBC.

But this appraisal ignores JN-T's contribution to the final days of the series. While it's true that JN-T gave great latitude to his script editors, the fact is *Ghost Light* only became the script it was when JN-T vetoed Marc Platt's original story idea, *Lungbarrow*, which used the same central concept as the televised version, only featuring the Doctor's family on Gallifrey. Fans bitterly complain about JN-T's call regarding this, but it's clear he was doing his job, providing dramatic boundaries for the series.

JN-T made the series work within the miniscule resources it was given: splitting the Outside Broadcast work and the studio work for one story into two separate stories (*Ghost Light* was the studio component of that deal). It is thought that he rearranged the broadcast order of the stories that season in order to make sure their best effort, *The Curse of Fenric* – which was made first and should have been the season opener – received the exposure it deserved when the BBC made no effort to promote Season Twenty-Six.

Rather than sink into defeat after denial by the BBC to move him off the series, JN-T went back and, instead of producing more of the same, John Nathan-Turner did the unthinkable. He radically reformatted the series he had radically reformatted seven years before. New titles. New theme arrangement. New incidental music. New costume and Doctor. New script editor who brought in new writers, with new directors to complement them. (Director Alan Wareing brings the same visual verve to *Ghost Light* that Lovett Bickford brought to *The Leisure Hive.*) JN-T did the 100% solution once more, and *Ghost Light* is the culmination of that.

It should have been a victory for John Nathan-Turner, a return from the brink of ignominy. Unfortunately, it turned out to be a period of decline, aided by indifferent scheduling, indifferent promotion and an indifferent BBC. But Seasons Twenty-Five and Twenty-Six have an incredible cult following from fans, making the triumph qualitative in nature; even the quality broadsheets gave *Ghost Light* positive reviews.

Once the Victorian mansion sets for *Ghost Light* were struck, *Doctor Who* would never again be made in Television Centre. JN-T would parlay his association with the series into some steady jobs: turning out special videos for BBC Worldwide, supervising the first missing episode audios, setting *Doctor Who* specialist questions for *Mastermind*. But, even in the relatively thriving post-TV series market of the early 1990s, JN-T was yesterday's man. The fans he tried so hard to please during his tenure had now grown up and were tending to the legacy of *Doctor Who* themselves in the era of BBV's *The Stranger* videos, *Thirty Years in the TARDIS* and the New Adventures. *Dimensions in Time* marked the last official *Doctor Who* work JN-T did for the BBC. However, his departure from *Who* was a gradual fade into the oblivion of convention appearances.

It was a most unfitting conclusion.

On May 1, 2002, we lost the star of *Doctor Who* in the 1980s. Perhaps appropriate for a man who loved to share the spotlight with his lead actors, his story of being on *Doctor Who* is an epic three-act tale of triumph, adversity and bitter-sweet moral triumph at the end.

It would have been the sort of *Doctor Who* story John Nathan-Turner would have loved to produce.

# The Maloney Era

by Jim Sangster

*From Enlightenment #136, November 2006*

In 1977, when I was six years old, Davros was the most fearsome being in my universe. No, not the gnarl-faced, wheelchair-bound creator of the Daleks; John Davis, the toughest lad in the school, known to one and all as "Davros" Davis. He wasn't a bully, but he could handle himself and he had a short temper. Six years old and named after the most evil being ever seen in *Doctor Who*. That's how influential that show was when I was little. Later, in the 1980s, I was laughed at for even watching the show but, when I was approaching its target age range, everyone watched it.

As fans, we divide *Doctor Who* into eras: the Pertwee Era, the Davison Era, the Paul McGann bank holiday. The more production-minded of us might instead talk of the Innes Lloyd era, the Graham Williams era or (in rapturous tones) the Hinchcliffe era. We all know that we're experiencing a "New Golden Age" in the "RTD era" (or "He's back – and it's about Wales!"), just as we all know that the Hinchcliffe era was a previous occasion where, generally, it all fell into place and everyone was at the top of their game. We know this to be true, just as we know that it was because Hinchcliffe was partnered with a script editor who was of a like mind to terrify the kiddies into becoming a nation of bedwetters. We can't divide directors into eras, because few of them ever worked on more than two stories consecutively. However, for my money, the Hinchcliffe-Holmes era was made all the more successful because of three specific stories – *Genesis of the Daleks*, *The Deadly Assassin* and *The Talons of Weng Chiang* – all of which were helmed by David Maloney.

(We'll sidestep for the moment *Planet of Evil*, which, while a decent enough story, rarely tops any polls. A shame really, as it's got a stunning jungle set and the electronic monster effect is very well handled, but it's also got Prentis Hancock, so...)

We might all have our favourite individual Dalek adventures, but only over-familiarity with the tale could prevent anyone from accepting *Genesis* as pretty much the best of the bunch. Yeah, yeah, we know about the Troughton stories, but none of us has seen either of them complete since original transmission, so *Genesis* it is.

We know the old maxim "show, don't tell" and that's what *Genesis* – sorry, David Maloney – does from the very start. I don't think there are any other scenes in the 40-plus-year history of the series that so graphically depict the horrors of war as effectively as that opening shot of the soldiers being gunned down. But here's a question for you: which side are they from? Both sides cannibalise whatever uniforms and equipment they can find, to the point where sides are barely distinguishable. I've just watched the scene again and, while I might hazard a guess that they're Kaleds, I can't be sure. If you can't work out which side is being gunned down, that surely tells us a lot about the pointlessness of war.

Terry Nation often waxed lyrical about how, for *Genesis* at least, he was thinking of the Kaleds as Nazis. So we get all the actors in nice, neat, grey uniforms and shiny jack-boots. But, outside of the Kaled dome, it's clear we're in the trenches of World War I, although, again, it's not clear which side of No Man's Land we're on. History generally agrees that The Great War was an exercise in madness and wastage, and so the Kaled-Thal war mirrors that. I'm going to hazard a guess that, actually, we're supposed to feel sorry for the Kaleds and their insane leaders. The Kaled soldiers are our own, just as the innocent Tommies in Maloney's *The War Games* had been. When we see the Thals later on in the story, they're depicted as even more brutal than the Kaleds. They fire the first devastating shot (courtesy of Davros and Nyder), having exploited mutos and prisoners alike to load their rocket with a substance that is so toxic no Thal will allow themselves to touch it. Nasty.

You can see just how important that first shot of the story is, how its very basic theme of the pointlessness of war reverberates through the rest of the story, and how the imagery comes from David Maloney, not Terry Nation. I don't know for sure, but I doubt Nation went as far as to specify a freeze-frame for the cliffhanger where Sarah plummets to certain death (or just a grazed knee, one level down).

Ah, the freeze-frame cliffhanger. That's what got *The Deadly Assassin* into so much trouble later on, as first the Doctor is seen to gun down the President of the Time Lords and then, two weeks later, Mary Whitehouse was so traumatised by the image of Tom Baker drowning that she began a campaign against the show that lasted long after anyone else was watching. *Doctor Who* fans instantly decided that Mrs Whitehouse was wrong to pick on our favourite show and, when she died in 2001, I'm sure there were more than a few fans who thought "well, we won that one". Never mind the fact that shows such as *Big Brother* show that, to some extent, she'd been right all along to say "if you tolerate this, your children will be next" (no, wait, that was the Manic Street Preachers), she targeted *Doctor Who* as something abhorrent, something to be condemned.

The funny thing is, while all kinds of debauchery go on over on Channel 4 in the UK, with teenagers shagging, fighting and drinking themselves sick live on *Big Brother* in the name of entertainment, *Doctor*

*Who* has in fact been affected by Mary Whitehouse's crusade; the BBC is no longer allowed to show the kind of Kensington gore that *The Brain of Morbius* gave us in the same timeslot!

So, if Mary was our nemesis, Philip Hinchcliffe, Robert Holmes and – yes! – David Maloney became our champions. They'd given us war, they'd given us graphic violence and for their swansong together, they gave us prostitution, institutionalised racism (and I don't mean the Chinese; I'm talking about the depiction of the Irish as stupid, cowardly drunks!), they gave us, in short, the story that possibly represents every single facet of the *Doctor Who* we know and love. *The Talons of Weng Chiang* has a sumptuous period setting, a complicated story, a sinister villain, an over-ambitious monster that doesn't quite work and a Doctor who we have absolutely no doubts about: he's in charge and will win the day.

How much of this is down to David Maloney? I don't care, to be honest. I'm possibly one of the few who is slightly disappointed that 2Entertain and BBC New Media came up with the idea of animating missing Troughtons, simply because my two favourite stories of that time will probably be pushed back in the release schedules now. *The Krotons* has many faults but, as the first Troughton story I saw (thanks to the "Five Faces of *Doctor Who*" season back in 1981), I adore it out of all proportion. True, the central aliens are a clumsy, unwieldy example of poor design work, but they're handled very well by the director. There are lots of innovative flourishes and generally it all rattles along at a fair old pace.

But *The Krotons* is not the most unfairly maligned story of the time either. Just because Target Books managed to novelise *The War Games* to the same page count as *Planet of Evil*, a story two-fifths its length, some fans (pah – fans?) have assumed that it was the original story that was padded, rather than the novelisation that was lacking. They'll see, when *The War Games* finally gets its much-deserved DVD treatment, that it's one of the most complex and perfectly structured stories ever; the onion layers that are peeled back each week to show that the villain is merely a subordinate of another villain, who in turn reports to someone else who is so powerful that the Doctor cannot defeat him and must... well, you know.

Again, I don't know how much of the production's brilliance is down to Maloney or whether it just happened that everyone fell into position because of the superb script from Terrance Dicks and Malcolm Hulke. All I can tell is that *The War Games* is yet another story at the top of my personal favourites that was directed by David Maloney.

I met him a couple of times at conventions in the late 1990s. Charming, easy-going and very good company. I told him about my school's champion brawler, how the images he shot had marked a generation (for the better, I should stress) and how so many of his stories figured so highly in fan favourites. He knew – about his popularity, at least – but went on to talk about Michael Wisher's performance, Philip Hinchcliffe's support and all those scripts that had benefited from being torn apart by Bob Holmes. Modest too.

It's sad that his talents will possibly be appreciated more now that he's no longer with us, but that they're appreciated at all is some comfort.

# CROSSING MIDNIGHT

1960s *Doctor Who* was defined by odd, askew, pop-art-before-pop-art design (look at the Daleks, Raymond Cusick's design, the entirety of *The Seeds of Death*). 1970s *Doctor Who* was defined by bright, bold colours and soft-focus filmic horror (look at Michael E. Briant's direction, Robert Holmes' scripts, the entirety of *The Stones of Blood*).

What of the 1980s, then?

*Doctor Who Magazine* published one of the most spirited defences (and explanations) of the decade in their "Watcher's Guides" to the fifth Doctor in *DWM* #411. "Britain in the early 1980s was a curious place, juggling shiny computerised futurism with soft-focus heritage-industry nostalgia... meanwhile the pop charts, ever a barometer of *Doctor Who*'s house style, were fusing futuristic sounds with swashbuckling historical foppery and glassy cocktail-bar chic... with the relatively newfangled phenomenon of rock video busy establishing itself at the cutting edge of experimental techniques in effects and art direction, it's scarcely surprising that some of the most memorable music clips from those avant-garde days bear such a preposterously close resemblance to the very things *Doctor Who* was doing at the same time." Thus Peter Davison's *Doctor Who* easily fits in a world of *Chariots of Fire* and videos by Visage, Adam and the Ants, and Kate Bush.

The plastic sheen, the nascent attempt at branding by giving identifiable costumes to the lead characters, the expansion into soap opera, the synthesised music; all these things perfectly reflect the decade it happened in. Even *Doctor Who*'s foray into grimmer realities – Rula Lenska's character, Styles, in *Resurrection* points out that the purpose of her whole existence is to blow herself up to stop the Daleks – is not out of place in a decade where the nuclear doomsday clock was at three minutes to midnight. The Doctor belonged on Varos and Karfel and Thoros Beta because, at the time, we did too.

The thing about the 1980s in *Doctor Who* is that it's a decade with a single producer and yet it's more complex: a series of often-overlapping sub-eras-within-eras based on script editors, actors playing the lead role, actors playing the companion and the whims of the BBC hierarchy. Probably more than any other decade in *Doctor Who*'s history, the program evolved at an accelerated rate – like *Ghost Light*'s Control – from a hard-SF serial to an adventure show with grim undertones to an adventure show with grim *overtones* to a whimsical science-fantasy show to a groundbreaking though somewhat flawed show that combined all of the above and turned its central character into someone bigger and more mysterious than we thought. *Doctor Who* did all that between 1980 and 1989.

The trouble with writing about "the 1980s" in *Doctor Who* is that you need to specify *which* 1980s. But isn't that also true of a decade that began with Rubik's Cube and Soft Cell, and ended with U2 and the 386 IBM Clone? *Doctor Who* was, as ever, just along for the ride.

# Don't You (Forget About Me)

by Sean Twist
*From Enlightenment #117, August / September 2003*

Of course the eighties were the best. Not only was it the last decade in which you could watch Duran Duran's "Hungry Like The Wolf" without irony, it was – for me – the high point of *Doctor Who*. I've always felt that one of the major bits of magic about *Who* is the element of change. For ten (occasionally) glorious years, *Who* was all about change – from Doctors and approaches to companions – finally culminating in the biggest change in the series' history: it vanished from our screens.

The eighties also represented the last decade in which I enjoyed the show by myself. I wasn't viewing the show through the prism of collective fandom, coming to each episode loaded down with several judgments before the logo flashed blue-white onto the screen. In fact, I hardly knew anyone who had heard of the show, let alone watched it. So my time with the Doctor from 1980 to 1990 was spent in the Southwestern Ontario snowbelt, trying to catch the TVOntario signal with a flailing television aerial, or hunched in front of a small television in a series of crap apartments. It is a testament to these fandom-free viewings that I actually thought *Time-Flight* was quite good. And I still do, damn you all.

But, getting back to the eighties... the one element that does connect *Doctor Who* to the pop culture of the time was the aforementioned element of change. This was especially evident in British music, as punk rock cleared its throat after its initial growl. The long-hair, prog-rock indulgences of the seventies now stared uneasily at the spitting fury of The Clash. Robert Smith (not our Robert Smith? – the other, less famous one) wore makeup on stage, singing songs about depression, while The Jam declared war on British complacency. Change was in the air, on the airwaves, and it couldn't help but manifest in *Who*.

*Logopolis* really depicted the end of the seventies in *Who*, courtesy of gravity and a very tall radio telescope. The lovable, lunatic fourth Doctor regenerated and everything changed. With his long hair, eccentricity and possibly chemically induced smile, the fourth Doctor could easily have passed as a roadie for Yes. His replacement represented the first of many changes in store for the show. Fortunately, this change worked: instead of a middle-aged Doctor, we had ourselves a young'un.

Peter Davison, looking positively lost in the jacket and scarf of his predecessor, brought a fresh energy to the show. Outfitted in a cricket jacket and scarf that screamed summer afternoons and tea, he still emanated the glow of Dear Old Blighty that is important in maintaining the show's magic. With his slight frame and gentleness, the fifth Doctor would not have looked out of place fronting a New Romantic band.

Teamed with Tegan and Nyssa, this Doctor formed my ultimate TARDIS team. (Yes, yes, there was Adric, but not for long.) Tegan's spark, Nyssa's strained innocence, along with the fifth Doctor's ancient soul peering out through a young man's eyes, made the TARDIS seem more like a home than it had since the Troughton era. It was – and let me say now that your sniggering doesn't hurt – sweet.

But more change was to come. *Earthshock* saw the death of a companion: Adric. Regardless of how you feel about it this event (joy, amusement or just mild happiness), it did introduce a new element into what had been a rather reassuring mythology: the Doctor can't always win. Sometimes, bad things can happen.

Undeniably more powerful than Adric's death itself was Tegan's reaction in the following story, *Time-Flight*. She demands the Doctor go back in time to rescue Adric. Deeply upset himself, the Doctor knows he can't break the laws of Time. "Don't ever ask me to do anything like that again!" he says, the pain evident in his voice. A wonderful moment! Suddenly, the universe is darker. Violence – and loss – has struck the TARDIS crew. Nothing is as safe as it was.

This violence rises again in *Resurrection of the Daleks*. Surrounded by Daleks, death and harsh brutality, Tegan herself leaves the TARDIS, unable to stomach any more. Her departure scene remains my favourite *Who* moment of all time: it's unexpectedly moving, both from Tegan's tears and the look of complete shock on the Doctor's face. Soon, the violence that sickened Tegan will also reach out and claim the fifth Doctor as well.

But not before another change, this one ill-advised. In *Planet of Fire*, we are introduced to a new companion, Peri Brown. Now granted, at the time, I wasn't complaining. A cute brunette, all curves, introduced to viewers in a bikini. But poor Peri has "marketing research" written all over her: busty to attract the casual male viewer, American to attract the North American audience, and... we did mention busty, didn't we? What was wrong with Peri (now thankfully redeemed by Big Finish audios, authors and Ms Bryant herself) was simple: her character wasn't subtle. She seemed created simply to pander to people who weren't watching *Doctor Who* anyway. As a result, the audience didn't like her, the Doctor seemed mystified by her and Peri had no resort but to start whining.

At this point, *Who* seemed to be on shaky ground. Then the Doctor sacrifices himself in *The Caves of Androzani*, another grim tale in which rubber monsters seem an afterthought and machine guns rule the day. Gone is the beloved fifth Doctor, dying to save a companion destined for a level of popularity not seen since the Adric days.

The subtle change seen in Davison's casting as the Doctor in *Logopolis* was thrown out the creative window when *The Twin Dilemma* aired. Colin Baker's loud, jarring portrayal of the sixth Doctor probably looked good on paper; perhaps even better after a few drinks. In reality, it flopped. Everything about the new approach – from Baker's mood swings to his patchwork coat – did not so much hint at change as threaten the viewer with grievous bodily harm. Gone was the idea of the TARDIS as a comfort zone, gone was the idea of the Doctor as a gentle soul. Now he was just a jerk, stuck in a loveless TARDIS with a woman who wasn't sure whether to hug him or claw his eyes out.

At this point, for me, the mythology of the show began to list. It was now I began to see that I was watching a show, with actors, and was not really able to suspend my disbelief. I began to notice the sets more – and boy, did they look cheap. Granted, it was evident Colin Baker was trying, as was Nicola Bryant, with scripts that would challenge Hepburn and Olivier. But, even with episodes like *Revelation of the Daleks* that seemed to at least aim the show in the right direction, there was always the feeling that maybe next time they'd get it right. Hopefully.

They didn't. Even with the bloated mélange of *The Trial of a Time Lord* – a desperate attempt to link cancellation-fear reality with the show's bruised mythology – it was apparent the magic was lost. I still have no idea how the show ended, and had to turn to the novels to determine Peri's fate.

When the Doctor regenerated again (another fall, this time of about eight inches, apparently) in September 1987, the show looked worse than ever. *Time and the Rani* introduced Sylvester McCoy to the role, whose initial interpretation seemed to draw on Harpo Marx and spoon playing. The set looked like a failed Duran Duran video. Mel – played by sixth Doctor holdover and apparent star Bonnie Langford – screamed a lot.

It now became rather masochistic to keep watching, at least for me. How bad can it get? But then it began to surprise me. It wasn't the intro-duction of Ace (another marketing meeting character: "We need street cred! Slap some bird in a leather jacket and have her blow things up!"), but a new reintroduction to the Doctor's mythology. Since there was no money for sets, the show had to focus on the writing. *Remembrance of the Daleks* made this comical Doctor a figure to reckon with, especially since he now didn't mind committing planetary genocide. Suddenly, there were dark spots in the Doctor's history, areas perhaps even he didn't know about. Was he Merlin, as hinted in *Battlefield*? Would he be Merlin? Was this an alternate-universe Doctor? Now that's cool, I thought – and I still do, damn you!

In *The Curse of Fenric*, we had a Doctor who played games over deep time and even Ace discovered a deeper gravity to her character. (Just ignore the lame Oz reference.) Sure, maybe *Who* wasn't dazzling the senses, but the story of the Doctor and Ace was far more intriguing than anything I'd seen in years.

And then it ended. With a story about cats.

Of course it didn't end. You know that. But the screen did go dark, and except for a brief flicker six years later, has stayed that way.

The eighties for *Who* began with change for the better, and ended with change for the worse. But it also began with something else, something that it still has, despite the changes forced upon it. It still has hope. And, because we're fans, so do we.

# Turning Eighteen
by Ari Lipsey

When I was a wee lad of four or five, I became a fan of *Doctor Who*. But in Toronto, where I grew up, there were two distinct *Doctor Who*s as far as I was concerned. There was "weekday" *Doctor Who*, shown on the American PBS channel right before dinner. This *Doctor Who* had a bass-heavy theme tune and a brown colour scheme that ran from the title sequence into the episode. This was a *Doctor Who* of giant slugs that could freeze the movements of the Doctor's companion, and laughing ventriloquist dummies that cackled as they rode into the night. But there was also "weekend" *Doctor Who*. That was the one with the starfield and the upbeat music where the Doctor was young and blond and could visit any one of the stars you saw at the beginning.

I preferred "weekend" *Doctor Who*.

Most people don't, of course. It has to be said that most fans of the classic series tend to be in their 30s or 40s and were evolving into fans when the only game in town was "weekday" *Doctor Who*: the Hinchcliffe-Williams years. That's the template they grew up with: a universe full of mystery. The apex for this kind of *Doctor Who* is *The Talons of Weng-Chiang*, which finds the Doctor in the midst of his own brand of Sherlock Holmes story. As many a fan will tell you, *Talons* is the natural place to set a *Doctor Who* story. Which, to borrow the British phrase, is complete bollocks. You have a show whose concept is to travel anywhere in time and space, and its perfect setting is the well-tilled soil of Victorian England? Would *Talons* have felt as natural in the Pertwee years, or with William Hartnell as the Doctor? In actuality, *Talons* is a self-fulfilling prophecy. Hinchcliffe and company saw *Doctor Who* as a science-fiction version of Sherlock Holmes, just as Barry Letts saw it as a science-fiction version of James Bond. Robert Holmes simply "wrote to type".

That *Doctor Who* ends in Season Eighteen, the dawn of the JN-T years – or, as many 1970s fans think of it, the beginning of the end. I'm not going to try convince 1970s fans that 1980s *Who* was better, mostly because they would reflectively respond "cause it wasn't, mate". But I'd like to show them why some of us think 1980s *Who* was more fun and why Season Eighteen begins this transition as to what we 1980s fans think of as *Doctor Who*.

Let's get the first issue of contention out of the way: production values. In a review of *The Leisure Hive* in *About Time 4*, one of the authors relates an experiment where he took several people with no familiarity with *Doctor Who* and showed his test subjects ten minutes of *Nightmare of Eden* and then ten minutes of *The Leisure Hive*. The subjects who lived to tell the tale claimed they could see no discernable difference in "production values", which is contrary to everything we "real fans" assume to know about the John Nathan-Turner era. But a modern-day test audience unfamiliar with *Doctor Who* sees everything through a contemporary lens: everything from the 1970s and 1980s looks "cheap". The effects use the same analogue technology and both are shot substantially on video, something unfamiliar to anyone not watching soaps.

The *real* reason we as fans thought the production values were higher around the time had less to do with how the money was spent and more to do with the outlook of the new series, which matched with the changing values of the decade. Most cultural historians dismiss the 1980s as a time of soulless capitalism, but in terms of art, it was a period of epic storytelling. The *Star Wars* trilogy sprawled over an entire galaxy. Opera-scoped musicals were the hit of the West End. One of the culminations of this attitude by the end of the decade was the American television network ABC's decision to shell out $104 million on a mini-series called *War and Remembrance* (based on the Herman Wouk novel), which attempted to depict every major event in World War II from Midway to Auschwitz. By the late 1980s, it was assumed that this was the way it had to be done: there wasn't any point in doing a World War II epic unless every major event is covered.

*Doctor Who's* evolution was following along these lines; the "things lurking in the shadows" became too small and irrelevant. The opening credits of Season Eighteen are of a starfield, a vast expanse with worlds to explore that the viewer is traversing through. The 1970s had a tunnel of mysterious shapes. The Season Eighteen theme music had a faster tempo and higher notes. It's shifting the focus of the series from the monsters that you don't see to the planets you can.

*Doctor Who* has always been a show about a man travelling through time and space, but here the scope of the journey – rather than enigma of the destination – has become the central theme of the show. The earliest indication of this change in sensibility is the music. Dudley Simpson's scores of long notes evoking organ music have been replaced by synthesized, high-pitched harmonies. It's less unsettling and more inviting. The theme tune once again plays the middle eight, the highest notes in the theme, hinting at a universe of our hero's triumphs and where the love of adventure can flourish.

But it's more than just stylistic innovations. Consider that Season Eighteen is the first season where none of the stories take place primarily on Earth. (For the objector who's going to bring up *Logopolis*, take a moment to consider that *Logopolis* is the only story to solely bear the name of an alien planet up to this point, which might suggest where the writers were focused.) This is why the TARDIS is more brightly lit in Season Eighteen; it's a ship for explorers, not a magic cabinet whose secrets remain hidden from us. Every planet is a new world of sensory opportunity. In such a universe, monsters are almost an afterthought. Season Eighteen features more alien cultures than monsters. In three years of Graham Williams *Doctor Who*, there was one race of (non-menacing) aliens that did not look like humans: the Swampies. In Season Eighteen, we get at least three, arguably five: the yellow-haired, green-skinned Argolins; the hairy, feline-like Tharils; and the cranially enlarged Logopolitans. (Both the Marshmen and the Foamasi play the roles of monsters until their true intentions are revealed, so we could make a case for another two.)

Of course, change in a long running series doesn't happen abruptly. It's clear that the leading man, Tom Baker, wanted to return to a universe that seemed to revolve around his character, where aliens were simply foils for his cleverness, and he had complete command of the technobabble. But the story that's widely regarded as the gem of the season, *Warriors' Gate*, works precisely because the Doctor is thrust into a universe whose workings he's unfamiliar with. He knows nothing of the great empire of the Tharils, or the purpose of the Gundan robots. The story's most dramatic moment occurs when the Doctor believes that Biroc has abandoned him. Biroc tells the Doctor not to worry, and in this moment, the Doctor is put into the position he has put many others – namely, that of being told, "I've figured it out. Trust me and you'll get out of this." Another of these moments happens in *Logopolis*, when the Doctor – right before he confronts the Master – laments about how circumstance has foisted responsibility (including his companions) on him unwittingly. This would have been unthinkable a year before, when, in *The Horns of Nimon*, Baker was holding on tight to K9's head while the TARDIS was about to collide with an asteroid, and then started to laugh it off with a bunch of wizardry at the TARDIS controls.

But Baker's baggage proves too much. He's not going to have fun in this environment, nor is the character he constructed suited to it, so he has to go. What is remarkable is that his replacement is so young, but that's precisely what this universe needs: a young Doctor who'll be exploring space with us. It's worth noting that our young Doctor will have a cadre travelling with him – a departure from the format favoured for the last five years prior (and arguably ten of the last eleven years) where the Doctor has one female companion. Interestingly, 60s *Doctor Who* was also very concerned with planet-hopping and also had several companions travelling with the Doctor. This actually makes perfect sense. The James Bond / Sherlock Holmes sensibility makes the universe palatable for "assistants", but the galactic adventure needs genuine companions, more people to explore different facets of larger landscapes.

When the new series was announced in 2005, I often found that most of the trepidation over the stories being primarily Earthbound came from the 1980s *Doctor Who* fans. Many of us thought that if you have a craft that travels through time and space but barely use it to travel through the latter, what's the point in bothering? But while we fans could be demanding of such things, Russell T Davies had the responsibility of a budget. It's worth considering, however, whether he thought travelling to distant worlds was necessary. Davies was 17 when Season Eighteen first aired. His formative years were watching Pertwee-Baker era *Who*. For better and for worse, it shows.

# Authorship in the John Nathan-Turner Era

by Dave Rolinson

*From Time and Relative Dissertations in Space, 2007*

In a way, *Doctor Who* fans were ahead of academic debates on authorship. Fans didn't need to be told that drama series are a "producer's
medium", as they always periodised the programme by producer ("the
Hinchcliffe era") just as much as by leading actor ("the Hartnell era").
John Nathan-Turner's era is a useful case study because there were such
visible, often public, differences of opinion between the producer and
others in the production team, and because fans attributed the programme's initial success and eventual failure to the producer's personal
input in a way that addressed what a producer should or shouldn't do.

*Doctor Who* attributed authorship to writers in its opening titles (*"The
Leisure Hive...* by David Fisher"), but this practice obscured the extent to
which writers' space for individual expression was contested. For
instance, Jonathan Bignell and Andrew O'Day – in their book on Terry
Nation – observe that because *Doctor Who* was an ongoing, episodic
series, "an individual writer's storyline or script must contribute to the
overall whole of a programme" and, because it was part of the science-
fiction genre, writers were expected to employ "specified generic characteristics". In other words, the "personal signatures" of writers were subsumed within "generically coded formats". In *The Unfolding Text*, John
Tulloch and Manuel Alvarado contrasted the "Great Tradition" of television "artists" like Dennis Potter, who were seen to assert their individual
voices within "serious" play strands like *The Wednesday Play* (1964-70),
with "the 'craft' tradition" of "craftsmen" who were "enmeshed within
the cramping restrictions of a ratings-oriented industry". Tulloch and
Alvarado discuss the tensions between these traditions in the making of
*Kinda*, in which Christopher Bailey tried to "appropriate a space for
authorship" and "serious creativity", and *Warriors' Gate*, in which
Stephen Gallagher's autobiographical references were hidden "to the
producer's satisfaction" within the format.

Fans have always accepted the "craft" tradition, celebrating features
which might be seen as obstacles to "artists". In 1995, future *Doctor Who*
writer Matt Jones called Robert Holmes a "Mastercraftsman" and argued
that "the skill in writing" such "formula television" as *Doctor Who*
"comes from exactly how the ingredients in the formula are mixed".
Jones was operating within what Tulloch and Alvarado described as the
"space for authorship" that is "appreciated by fans" because it "works

within and expands the mythology of the institution". Therefore, fans responded to writers who adhered to the formula like Nation or Terrance Dicks – who once said that, in his New Adventures, unlike more experimental fellow novelists, "I'm still selling you steak and chips." Writers who combined a distinctive voice with an adherence to the formula were highly valued, like Holmes, Brian Hayles or Malcolm Hulke (whose book, *Writing for Television*, was clear about the function of writers in popular drama series). This reading of authorship is shaped by the acceptance that viewers of series, like spectators of genre cinema, derive pleasure from (in Tulloch and Alvarado's phrase) "novelty-within-convention": getting more of the thing you like but with interesting variations. If success is defined by the extent to which writers serve existing generic features, to an extent writers both write *Doctor Who* and are written by *Doctor Who*.

However, there are problems with the opposition between "craftsmen" and "artists". Writing about Dennis Potter, Rosalind Coward disputed the use of the "author" construct, imported from other disciplines such as English Literature, because the idea of "transparent communication" between authors (even in "serious" drama) and audiences is oversimplistic. Literary study must respond to Roland Barthes' discussion of the Death of the Author: instead of simply working out what the author intended or researching their lives as the key to understanding their work (and vice versa), we move towards the Birth of the Reader, where readers are not passive receivers of an artist's directly transmitted vision, but are instead active participants in the creation of meaning. Added to this, the specific working conditions and reception of film or TV productions cause further trouble. *Doctor Who* fans know so much about the programme's inherent collaboration and resist critical readings of the programme by repeating as a mantra (often over-defensively, to the point of obstructive anti-intellectualism) its populist, entertainment remit (as if entertainment and seriousness are somehow separate genres).

Despite these restrictions, we still discuss *Doctor Who*'s authors. Tulloch and Alvarado noted that, within the "continuity of professional concerns" there is still a "variety of signatures". Fanzines have isolated individual figures for study, aware of the differences between stories written by Dicks and Douglas Adams or directed by Graeme Harper and Fiona Cumming. One of the consequences of fandom's displacement of the "canon" inadvertently established by Jeremy Bentham during the growth of organised fandom in the 1970s has been the re-evaluation of individual contributors. *DWM* has interviewed and profiled individuals, including Philip Macdonald's features on Hulke and Holmes. Academic books have slowly warmed to this, with Bignell and O'Day's book on

Nation, or Andy Murray's chapter on Holmes in *Time and Relative Dissertations in Space*.

Auteur theory emerged when French auteur critics – future directors like François Truffaut and Claude Chabrol – looked at the studio system which seemed to stifle individual creativity, and found directors who still produced distinctive work. *Doctor Who* fans went through the same process, in effect substituting "studio system" with "*Doctor Who*". To pick a 1990s fanzine piece at random, Theo Robertson elevated Hulke above others who treated *Doctor Who* as a children's programme and argued that, given the moral complexity of his work, Hulke could be set against writers like Terry Nation and described as an "exception". If the French critics' adulation of (for instance) Alfred Hitchcock legitimised Film Studies as a serious discipline – if cinema produced artists, it was an art – then identifying personal work might open up *Doctor Who* to the kind of critical respect shown to authors of "serious" plays.

But celebrating authors is trickier these days. Just as Barthes stopped us fetishising authors as centres of meaning, so film theory since the late 1960s argued against / replaced / destroyed (delete according to taste) auteur theory. Television Studies developed after auteurism's decline and so was slow to identify important creators. So, books about directors / writers often start with an explanation of how they're not just going to use outdated auteur ideas because theory, rather than the taste / personality of the director / writer, is king. (Author-based books usually fudge this by explaining in the introduction how author studies are problematic, before carrying on as normal.) Anyone keen to imagine Nation as tortured artist devising killer clams and icecanoes as metaphors for the human condition to communicate to his audience (by the way, good luck with that) may be frustrated as Bignell and O'Day must first clarify their study with theory and explain how it makes us question where "authority" can lie in a collaborative medium. And yet, Nation's "agency" as author cannot be entirely displaced. John R Cook responded to Rosalind Coward by arguing that the "complexity of production" which Coward argued invalidated "notions of authorial expression" can "be seen to resolve itself into a clear hierarchical system of creative power relations whereby traditionally in British television, the writer was privileged". This is true of certain writers of single plays, but does the more regimented "hierarchical system of creative power relations" in series drama resolve itself in this manner?

Nathan-Turner's first broadcast story, *The Leisure Hive*, would suggest not. It introduces Season Eighteen's defining tone and themes. There's a conceptual pun typical of the season: the recreation generator which one citizen of Argolis uses to attempt the re-creation of Argolis by building a new generation to replace Argolis' post-nuclear-war sterility. Foreshadowing later Season Eighteen ideas, the story features recursion (trying to recover from the aggressive use of technology by making an aggressive use of technology) and an embattled society in thrall to its own history, like the underground society of *Meglos*, the querying of descent which reveals evolutionary recursion in *Full Circle*, the apparent retreat into medievalism and vampire legend of *State of Decay*, or the Gateway as temporal focal point in *Warriors' Gate*. Philip Macdonald observed that Season Eighteen stories show "objects, societies and planets... being dragged backwards by their very efforts to move forwards", reinforcing the season's dominant themes of entropy and "reclaiming humanity from the ravages of corrosion".

But can we say that David Fisher is responsible for this story's introduction of Season Eighteen themes? The credit "by David Fisher" suggests so, but the programme's "creative power relations" bring it into doubt. Many books have used *The Leisure Hive* to itemise the impact that Nathan-Turner had on the series. These include his experience of BBC budgets as production unit manager to "put the money on the screen" and improve production values (as Lawrence Miles and Tat Wood point out in *About Time*, we shouldn't underestimate that as "bean-counting", because higher production values involve "understanding how to use a visual form to tell a story"). There were changes in style: adding a new title sequence and theme arrangement, replacing Dudley Simpson's incidental music with the Radiophonic Workshop's electronic scores, and insisting that Tom Baker perform in a "more sombre" way than under Graham Williams, reflected in his new costume and in the tone of scripts.

Nathan-Turner and script editor Christopher H Bidmead asserted their agency (for instance, in Tulloch and Alvarado's book) by contrasting their "serious", hard science fiction with the "undergraduate humour", "childish silliness" and poor production values under the previous regime of Graham Williams and Douglas Adams. Bidmead aimed for the "scientification" of *Doctor Who* and a greater thematic unity which resulted in, according to Macdonald, "probably the most consistent and carefully constructed progress" of any season. So, although Seasons Sixteen and Twenty-Three have season-long arcs (*The Key to Time* and *The Trial of a Time Lord*, respectively), Season Eighteen's use of running themes is more sophisticated and authored. Privileging Bidmead's authority throughout the season, Macdonald credited the Bidmead-scripted season finale, *Logopolis*, with "bringing to a climax the mood and the themes of the preceding six adventures".

The attention paid to script editors by fans is fascinating. Within the usual TV hierarchy, script editors are often relatively junior and lack creative autonomy. But *Doctor Who*'s specific production circumstances and the format's balance of generic rules with a lack of fixed recurring features seem to give its script editors influence over style. After all, we use them as markers of sub-eras that are more accurate than splitting the show into eras by producer alone: surely Nathan-Turner was criticising Williams / Adams rather than Williams / Holmes or Williams / Read? It's hazy: Bidmead felt his job title was "utterly undefined". A BBC Editor's Guide said that the editor's "primary function" was to "find, encourage and commission new writers": "encouraging writers to practise their art with as much freedom as possible" but also guiding them on "necessary disciplines". Bidmead estimated that he wrote 70% of Season Eighteen, in two distinct ways: the "legitimate" authoring which took place in "brainstorming sessions with each of the writers" to which script editors would "contribute at least half the ideas", and the "less rewarding" work of substantially rewriting material which did not "achieve what was required". This is a paradox of Season Eighteen: its "intellectual" scope suggests more freedom for authors, but Bidmead's desire to apply his dominant themes restricts the agency of individual contributors.

Bidmead once sympathised with writers who interpreted the process as "that bugger Chris Bidmead took my stuff and did it his own way". Indeed, Stephen Gallagher once complained that *Warriors' Gate* was "heavily edited between leaving my hands and appearing on air". However, Gallagher discovered that he had not been "singled out" as this practice was typical: "I found out that every writer who worked on the show in those couple of seasons had the same complaint." Eric Saward once argued that "I could have gone up as co-author on almost every story." Bidmead hit upon a more amenable job description when recalling his rewriting of *Full Circle* after discussions with writer Andrew Smith: "I just incubated the script we had originally hacked out between us."

This "brainstorming" is closer to Andrew Cartmel's definition of his work as script editor. His strategies, which included restoring mystery to the Doctor's character and bringing depth to the companion's characterisation, affected the narrative structure suggested to writers, who employed the "plot device" of the Doctor as "a distant mountain range seen through a mist... manipulating everything" and based plots around Ace. However, despite proposing a controversial re-visioning of the Doctor's past (in fan-speak, the "Cartmel Masterplan"), this was never imposed as an authorial framework like Bidmead's recurring themes or structures like the E-Space Trilogy. Indeed, Cartmel stressed his writers' autonomy: noting Rona Munro's "feminist / occult symbology" in

*Survival*, he argued that Munro was an example of "someone writing from her own obsessions and inspirations on a path that was parallel to *Doctor Who*; that was what I wanted". However, Munro also experienced the generically coded format. She recalled Cartmel discussing the "*Who* Concept... where the writer comes up with the story and the production team make it fit into the world of *Who*". (The impact of this on the story's feminist ideas is discussed in "Is *Who* Afraid of Virginia Woolf?" elsewhere in this collection.)

Sometimes script editors rewrite so much that stories nominally by other people say more about their ideas than scripts with their credit on. But their own scripts give cues to help us read their script-edited work. Bidmead's script for *Castrovalva*, although written to start Season Nineteen and the Davison era rather than appearing in the Bidmead-edited Season Eighteen, can be read as the culmination of Season Eighteen. It closes a themed trilogy, as Shardovan sacrifices himself to thwart the Master just as the new Keeper and the Doctor did in *The Keeper of Traken* and *Logopolis* respectively. *Castrovalva*, like the Cartmel-edited *Survival*, has the Master lure the TARDIS crew to a world over which he appears to have creative agency until it turns on him. These ideas of agency and escaping history could be read as a comment on the programme's need to emerge from Tom Baker's long era, symbolised by the new Doctor's unravelling of the fourth Doctor's iconic scarf while mapping the labyrinthine TARDIS. The Doctor is trapped in Castrovalva, whose history and the memories of its people are false because they were invented by the Master. Echoing the self-perpetuating tasks of *Full Circle* and the TARDIS-within-a-TARDIS of *Logopolis*, the Doctor is trapped within a recursive landscape. Escape from *Castrovalva* requires a dynamic individualism which closes the Bidmead arc of Season Eighteen, in which individuals battle the universal scale of entropy and are unable to escape; this is personified by the Watcher, a harbinger of doom from which the Doctor cannot escape.

This individual inability to escape (although it would be wrong to call Season Eighteen just a study of scientific determinism) is exorcised in redemptive ways in *Castrovalva*, in which individuals discover their free will. Escape from Castrovalva is foreshadowed in the TARDIS' escape from Event One, a site of history and creation (the "big bang"). Observing that "people escape from gravity all the time", Nyssa and Tegan learn that "if" must be turned "into a fact", because freedom as an aesthetic concept must be understood imaginatively before it can be enacted. This idea is grasped by Shardovan, who negotiates Castrovalva's bafflingly recursive spatial topography "in my philosophy" and ultimately revolts against his creator, the Master, in a sacrifice which asserts individual agency and, unlike the sacrifices which closed *The Keeper of Traken* and *Logopolis*, leads not to the perpetuation of the status quo but to the realisation that "we are free!"

Like Shardovan, writers attempt to assert their agency from within Bidmead's creation, as his themes unify the stories from *The Leisure Hive* to *Castrovalva*. Looking through the Stephen Gallagher archive at Hull University, with its notes from script meetings and an exchange of letters with Nathan-Turner hoping that his later story *Terminus* won't be as messed around in the studio as *Warriors' Gate* was, I wonder whether the credit "Stephen Gallagher" should be read as referring to the noted horror novelist Stephen Gallagher or instead to a nominal "Stephen Gallagher" in quotation marks, if we use the language of auteur-structuralism, with which film theorists discussed auteurism by contrasting, for instance, John Ford the director of Westerns with a quotation-marked "John Ford", the agent constructed by critics: a way of organising and thinking about the works with that person's credit, an organising structure.

Is there, then, a distinction between Gallagher, Fisher and David Agnew, that most elusive *Doctor Who* writer? Any critic seeking Agnew's authorial signatures would struggle, given that, before writing *The Invasion of Time* and *City of Death*, Agnew wrote such "serious" plays as "Hell's Angel" for *Play for Today* and *Diane* for director Alan Clarke (it would be remiss of me not to add: see my book on Clarke). Of course, this auteurist reading is indefensible because, like Norman Ashby, Robin Bland and Stephen Harris, "David Agnew" did not exist; the name was a pseudonym for disputed credits. The idea of constructing an "Agnew" signature seems laughable; Mark Shivas, the producer of *Diane* (from which Jonathan Hales removed his credit after extensive revisions by Clarke), was amused by "the idea of someone doing a PhD thesis on 'Agnew's' work some years down the line". However, is it more sensible to try to construct a "Gallagher" or "Fisher" signature, when discussing serials that have been so reworked? Do we need a different form of credit which does not, in Coward's terms, "hide knowledge of the media"?

The way that *The Unfolding Text* asserted the agency of Nathan-Turner / Bidmead has been questioned. Gareth Wigmore satirised the standard view: "And lo, the great Hinchcliffe had his power cruelly ripped away... [under Williams]. Anarchy was loose: robotic dogs, gigantic prawns, dancing bulls, glowing green phallus-monsters, yay, even unto Catherine Schell", until Nathan-Turner "dragged things back from the brink of disaster". It's more complicated than that, argued Wigmore, because *The Leisure Hive* and *Meglos* were "written for the Williams house style" and were arguably weakened by their "serious" treatment. Philip Macdonald (hmm, itself a credit we could debate) started a review of *The Leisure Hive* with a plot synopsis that could have been for that story but was from *The Horns of Nimon*, stressing their similarities: "a complex cautionary tale of scientific hubris" full of "iconic images" including "lurking alien infiltrators" in a landscape devastated by war and "the neurotic remnant of a once-proud race of conquerors [...] retreating to the insular protection of their many-spired city". These similarities proved to Macdonald that *The Horns of Nimon* has a poor reputation because of markers of the Williams style (camp atmosphere, unconvincing production values), whereas *The Leisure Hive* is valued because of Nathan-Turner's markers (glossier production, "serious" tone). Disputing this, Macdonald argued that Season Eighteen is less authorially discrete – and the Williams era more sophisticated – than is often thought.

*State of Decay*, for instance, features an abundance of signatures: a script by Terrance Dicks (Pertwee-era script editor and writer for several eras), a concept created for Season Fifteen (but withheld because of the BBC's sensitivity over *Count Dracula*), vampire iconography redolent of Hinchcliffe's "Gothic horror" era, simultaneously inflected by the dominant themes of Season Eighteen as overseen by Bidmead (including decay, hence the retitling from *The Witch Lords*) and witty interplay between Tom Baker and Lalla Ward largely unseen since Season Seventeen (apparently preserved by director Peter Moffatt despite Bidmead's attempted rewrite). Another way to test the impact of new production teams is to look at cusp *Doctor Who* stories overseen by figures from previous eras. There's *Robot*, which opens the Baker / Hinchcliffe Season Twelve but is a UNIT romp written by Dicks and produced by Letts at the end of their era. Or *Time and the Rani*, written by Pip and Jane Baker in a way that jars with the Cartmel era it opens (and Cartmel regretted his doomed attempts to synthesise their separate aims).

With these qualifications in mind, maybe we can recover David Fisher from debates over how different production teams reshaped his work. Macdonald noted that *The Leisure Hive* revisits themes from earlier Fisher stories, including time-bubble experiments from *City of Death* (itself a Williams / Adams rewrite of a Fisher concept), "inter-species communication" from *The Creature from the Pit* and "space-age courtroom drama" from *The Stones of Blood*.

In this reading, Nathan-Turner's "signature" seems less creative than administrative, in keeping with Bignell and O'Day's definition of TV as "a producer's medium" in which the producer "controls the process of making a programme and fulfils a responsibility to the television institution... by overseeing the format, budgets, personnel, the production schedule and the delivery of the finished product". Fans welcomed the improvement in production values despite the low budget, but his reputation declined when Nathan-Turner blurred the roles between producer and script editor. Fans' interpretations of a producer's duties were explored publicly following the "cancellation crisis" of 1985 and Cartmel's fraught first season. Nathan-Turner was criticised by disgruntled fans on TV (including future *Who* and *Torchwood* writer Chris Chibnall) and by his former script editor Eric Saward in the press. Saward felt that he and his writers were constricted by the producer's influence over scripting, particularly increased reference to the series' past. Saward disliked the "very heavy brief" given to Peter Grimwade for *Planet of Fire*, as he "had to write out Turlough, introduce Peri... use the Master and... the Lanzarote location", while Robert Holmes' brief for *The Two Doctors* included an overseas location, a multi-Doctor reunion and the Sontarans.

Discussing the producer's role and how others on the production team asserted their individual roles is partly helped by the itemisation of responses to Nathan-Turner's decisions and even, to a limited extent, off-screen gossip. Given *DWM*'s current stress on constructive, jovial collaboration and the wisdom of executive involvement, Bidmead's 2009 interview may have surprised its modern consumers with his criticism of Nathan-Turner, both professional ("Stuff came in from John that I just found unbelievable") and personal ("You f—ing idiot, you don't understand stories! You're pissed all afternoon anyway, so I don't know why I'm even arguing with you!"). But what interests me is how often Nathan-Turner was criticised for exercising his legitimate powers as producer: for instance, interviewed alongside Saward in *DWB* in 1992, fan and unofficial adviser Ian Levine attacked Nathan-Turner's casting, his choice of writers and directors, and was disappointed that Nathan-Turner decided on the sixth Doctor's tasteless jacket "against the advice of the costume designer *herself!*" Levine alleged that Nathan-Turner excluded writers and directors from the series' past so that his control (or agency) was "untempered by anyone else". This contradicts the praise that Nathan-Turner had received for supporting new talent in responses to the perceived success of Season Eighteen.

In considering Nathan-Turner's attempts to use new talent in Season Eighteen and criticisms of his choice of directors later in the decade, we can move on to this essay's final example of the creative team: the director. *Doctor Who* directors remain critically neglected, but this is true of television directors in general. When John R Cook argued that the creative "hierarchy" resolved itself in favour of the writer, he added that writers were prioritised over directors, who were "relegated to the secondary role of interpreter" of writers' ideas. Although Film Studies discussed writers "serving" directors (Hitchcock often used several writers interchangeably on a single film), in TV during much of *Doctor Who*'s lifetime there was a belief – among programme makers as well as critics – that directors served writers. This was changing by the 1980s: take *The Singing Detective* written by Dennis Potter, which Joost Hunningher later explored in a rare academic investigation into a TV director (Jon Amiel)'s impact upon a script.

How we might write about television direction without simply copying Film Studies ideas (which often don't fit TV) is something I discuss in my book on Alan Clarke. Can we pay more attention to *Doctor Who* directors? Although Clarke benefited from being able to direct some plays entirely on film as a result of institutional support denied to *Doctor Who* (*Spearhead from Space* was the only all-filmed serial, and an emergency measure at that), he also worked within the same restrictive structures which affected *Doctor Who*, and yet was skilful enough to assert a level of creative authority over and above that of *Doctor Who* directors. They too faced the stressful time restrictions of multi-camera studios (throughout the programme's history), "piebald" productions which combined studio interiors with a small amount of location material shot on film (*Doctor Who*'s dominant form between its first filmed location material in 1964 and its last in 1985), and video location material shot on Outside Broadcast. Location video featured experimentally in Season Twelve's *Robot* and *The Sontaran Experiment*, then on other occasions as its use became more common across drama – but only became the norm for *Doctor Who* from 1986 onwards for budgetary reasons. Filmed drama was the Holy Grail for many directors, as in the small number of *Play for Today* productions allocated all-filmed slots: indeed, Stephen Frears once remarked that Clarke's willingness to take on "tape" and "studio productions" risked making him seem a "bread-and-butter director" because they were "somehow looked down upon in a rather silly, snobbish way". Similarly, *Doctor Who* director Darrol Blake once argued that making video drama, notably soaps, so restricted his offers of work that "I haven't stood behind a film camera for many years and that's silly, because the same eye that directs film directs video." The irony is that today, in the digital age, video (albeit a different kind) is the norm in TV and cinema.

To identify interesting *Doctor Who* directors, do we just, as with writers earlier in this essay, separate "craftsmen" who skilfully serve the format from those who exercise true individuality? For Holmes and Hulke, read Douglas Camfield and David Maloney? But how "individual" can they be on *Doctor Who*? Lawrence Miles and Tat Wood compiled a list of "auteur" directors: Camfield, Maloney, Derek Martinus, Alan Wareing and Graeme Harper. Their criteria involved "a recognisable style, a readiness to adapt the script to [a director's] own ends, a reputation sufficient that producers and script-editors will angle stories specifically for him and a willingness to see working on *Doctor Who* as a challenge rather than a day-job." Therefore, Camfield had recurring features ("a repertory company... military detailing... stock-footage [and] a cinematic flair"); Maloney "innovated in areas such as the use of animation" and was given "projects that allow him free reign"; Martinus made *The Ice Warriors* as something that "looks like nothing else"; Wareing made stories look better than they might have done in that period; and Harper brought a more dynamic visual style, inspired in part by Camfield.

However, auteurs are tricky to identify in a series, which depends upon directors subordinating their technique to house style, genre and rigid production circumstances (if Ken Loach directed *Hustle* or John Woo directed *Heartbeat*, regular viewers might feel lost). None of the directors listed by Miles and Wood qualify as auteurs using François Truffaut's distinction between the sort of film director called a "metteur-en-scène" (someone who faithfully transfers someone else's work) and an "auteur" (who transforms material into an expression of their own personality). Miles and Wood highlight Camfield and Maloney's space to "borrow ideas from other directors" but, given that their quotations are hardly intertextual (or else we can get excited by Chris Clough's Akira Kurosawa detail in *Delta and the Bannermen*), this reinforces the sense that they are lesser directors. "Making scripts work" is a sign of an efficient director rather than an "auteur" (although given some *Doctor Who* scripts, it's sometimes a genuine feat).

But then, no *Doctor Who* directors would qualify if we use Film's metteur-en-scène / auteur distinction. By definition, a successful series director is a metteur-en-scène, as they are recruited to skilfully serve scripts, producers, genres and house styles. However, Miles and Wood are right to note, in the context of *Doctor Who* as a series, that some directors were consulted early in the process: it's an important point in the identification of a creative hierarchy. When Miles and Wood claim that Graeme Harper's "foregrounding of the camera almost as a character" stands out from "what BBC drama looked like in 1984", they're wrong about BBC drama in general (single drama contained exceptions like Clarke), but absolutely accurate about BBC series drama and *Doctor Who* in particular: therefore, recognisable signatures (such as "the real Camfield inheritance, occasional slow, lingering, dissolves") are noteworthy even if they're rooted in serving the format and script. Where their contribution shapes the possibilities of the series beyond their individual episodes (as Camfield, Harper and Waris Hussein could all claim), we can measure their impact relative to the specific limits of *Doctor Who*. So, the specifically *"Who* auteur" is an interesting idea that deserves following up.

It's more interesting that Miles and Wood have excluded directors who were only hired once: the nearer a director gets to being an individual or an auteur, the less "successful" they are as far as the producer is concerned. Idiosyncrasy is not valued in series, yet examples might include Michael Imison's fluid work on *The Ark*, Ken Grieve's inventive compositions and use of steadicam on *Destiny of the Daleks* and, most memorably, the work of Lovett Bickford and Paul Joyce on Season Eighteen. Bickford and Joyce provide interesting case studies of directors who challenged their places within the "creative power relations" of the programme, bringing a greater visual emphasis and also claiming to have rewritten their respective scripts.

Bickford's direction of *The Leisure Hive* was a vital part of Nathan-Turner's attempt to establish a signature of modernity. Bickford opens with a long pan across a deserted out-of-season Brighton beach, which eventually finds the Doctor asleep in a deck chair. Bidmead's response – "It was full of great meaning for Lovett... but I think at the expense of the rest of the episode" – seems surprising, because the shot establishes an atmosphere of regret and desolation in leisure and reinforces the theme of "doing nothing", which comes up throughout the season and becomes the Doctor's defence against entropy. Bickford brought what he described as his "particularly idiosyncratic visual style" to give a semantic weight to visuals which was almost unique for pre-1996 *Doctor Who*. This sequence ends with a highly unusual transition between Earth and Argolis, a zoom out from Earth, across space to Argolis, using a light as a metonym for a sun, before the camera seems (due to an inventive edit) to move through a wall.

Similarly, *Warriors' Gate* opens with a disjointed montage of tracking shots which sets the mood and heralds one of *Doctor Who's* most inventively directed serials. The feature on the story's 2009 DVD release is an excellent case study of debates from this essay: director Paul Joyce was brought from more "serious" drama, having written and directed a *Play for Today* called "Keep Smiling" (but other future *Doctor Who* writers and directors did too, and in this period crews were rotated around different types of drama; in the 1970s, several directors of photography and editors moved between harrowing Clarke dramas and *Doctor Who*). Interviewees praise Joyce for taking more interest in the whole process (for instance, effects) than other directors, some of whom are described by Joyce as "just calling shots, really" (i.e. hacks).

Multi-camera studio has been criticised by many practitioners for its fraught atmosphere, which can now be sampled on DVD extras. Time restrictions compromised directors' ability to assert a personal signature in terms of composition and editing, as they had to mix between cameras recording simultaneously rather than composing and lighting each shot separately and editing them together. Just as Clarke was able to make distinctive work within this system, so Bickford recalled "pushing the boundaries of a studio-based system that wasn't ready for it". The *Warriors' Gate* DVD details problems with rotating BBC camera crews who may be more familiar with light entertainment than drama (the best crews would work on more prestigious dramas), let alone dramas with challenging visual ideas. Joyce's attempt to use the multi-camera studio in more inventive ways caused friction, but earlier the producer had welcomed Bickford's single-camera approach, as time-consuming as it was, because it served as an assertion of his own signature, judging by Bickford's comment that "John Nathan-Turner and I were striving to do something new and different".

Directors are, then, central to the modernity which Nathan-Turner brought to *Doctor Who* (and which is so hard for contemporary fans to gauge). Miles and Wood noted the shift in the way that *Doctor Who* constructed visual / mental space from the theatricality of 1970s "space opera" stories to, for instance, Peter Grimwade's direction of *Earthshock* and cite *Warriors of the Deep* as a regression to looking "as if it's shot on stage-sets again" once a 70s director returns. A clash of eras similarly occurred with Joyce, who describes arguments with executive producer Barry Letts about attempting a "cinematic" approach, in Joyce's belief that TV would move closer to cinema.

Distinctive drama was possible in the studio. But if single dramas could afford a little more time in the studio, and could experiment with conventions of narrative and genre, Bickford and Joyce discovered that a popular drama series could not. Expressive visuals that required overruns were not welcome: the treatment of Joyce on *Warriors' Gate* is still being documented. Graeme Harper (who covered for Joyce on *Warriors' Gate* during his, shall we say, enforced absence) brought a distinctive approach to *The Caves of Androzani* and *Revelation of the Daleks*, with striking visual ideas, unusual compositions and editing strategies, and a use of hand-held camera in the studio which reinforced the scripts' themes of paranoia and changing identities but, unlike Bickford and Joyce, produced "novelty-within-convention".

However, if we're to accept the limitations of "house style" in series drama, then we can see how the creative hierarchy is again resolved in favour of the producer, because producers shape the house style. Indeed, criticisms of the programme's directors in the mid-1980s were related to Nathan-Turner: while Bickford and Joyce's dynamism reflected his search for modernity in Season Eighteen, criticisms of Peter Moffatt's direction of *The Two Doctors* were used to reinforce criticisms of the producer. Moffatt initially withholds the identity of an alien aggressor through a shot of them looming (almost but not quite point-of-view) over the Doctor, but if this builds mystery, the later revelation that the aggressors are the Sontarans has little dramatic impact, because the first Sontaran is framed (in the location footage) in a very placid long shot. Criticisms of this shot constitute it metonymically as the producer's privileging of style over dramatic content, as its display of landscape maintains the languid, travelogue pace of the scenes shot on location in Spain. Eric Saward queried the dramatic value of Nathan-Turner's use of overseas locations, telling *DWB* that a video recce of Singapore locations for a proposed Auton story was shot at the last minute after the producer had enjoyed "a good time... at the BBC's expense". Equally, the gruesome stabbing of Oscar in *The Two Doctors*, which jars unpleasantly with the story's frivolous tone, reinforced criticisms of violence which Michael Grade used to defend his attempt to cancel the series. The producer was, therefore, being held accountable for production values (in a reversal of earlier praise, for their glossiness rather than poor quality), elements of directorial style and narrative tone.

But is it possible to identify the Nathan-Turner style? In *DWM* in 1988, he contested the idea that he imposed a "house style" on directors. He said he was "very keen that directors bring their own interpretation to it", noting that, unlike on *Rockliffe's Babies* and other series, on which directors "are told the house style is this, and that is how you should shoot it", there were "no house rules in *Doctor Who*" apart from "favour the Doctor", "shoot a cliffhanger in a certain way" and "start a first episode in a certain way". However, former collaborators noted his influence on the series' pace and style. Bidmead argued that "He was still stuck with the language of the sixties. If you cut from you and I sitting here [...] to the same situation two hours later, John would say that in order to understand that time had passed you had to put in a cutaway [...] if nothing happens, why are we messing about with it?" There is a jarring example of this during *Dragonfire*, when we cut away from the core plot for a very brief scene of Mel and Ace playing "I Spy".

Andrew Cartmel had a more positive view: "Probably half the battle in television is getting the script and shooting it [...] Editing is a whole separate creative process. John was fantastic at it. He'd say, 'Cut all that, reverse the next two scenes, put that there,' and it would work." This editing practice has a distinct impact upon the pace and style of *Who* in the late 1980s, as you can tell by comparing the original version of *The Curse of Fenric* with the DVD special edition. The original featured scenes which were halved and moved around, which enables it to pack in lots of information from an overlong script and results in a frenetic pace with, arguably, a dissipation of moments of atmosphere and characterisation by these devices and "topping and tailing" the beginning and ending of scenes for timing reasons.

Other perceived failings of the era's visuals were rooted in technological restrictions. Responding to fan complaints of "pantomime" style, Cartmel blamed the studio's "bright, artificial lighting" which gave images "a brashness and a lack of depth". For Cartmel, shooting entirely on videotape restricted atmosphere (as Miles and Wood suggest, Alan Wareing stood out for his handling of it). As the Darrol Blake quotation indicated earlier, directors rarely built reputations on video. Just as film critics have neglected TV directors, *Doctor Who* fans rarely discussed directors' contributions, at least until the 1996 TV movie, which as a 35mm all-filmed production inspired detailed analyses of director Geoffrey Sax's substantial personal contribution. Of course, post-2005 *Doctor Who* is also shot largely in a studio, albeit on single camera and with increased time and money.

The authorial discourses which circulated around Nathan-Turner help us to think about roles in television drama, but also motivated an anti-JN-T campaign whose impact lingers in the DNA of fandom, in the "pro" and "anti" camps and wearying catchphrases ("RTD must go!") resurfacing in responses to the Russell T Davies era. Davies' role has both resolved and further problematised this essay's investigation into agency. As executive producer / lead writer (on screen) between 2005 and 2009, Davies has had an unprecedented degree of control within the "hierarchy" of "creative power relations"; *SFX* in 2005 called him the "most powerful" producer in the programme's history, to the extent that the show was now "auteur television". As this implies, Davies' highly distinguished pre-*Who* career creates new fissures in the attribution of agency, because, although this is a popular drama series with a "generically coded format", it is also an artefact from a writer in the "artist" tradition. As a writing "show-runner" (commonly attributed to American series such as *Buffy the Vampire Slayer* under Joss Whedon or *The X-Files* under Chris Carter, which neglects British precedents such as *Robin of Sherwood* under Richard Carpenter), Davies is not a script editor (they exist, in a junior role more typical of the industry) but has rewritten as widely as Saward or Bidmead; he is not a producer with Nathan-Turner's business acumen (there are producers dedicated to that side) but has provided "shopping lists" to writers as Nathan-Turner did.

*Doctor Who Confidential* provides immediate behind-the-scenes accounts (including of collaboration) undreamed of in the 1980s and its success (not to mention that of the series itself) dwarfs Nathan-Turner's impact on the fan circuit. Complaints about the scale of his input and negative rumours about so many standard production developments suggest that the best-informed fandom in the programme's history has regressed in its understanding of television authorship.

# Dwellings of Simplicity

**by Jason A Miller**

*From Enlightenment #108, February / March 2002*

Last week, my boss took me out to lunch at a lower Manhattan bistro. Seated at a booth nearby was Michael Imperioli of *The Sopranos*. My boss and I are healthy *Sopranos* fans, although only I watch, and quote from, *Doctor Who*. We were both amused to note that Imperioli in real life, or at least on that day, dresses exactly like Christopher, his TV character, a mobster screenplay-writer wannabe. All black: coat, shirt, pants and shoes. We're talking black as Anthony Ainley's jumpsuit, blacker than the original cover of the Target novelisation for *Castrovalva*.

Only a few days beforehand, I'd watched *Castrovalva* for the first time in years. There was a time when I'd watch TV *Doctor Who* on a weekly basis, but over the past few years, as cutting-edge television evolved and my videotapes didn't, I watched even my favourite episodes less and less. This was the first time I'd seen the story since another celebrity sighting I had, at a *Doctor Who* convention in Chicago in 1997, when Peter Davison was the lone past Doctor in attendance.

That weekend, my convention friends and I sat in the hotel bar into the very late Saturday night, until at long last there were left only ourselves, and Peter Davison. One of us had brought a home-distilled bottle of mead to Illinois, and it was quickly decided that we needed to go up to Peter and ask him to try some of our spirits. To his credit (and to what appeared to be a hangover the next morning, when he appeared in the autograph room wearing sunglasses), he drank a small cupful. And when he did so, he winced, the same way I'd seen him wince in episode four of *Castrovalva* dozens of times before.

You remember the scene: Mergrave the physician (Michael Sheard) offers the ailing Doctor a blue concoction, whereupon the Doctor downs it in one gulp, and winces dramatically. That same wince he later showed us in Chicago. A combination of this memory, my watching *Castrovalva*, and seeing another TV actor in person yet barely out of character, all brought back my grand nostalgia for the fifth Doctor, and Peter Davison in general.

There's a mild argument to be made that *Doctor Who* really grew up in Season Nineteen. That was the first year the show didn't air on Saturday nights. The first year after nearly a decade of Tom Baker. Season Eighteen, with its new opening titles, synthesiser incidental music and 1980s production values, may have started the shift, but a year later we had a Doctor barely out of his twenties, and a female companion who actually used the words "Hell" and "pathetic", nouns that would have never been an issue when Leela or Romana were in the script.

*Castrovalva*, then, is almost the pilot episode for a new format of *Doctor Who*. I was surprised to remember that Peter Davison's Doctor needs rescuing at nearly every turn of the story. Tom Baker was rendered unconscious in every adventure during his first three years as the fourth Doctor, but he never needed rescuing. In Davison's premiere, he's pushed in a wheelchair, carried in a box, medicated by the Master and nearly squashed by a falling door. Not to mention, pill bottles fall on his head. This is the vulnerable Doctor, a Doctor who's man enough to wince when he drinks the blue stuff.

I also love Christopher H Bidmead's dialogue. Once the Doctor has entered the city of *Castrovalva*, he befriends the unlikely trio of Mergrave, Shardovan the librarian, and a tiny little man named Ruther. Mergrave is warmly played by Michael Sheard, who acted in so many *Doctor Who* stories that you'd almost think he was created, through block transfer computation, specifically for the show. Then there's Ruther. Remembering that *Castrovalva* is billed "The Dwellings of Simplicity", I always found it funny that such an officious little man, a bureaucrat, could even exist there. Nasally, he proclaims "Some stairways rise from the square. Others descend to it. Still others debauch laterally. Surely an equitable arrangement, allowing for much variety of movement." Yes, well, that's democracy for you.

Shardovan is the sinister one, the tallest man in town and the one who dresses in black. In many ways, you could believe that this is the kind of person the Master used to be, before he became evil. Only Shardovan sees that something is amiss with *Castrovalva*. One of my all-time favourite exchanges – indeed, one of my all-time favourite *Who* moments – occurs in episode four when the Doctor and Shardovan discuss the library's history volumes. The books are old – but they chronicle the rise of *Castrovalva* to the present day. This is a delicious paradox, a virtual-reality plot twist that would go on to inspire nearly a dozen Justin Richards novels.

Finally, there is Peter Davison's stamp on the story. His Doctor may be ill and queasy for the full four episodes, but Davison's versatility means that he never quite sinks into the background, never manages to become irrelevant. Even moving beyond his Hartnell, Troughton and Pertwee impressions in the opening minutes, here's a thirty year old who plays old and crotchety, and young and sweet, all at once. The moment that crystallises it all for me is in the escape from the city after the equations have fallen apart. Adric has just led the group to safety... and the Doctor charges back into the dwindling city to try and rescue Mergrave, the fictitious inhabitant. Compare and contrast with Tom Baker's cold dead-with-honour assessment of the final casualty of *Horror of Fang Rock*. I thought it was neat that the Doctor could be this compassionate.

I doubt I'll ever run into the fifth Doctor in a hotel bar again, or watch him make an amusing face when drinking mead. Working in Manhattan, I'm far more likely to stand in line behind Scott Glenn in the corner drugstore, which won't bring back any memories at all. But Davison remains my favourite of the Doctors Who and, while I don't watch *Castrovalva* as much as I used to, I'll still whistle Paddy Kingsland's incidental score while hiking through the woods (without a wheelchair), still recite passages by heart, still thrill when Peter Davison holds up the little bottle and says: "The Solution! Oh, my little friend, if only you were..."

# Untrue Grit

by **Mike Morris**
*From The Doctor Who Ratings Guide, April 2002*

One of the great things about *Doctor Who* is that it very rarely produces something that's completely without merit. As a programme that can't rely on visuals, it is – for SF – extremely intelligent; most stories have something to offer. Ditto the seasons. There hasn't been a season ever that's got nothing going for it.

Season Twenty-Two has a lot going for it. A lot. Not only that, but it is such a change from what went before that it's easy to find an awful lot to admire. There's more real content in Season Twenty-Two than Season Twenty or Eleven, for example. It's more thoughtful, more daring, more interesting.

I don't like it.

I don't get any pleasure from not liking it, mind you. I want to like it, I really do. Too many times it's dismissed as derivative, overly violent, gaudy rubbish, which just isn't fair. But we have to accept something: the damn thing didn't work. *Doctor Who* got cancelled after it aired, for god's sake, and there's such a queue of people who don't like it that they can't all be wrong. Before Season Twenty-Two, *Doctor Who* was, overall, in reasonably good shape; it was popular, the Doctor was liked, the stories were (vaguely) consistent and the ideas were deceptively thoughtful. Yes, Season Twenty was mostly rubbish; but Season Twenty-One had a freshness, a confidence and a thematic consistency that overrode the odd dodgy story. Afterwards came *The Trial of a Time Lord*, a confused and desperate mess which was symptomatic of the show suddenly finding it no longer had a niche.

Something went wrong in between, and that something was Season Twenty-Two.

Why? Why? What's wrong with it?

"The continuity links!" some people may cry. "The violence!" others will say. "The portrayal of the Doctor!" is another element. There's a grain of truth to all these, but they aren't the core reason. Season Fourteen is probably more violent than Season Twenty-Two, *The Seeds of Doom* showcases the most violent Doctor the world has ever seen (as well as a mercenary who wasn't created by Eric Saward) and *Genesis of the Daleks* is continuity-obsessed; these things aren't unpopular.

In particular, the continuity of Season Twenty-Two is somewhat overstated. Admittedly, there's only one story that doesn't have a reference to previous *Who*. But let's not forget it was the sixth Doctor's first season and it made sense to bring the popular monsters back (it's the same idea as Season Twelve, as *The Power of the Daleks*, as Season Twenty-Five). People like Daleks, they like Cybermen and they like Pat Troughton! Why not bring them back to aid the new Doctor's settling in?

To say it's derivative is also misleading. The old mythology was actually re-interpreted every bit as much as it was during the McCoy era, which takes so much credit for re-defining the old mythology. The Cybermen were given a new edge; the process of "cybernisation" was examined in detail for the first time; "rogue" Cybermen; there's a lot of new stuff there. The Daleks were revolutionised too, and all the "invention" of *Remembrance of the Daleks* was actually invented here. The presence of the third Doctor in *Timelash* was another new departure, an attempt to give the Doctor a past beyond the televised programmes and to examine the consequences of his actions. In addition, the crucial idea of the "Web of Time" was actually first examined here. Yes, it went too far, with too many touches (having *The Invasion* Cybermen in *Attack* was too much), but many elements were incidental. The Totter's Yard scenes in *Attack* aren't offensive, so why criticise them and not criticise an equally meaningless reference in *Remembrance*?

(Yes, the return to Totter's Yard in *Remembrance of the Daleks* is meaningless. Just because there's a gunfight there doesn't mean there was any reason to go back.)

Derivative? Vaguely. But not, as yet, offensively so; that came next year.

I'll return to the question of violence and the Doctor later. They were important, yes. But not as important as a much more fundamental flaw; namely, that the stories of Season Twenty-Two display astonishing deficiencies in plotting, logic and characterisation. This is the only season of *Doctor Who* where the programme seemed unable to tell a story well and I'd argue that this is the real, primary reason it's disliked.

Admittedly, this trend didn't start in Season Twenty-Two, but during the Davison era, and probably took root in the Big Stylistic Change of Season Eighteen. Set pieces and good visuals became more important then than previously. But most stories had an internal logic at the least. For every *Resurrection of the Daleks* there was a *Frontios*. Plotting, structure, motivation; these remained important.

Every single story of Season Twenty-Two is deficient in this area. *Attack of the Cybermen*, for all its good points, is an utter mess. Here are a few questions: how in the name of physics did Lytton pick up a Cryon distress call from the future? Why is his distress call still signalling after they've hired him? What are the Cybermen doing on Earth anyway? If they're rescuing leftover Cybermen from *The Invasion*, why have they set up a base there and why don't those Cybermen look different? Why send out Cyber-scouts when their base is so well-concealed? How does Lytton know who Stratton and Bates are? Why do the Cybermen lock the Doctor in a room full of explosives? Why are the Cybermen mining the surface of Telos anyway?

*Doctor Who* has always had plot holes; in fact, some of the best stories are full of them. But never have they been so constant, so blatant – and when the plot holes weren't obvious, the motivations were daft. *Revelation of the Daleks* is ultimately based on a very stupid premise: namely, that Davros has lured the Doctor halfway across the universe to drop a fake tombstone on him. *The Mark of the Rani* hinges on another daft notion: three Time Lords have coincidentally arrived at the same point in history and two of them have meaningless motives. Quite why the Rani has to take brain fluid from so many points in history is anybody's guess and the Master's plan is ludicrous even by his standards. In *The Two Doctors*, it's hard to see why Dastari and Chessene have allied themselves to the Sontarans, why they brought them to Earth and why they've decided to set the Time Lords up anyway; the Time Lords were giving them all the trouble, and they can hardly expect to fool the Time Lords into thinking the Time Lords destroyed the space station!

In the last two examples, the returning villains are very much tacked on; hence the "derivative" tag, when it's really just bad scriptwriting. In *Revelation of the Daleks*, by contrast, it's the Doctor who seems added at the last minute. *Revelation* is the best story of the season, simply because the plot without the Doctor is quite logical – and largely, it's the Doctor / Davros story that lets it down.

Side by side with this is another issue: padding. I might accept that hey, these stories are fun runarounds, if not for the fact that nothing happens in them for long periods of time. In *Attack of the Cybermen*, *Vengeance on Varos*, *The Mark of the Rani* and *Timelash*, the Doctor and Peri seem to spend half the first episode in the TARDIS arguing. Eric Saward has said that the 45-minute episodes (another brave and positive move) allowed for a more "relaxed" opening, which is fair enough, but this is counterpointed by another factor: that the conclusions of these stories looked rushed (*Attack*) or lacked sufficient depth (*Vengeance*). *Attack of the Cybermen* is the greatest offender. The slow pace of episode one is actually quite nice. But then the events of episode two are so hurried that episode one looks indulgent, particularly given that the Earth-based segments of the story are completely unnecessary to the main plot. And *Timelash* is taking the piss utterly, treating us to Scottish detours and TARDIS "safety" belts before we get anywhere near the famed Planet of Tinsel.

These are merely the most blatant examples of the way that, in this season, the Doctor and Peri spend a lot of time running up and down corridors, getting captured, escaping, getting recaptured and hanging around in the TARDIS for half an hour. Padding, of the best Pertwee tradition.

Without the traditional focus that *Doctor Who* had always had – narrating a story – the principal energy had to be derived elsewhere. It came sometimes from allegory (*Vengeance on Varos*), sometimes from continuity developments (*Attack of the Cybermen*, *Revelation of the Daleks*), but largely from action, explosions, and – by extension – people getting hurt. This, I feel, is where the violence accusations kick in.

Here's a quick list of some of the more cited "violent" scenes of the era. The hand-crushing of Lytton; the laser-rigging, acid bath and plant-traps on *Vengeance on Varos*; Shockeye eating a rat, bits of Sontarans all over the place, the murder of Oscar and the killing of Shockeye in *The Two Doctors*; Grigori's interrogation and Davros' hand getting shot off in *Revelation of the Daleks*.

Each of these scenes has been defended elsewhere, and I won't duplicate those arguments here. I will say that some have less of a case to answer than others; I consider the death of Shockeye, and the chase-scene leading up to it, one of the most frightening and effective scenes of the season. Suffice it to say that, in themselves, none of those scenes are that bad. Certainly they're no bloodier than, say, Condo's death in *The Brain of Morbius* and no more sadistic than Sarah being dangled over a sheer drop in *Genesis of the Daleks*.

The issue isn't the violence; it's the use of it. It's unnecessary except in itself. Condo's death is a necessary plot-point, whereas Oscar's death is not. In the absence of linear stories, the violence became the point rather than a story element. There is no plot reason, none at all, that we get a shot of a Sontaran leg in *The Two Doctors*; it's there to shock us. The impression given is that the whole long, messy death of the Sontarans was there just so we could see their blood all over the place.

This isn't a more violent philosophy, just a more witless one. It's no different, really, to the way that the last ten minutes of *The Mark of the Rani* episode one are there just so the Doctor can roll down a hill on a trolley; it's just more uncomfortable. Plots aren't as important as moments in Season Twenty-Two. Hands get crushed, people turn into trees, dinosaurs grow in TARDISes, guards die in acid, Daleks fly; these are set-pieces good and bad but they aren't linked into a story in any meaningful way. It's no coincidence that Grigori's interrogation and Davros having his hand shot off are often not mentioned, simply because they take place in the best story of the era. *Revelation of the Daleks* actually makes perfect sense – or rather it would, if it didn't have to include the Doctor.

Oscar's death is a blatant example. *Doctor Who* has killed countless characters but never like this. The whole "Shockeye goes to a restaurant" jaunt is meaningless, a quick chase through Seville that doesn't add anything to the story. It's then ridiculous to assume that Shockeye (a chef!) wouldn't understand the concept of a bill, or wouldn't know that Nargs are not negotiable currency on primitive planets. And it's a hell of a coincidence that, out of the hundreds of restaurants in Seville, Shockeye just happens to go into Oscar's. What disturbs me about that scene is not the death (it's well acted and even poignant on its own merits) but that the last fifteen minutes seemed to have one purpose: to kill off a character. It's not there to show the horror of random death, as has been suggested elsewhere, because Oscar's death is not random. In fact, the story goes to extraordinary lengths to kill him. The scene makes the programme feel cynical, contriving a hollow way of manipulating the audience's emotions because it can no longer think of anything better.

In a season where the show became notably more intelligent in its ideas (examining television, profit-making monsters, meat eating), it was notably less so in its plotting. The wit, invention and structure went out the window and was replaced with bigger explosions and more deaths. The violence isn't the problem in itself; it's a result of the root problem, that *Doctor Who* can't be bothered telling a story any more.

The final issue is the Doctor. Of course, we all know that the sixth Doctor was great, really, and that Colin played him brilliantly and that it wasn't his fault the scripts weren't very good.

Hang on a minute. You know what? I don't really agree. I don't think that Colin Baker played the sixth Doctor brilliantly. I think he lacked screen presence and charisma. His performance verged on the pompous and I often don't believe in the character.

There. I've said it. Sorry.

I just don't fully subscribe to the Doctor-was-great-but-scripts-were-bad theory. I think that, at times, Baker's performance was over the top and misjudged. That's not to say he isn't a thoroughly good actor; not to say he wouldn't have been a great Doctor given more stories (Colin is apparently proving this in the audios and I'm glad). Most Doctors had an initial run of good, energetic stories and eased their way in. It's not Colin Baker's fault that, by contrast, his character was the focus of the programme from the start and that the programme was poorly written at the time. Anyone would have struggled, but the fact remains that if you compare Colin's "unlikeable Doctor" with the rude, arrogant Doctor of *The Seeds of Doom*, there's not much competition as to who's better. Tom is loud, prescriptive, bossy and generally not very nice – and yet we like him. This is partly because the story's better and one feels that the Doctor's being rude because he's genuinely concerned about a real menace; it's partly because Tom is simply a better actor.

I'll put it another way. A flatmate of mine has seen quite a few of my videos by now and he likes the programme, sort of. His analysis of what I show him is sharp and the points he makes are valid. He's never going to be a fan, but I respect his opinion.

He describes the sixth Doctor as, "that obnoxious little man".

I've argued in the sixth Doctor's favour; I've said how that was part of the point, that the interesting aspect of his character was that his brashness was a veneer covering up a very heroic figure. And yet, I find my arguments fading when I watch the programme, because I frequently find myself watching an obnoxious little man.

There are attempts at comedy and they tend to make this worse. I find that I can like completely obnoxious bastards, but it's harder to like obnoxious bastards who keep trying to be funny. The inherent stuffiness in his character (all that quoting, the pomposity of his speech) means he might have been funnier if he was more humourless. But:

Colin. Baker. Isn't. That. Good.

Having said all that, there are many occasions when the sixth Doctor is wonderful. My favourites from this season are the oft-cited mutant death scene from *Revelation*; his outrage at the Rani, which rises against the obvious limitations of the tree scene; the energy of his striding around London in *Attack*; the downbeat finale of that story; the aforementioned chase scene with Shockeye; "no 'arm in trying"; in fact, all the scenes with Davros. I'm not saying he's awful, but he wasn't great either. He was great, sometimes. Just as he was awful, sometimes.

I'd kind of forgotten about Peri but, since the writers usually did as well, that's quite appropriate. I should say there are sharp retorts as well as annoying whines and that her relationship with the Doctor could be very funny indeed ("watch it, Porky!"). Like the rest of the season, however, the bad bits tend to conceal the good. What damages Peri isn't her arguments with the Doctor, it's her sheer uselessness. The bloody girl spends the entire season being rescued and screaming, so whining at the Doctor every five minutes is adding insult to injury. In *Vengeance on Varos*, she says, "I was supposed to have a cold supper," expecting to be waited on hand and foot. In *The Mark of the Rani*, she discovers that the Doctor's not dead and says "I could have been stuck in the eighteenth century forever." The Doctor would be forgiven for telling her to jump down a mineshaft. In the entire season, she does two constructive things: hit a mutant with a stick and collect some plants. She didn't even hit the mutant convincingly and her plant collecting is in its own way an admission of defeat, the authors unable to come up with a character beyond She's A Botanist.

No, it's not the whining. It's just that Peri seemed incapable of anything but whining. She has some great scenes, but they're outweighed by scenes that make me want to hit her. And, while we know that Nicola Bryant is a bit pretty, there's no need to have every bloody story revolve around her being a bit pretty. The poor girl even gets lusted after by the Borad, who then wants to change her appearance; what, he loved her for the beauty within when he hadn't even met her? At least it's an improvement on the hermaphrodite slug that fancied her in *The Twin Dilemma*. Ultimately, the problem's basic: no plots for her to engage with. No motivations given to her. No imagination beyond "she whines and she's got big tits" – and really, she only argues because it's the easiest filler material to write.

As a whole, the season deserves some – but not all – of the criticism it gets, and ditto the praise. It tries new things and it pushes a lot of our buttons, so it's hard to be objective about it. I just think that the thought and intelligence put into plotting, environments and characters has always been what distinguished *Doctor Who* from other SF shows and the lack of these aspects is primarily what makes me dislike it – and, moreover, what gives rise to all the other faults. I can't tolerate plotting and logic this bad. This is, maybe, a personal thing. Other people can look beyond the problems and enjoy Season Twenty-Two. Good for them, because it does have a lot going for it. It's important. It's the point where the writers tried to make the programme grow up. It has some great scenes. *Doctor Who* might not exist as it does today without this season. I don't care.

The complexity of Season Twenty-Two means it should be looked at beyond "it's crap" / "no it isn't" / "is too". I try, honest I do. But I just can't like this stuff, and there my opinion will always begin and end.

# Dark Humour in Revelation of the Daleks

by Kyla Ward

*From Burnt Toast #2, April 1990*

*Revelation of the Daleks* is the story when, faced with the impossibility of playing the usual game with the audience of "the unseen monster", *Doctor Who* took the fact that Doctor and companion were the only ones who didn't know the place was crawling with Daleks and made it funny.

The entertainment lay, particularly for Davros, in watching "his own curiosity deliver him into my hands"; an actually quite dreadful idea that puts the viewer in the unnerving position of Davros' viewpoint. Or, it would be unnerving if the Doctor tripping into the trap wasn't acting like such a fool. There are other fools in the story: the pair bent on retrieving the body of Natasha's father for example. They are introduced in a classic comic sequence, sneaking with guns and all quietly across the hall behind Jobel and his friends. What is a fool? And what is their function? Another interesting character in the story is the DJ, who also acts, in spite of his omnipresent video screen and the knowledge it gives him of the situation, in an incredibly foolish way. His running commentary certainly irritates Davros: "Bring the girl here. And while you're at it, kill that foolish DJ." Davros also considers the Doctor a fool. The thing is, the Doctor agrees. When Orcini, with the Doctor's help, manages to blow off Davros' hand, he turns on him: "That was a foolish waste of energy!" The Doctor answers "No 'arm in trying." And Davros again: "When you become a Dalek, you will suffer for every indignity you have caused me!"

That is the crux. It is the answer to the viewer's acceptance of their positioning and a prime example of comedy showing dangerous things, like different points of view. The "bodysnatchers" are foolish, and would come into the category of "innocent fools" whose naïvety can be laughed at as they bumble round the catacombs, just as their "rightness" is appreciated. All under the DJ's monitors. The DJ is also foolish but from a position of knowledge. He knows so much he can simply watch the bodysnatchers with curiosity, while their presence causes such deadly seriousness among the rest of Tranquil Repose. The DJ sees the full ridiculousness of his position, reading dedications to corpses – "And you know that I get as much of a kick as you do hearing them" – and sets himself up to be laughed at, whereas the bodysnatchers are laughed at for their innocent earnestness.

The Doctor is another knowledgeable fool, so knowledgeable he seems innocent. But he extends the role to fulfil his ideological role in the series. The purpose of his foolishness is to reveal not only what is foolish but what is indeed worthwhile. This is also Orcini's role, the assassin who wishes "to kill once more for honour". Note, however, that he, like all other Necros characters, is a dealer in death. The difference that enables him to be a noble character is that he knows it and makes no apology, let alone trying to disguise it. That is, of course, the entire purpose of Tranquil Repose. This is where the comedy becomes black.

As indicated above, comedy can act to expose and show up the "real" follies in a situation. A fool in this action is a character. These follies often surround painful or damaging truths. When the truth regards an individual, i.e. when a character like Davros is isolated sufficiently from the rest of the social order, their pretensions can be exposed and the character humiliated in all good fun. But when the truth is one of those that would, or that is presented in a way that would, damage the social order, it is a different case entirely, and here "good" and "bad" taste, as well as black humour, are generated.

*Revelation of the Daleks* weaves the comic dilemmas of all characters, from the bodysnatchers to Jobel's crawling little admirer, around one of our society's most painful truths. It explores through these characters the attitudes and constructions – some of which can be harmful, as in the case of the bodysnatchers – around it. Those attitudes and conventions I have previously referred to as "follies". It manages to get to the closeness required for analysis through comedy. By treating them as follies in the way described, it slips under the social and even mental guards of "good taste" and "respect". It is a dangerous game and does not always work; black comedy is not to everyone's taste. But the heroes in black comedy must be these strange "wise fools", who can laugh at themselves and thus save themselves from the pitfalls awaiting those who can only laugh at others (a *Doctor Who* villain's prerogative, and frequent trademark).

The tone of darkness in *Revelation of the Daleks* is set when Peri and the Doctor are walking towards Tranquil Repose and Peri remarks on the purple flowers they are passing. The Doctor gives their botanical name, "the Staff of Life" and their common name, the Weed Plant. They have, he says, a similar protein content to the Earth soya bean and he can't understand why the plant hasn't been cultivated. The reason is implied as the body of the President's wife is arranged, the purple flowers used as decoration. The Staff of Life subordinated – largely ignored, in fact – in favour of covering up death. At the close of the story, the Doctor presents it to Takis as the solution to the sudden shortage the loss of the protein concentrate extracted from bodies will cause. This is his action, that which he sustains throughout all stories, all seasons, one of the bases of the character. *Doctor Who* frequently exposes societies that have gone wrong. But it does this while positing an ideal society, that those he encounters have simply strayed from. This is not necessarily bad, given that the alternative to adopting some sort of ideology and organisational structure is anarchy. *Revelation of the Daleks* exemplifies the possibilities of black comedy as the breaker of ground.

# Greater Than the Sum of its Parts

by **Emily Monaghan**
*From The Doctor Who Ratings Guide, November 2008*

I bloody love *The Trial of a Time Lord*.

Yes, really. I think it's wonderful. Last night, I screeched to the end of *The Ultimate Foe*, beaming all the way through, hiding behind a cushion in excitement and swearing under my breath. And that was but the last hour of a month I've spent in similar fashion, getting increasingly more excited from, oh, *Mindwarp* onwards.

I've put my cards on the table, and I can safely assume you disagree. If overanalysed, this does look pretty ropey. Even I can't defend Mel; the individual adventures are desperately generic; the court scenes in *The Mysterious Planet* are pointless; and the Valeyard could surely have found episodes to air which show the Doctor in a worse light (I could have convicted him on *The Caves of Androzani* alone). In other words, it's very hard to refute half the charges thrown at it.

But the final product is far greater than the sum of its parts – and I'm not making a critical judgement, I'm making an emotional one. A lot of people can't detangle the episode from the era and judge it on its merits without the intrigue (stop me if this all sounds familiar; I'll be telling you my essays have been manipulated next!). But I wasn't there then – and, taken out of its original timezone, it's a fine piece of work.

Criticising Colin Baker himself has long been out of fashion – personally, I never saw why it was in. He's pretty much everything a Doctor should be, just wonderful in every way. Watching his interplay with the Valeyard is priceless. The key to their double act is that the Doctor changes, but the Valeyard never does. He's always calmly malevolent; while the Doctor passes from arrogant, to worried, self righteous, passionate defence, angry, upset and back to arrogant confidence again as the situation changes. Most tellingly, as the situation gets worse, he suddenly remembers the Valeyard's name – and then, in *The Ultimate Foe*, when he starts regaining his confidence, he's back to calling him Railyard again.

The conflict between them is a horrible perversion of the squabbling usually sparked off by multi-Doctor confrontations. The Valeyard is scarily implacable, only just revealing his anger, an immovable object to the Doctor's unstoppable force. One wonders which bits of the Doctor he got, for him to be able to sit so still and quietly (two qualities no Doctor has ever had). The third, perhaps, as his voice often resembles Pertwee's. I liked the way he inherited a penchant for quoting literature – his distaste when he comes out with a snatch of Hamlet and the Dickensian Matrix formed by his subconscious – and the sinister fact that he's the only Time Lord in the room who understands the Doctor's Earth colloquialisms "bugged" and "framed".

The Doctor's relationship with both companions is just too cute. Particularly with Mel. Now, I wasn't that fond of her either, but I did like what she represented. I've always seen the Doctor's lives as different parts of one extended life: Three's the schoolboy whose tree-climbing antics are curtailed by his parents and teachers; Four is the adolescent, all confidence and self belief; Five is something of a mid-life crisis, unable to strike the same balance in his actions that he always took for granted. Which brings us around to Mel and Future Six. Usually, it's the Doctor's job to protect his companion. But with her doing the investigating and being loudly proactive about his rescue, I get the impression she's taking care of him. Look at him in *Terror of the Vervoids*: very mellow, not looking for trouble, with her taking the lead with the mystery and making sure he stays fit. I think he's earned it; some semi-retirement, with Mel taking on a wifely role. Not romantically, I hasten to add, just in terms of the sense of equality they have.

But not even I, an Adric fan, can exonerate her completely – and my admiration is based entirely on my thoughts about the character, not on exactly what was on screen. And her voice grates through my nerves; give me a Dalek any day.

The Doctor and Peri have their moments too, but particularly his reaction to Peri's apparent death is terribly moving. I actually found it more so than *Earthshock*, and anyone who was with me on the drinking binge that occurred an hour after finishing the episode will know I was pretty upset. Even with the foreknowledge that Peri would be fine, the Doctor's reaction still has a real emotional kick. I'd say it took less alcohol to get over than Adric – but actually, I'm not over it, and maybe the lack of booze is why. Going out in public after watching Colin Baker has proved to be a bizarre experience on more than one occasion; he's that wonderful, yet also that unpopular that I feel I'm the possessor of a wonderful secret nobody else knows.

Hell, I even loved the Master's involvement. Again, my minority opinion is that Mr Ainley's performance as the Master has never been better than here. As a Master-centric episode, I still prefer *The King's Demons*, but here he demonstrates the kind of cool, amused menace that really make the character great. At times, he's even scary. And that's not a word I tend to apply to the Master outside of *Utopia*. I like his motivation too: the last thing he wants is a Doctor, with all his ingenuity and dislike of him, freed from those moral scruples.

If we look at the individual adventures, *The Mysterious Planet* was my least favourite of the four. I liked the individual ideas, of course – Drathro's two blonde buddies were cool, the underground set was very eerie and the Doctor had some lovely lines – particularly "Is there any intelligent life here?" "Apart from me?" – but it had very little momentum and I had little difficulty waiting between episodes. But this was also the point at which it got scary.

There are three things going on with the Doctor's behaviour in *Mindwarp*. His brain has been fried by the bad guys and he is acting evil. He's deliberately deceiving everyone (shades of the coming seventh Doctor?) to get to the bottom of the plot. And meddling in the Matrix is twisting the evidence to show him in the worst light. But which is where is anyone's guess. It's scary at the time, because you're not sure what he's up to. It remains unsettling because it's never explained. His treatment of Peri is, accordingly, tragic, cruel or incorrect. It's still hard to watch; pop *Mindwarp* on after *The Caves of Androzani* if you really want to appreciate the shock factor.

Much like *The Mysterious Planet*, I can see that *Mindwarp* is a bad episode. An unrealistic, manufactured society, bad locations, a plot that consists of running around and getting lost. In addition, I have never believed a room of Time Lords who fried Earth to hide dodgy paperwork would convict on the grounds that the Doctor puts his companion in peril. But it too had highpoints: the opening scene on the beach with the pink sea was wonderful, the dog-man effect was unpleasant and I really liked some of the music cues. In addition, it appears that *The Trial of a Time Lord* was the career move of choice for morally ambiguous blond scientists: there's another one in *Mindwarp* and I like him even more than the first two. In terms of the Doctor, however, this is one of the *Trial*'s true highlights.

*Terror of the Vervoids* is also pretty good. Again, the physical effects were really quite unpleasant. I like the captain appearing as the Doc's old friend; there must be people like that all over the galaxy. I particularly enjoyed the scene at the end where they blow the things up, which is wonderfully played by everyone. Even though my views on *Who*-shipping swing wildly between shipping all four regulars in *The King's Demons* in several combinations at the same time, and taking out fatwas on people who even dare breathe the suggestion, I always think there should be companion hugging. And the image of the Vervoids going through a speeded-up autumn, winter and rotting to nothing was smart, unpleasant and bizarrely moving.

Of course, the best thing about *Terror of the Vervoids* is that, while all that stuff on the ship is going on, the courtroom is getting to the apex of tension. The Valeyard's arguments are starting to hit home – in *The Mysterious Planet*, they were roundly unconvincing, but from the suggestion in *Mindwarp* that "companions are statistically in danger twice as often as the Doctor", he starts getting scary – if for no other reason than we, an audience of fans, know he's completely right.

Accordingly, the best episode of *The Trial of a Time Lord* is the trial itself. One of the key problems of *Doctor Who* is you rarely believe the Doctor is in danger. How can you? They ain't gonna kill him, not permanently; at the end of the episode, you know he's going to go trudging back to the TARDIS. The best episodes allow you to forget this, whether through the character's performances or sheer direness of the situation. As a framing device, the trial heightens tension by putting the Doc in danger the whole while.

The Time Lords have always been a scary bunch, but never more than here. Normally, the sense of power, dignity and callous practicality is let down by actually getting to see the council – inevitably dull squabbling and a game of spot the traitor. Neil Gaiman is right when he suggests they should be "distant and unknowable". Their behaviour in this one really takes the biscuit: manipulating Yrcanos for their own ends, letting Peri become collateral damage (sort of), destroying the Earth for a cover-up, and making the Doctor a scapegoat for interference and genocide like their own hands are whiter than white. The worst part is, none of it is hard to believe and their physical absence makes it all the more sinister.

Of course, these days the Valeyard's identity will come as no surprise, but I can still admire the skill with which the reveal is done: the Master's utterly casual, sans-melodrama delivery of such an important fact; blink and you'd miss it entirely. It's nice to know that part of the Doctor's sub-conscious is given to wearing black and cackling after all.

I've always loved the revelation about Peri too. It's taken a lot of flak but, for me, this isn't just another unlikely companion romance. There's something sinisterly tragic at work too. You're a normal Earth girl, who finds herself suddenly stranded in the future. Your only friend has van-ished and hasn't come back for a long time now, and he was acting very strangely before anyway. (Peri and the Doctor's final scene, anyone remember it? Tears on Bad Wolf Bay, blue crystal wedding presents, that sort of thing? Actually, the last time they appear on screen together is the second cliffhanger of *Mindwarp*, when Peri prevents Yrcanos from killing him. As far as she knows, the Doctor has turned incurably evil and aban-doned her for good.) Someone wants to marry you and give you a home in this world you don't understand – and from a warrior king, it's hard-ly a mean offer. What the hell else was she supposed to do? Say no, because she doesn't fancy Brian Blessed, and then do what? She can't fly spaceships, she has no currency, no idea of how the system works on that planet or any other. It's not a situation in which a girl can be picky. And as for the Doctor's smile at the end, just like neglecting to pick up Sarah Jane after *The Deadly Assassin*, you can be sure he never went back to check how she and Yrcanos were getting along. If her desire to get back to Earth in *Mindwarp* is anything to go on, I imagine she'd want to get out of there at once.

By the time we got to the denouement of *The Ultimate Foe*, I barely cared that the ending was rushed, because I was just having so much fun. Final shot = priceless. The best thing about *The Trial of a Time Lord* is its length: by the time you get to the end, you're almost ready to watch it all over again. I certainly am.

I've always been happy to have controversial opinions and I'm always pleased to discover many of them aren't that controversial any more. There is a healthy base of Adric fans, for example; nor is *The King's Demons* as universally despised as you might think. *The Trial of a Time Lord* is the exception, though: it is still hated. And, without even engag-ing with the 1980s politics which surrounded the episode, I can see why – but it would be a colossal St. Peter to even try and rationalise my reac-tion in light of other opinions.

I'm not an apologist. I'm not a lone defender. Maybe I'm not a defend-er at all. I just genuinely loved this piece of television.

# Why I Like Cheese
by Mike Morris

Season Twenty-Four probably showcases *Doctor Who* in the depth of its greatest identity crisis. *Doctor Who* has had wobbles before – the short-term uncertainty of Season Fifteen is a good example – but, in Season Twenty-Four, it was painfully obvious that *Doctor Who* didn't know what it wanted to be. The end of the Saward era marked the final implosion of an era that had, at its best, had a marvellously cohesive (if sometimes cynical) worldview. Yet the unapologetic grimness of Season Twenty-Two had given way to the tired confusion of *The Trial of a Time Lord*, at the end of which Johnny and Eric weren't friends any more. By the time *Delta and the Bannermen* came around, *Time and the Rani* – the absolute nadir of the programme – was already in the can and best forgotten, Andrew Cartmel had the job as script editor shortly after he started shaving and new writers – the ones that Eric Saward had been unable to find – were suddenly sprouting from the trees. *Paradise Towers* feels like a series that has shaken off its past, but at the same time doesn't really know what to make of its future; there are some lovely basic ideas, but the presentation is uncertain. Then came *Delta and the Bannermen*.

Well, it's just brilliant, isn't it?

Ah.

Okay; it would be disingenuous to claim that *Delta and the Bannermen* is flawless. Belinda Mayne and David Kinder give wooden performances in important roles, and there's no getting around the fact that it simply looks cheap. Ken Dodd is, contrary to popular opinion, perfectly fine, but that bloke from the Flying Pickets (that'll be Brian Hibbert, that will) is the least convincing assassin since Maggie Simpson shot Mr Burns.

Still, it's thoroughly charming and also gloriously entertaining. It's a story in which silly, ordinary people triumph over nasty bad guys, and that's ultimately what makes it great. Later Cartmel stories may have been more ambitious, but none of them were as uplifting or so certain of themselves. Its heroes include an old man who will take care of an alien baby without batting an eyelid, and the lovely Mr Burton, who will endanger his life for a woman he barely knows. True, the script isn't short on nostalgia, but it escapes the slightly tawdry feel of "ooh weren't things nicer back in them days" because – well – because it's got alien armies in it, frankly.

It's also got Sara Griffiths in it. (Sighs. Sighs again. Oh, how I love Ray.) She's possibly the best example of what this story does so well, and indeed what *Doctor Who* historicals have always done well; a stereotype who leaps happily from the screen and demands acceptance. The performance is wooden, in its own way, but that seems somehow to help; she's a lovable cute character who parrots "he's been ionised!" to heart-stealing effect. Billy is an attempt at more or less the same thing, but the performance is too laboured to work. The shameless glorification of period stereotypes has a healthy history in *Doctor Who* – Jago and Litefoot are probably the most celebrated example – and Ray is a positive triumph of a character; I do think that watching her trip around Iceworld with the Doctor would have been a joy.

(In fact, the locked-in insistence on a single companion is what we never question about the uncertainty as to whether Ace or Ray were decent companion material. Ace certainly had more mileage than Ray, but the thought of the two of them forming an odd-couple relationship is certainly interesting – if one which would have been difficult to sustain in the later, darker seasons.)

Even the CIA are cute, which is admittedly a tricky one to wrap your head around these days. Stubby Kaye is even less convincing a spy than Flying Picket-Man is an assassin, but he gets some cracking lines ("calling from Wales – in England!"). Hawk and Weismuller are funny and surprisingly empathic. The scene where Gavrok is on the point of shooting them is improbably and shockingly effective; for them to be killed seems so horrifically out of place, so unfair.

There is something extraordinarily grotesque about the Bannermen, quite apart from their leader munching away on raw meat. They're the ultimate Thatcherite baddies, with no morals and a job to do. We're never told why they're so zealous in their pursuit of the Chimerons, but it hardly seems to matter; the Bannermen's motivation is really not the important factor. You wonder why the hell they care so much... but I've always wondered why stockbrokers care about playing the markets, why supercapitalists keep working eighteen hours a day. The sheer unfathomable obsession, the viciously masculine single-mindedness, is really part of the point. These are people prepared to travel across the galaxy just to destroy a woman and her child, and who will blow up a bus full of people on the off-chance she's there. They are, quite simply, obscene.

The Doctor's rant at episode two's conclusion, one of the finest scenes of the era, manages to be somehow valedictory: "What do you know of life, Gavrok? You deal in death. Lies, treachery and murder are your currency. You promise life, but in the end it will be life that defeats you." Viewing this story recently made me wonder whether this is actually McCoy's best performance. He's still saddled with the malapropisms of his earlier stories (although he does get the only funny one of the lot –

"there's many a slap 'twixt a cup and a lap"), but carries them off as well as can be expected and seems thoroughly at home with the story's aesthetic. There are some lovely moments of physicality; his awkward dancing with Ray, his hugging a Stratocaster, or his repeated failure to eat an apple in episode one. That grand cosmic manipulator of the later seasons and the New Adventures is all very well, but this story reminded me why I liked him, too. Scruffy, curious, goofy, friendly and yet oddly wistful; he's marvellous, just marvellous.

The plot is, in the best McCoy fashion, simple but fragmented. A bunch of aliens chase a woman to Wales in 1959 and humanity gets diced in the crossfire. However, it opens with three settings – the Chimeron battlefield, the toll station and Wales – and introduces so many characters that we actually have more layers than one might expect. Goronwy manages to be both funny and enigmatic, and other elements – such as the holiday camp's evacuation – are given more weight than you might imagine. It's a rickety but oddly compelling structure, even if the last half of the story is really just the Doctor and Gavrok trying to outfox each other; the rough-around-the-edges knockabout narrative seems curiously appropriate.

For all its light-heartedness, *Delta and the Bannermen* isn't without moments that are disturbing. The slaughter of the tourists on the bus is the obvious example; it's really shocking, boosted no end by – and these are words you don't get to write often – Bonnie Langford's terrific performance. She's great in this, a story that perfectly suits her aesthetic; Mel is precisely the sort of girl who would join in sing-songs on a tour bus, dance enthusiastically to dodgy fifties cover-bands, and then quickly lie when threatened with death. One thing Langford can portray, superbly, is terror; the scenes between her and Gavrok carry a genuine threat. Don Henderson chews the scenery in his own way, but he scores points by playing his character so straight. It would be tempting to send Gavrok up, but it would have given the story a smug edge that would have damaged it horribly.

Call it the big lie if you will, but this is one of those stories where the good guys win; not only that, but their victories come courtesy of bees, honey and the song of a little girl. A constant diet of this would be sickly sweet, but it's so atypical that it works. It champions idealism and the wonders of the universe; contrast Burton's simple "I don't know what I saw in that police box, but I cannot risk my staff for it" with Hawk's constant cynicism and closed-mindedness, culminating in him quite literally getting burned. He finishes up the story listening to Goronwy, nodding and saying "that's amazing". Just about the only moral the story's got, cheesy as it is. And the parallel between the Chimerons and the bees is deceptively clever.

*Delta and the Bannermen* is a rubbish title, sure, and it's almost impossible to know why they didn't go for *Flight of the Chimeron* instead. And yet, that aside, I find this to be somehow beyond criticism. There are scenes that should fail on every conceivable level; the opening scene is a supposed war sequence, but is shot with a dozen extras and awful video editing, in what's very obviously a quarry. And yet, this was a different time for *Doctor Who*. These days, we're accustomed to it being a commercial televisual juggernaut, flattening everything in its path and giving us technically perfect scenes. That's not to criticise the new series, but there was (and is) always something affirming about olde worlde *Who*. The Graham Williams era is the best example, I feel, of this; it has a heroism, a derring-do bravery and carefree wit that its richer cousin can't achieve.

*Delta and the Bannermen* is maybe the only story of the late 80s that manages to achieve this feeling. Rough and ready, armed with nothing but its convictions, it's unrealistic and naïve and silly. But hey, so's the Doctor. Which is why, if you criticise it, you aren't just missing the point. You're Gavrok.

I viewed this story prior to writing this review for the first time in, oh, a couple of years. I was nervous, truth be told, that my older and more cynical self would be disappointed. Truth is, I loved it more than ever. (Although love has never been known for its rationality, right?) It's simple and happy, and ends up with that wonderful "Here's to the Future" farewell. It might be creaky, but that's part of the joy and it knows it. "I was just speculating what this vehicle would be like with more sophisticated braking and suspension systems," muses the Doctor. "Are you kidding?" replies Ray. "This is the best there is!"

And she's right. She's so wonderfully right.

# Ghost Light: Four Views
*From Dark Circus #4, Summer 1990*

### 1: Biology
### by Kate Orman

**Precambrian Era (more than 570 million years ago):** Life begins on Earth. Simple organic molecules ("sugars, proteins and amino acids") are created when ultraviolet light from the sun strikes the oceans. This forms "primordial soup: the most precious stuff in the universe, from which all life springs." When the Jagaroth's spaceship explodes, it provides the extra energy required to start life on Earth ticking.

Primitive DNA molecules appear, as the smaller molecules which make up deoxyribonucleic acid join together. DNA has the almost-unique property of being able to make copies of itself. However, some DNA strands are better at reproducing themselves than others. By gobbling up the molecules needed for reproduction faster than the other strands, they eventually force those strands into extinction. Natural selection has begun.

After some time, very simple, one-celled lifeforms appear. When they die, a few sink into the sediments at the bottom of the ocean. Those sediments turn to rock, as do the tiny corpses they contain. Millions of years later, human beings will find these fossils, evidence of the very earliest life on Earth.

**Paleozoic Era (570 million years ago):** *Cambrian period (570-500 million years ago):* Some of the one-celled creatures develop the ability to absorb light-energy from the sun and use it to make food. This "photosynthesis" changes the entire planet. The process produces oxygen, which is poisonous to most of the existing lifeforms. Soon, they are all but extinct; the primitive plants – and other organisms which can survive the oxygen – take over. The sun's ultra-violet light converts some of the oxygen into ozone.

*Ordovician period (500-430 million years ago)* and *Silurian period (430-395 million years ago)*: Plants and animals begin to invade the land, protected from the sun's UV radiation by the newly formed ozone layer. The first creatures with backbones appear.

*Devonian period (395-345 million years ago)*: Their backbones help the fishes to become the most important lifeform in the oceans; scientists will later nickname this period the "Age of the Fishes". Some of the fishes develop swim bladders: special sacs the can fill with air to help them keep afloat. When lakes dry up, some fishes use these sacs to breathe and flop across the land on their fins to find new lakes. Eventually, fins evolve into legs and the swim bladders become lungs. The first amphibians have been born.

Insects also appear. Some grow in stages, shedding their old skin and growing a new one at the end of each stage, until they reach their final, adult form. The old skins are left behind like the husks of fruit.

*Carboniferous period (345-280 million years ago)*: The "Age of Amphibians". The plants of this period, instead of becoming fossilised, are turned into coal. Later, humans will discover that coal can be burnt to produce energy – and pollution.

*Permian period (280-225 million years ago)*: Some amphibians develop eggs with water-tight shells and scaly skins which don't dry out in the sun. They no longer need to stay near water. These reptiles take over from the amphibians. They are very successful and some grow to enormous size. The dinosaurs have arrived. They will rule Earth for the next 160 million years.

**Mesozoic Era (225 million years ago):** Some reptiles are becoming more and more able to control their body temperature; instead of having to become inactive at night, or when it becomes too hot during the day, they can be active at all times. These are the first "warm-blooded" creatures: the mammals. The birds appear shortly afterwards.

Light arrives on Earth during the last part of the Mesozoic era, *the Cretaceous Era (136-65 million years ago)*, and starts cataloguing the native life – "from the smallest bacterium to the largest Ichthyosaur". As well as taking specimens and putting them into Quarantine Cubicles, he probably dissects some, as he later will one of the maids in Gabriel Chase.

Light's catalogue takes centuries to complete. During that time, life on Earth has been evolving. Light find to his frustration that his catalogue is out of date. Possibly, he keeps trying to catalogue life, but is unable to keep up. Eventually, he becomes dormant in his spacecraft. He does not wake up for over sixty million years.

**Cenozoic Era (65 million years ago):** *Tertiary period (65-62 million years ago):* Despite Adric's best efforts, the anti-matter-fuelled spacecraft he is on crashes into the Earth. Millions of tons of dirt and dust are thrown into the atmosphere, causing a "nuclear winter"; the dust screens out the sun's heat and the temperature of the Earth plummets. The dinosaurs, unable to cope with the cold, become extinct. Earth is inherited by the dinosaurs' warm-blooded children: the mammals and birds.

During the *Eocene epoch (54-38 million years ago)*, Earth's moon arrives from outer space. The Silurians and Sea Devils believe it will strike Earth and go into suspended animation to avoid the disaster. In fact, the moon is captured by Earth and goes into permanent orbit. The Silurians leave behind their pets: ape-like creatures which are the ancestors of humanity. When the Fendahl arrives, during the *Miocene epoch (about 12 million years ago)*, it goes to work on the pets, influencing their evolution into humans.

During the *Stone Age (about 30,000 years ago)*, Neanderthal man becomes extinct ("At least they knew when to stop evolving"). Light is awake again, and takes up Nimrod as the last example of Homo Neanderthalis. Other cavemen continue to develop; they make stone tools and paint cave pictures of Mammoths, which will soon become extinct.

About 10,000 years ago, the *Recent epoch* begins: human civilisations appear. Human beings start to wonder where they came from. As yet, they have no way of knowing about Earth's millions of years of change and development.

**1859:** Charles Darwin publishes *Origin of Species*. He has been around the world collecting information on different plants and animals. Though he is not the first biologist to realise evolution has happened, he is the first to realise that it happens by natural selection. Biology, geology, astronomy and many other branches of science at last begin to make sense in the light of evolution. By the end of the century, almost all scientists have accepted evolution and natural selection. But, despite the evidence, a very few – plus a number of lay people – cling to the idea that life on Earth was created all at once. These "creationists" are still active today. Like Light, many don't favour the idea of evolution because they would prefer a static, stable universe to one which is constantly changing.

**1881:** Josiah Samuel Smith emerges from his Quarantine Cubicle. After releasing Nimrod and taking over the Pritchards' household, he begins to publish papers about evolution, possibly using Light's catalogue for information. This attracts the attention of a creationist, the Reverend Ernest Matthews.

**1883:** Krakatau, an island volcano between Java and Sumatra, erupts; the tremendous explosion and the resulting tidal wave kill 36,000 people. The island containing Krakatau is completely wiped clean of life and the coast of Java is devastated.

Josiah continues his efforts to develop into what is considered to be the pinnacle of nature: a Victorian gentleman. He has gone through many stages of development, leaving behind a husk at each stage. This development resembles evolution; he must go through many forms, such as an insect and a reptile, before becoming human. This is similar to the way that a human embryo goes through stages which resemble fish, amphibians and reptiles: the embryo even has gills at one point. This development recounts the evolutionary story of human beings.

Meanwhile, Control is also attempting to develop – in her case, into a "ladylike" – but is being held back by Josiah. "World only changing for him. Now he's Josiah. Big man now. Leaving Control behind."

Both Josiah and Control are part of Light's equipment. Apparently, it is Josiah's function to evolve, while Control acts as an experimental control; that is, she does not evolve, so that Light can compare the two.

Josiah completes his final metamorphosis with the unwilling help of the Reverend Ernest Matthews. By turning back Matthews' evolutionary "clock", Josiah is able to turn his own clock forward. At last, he becomes a Victorian gentleman, leaving behind one more husk and turning Matthews into an ancestral ape. Earlier, Control has tried to use Ace for the same purpose.

The Doctor promises to free Control from Light's service if she will bring Light out of his hibernation in the spaceship. Light emerges, taking on the form of a human being. However, Light is not a flesh-and-blood organism, but a creature made of energy. As the energy from both Light and his spacecraft spread out into the house, many of the specimens come to life. "It's the energy from Light's ship. Invigorating, isn't it?"

Redvers and Ace both help Control to evolve. Her development seems to rely on the energy from Light and his ship, and does not produce husks as Josiah's did.

Control eventually does to Josiah what Josiah did to the Reverend Matthews: she absorbs his "evolved-ness" into herself, at last becoming a fully fledged ladylike. "There go the rungs in his evolutionary ladder." Josiah reverts to a more primitive state.

**1937:** E.B. Ford of Oxford University has been studying the peppered moth. During the mid-nineteenth century, these moths were grey, but they gradually became black, until by the 1890s hardly a grey moth could be found. Ford realises that the grey-coloured trees the moths lived on have become covered in soot, produced by industrial burning of coal. Their camouflage ruined, the grey moths were mostly eaten by birds, while a very few mutant black moths were hidden on the soot-covered trees and survived. The peppered moth becomes the textbook example of natural selection. Little does Ford know that Josiah has beaten him to the theory by nearly forty years: "Even in a single species there can be a wide variation in colouring from countryside to town. I'm certain they're adapting to survive the smoke with which industry is tainting the land."

**1983:** Manisha's flat is fire-bombed. Ace burns down Gabriel Chase.

## 2: Literature
## by Steven Caldwell

Marc Platt must be a Victorian junkie! As research for *Ghost Light*, he has not only read the traditional Gothic stories like *Dracula* and *Frankenstein*, but he has also drawn from the popular music and magazines of the age. Even some of the characters have been inspired by, or taken directly from, other Victorian works.

Mrs Grose, for example, is taken from *The Turn of the Screw* (1898), a ghost story by Henry James (watch for the references to this in the novelisation). Gwendoline is borrowed from *The Importance of Being Ernest* (1895), a play by Oscar Wilde. Redvers Fenn-Cooper's name bears a strong resemblance to the American adventure writer James Fenimore Cooper, who wrote *The Last of the Mohicans* (1826). As a big-game hunter, Redvers is part of the popular culture of the time, and even refers to Sir Henry Stanley's famous 1869 expedition into Africa in search of the lost Dr Livingstone.

There are a number of obscure references which are used to flesh out the Victorian background. The popular Music Hall tradition is represented by Gwendoline's ominously placed song, "That's the Way to the Zoo", a song based on a children's rhyme of the time. Equally sinister is Gwendoline's use of the old rhyme Oranges and Lemons: "Here is a candle to light you to bed..." The next line is "Here comes a chopper to chop off your head!"

The famous W.S. Gilbert and Sir Arthur Sullivan, best known for their light comic operas of the time, are also represented by a (sort of) quotation: "The line of my ancestry can be traced back to a protoplasmic globule." This comes from *The Mikado*, Act I (1885).

There are several references to Lewis Carroll's *Wonderland* stories (1865), which serve to stress the fact that there is something wrong in Gabriel Chase. Ace is paralleled with Alice when she goes down the lift shaft – or, as the Doctor later puts it, "the rabbit hole" – and she encounters animals dressed as people (the husks). Gabriel Chase is also called a madhouse or asylum which could be a reference to the mad people that Alice meets in Wonderland. The Doctor quotes Lewis Carroll's gibberish poem "Jabberwocky" (1871) in his final confrontation with Light, when he informs him of "gaps" in his catalogue. The novelisation heightens the significance of the Wonderland stories with a chapter titled "Ace's Adventures Underground".

Charles Darwin's *The Origin of Species* (1859) is central to the discussion of evolution in the story. Evolution is essentially change over time. The sources Platt has chosen all have "change" as a major element in their plots. For instance, *Pygmalion* (1913), the play by George Bernard Shaw (which has been popularised by the 1956 musical *My Fair Lady*), is concerned with the creation of a refined lady from an uneducated flower-seller by the name of Eliza Doolittle. The Doctor calls Ace Eliza at one point when she is behaving in a less-than-cultured fashion. The rhyme which Ace teaches Control is a direct parody of the one taught to Eliza ("The rain in Spain falls mainly on the plain"). The parallel between

Control and Eliza is obvious.

Mary Shelley's *Frankenstein* (1818), Bram Stoker's *Dracula* (1897), Robert Louis Stevenson's *Strange Case of Dr Jekyll and Mr Hyde* (1886), as well as Edgar Rice Burroughs' *Tarzan* (1912) are important stories. Ace sees parallels between the vampire Count and Josiah ("Stitch this, Dracula!"). The Doctor uses the Dr Jekyll / Mr Hyde relationship to explain the bond between Josiah and Control; meaning, which of the two is the monster? They are both part of the same experiment (like Dr Jekyll and Mr Hyde are, in fact, the same person), yet one has changed for the worse.

Josiah is something like Dr Frankenstein's monster. He tries to be human, but he is unnatural and is denied true humanity. The fear of light and flame that he and his husks share may also be a reference to the Frankenstein monster's similar fear.

In each of the stories listed above, the main characters are slightly out of place in the world. Count Dracula imitates the hero, Jonathan Harker, in the hope that when he gets to England he will pass as a normal man. Underneath that, however, he is still a depraved monster. The Frankenstein monster is made of human parts, but lacks a compassionate soul and is unable to lead a normal life. Even Tarzan is cut off from society because of his upbringing in the jungle.

It is Josiah's desire to be a proper Victorian gentleman that causes all the problems in Gabriel Chase. He, like the characters above, has only absorbed part of the human essence: the destructive side. William Blake, an English poet of the late 1700s, wrote the following lines which could be used to describe Josiah Samuel Smith:

Cruelty had a Human Heart,
And Jealousy a Human Face;
Terror the Human Form Divine,
And Secrecy the Human Dress.

—"A Divine Image" (1789), lines 1-4.

William Blake has been a great inspiration to Marc Platt. The author has said that Light was drawn from Blake's Angels in his visionary poems. The poems, such as "The Book of Urizen", "The Angel" and "Auguries of Innocence", deal with the combat between the forces of light and darkness. The Angels are not always good in these metaphysical poems. They are often destructive forces seeking the revenge of God.

There are several Biblical references in *Ghost Light* beyond that of Light (Lucifer, "bringer of light", was the name of the fallen angel who became the Devil). Gabriel Chase is a reference to the angel Gabriel who was the messenger of God and "chief of the Angelic guards" (*Paradise Lost* by John Milton, 1667, Book IV, line 561). Nimrod is also a name drawn from the Bible, as is the Reverend Ernest Matthews. Matthew was one of Jesus' most fanatical apostles. The addition of "earnest" to his name only heightens this.

A quote from Douglas Adams even makes its way into *Ghost Light*, also illustrating the evolutionary theme: "Earthmen are not proud of their ancestors, and never invite them round to dinner."

Marc Platt gives us a story that is thick with glib references to his sources. These are used to heighten the mood, and to illustrate specific characters and their relationships with one another. Judging by the results, all of his research has paid off.

## 3: Puppet Shows
## by Nathan Bottomley

*Ace gleefully picked up the tin model of a skating rink. The clockwork skaters immediately began to whizz merrily around in circles. She giggled. "It's well safe, Professor."*

– *Ghost Light* novelisation by Marc Platt, page 18

*"It's a laboratory... or it could be a nursery. But the kids'd have to be pretty advanced."*

– *Ghost Light* by Marc Platt (televised version), episode one

If you think back to 1977, to Chris Boucher's *The Robots of Death*, you'll remember why Leela found the Sandminer's crew of "creepy mechanical men" so disturbing. Although they were human in shape, they had no human movements, no body language. Living with them for a few months was enough to drive someone mad with "robophobia".

That's one of the things that makes *Ghost Light* such a disturbing story to watch. When Ace puts down the toy ice rink and goes downstairs with the Doctor into Gabriel Chase, she enters a world of creepy mechanical men or (if you want to avoid the anachronism) sinister clockwork figures, whizzing around in circles. These figures are the human inhabitants of the house: the Pritchards, the maids and Nimrod; and three visitors: Redvers Fenn-Cooper, Inspector MacKenzie and the Reverend Ernest Matthews.

Three things give us the impression that the human characters in *Ghost*

*Light* are nothing more than clockwork automata under the control of Josiah Samuel Smith.

One, their movements are strictly regimented and choreographed: maids emerge mechanically from sliding doors and stand in neat rows on the stairs, and the Pritchards rise mechanically from under their dust-sheets in the Upper Observatory at exactly six o'clock.

Two, they are only partially aware of their surroundings: Mrs Pritchard ignores the Doctor's introductions when she enters the study to get Redvers; Nimrod does the same just before he takes the Doctor's hat and umbrella; and Inspector McKenzie enters a room inhabited by an angel and a caveman and sees nothing to be surprised at.

And three, the Pritchards at least show affection and sympathy for Josiah: Mrs Pritchard's evil complicity in Josiah's scheme to destroy Reverend Matthews, her concerned reaction to the Doctor threatening Josiah with a radiation detector, Gwendoline's "lucifugousness", and the almost sexual relationship between her and her "dear uncle", Josiah.

And it seems that Josiah can do anything he likes to any of them. He makes Lady Margaret Pritchard his housekeeper, Nimrod the Neanderthal his butler, Redvers his executioner and Matthews his pet chimpanzee. "They're toys. They're just Josiah's toys," says Ace. "Your puppet show doesn't fool me, Josiah," says the Doctor. In the novelisation, Josiah himself revolting refers to the Upper Observatory where he keeps them all as the "toybox".

So how is Josiah doing it?

*He stalked out of the study. Selective hypnosis was just the sort of crude device the Doctor had expected from Josiah. It was typical of the contempt in which Josiah held the humans he treated so cruelly as playthings.*

– *Ghost Light* novelisation by Marc Platt, page 81

Josiah is a hypnotist, exerting different sorts of control over the different inhabitants of Gabriel Chase. He controls the night maids completely; he allows the Pritchards some freedom to act independently, although he forces them to be concerned for his welfare and intentions; he lets Redvers and Nimrod wander loose in the house until he needs them; he even allows Ernest Matthews to argue with him, knowing that of course he can easily defeat him.

But, like the Victorian stage mesmerist, he can only make people do what is already in their nature. Mrs Pritchard and Gwendoline are "lost" – damned to perdition – for what they have done, because, despite Josiah's conditioning, they are still responsible for their actions: "I could have forgiven her for arranging those little trips to Java," says the Doctor, "if she didn't enjoy it so much." Gwendoline's joy at the prospect of sending Ace to Java reflects something evil in her character. ("I'm sure she'll enjoy Java, Uncle. Once she gets there.") And this is all the more shocking when she appears to be so innocent and untouched at the beginning of episode one.

The only person who successfully resists Josiah is Redvers, and that's because he has been driven mad by something much more powerful: Light. While Light is asleep, Josiah can play with his toys as much as he likes. When it wakes up, it's Game Over for Josiah, as Light goes around breaking and destroying all of Josiah's playthings.

So when you next watch *Ghost Light*, watch the first scene with Ace and the Doctor very carefully. The Upper Observatory is full of Victorian playthings right from the very beginning – but by the end of episode two it is filled with toys that are much more sinister than ice rinks and rocking horses: the human inhabitants of Gabriel Chase. After all, the kids in this course are "pretty advanced – and creepy", aren't they?

## 4: Aliens
## by Dallas Jones

The crux of the story *Ghost Light* are the questions:

1. Who is Light?
2. What is he doing?
3. And why is he doing what he is doing?

In *Doctor Who Magazine* #158, Marc Platt, author of *Ghost Light*, says in an interview that "The answers are all there." So the answers to all these questions should be in the story.

Now, this does not mean that the answers have to be spelt out in black and white, but if we can deduce the answers from the information that Platt has provided, then his statement about his story is truthful. The only trouble is that it is quite easy to deduce different, conflicting answers, because all the information is not there, or it is cryptic and vague. Anyway, let's try and find the answers.

The second of the questions ("What is Light doing?") seems to be the easiest to answer, so we will look at it first – but it will quickly lead us into trying to answer the other two questions. Basically, Light catalogued all life on Earth. For some reason "he" went into hibernation, and when he woke up found that not only was he still on Earth, but as the local life had evolved to produce new species, his catalogue was not complete.

Light sets about making sure his catalogue will be accurate by planning to destroy the Earth when the catalogue update is completed. Thus, the catalogue will always be correct.

The biggest clue about what Light was doing is that it is hinted that he did know about evolution. He says of Nimrod, "He was the last of his kind." To make this statement, Light must have some knowledge of evolution, as the extinction of species is part of the Darwinian evolution theory.

Of course, it cannot be taken seriously that something with Light's power, who has a mission to catalogue all life on a planet, would not know about evolution; this is plainly ridiculous. If we accept that Light did know about evolution when he was doing his catalogue, but he doesn't know about it now, then we must assume that something has gone wrong.

This is confirmed by Light not believing that he was still on Earth. Of course, the question of who or what Control and Josiah are come into the spotlight at this point. The answer is easy: they are part of the original experiment, which, as well as cataloguing the planet's lifeforms, was also looking at the nature of evolution on the planet. If this is not the case, we are left with the question of why Light was cataloguing the planet.

Control, as the name implies, is the "control": a standard of comparison not acted upon by the experiment. Josiah is the subject of the experiment (the "survey"), with the husks being the different stages that he has gone through. They mimic the evolutionary path from lower to higher animals, i.e. from insect to reptile to mammal (though this isn't exactly the correct pathway). The change from the Josiah we first see to the more refined Josiah is a reference to the evolution of intelligence and culture that mankind has gone through.

This is backed up with the evolution of Control, once she is no longer a "control". We do not see much of her physical evolution, but we have the "Eliza Doolittle" evolution of her character from gutter snipe to lady.

What went wrong to cause Light to forget about evolution and to leave Josiah in charge is not spelled out. All I can say is that it really doesn't matter, as it is not important to the story. The results of whatever happened are important, however, as they are, in fact, the story.

That leads us back to our first question. Who is Light? We know of the various religious allusions that Platt has ascribed to him: Ace calls him an angel, and I would go so far as to say he is the Archangel Gabriel, one of the angels who will blow their trumpets to signal the end of the world. It is also interesting to note that Light, Control and Josiah make up a triumvirate; an allusion to the Trinity (God the father, the son and the holy ghost)?

What is clear is that Light is an ethereal being (i.e. he has no physical body), who, as the Doctor says, "travels at the speed of thought". Thoughts aren't physical things, but electrical impulses, suggesting that he is an energy being. Another possibility is that Light is not a "being", but a construct. Something built to carry out the mission of cataloguing all Earth lifeforms and performing experiments to understand the path of evolution on the planet. This could easily explain why things went wrong, because if Light was a construct, all we would need to say is that something failed or interfered with its "programming", along the lines of Nomad or V'Ger from the *Star Trek* universe.

You can see that many of the questions raised by *Ghost Light* can be answered from the information in the story, but, I feel, not all of them. Some are relatively unimportant, like "What happened to cause things to go wrong?", but others are very important, such as "Who is Light?" So, despite what Platt says, I do not think all the answers are there.

But there are a lot more answers and explanations in *Ghost Light* than you would think from a cursory viewing, and this is one of the strengths of this story. Unfortunately, to a casual viewer, it is also one of its weaknesses.

# INTERLUDE

## The Key to a Time Lord - 5
**by Scott Clarke**
*From Enlightenment #124, November 2004*

**Episode Four: Humour**
*"Eureka is Greek for 'this bath is too hot'"*

Episode five of *The Talons of Weng-Chiang* offers the payoff to one of the longest gag setups in *Doctor Who* history: Professor Litefoot opening his front door to Henry Gordon Jago. Okay, I'm probably stretching the definition of a gag, but the essence of all good comedy is that delicious blend of the expected/familiar and the unexpected. Throughout the story, we'd come to know these two characters individually: Litefoot's unflappable nature being used as excellent foil to Leela's Eliza Doolittle; Jago's comedic bluster used to side-splitting effect alongside Casey and the Doctor. As when chocolate met peanut butter, their inevitable collision is both satisfying and surprising.

Immediately, Henry mistakes Litefoot and his dustpan for the butler. Upon being set straight, Jago exclaims, "By dash me optics," and addresses Litefoot as the "peerless premiere professor of pathology." Robert Holmes is at the top of his wit. A moment later, Litefoot escorts Jago into the parlour, carrying his stick for fending off ruffians; it's a wonderful, subtle sight gag. All that we know about these characters thus far contributes to our delight and anticipation. Later, when the Greel captures the dynamic duo, we're treated to a hilarious bit of three-way interplay where the villain questions Jago while throttling him, and Litefoot carries on the exchange with Greel:

> Greel: Why were you waiting at the theatre?
> Jago (looks at Litefoot): Why were we at the theatre?
> Litefoot: I refuse to answer.
> Jago (to Greel): There you go, he refuses to answer.

Humour diffuses an exceptionally intense scene, both in the scripting and direction. A simple bit of dialogue and plot exposition are transformed into something quite funny. In fact, much of episode five is quite talky and expository, getting characters from point A to B. And yet, it's quite memorable for its comedic flourishes. Essentially, when Litefoot and Jago escape through the dumbwaiter, all we're getting is traditional *Doctor Who* escape/capture padding. But the sight of the "peerless, premiere pathologist" and the blustery theatre owner crawling into the cramped conveyor of Victorian vittles is priceless!

Humour is laced throughout the various eras of *Doctor Who* in a variety of styles: there's slapstick ("when I say run, Jamie... run"), satire (tax forms in *The Sun Makers*), black humour (more ketchup with Auntie Wineva please, in *Revelation of the Daleks*) and farce (*The Romans*). These serve a variety of purposes, such as comic relief in frightening stories, character development, or soft pedalling social commentary. Tom Baker and Patrick Troughton were particularly effective in employing humour to define their characters and to lighten grim encounters with baddies.

As *Doctor Who* has always been classified as a "family program", humour has been vital during various points in the program's history. When the BBC programmers found the show to be excessively violent after the 1985 Colin Baker season, the strategy was to tone down the violence and "up" the humour quotient. A rather misguided directive, as *Doctor Who* has always been a fine balance of both heavier and lighter elements. Ironically, it was Robert Holmes himself who delivered the rather weak comedic antics on display in *The Mysterious Planet*. Much of Glitz and Dibber's dialogue is a little forced, and some of the more slapstick material with the food processors shows signs of chronic fatigue. Ditto Sylvester McCoy's debut in *Time and the Rani*, which is forced and self-conscious, never really "spooning" smoothly with the action.

Early attempts at humour in the program were rare and had mixed results. *The Reign of Terror* shows us the Doctor (shanghaied into a work party) tricking a foreman into bending over for a coin and then cudgelling him senseless with a shovel; it's a nice little jewel of a set piece, enabling us to see the first Doctor in a different light. Full-on farce erupts in *The Romans* as Dennis Spooner unleashes Nero onto a long-suffering Barbara through the corridors of Rome; it's quite a shock, after the intensity of the previous two stories. I love the sense of experimentation evident in the story, proving the mould would never set on *Doctor Who*.

Troughton infused regular doses of clownishness into the offices of overbearing authority figures under siege, and his ongoing double act with Jamie provided a canvas for all manner of comedic potential. One always delighted in observing how he would "let the air out" of various gasbags. But there were very practical reasons for all the clowning: the

Troughton era contains some visceral imagery and situations.

Douglas Adams first teased viewers with his popular brand of imaginative, undergraduate humour in *The Pirate Planet* and then assaulted them full on with Season Seventeen. It gelled nicely with Tom Baker's larger-than-life lunacy. But look a little more closely at what's going on. In the rather routine opening of *Destiny of the Daleks*, Adams "subverts the familiar" with the Doctor's comment, "Oh look, rocks!" Suddenly, the same old, same old is imbued with freshness. In the following story, witty dialogue enlivens what could have been familiar delivery and sharpens our delight in the characters ("It'll be so much the worse for you, for this young lady, and for thousands of other people I could mention if I happened to have the Paris telephone directory on my person"). Of course, some would argue that Adams went too far with his sendup of *Who* itself ("If you're the conquerors of the universe, why not climb up after me?"), but good comedy often does just that: externalises the unspeakable – and unthinkable.

After the iconic imagery in *Doctor Who*, I would argue that the humour is the second-most-memorable element of the program. Certainly, it was what kept me watching the predictable plotting and dodgy production values in *Robot*, one of my earlier *Who* viewing experiences. The sight of Tom Baker in the Viking outfit had me in stitches; I don't particularly know why. There is an element of magic to humour that makes it very risky. Why did Sylvester McCoy fail so badly for me at first? Humour is a matter of taste, of course, and the person who enjoyed Troughton's clowning is not the same one who delighted in Orcini's dark wit in *Revelation of the Daleks*. Perhaps *Doctor Who's* ability to try on different comedic traditions is yet another tribute to its staying power.

Weaving humour seamlessly into an intense and gothic story like *The Talons of Weng-Chiang* is certainly the key for me. I'm not opposed to a silly romp like *Delta and the Bannermen* or even to the Doctor battling a dancer in an oversized bull's head, but when you can deliver me a terrifying villain who is throttling a hero, and make it funny, you've got me!

Russell T Davies obviously thinks humour is essential to the new series, even in the choice of writers he's selected for scripting: Mark Gatiss (*The League of Gentlemen*), Steven Moffat (*Coupling*), Rob Shearman (*Jubilee*, *The Holy Terror*). And Davies was recently quoted in the *Manchester Evening News* as saying, "I think it's magnificent and it's very funny... It's not a knock-about farce, but it's laugh-out-loud funny. That's partly because Christopher Eccleston knew he had a reputation as a very serious actor and wanted to do it because he wished to reinvent himself and show how funny he could be!"

Here's to hiding behind the couch... or falling off it!

# DARKNESS

For a long time, *Doctor Who* was defined by stories where good people came into evil situations, overcame adversity (monsters, villains, guns, super weapons, giant clams) and became triumphant in the end.

Except it's more complex than that.

One of the great contradictions of *Doctor Who* is that it's a show whose identity is founded on optimism and morality, even as the *Doctor Who* universe itself is a dark and disturbing place.

Then there's the Doctor himself. By the late 1980s, the *zeitgeist* in popular culture virtually demanded that viewers question the motives of their heroes, whether that be to ask why a man would dress like a bat and fight criminals or what a self-professed Lord of Time might be actually capable of doing. In *Doctor Who's* case, the last couple of seasons of the classic series opened to the door to that question by having the Doctor become more enigmatic and more willing to play the game at all costs.

And yet, the series always had that particular door wide open. The Doctor is our beloved hero, but is still willing to split a caveman's head open, still willing to coax a human/Dalek hybrid into existence only to immediately dispatch these new lifeforms into a war with the Daleks that will wipe them out, still willing to do to the Sea Devils what he admonished the Brigadier for doing to the Silurians, still willing to go back to the Dalek embryo room and blow it up (no matter how many times documentaries proudly show the clip of him agonising over it earlier).

The truth is clear in the new series (and the novels of the 90s before it): the Doctor is a mess of contradictions. He's a clown who hides his ruthlessness. A god-like alien who uses human qualities of warmth, humour and curiosity to deflect his true nature. The Doctor can be as dark as the universe he lives in. However, what makes him so heroic, and so loved, is that he's frequently much better than the universe he's in. Often in spite of himself.

# The Doctor's Darker Nature

## by Lou Anders

Do you know what the most interesting scene in the entire history of *Doctor Who* is to me? I'm talking the absolutely, hands-down, most fascinating thing the program did, in both its 26-year original run and its new, heading-into-a-fifth-year incarnation? The thing that blows me away the most, that I keep coming back to in my mind again and again and again?

Okay, I'll tell you. It's that scene in the very first storyline, *An Unearthly Child*, where the Doctor picks up a rock and Ian barely stops him from using it to pulverise a caveman's brains. In the scene, the TARDIS crew are running for their lives, and the Doctor selfishly insists that an injured stone age man is slowing them down. Ian and Barbara make it perfectly clear that the merciful thing to do is to take the man with them. The Doctor is overruled, unhappy about it and, left on his own for a moment a little later, decides to remove their objection by killing the man.

That's right: the Doctor. Not a Dalek or a Cyberman or the Master or even one of his less-likeable companions like Turlough or someone. But our hero, the star of the show, the star of what was supposed to be (and is still often regarded as) a children's show, is planning on splattering the contents of an injured man's cranium all over the ground for nothing worse than the crime of inconveniencing him.

Wow.

Can you imagine that happening today? On any show? Let alone *Doctor Who*, the show that lately can't seem to stuff enough Christ-figure metaphors into its main character? And yet, here at the premiere story of *Doctor Who*, our lead is about to commit cold-blooded, calculated murder. And as out of character as this may seem for "the Doctor" that we have watched through five decades of heroism and self-sacrifice, it isn't actually *that* out of character for this strange man we've just met. After all, his human companions – the ones so intent on saving the wounded man – are only along for the ride because he kidnapped them, throwing a time machine he couldn't pilot into the past as a way to prevent them from taking his granddaughter away, when it became clear the granddaughter herself wanted off the bus.

He endangers all their lives again in the second story, *The Daleks*, when, outvoted on whether or not to explore a mysterious, potentially deadly (and, although they do not know it yet, radioactive) city, he empties a "fluid link", forcing them to scout out the missing components (mercury) to fix the TARDIS. He's basically an utterly selfish and self-interested bastard, who thinks nothing of risking the lives of those around him when it suits his purposes, or even his whims. He's hardly a hero at all. And that's what I love about *Doctor Who*. The Doctor didn't start out a hero, he didn't even start out as "the Doctor". When his granddaughter, who's been using the name "Susan Foreman", leads the teachers into Foreman's Yard, they mistakenly refer to him as "Doctor Foreman", causing him to react, "Doctor who? What's that man blathering about?" And thus was born the conceit that we don't even know our lead's real name.

Now, over decades of real life and hundreds of hours of television, the Doctor did become a hero, and bits and pieces of the mythology begin to almost organically accrue. He's a Time Lord, he's from Gallifrey, he has two hearts, yada yada yada. But the one thing that stuck and never got messed with was the idea that before we met him in *An Unearthly Child*, he had been someone quite different.

In the unfinished episode *Shada*, for instance, we learn that the Doctor's childhood hero was a criminal. In *The Keeper of Traken*, the fourth Doctor muses that the planet's nature – which makes it inimical to evil – might be the reason he never visited. We learn in *The Five Doctors* that the early days of the Time Lords were full of cruelty: they were essentially über-powerful tyrants who played with lesser races for their own amusement until Rassilon experienced a change of heart and established their equivalent of the Prime Directive against non-interference. This in itself isn't as significant until you get to all that unfulfilled hint-dropping in the seventh's Doctor's brief reign, where they go out of their way to suggest that Rassilon and Omega had a third, lost-to-history accomplice. Now, leaving aside all the fan speculation, various theories put forth in the New Adventures and BBC books, etc, and sticking simply to the show itself, it doesn't take a genius to work out that where they were going with this was that before he was "the Doctor", he was one of those rather powerful, rather cruel tyrants from the early days of Time Lord history and that perhaps the reason he doesn't want his name known is because he's got an evil past to go with it.

Whether this is true or not, it is certainly true that the Doctor's nature improves over time, and I think there's some pretty strong evidence that the intent of the series is to suggest that it is his exposure to his human companions that is responsible for his walking deeper in the light. Whether it's the first Doctor telling Barbara that he learns by observing her, or the seventh Doctor reciting the names of all of his companions to create a psychic shield against the Haemovores, or Donna holding back the tenth Doctor from pouring the entire Thames down to the centre of the Earth (which he sort of did anyway), there's a five-decades-long understanding that maybe what makes the Doctor a good person is who he chooses to surround himself with.

Conversely, there's a subtler, parallel theme at work, one which may not be conscious in the minds of the writers, but is certainly there. Which is that, despite his companions, he's slowly turning dark again anyway.

The clearest example of where this can be seen is in his relationship with Davros and the Daleks. In *Genesis of the Daleks*, the Doctor is sent by the Time Lords to prevent the Daleks' creation. And, even though he's been told that nothing less than the fate of the entire universe is at stake, he can't bring himself to make such a major change in history. It's just too much. One incarnation later, in *Resurrection of the Daleks*, the Doctor grabs a gun and almost manages to kill their creator. Almost, but again, he can't do it. However, he's apparently had enough by the time of *Remembrance of the Daleks*, where the seventh Doctor programs the Hand of Omega to destroy not only the Dalek mothership, but their entire homeworld of Skaro as well. And, of course, by the time of the Time War that forms the background for the new series, he's seemingly wiped out all Daleks everywhere and, it's implied, been responsible for the eradication of his own people as well.

So yes, I'd say he's getting darker as he grows older.

I'd go so far as to say that the way he eschews guns and deplores violence so loudly sounds to me like nothing so much as the way an alcoholic reacts when you offer him a drink. The Doctor isn't nonviolent – he's unbelievably violent – but he hates it with a hatred that only self-loathing can explain away. "It takes one to know one," as they say. Whatever he did back then in the dark days of Time Lord prehistory, he's terrified of a return to it.

But you've got to stand up to evil when you see it, right? I mean, that's one of the abiding themes of the show.

Which is how he's come to evolve his current, tenth Doctor code, of having to always offer the Bug Eyed Monster a choice. One chance to stand down (and how cool was it when the Vashta Nerada actually took him up on it?), and then he's not responsible for the violence that follows. Of course, we all know that 99 out of 100 times the BEMs aren't going to take the easy way out and, as smart as he is, he must know it too, but offering the choice allows him to unleash his violence with a clear conscience.

That's pretty dark, when you think about it!

What's fascinating to me is how this actually fits with both the original series and new series continuity. In that mess of a season-long story, *The Trial of a Time Lord*, we meet what could have been the ultimate adversary, the Valeyard, who is said to be "an amalgamation of the Doctor's darker side, somewhere between his twelfth and final incarnation."

Say again? Yup, the Valeyard is none other than a piece of the Doctor, broken off and given independent life. Maybe as it grew, he realised the only way to deal with it was to physically expel it. (There is some wonderful speculation in *The Discontinuity Guide* about things being projected out of Time Lords during their regenerations.) Whatever the rationale, I hope the series will deal with it when we get there, because that line right there – "an amalgamation of the darker sides of your nature, somewhere between your twelfth and final incarnation" – well, that's the second-most-interesting thing about the entire series to me.

Because, when you get right down to it, *Doctor Who* is a series about the battle between good and evil. That the front line of this battle takes place inside the head of the same man, that's what I find so compelling. He may wrestle with monsters throughout time and space, but it's the internal struggle going on behind his eyes that keeps me watching. And I suspect it always will. After all, a universe without the Doctor scarcely bears thinking about.

# The Day the Animals Learned About Death

by **Cameron Dixon**
*From Enlightenment #110, June / July 2002*

Death on *Doctor Who* used to be fun. It was a plot device, something you could count on. In fact, something you could literally count. You start the story with a certain number of characters, and that number slowly gets reduced as the story goes on. Ooh, I wonder what happens next! Palmerdale gets electrocuted, and thrown over the side of a lighthouse! Harker's the next to go, then Vince – poor Vince, tee hee hee. Adelaide goes screaming, big surprise there, and Skinsale dies scrabbling for diamonds. Tick, tick, tick; checkbox empty, roll on the next exciting adventure!

Fun stuff. Kids' stuff. In the novelisations, you could always count on someone dying in the opening bit, before the TARDIS showed up: *Planet of Evil, Death to the Daleks, Image of the Fendahl*. The hiker screaming in terror as his life-essence was sucked out of him; isn't that neat? I actually remember showing that bit from the novelisation of Fendahl to my grandmother, back when I was eleven. I think she was quite polite about it.

It's fun because it's not real. These aren't real people dying. That much is obvious to anybody. These were all fictional characters, there to populate a plot; nothing more. As a kid, I knew that much. What I didn't know was that there could be any other way of looking at it.

## 9. Darkness

I would have been about fifteen or so when *Resurrection of the Daleks* aired. Resurrection. Funny title, that, all things considered.

Back then, [insert typical tale of formative teenaged angst], but the bruises faded eventually and I've never seen them since. I knew that I needed something to escape to, but at the time I couldn't find the words for what I really wanted: a tale of good defeating evil. Real evil, not the wussy kind of first-season *Star Trek: TNG* evil that said "Oh, you mean what we're doing is wrong? Okay then, we'll stop." Show us evil with no remorse and whip its arse.

And that was what I was getting from *Doctor Who*, for a while there. That was what I thought I was going to get from *Resurrection of the Daleks*. Plus, it had Daleks in it, so it had to be cool, right?

Wrong. It's amazing what effect a slight error in post-production can have on a young man's upbringing, if by "slight" you mean "the complete absence of sound effects and music from the second half of the serial." Part of the version of *Resurrection of the Daleks* broadcast in North America was accidentally lacking in certain audio qualities – which, in short, means that for about 46 minutes there in 1985, I was watching people walk through various metal corridors and shoot each other with guns that didn't even have the decency to go "zap" when they killed someone.

It was... boring. Watching people die was boring.

Watching people die.

Perhaps if it had actually had a soundtrack, there would have been some tension to it. The extras actually would have been extras, falling over on cue in an action-adventure piece. But, without the music, without the audio effects, they were just... people. This wasn't calculated, manufactured grimness; this was just grim. The soldiers on screen were reduced to the level of children, running around in the schoolyard, pointing sticks at each other and saying "bang".

That spoiled it for me. The lack of interest meant that the complications thrown into the storyline just became confusing; for quite a while there, I couldn't even have told you what *Resurrection of the Daleks* was ultimately about, just that it had people running around shooting each other. But the worst was yet to come.

You know the scene I'm talking about. Already bored with the story, waiting for it to be over, really not enjoying this, but watching anyway, because it's *Doctor Who*. On the docks. Tegan, looking for help. Policemen arrive. Salvation! Until one of them pulls a gun out from under his coat. Tegan runs to the edge of the docks, looks over the side. There's someone down there, a man with a metal detector, a potential ally. She calls; he doesn't even notice. She's caught. She looks at the man in the distance. He hasn't looked up. Doesn't even know she's there.

They shoot him.

She screams.

That's not the word. This wasn't a cheap companion shriek, a Leatherlungs howl, the prelude to "Mel vs. the Tetraps". This was a cry. A raw, throat-scraping shriek. This is Janet Fielding pulling out all of the acting stops and giving us pure, animal, This Is Not Happening denial. This was real.

Eric Saward has gone on record as saying that he wanted to show the consequences of violence; that when you got hit, it hurt. This is the one that did it for me. This is where death stopped being fun, where extras stopped being extras, where fictional characters acquired depth. Death was no longer a checklist. When people got hit, it hurt; when they got shot, they died, and they never, ever, ever came back again, from anywhere. Ever.

He didn't ever know they were there. That's why Tegan screamed, that's why I recoiled and am still, on some level, recoiling. He was just out trolling for loose change, and bam, he was... just out. No name. No face. No role to play in the grand scheme of things. No idea whether or not he had a moustache. Gone.

That shriek, the look on her face; that's what changed *Doctor Who* for me, and the concept of death, while we're at it. Death stopped being fun. Loss and grief acquired real emotional weight; scars lasted. Absence became lasting, not something to be shrugged off lightly with a promise of a visit to the Great Victorian Exhibition.

This concept of gravitas reshapes the world; the idea that every life really, really matters. That the people you pass on the street have their own lives as rich and full and precious as your own. That there are no extras. That death strikes with no warning, takes away something special and never, ever gives it back.

It's a more mature point of view; it kick-started me out of childhood, and Eric Saward and Janet Fielding helped to do that for me. Or to me.

I wish I could thank them for it. Really, I do.

# The Two Clowns
# With Skeletons In The Closet

by James Bow

*From Enlightenment #64, September / October 1994*

Recently, I was speaking with a friend who was also a fan of *Doctor Who*. As friends who are fans are apt to do, our discussion soon turned toward the series, and our subject matter ranged through a wide variety of topics. In due course, it was during this conversation that I was struck by the similarities between the second Doctor story *The Evil of the Daleks* and the seventh Doctor adventure *Remembrance of the Daleks*. Obviously, both are Dalek stories; both also feature an Emperor Dalek, different Dalek factions and a Dalek Civil War. Both feature events which could be construed as the final destruction of the Dalek race.

But I was also startled by the similarity between the characters of the second Doctor and the seventh. Both are under 5 feet 10 inches tall, both have clownish exteriors that shield a deadly serious core and, most surprising, both characters have dark sides, and are willing to manipulate events and people, including their own companions, to meet their own ends.

Though I have generally enjoyed the stories that featured in the twenty-fifth and twenty-sixth seasons of our program, I have been annoyed at the drive by the production team to make the Doctor more than just a Time Lord. The Doctor is alien, yes, but to have him being dark and manipulative all the time, knowing what is going on before anybody else does gets distracting after a while, and detracts from the drama of the series.

So, you can imagine my surprise when I saw the second Doctor exhibiting the same dark attributes as the seventh. A reassessment of my perceptions of the two characters may be in order.

Critics suggest that the negative characteristics of the seventh Doctor include his knowing what is going on before other people and bending the laws of time to gain this knowledge. They also state that his dark and manipulative nature, having the ends justify the means, is out of character for the Time Lord we know and love. He misleads his companions and is not above sacrificing people so that a greater good is achieved. This makes the Doctor alien. However, I and others don't really want to watch a program about an alien. We want to see a program featuring alien technology, yes, but the main protagonist should be somebody we can sympathise with. How can we sympathise with someone who destroys planets, who knows what is going on before anybody else, yet is unable to prevent innocent people from being hurt?

Yet, this is exactly what the second Doctor can be charged with in *The Evil of the Daleks* and, to a lesser extent, *The Tomb of the Cybermen*. Despite this, some fans remember the second Doctor a lot more fondly than they are willing to remember the seventh. Why?

As Ace was manipulated to help bring down Fenric in *The Curse of Fenric*, the second Doctor deliberately alienates Jamie. The Highlander desperately wants to rescue poor Victoria, and is infuriated by the Doctor's apparent compliance with the Daleks. Defiant, he heads out on his own, as the Doctor expects. The Doctor stands idly by and monitors Jamie as the young man risks his own life to save Victoria. From Jamie's reactions to the very real dangers he faces (including a powerful strongman named Kemmel, booby traps and the Daleks themselves), the Doctor discovers the elements that make up the Human Factor. This he willingly injects into the test Daleks, despite the pleas of a remorseful Edward Waterfield who fears the invincible super Daleks that may result.

How questionable is the second Doctor's conduct? Edward Waterfield seriously considers attacking the Doctor from behind with a lead pipe to prevent him from implanting the Human Factor inside the Daleks. Jamie himself condemns the Doctor with the strongest words used by a companion in the show's history:

*"Well, Jamie!" the Doctor exclaimed happily. "The experiment's nearly over! I've got no sleep. I've been up all night, but it's been worth it!"*

*Jamie stopped in his tracks and drew back from the Doctor in disgust. "Get away from me!" he hissed.*

*The Doctor gazed at Jamie curiously. "Now what's the matter?"*

*"Anyone would think this was a little game!"*

*The Doctor's expression soured. "No, it is not a game."*

*"Of course it isn't, Doctor!" Jamie shouted. "People have died! The Daleks all over this place picked them out of the lot of us and all you can say is you've had a good night's work!"*

*"Jamie, I—"*

*"No, Doctor! Look, I'm telling you this: you and me, we're finished! You're just too callous for me! Anything goes by the board, anything at all!"*

*For a moment, the Doctor hesitated. He spoke nervously. "That's not true, Jamie! I've never held that the end justifies the means."*

*"Och, words!" Jamie sighed in exasperation. "What do I care about words? You don't care about a living soul except yourself!"*

*The Doctor's face hardened. "I care about life! I care about human beings! Do*

*you think that I let you go through that Dalek test lightly?"*
*Jamie didn't know what to think. "I don't know, did you? Look, Doctor, just*
*whose side are you on?"*

The above was transcribed directly from an audio copy that exists of this story's soundtrack. This stunning conversation mirrors a similar condemnation voiced against the Doctor by Ace in *The Curse of Fenric*, here novelised by author Ian Briggs:

> *The Doctor saw the anger burning in Ace's eyes.*
> *"You know what's going on, don't you?" she hissed...*
> *... "Yes," he said, and turned to the shadows.*
> *"You always know! You just can't be bothered to tell anyone!" Ace's anger*
> *flared.*
> *"Like it's some kind of game, and only you know the rules! You knew all about*
> *the inscriptions being a computer program, but you didn't tell me! You know all*
> *about that old bottle but you're not telling me! Am I so stupid?"*

In *The Evil of the Daleks*, the second Doctor knows a lot more about the events than he is letting on. He knows that implanting the Human Factor into the test Daleks will achieve results the Daleks never anticipated. As with the Hand of Omega and Skaro, the Doctor knew what he was doing and manipulated events to make sure everything turned out very much as he expected.

These are not the only examples of similar things happening to both incarnations. Three stories out of the four that make up Season Twenty-Six feature the seventh Doctor knowing more than he is letting on; but he lets events carry themselves out before resolving them, inadvertently letting innocent people die. Similarly, in *The Tomb of the Cybermen*, the Doctor knows the tombs are dangerous, that Klieg has something nefarious planned, but he accompanies the expedition into the chambers anyway, and does nothing to solve events until they are almost out of control. Here too, innocent people end up dying as a result.

As far as I can see, this may be the last time the second Doctor's darkness shows itself, though I have my doubts. In *The Enemy of the World*, the Doctor again depends on deception to achieve victory, although here circumstances demanded it, what with the would-be World Dictator looking exactly like him. I'm also told that attempts are made to make the Doctor, as well as Colonel Lethbridge-Stewart, suspects in the investigation to find out who is the spy for the Great Intelligence in *The Web of Fear*. This attempt doesn't come off very well for an audience which is unwilling to think ill of the impish Doctor, but he does deceive his companions to try and finally defeat the Great Intelligence. Both these examples are minor, however. The major shocking similarities between second Doctor and seventh can be found only in *The Evil of the Daleks* and *The Tomb of the Cybermen*.

So, has memory cheated? Have we forgotten darker elements in earlier Doctors that the seventh Doctor is simply playing off? Have we overlooked the first Doctor's adamant unwillingness to alter the tragedies of history (evoking a condemnation from Steven similar to those above), or the fourth Doctor's apparent callousness over the death of Lawrence Scarman in *Pyramids of Mars* and his rationalisation that if nothing is done, trillions more will die?

Although dark elements have manifested themselves in our Doctor throughout history, none of these dark phases have been as intense as the seventh Doctor's. Even when he was at his most unpleasant, Colin Baker's Doctor still had his caustic wit, and his undeniable concern for Peri to redeem him. Peter Davison's Doctor was clearly shaken by all of the violence and death that occurred around him that he could not prevent. Tom Baker's Doctor may have been cool and distant at times, but this was balanced by more caring phases elsewhere during his tenure. Jon Pertwee's Doctor was a gentleman, and adamant that the ends never justified the means. William Hartnell's Doctor was undeniably affectionate to his companions like Susan, Vicki and Dodo.

Where the second Doctor and seventh Doctor diverge is in the matter of redeeming features, and extenuating circumstances. The seventh Doctor is lacking in both. The second Doctor had his affection and clownish exterior to balance his darker moods. Unlike the seventh Doctor, he would never go so far as to hurt his own companions, even though he upset Jamie enough to make the Highlander wonder whose side the Doctor was on. The second Doctor, however, never forced a companion to relive an intense childhood trauma as the seventh Doctor did to Ace in *Ghost Light*, despite ample opportunity and reason to do so (Victoria and – even earlier – Vicki were both orphans, and probably still quite messed up by the events that led to their fathers' deaths).

But the most important difference that separates the darker versions of the second and seventh Doctors is that the second Doctor didn't know any better, whereas the seventh Doctor most certainly did. The second Doctor had no way of knowing that the Daleks he had hoped to trick had tricked him in turn, using his discovery of the Human Factor to find what the Dalek factor was and start implanting that in the human race, instead of the other way around. Although the second Doctor had suspicions about what the Tomb contained and what Klieg was after, he had no way of knowing for sure, and was arguably compelled to let the action carry on further to solve the situation then and there, rather than have another expedition stumble upon the site later, with worse results.

The seventh Doctor has entered into events like the Hand of Omega, Silver Nemesis, the Excalibur affair and Fenric with a good idea of what he was up against. Despite more than adequate foreknowledge, he let events play themselves out (mostly for contrived dramatic tension) and, as a result, innocent people were hurt or killed. The end results were an achievement, true, but is this the same Doctor who said in an earlier incarnation that the ends never justified the means?

# Death

**by David Carroll**
*From Burnt Toast #6, December 1990*

*"Oh marvellous. You're going to kill me. What a finely tuned response to the situation."*
—the Doctor, *Frontios*

Death permeates *Doctor Who*. The universe in which the show is set is not the most pleasant of places; violent death strikes suddenly and often. The first death of a *Doctor Who* character was the Old Mother in episode three of *An Unearthly Child*, killed by Kal for her supposed betrayal of the tribe by the release of the time travellers. The last (for the time being and foreseeable future) was Karra, killed by the Master after saving Ace's life in *Survival* episode three. In between, there is only one story I am aware of that contains no deaths, 1964's *The Edge of Destruction*, a story without any cast members besides the regular travellers. *Kinda* comes close, with only the natural death of Panna, the wise woman of Deva Loka, to account for, and that was bodily and not spiritual death anyway.

Being a member of the regular crew certainly doesn't exclude you from a violent end, as Katarina, Adric and Peri discovered, though Peri's death became a wimp-out, later revealed to be a fictional incident created by the Matrix. Interestingly enough, while the two latter incidents were both very emotional events, they occurred to two of the least popular companions. The story with the most fatalities is easily *Logopolis*, with something like a third of a galaxy destroyed by galloping entropy, but it's stories like *Horror of Fang Rock*, *The Robots of Death* and *Resurrection of the Daleks* that have the bloodiest reputations, with nearly everyone except for the Doctor and companions dying. The story within which the concept is most entwined is *Revelation of the Daleks*, a black comedy where each of the characters is involved in the death industry.

Does all this signify anything? After all, we're talking about an adventure show where the bad guys aren't about to tie people to train-lines for the Doctor to rescue. They are going to kill people and some of them do it for fun; sometimes, the Doctor has to kill them in return, if it is the only way of stopping them (and shows like this love the baddies to get their just deserts). But fiction, to me anyway, is far more than simple (or indeed, convoluted) plot-lines; it is about characters, their defeats and victories, and their handling of situations outside the norm. The best of fiction creates an emotive bond between viewer (or reader) and character; if one dies – preferably the character – the other should care about it.

It is for this reason that I believe horror is one of the most ideologically sound genres when it comes to this sort of thing. The detective mystery reduces death to a puzzle, a polite affair overcome with the application of logic, while the overly action-oriented story personified by *Rambo* or *RoboCop 2* treat death in their own "comic-book violence" way; something either exciting or gross to occupy a few seconds of screentime. (It is interesting that few comic books, at least of those I've read, contain comic-book violence. Again, that's hardly surprising with today's comic market being orientated more towards characterisation and horror.) Horror may have a larger fatality count, and indeed can kill off its characters in some incredibly nasty ways, but it seems to care about its characters in ways others genres don't. Note that here I'm talking about true horror, not excuses for bloodletting such as the *Friday the 13th* series.

Why do characters die in fiction? Lots of reasons: for plot purposes (for example the milk-man in *Survival*, who dies to provoke the Cheetah people into attacking the Doctor's party), to demonstrate how nasty the bad guys are (Inspector McKenzie's death shows us both how far Light can and will go, and Josiah's capacity for really bad jokes), to provide a motivation for the good guys (Harold V died in *The Happiness Patrol* for the purpose of getting Ace emotionally involved in proceedings), to make a story more exciting (any battle scene you care to mention, e.g. *Battlefield*), to receive their just deserts for the satisfaction of the audience (Gavrok in *Delta and the Bannermen*), to provide a heroic ending (Pex in *Paradise Towers*), to highlight the danger to our heroes (Daphne S' demise in *The Happiness Patrol* auditions), or simply because they were in the wrong place at the wrong time (guards are really good at this; for example, Delta's bodyguard).

I'm not trying to give the impression that any of this is necessarily bad, and in there are a lot of the reasons why people watch the show in the first place. Where a possible cause for contention arises is in the use of characters whose only purpose within the plot is to die, usually horribly. *Fear* magazine refers to these characters as Shreddies and says of them that "shredding characters for the sake of plot can be an enriching tech-nique... but all too often becomes transparently a means of writing mate-rial to fill a book and schlock the reader out". A more familiar term for these characters is "redshirts".

*Fear* uses Shakespeare's Rosencrantz and Guildenstern as its prime examples, but my own personal favourite comes from Alan Dean Foster's novelisation of the movie *Krull*. The first three pages of the book concern themselves with a young shepherd, giving details of his family, his life at home, his cousin in Banbreak, his father's approval of the uni-fication of towns into kingdoms, his expectations for the coming year. At the end of the third page, the Fortress of the Beast lands on top of him and obliterates both him and his flock entirely.

Sometimes they're not that obvious. Take the hiker at the beginning of *Image of the Fendahl* for example. Walking in the woods he grows steadi-ly uneasier until he suddenly finds he cannot move his legs, and is killed by some as-yet-nameless horror. A redshirt? No, because later on in the story his body becomes a vital clue for the Doctor, its disposal increases the tension among the scientists at Fetch Priory and the scene provides extra tension when the Doctor is attacked in a similar manner later on. He might not have enjoyed the experience too much, but our unnamed hiker was an essential ingredient in the story.

Well, what about the two guards in the prologue of *Slipback*? Checking the ducting of their ship after the computer has detected an intruder, Bates and Wilson soon get involved in "a great deal of unpleasantness": they get eaten by said intruder. Redshirts? You better believe it. Never mentioned again, they simply provide an effective hook into the opening credits. Indeed, Eric Saward, who penned the tale and is a very good writer (though not as good a script-editor), is notorious for high body counts and redshirts, his variety usually found in pairs.

What about these days? Season Twenty-Six is justifiably notorious for a very nasty content, with people dying left, right and centre. Are there any redshirts among the ranks of its fallen? I'm tempted to say no, though a friend of mine disagrees, pointing to some of the teenagers in *Survival*.

The last two seasons have had a mature attitude towards matters of death and destruction. Characters die, and the effects of their death are fully felt by both the audience, through good direction and writing, and the TARDIS crew. Indeed, it is my theory that much of the Doctor's cur-rent "darkness" can be attributed to his finally becoming sick and tired of the amount of death he meets on his travels. Wherever he has gone, innocent people have been killed at the hands (metaphorically speaking, in some cases) of the Daleks, the Cybermen and many, many others. He has finally decided to do something about it, take an active role rather than simply reacting. In *The Happiness Patrol*, he has heard nasty rumours about Terra Alpha and decides to take a look, finding the list of Helen A's victims running into the tens of thousands, perhaps millions with her eradication of entire towns. Does he single-handedly save the planet? No. But he does act as a witness to the atrocities and guides the course of the rebellion that would have happened anyway into less bloodthirsty paths. And, finally, he brings Helen A to justice, showing her the emptiness of her ambition as well as the weight of her crimes. Are the Doctor's actions in this story, *Remembrance*, *The Curse of Fenric* and many others, immoral? A very difficult question, and one made almost impossible because of lack of information. Whatever is happening (and, of course, the fact that he seems to have recognised Ace as a wolf of Fenric somewhere between *Dragonfire* and *Remembrance* certainly helps), the Doctor is angry, and it is far from unlikely that innocent death makes a significant contribution to this anger.

This mature attitude was, by no means, always the case. In the general silliness of *Delta and the Bannermen*, one of the things that really bugged me was that an entire busload of Navarino tourists was slaughtered by Gavrok and his band of merry men, yet not one of the good guys, save Mel for a couple of seconds, seemed to care in the slightest. A far cry from Ace's almost suicidal reaction to Harold V's execution a year later. Indeed, it is her presence, her questioning, that overcomes any problems created by our lack of information concerning the Doctor, as mentioned above.

Drama does not rely on death, but fiction these days is about high stakes and any sustained absence of bodies would become unbelievable and uninteresting. Death happens for many reasons and sometimes, just sometimes, death happens for no reason at all. Just like what happens to us non-fictional characters, in the real world.

# Don't Tell the Sisterhood

**by Sarah Groenewegen**
*From Bog Off One Hundred, November 1993*

Lady Peinforte: *"Doctor who? Have you never wondered where he comes from? Who he is?"*
Ace: *"Nobody knows who the Doctor is."*
Lady Peinforte: *"Except me."*
Ace: *"How?"*
Lady Peinforte: *"The statue told me."*

Ace: *"... He's a Time Lord. I know that."*
[Later, to the Doctor] *"Who are you?"*

—*Silver Nemesis* episode three

Perhaps more than any other series, *Doctor Who* manages to sustain a central character who remains an enigma. When the program started, three decades ago now, the title begged a question: *Doctor Who?* Who was that grumpy old man who lived with his "teenage granddaughter" in a junkyard that hid a space / time ship called "TARDIS" disguised as a police box? Twenty-five years later, in the anniversary story *Silver Nemesis*, the question was raised again. Despite the hints in all the TV stories and New Adventures to date, the Doctor still remains a mystery.

So, who is he?

As Ace says, the Doctor is a Time Lord. And, like Ace, we all know that. At the risk of being facetious, we also know why he (and the Monk, the Master, Professor Chronotis, the Rani, etc) left. The bits of Gallifrey seen in *The Deadly Assassin*, *The Invasion of Time*, etc, show the Doctor's home planet populated by insipid cut-outs who fawn at anything more powerful than them and, despite their grandiose title, that seems to include a hell of a lot of races. Plus, the planet itself is so fucking boring (though the Gallifreyans of *Cat's Cradle: Time's Crucible*, on the other hand, show much more life).

As a bit of an aside, I know some fans who used to whinge about *The War Games* and *Spearhead from Space* when they were first on. To them, the references to Gallifrey and Time Lord physiology destroyed the central mythos of the program. Now everyone knew the Doctor was a Time Lord from Gallifrey with two hearts. Why should we keep watching? But, just because we now knew it was possible for the Doctor to survive asphyxiation because of his respiratory bypass and the name of the planet he came from, doesn't mean to say we know who he is. And it still doesn't really answer the central question, therefore not really harming the mythos of the main character. We still don't really know why he left Gallifrey, taking someone who claimed to make up the acronym TARDIS, not to mention the hints that the Doctor had a hand in inventing the machine.

However, these fans who thought the central mystery had disappeared from the third Doctor on might have had something to their argument. From the Pertwee era through to the Colin Baker era, the emphasis of the stories was firmly in the adventures the Doctor and his friends were caught up in. Nobody, except some fans, was at all bothered about finding out more about the eccentric Time Lord. However, in answer to the low ratings of the mid-eighties, *The Trial of a Time Lord* was made. One of the things attempted was a return to first principles. Who is the Doctor? Think of the way the Valeyard was set up as the Doctor's final regeneration (or near enough).

And then came the seventh Doctor and things became mysterious again. Not immediately, mind. Season Twenty-Four was more akin to light comedy, albeit hiding a dark interior. (See *Paradise Towers* for what I mean. Actually, just watch it for the hell of it.) Then Ace came along and the Doctor changed. Subtly at first, then overtly by the time his coat changed from beige to dark brown. By Season Twenty-Six, and onward in the New Adventures, the Doctor is a manipulator. A meddler in what is his universe. The question that forms the title of the series is important again. At the risk of being repetitious, who is the Doctor?

Perhaps an analogy might be in order to explore this semiotic question. Though, like all analogies, be aware that it is not perfect. And, for the less bright readers out there who may take this dreadfully seriously, none of this is meant to be taken in such a way. If you do, it's your problem, and I suggest to you to skip the next bit, go to the end, and come back to this point if you're in a good mood.

"God" was a song by John Lennon. God is also an Anglo Saxon word of Teutonic origin. Most importantly, God is the focus of many of the world's major religions. In the interests of my sanity, I'm going to limit this analogy to the one I'm most familiar with: the Christianity I grew up with as a Presbyterian.

*The Encyclopaedia of Religion* quotes a whole heap of Bible references describing God. For a start, the Hebrew spelling is YHWH. It means the familiar "Lord", as well as the more interesting "ghost". There is a lot of conflict about what he looks like. He often vanquishes enemies, or just visits his chosen people without revealing he is there. He acts as the guarantor of justice. He's slow to anger and forgiving of sin. He's more in the Old Testament than in the New, where Christ takes centre stage. God's mainly relegated to the back scenes: omnipotent, but usually referred to as the father of Jesus Christ, the Messiah.

In the Western tradition that grew out of what is described in the New Testament, via Rome, God is firmly regarded as a being who created the universe and man. Anything more about who or what God is has kept theologians in business for millennia. St Thomas Aquinas, in his *Summa Theologica*, argued "God is in all things, not, indeed, as part of their essence, or as a quality, but in the manner that an efficient cause is present in that on which it acts. Hence God is in all things, and intimately."

Another major facet of God within Christianity is the presence of the Devil, and with it the conundrum of go(o)d versus (d)evil. This is an eternal battle common to many religions and mythologies the world over. It is a major theological problem centering on the point that because God created everything, he's already got evil sewn up and will eventually vanquish what he unleashed on a sinning world. One of the crucial points about the seemingly contradictory existence of good and evil in a universe of good's making is neatly summarised by Giordana Bruno: "It would not be well were evil non-existent, for it makes for the necessity of good, since if evil were removed the desire for good would also cease." In other words, God created evil and keeps it here not only to punish sinners, but as an example for Christians to fight against. As such, it is an eternal battle that will cease only when God decides it.

So much for that crash course in theology. It is very roughshod, but I've had much less training in such matters than Tom Baker or Sylvester McCoy, and there isn't room enough in this fanzine to even contemplate going into it in any more detail. Two questions now remain: one, what am I getting at; two, is this analogy sustainable? The first question is easy to answer and is inexorably linked to the second question. I am suggesting that there was a profound change in the Doctor's character from about *Dragonfire* on. Rather than just be a mysterious Time Lord, he became like God (God-like).

We all know that the central conflict of *Doctor Who* is the eternal battle between good and evil. Just look up a listing of all the episodes and you will see this conflict being fought. So what? Much popular culture is embroiled in that battle, either overtly as in superhero stories, or more subtly as in stories that question the hero's morality as well.

In the seasons that heralded the change from eccentric traveller who gets into trouble to the galactic meddler, the Doctor comments on this fact. In *The Greatest Show in the Galaxy*, the Doctor stated "I have fought the Gods of Ragnarok all through time." In *The Curse of Fenric*, it's implied that the Doctor has been battling Fenric since the "dawn of time". In other words, he was saying he'd fought evil all his life and now was the time to actively destroy it. It is in this context that the seventh Doctor becomes more than just a mere Time Lord from Gallifrey.

Note the way the nature of the battle alters from all the previous adventures. It has been argued pretty convincingly elsewhere, I think, that most of the televised Ace stories were preparing her for facing Fenric (or, the Devil). Accepting that, watch how the seventh Doctor behaves with his "new consciousness" of what he has to do. He destroys the Daleks and Cybermen with none of the qualms shown in *Genesis of the Daleks*, and in *Survival* he treats the Master for what he is: a wimp. The Master is certainly no match for him any more. Note the way the Master has succumbed to the planet's influence, but the Doctor doesn't. At time of writing, the Master has yet to show up in the original novels – has he really been vanquished now? Personally, I hope so.

But it isn't just this change in the nature of the Doctor's battle against evil that makes the seventh Doctor so different. Many people have commented on how this Doctor is manipulative, in control of his pawns (Ace, and anyone else he can use); in a word, omnipotent. There are oodles of quotations to back this view:

Mel: *"Oh, all right. You win."*
The Doctor: *"I do. I usually do."*

—*Dragonfire* episode three

*"I can do anything I like."*
—the Doctor, *Remembrance of the Daleks* episode four

*"It was your show all along, wasn't it?"*
—Ace, *The Greatest Show in the Galaxy* episode four

*"Doctor, something tells me you are not in our catalogue. Nor will you ever be."*
—Control, *Ghost Light* episode four

Ace: *"You know what's going on, don't you?"*
The Doctor: *"Yes."*
Ace: *"You always know. You just can't be bothered to tell anyone. It's like it's some kind of game and only you know the rules."*
—*The Curse of Fenric* episode three

And there are all the references in the New Adventures, but you can look them up. The TARDIS obeys him (almost) without fault; *Ghost Light* is about the only exception, and that's minor. In the New Adventures, there seems to be a spot of rebellion going on, but pretty much the old days of "This isn't where we're supposed to be" are gone.

God is also famed for caring for us people, despite all our flaws. In Christianity, the big thing is that he sent his Earthly son to die in atonement for what humanity had done. There is no argument to suggest that the Doctor's done that, nor ever would. But the Christian conception of God's relationship with his people is far more complex. Take the following as an example:

"It is even a great part of God's wisdom, in casting the plan of our life, that he has set us in conditions to bring out the evil that is in us. For it is by this medley of that we make of our wrongs, fears, pains of the mind, and pains of the body, all the woes of all shapes and sizes that follow at the heels of our sin – by these it is that He dislodges our perversity and draws us to Himself."

Ace is important in all this. She is arguably the strongest companion the Doctor's ever had. In spite of her flaws (hatred of Audrey, penchant for blowing things up, etc), she has a well-developed sense of good (caring about Manisha, Mags, fixing the iceflow on Iceworld, etc, and she knows her hatred of Audrey is wrong). Note that the seventh Doctor's all-knowing nature comes to the fore once Mel has gone. Perhaps, as the companion is wont to be, Ace is the embodiment of humankind, and as such fits the quotation above. Do I have to remind you how the Doctor tested her, threw her in the deep end on numerous occasions, and still she's come back, and more loyal? Sure, she's a bit rebellious, resentful, etc, but she does come through in the end. Like we're supposed to in Christianity.

Now, of course, it is quite a common device to compare the whole science-fiction thing to religion. The very word "fan" conjures the idea of fanatic devotion. Think also of the theological debates that rage over what is "canonical" *Who*. Are the New Adventures part of canonical *Who*, or are they apocrypha? What about the radio plays, the extra / changed bits in the novelisations? You know what I mean. We have our own holy relics, too. Go on, admit it. You have at least one scribbled autograph in your collection, or a prop maybe, or some merchandise that other people would absolutely kill for. We even have our own moral codes, though they're not found spelled out in the 158 volumes of our "Bible". We have our own saints and heretics, though we don't have any martyrs. (Which is just as well. It would be a very sad person indeed who would give their life to a TV show.)

So, is it any wonder that we should actually try to work out who our gods are? In a purely metaphorical sense, of course. Or maybe we should all have a laugh and not take this 30-year-old series so damn seriously. Just because our language is limited and the words we use to describe us have some extraordinary connotations does not mean that we should live up to those connotations. Sure, we might be called fans, but that doesn't mean that we are fanatics. It might look like we're worshipping when we put on *The Curse of Fenric* for the millionth time and intone the words along with the characters, but is it? It might seem dreadfully important to prove that the Vogans are actually Time Lords, or that sex, drugs, the word "fuck" and *Star Trek* are not part of *Doctor Who*, but it isn't. Nope, most of the time we're just having fun, playing intellectual games – which is what SF is all about.

And none of this is to suggest that the Doctor really is divine, even though he might play God on occasion.

# 20 Handy Tips for Survival in the Doctor Who Universe

**by Mike Morris**

*From The Doctor Who Ratings Guide, October 1999*

It could happen to anyone... a blue box vworps into your neighbourhood, an eccentric stranger starts babbling to you about time travel, and before you know it you're lost in the *Doctor Who* universe. Don't panic, though. Just follow these simple rules and you won't be killed off like all the other supporting characters.

1. People who dress in black are charismatic, but evil. Steer well clear.

2. People who dress in white are nice but dull. They also tend to have unimaginable powers and will sacrifice you for the greater good. Steer well clear.

3. Green lifeforms are, without exception, psychotic creatures intent on destroying mankind. Steer well clear.

4. When faced with the threat of nuclear annihilation, jeeps make for good cover.

5. All that stuff about "they can't go up stairs" is just wishful thinking. If trapped by a Dalek, however, don't panic; it will invariably shout "Exterminate" at you for five minutes, giving you ample time to escape.

6. Guns are absolutely useless; approximately 90% of alien lifeforms are impervious to bullets. Just run away instead, as the same 90% are generally incapable of moving at speeds faster than a lumber.

7. If faced with an enemy from a low-gravity world, with the strength of ten men and an impenetrable suit of armour, a simple arrow to the back of the neck should suffice.

8. Be careful when walking, as it's possible to twist your ankle just about anywhere.

9. Nasty monsters tend to hide out in a) the sea b) sewers or c) a handy cave. Steer well clear.

10. Plastic is evil. Steer well clear.

11. If you find yourself aboard a spaceship destined for a new home planet, be sure to send someone outside to check. It may well be part of a grand plan to roll back time and populate your original planet with dinosaurs. Then again, it may not, so best to suit up first, just in case.

12. Alien lifeforms are not, repeat *not* all evil, in spite of the overwhelming statistical evidence to the contrary. The exception to this rule is intelligent vegetable life, which will invariably try and destroy all animal life in the universe. Steer well clear.

13. Generally speaking, any metal lifeform is bad. Steer well clear.

14. The military have extraordinary powers of making people forget the most astonishing events. Examples include huge sea monsters attacking Parliament buildings and dinosaurs roaming about London. Don't let this worry you, though; splendid chaps, all of them.

15. Jelly babies are an invaluable tool of interplanetary diplomacy.

16. Fitting a Fast Return Switch in your time machine is, generally speaking, A Very Bad Idea.

17. Making vital pieces of equipment out of mercury is also, generally speaking, A Very Bad Idea.

18. Temporal paradoxes are, of course, impossible. However, they exist all over the place. Steer well clear. While I'm on the point, if you ever wake up to find yourself surrounded by impossibly nice people in silly uniforms, the chances are that you've landed in the *Star Trek* universe. If so, watch out for "Space Time Anomalies"; the bloody things are so common that they shouldn't really be called anomalies at all.

19. Generally speaking, most alien lifeforms are evil. Steer well clear.

20. In fact, almost everything you come across will be evil, or dangerous, or both. Steer well clear. In fact, if I were you, I wouldn't leave the house.

# THERE ARE WORLDS OUT THERE...

And then we were left to ourselves. *Doctor Who*, the television series, was no more. When the strains of Keff McCulloch's remix of the familiar theme music juddered to an end on BBC 1 on 6th December, 1989, the *Doctor Who* fan was now like the Doctor himself in *An Unearthly Child*: alone, unprotected, in exile.

During the classic series' last decade, the notion of a "*Doctor Who* fan" as a distinct species took hold. They began to define themselves through organised events like Longleat's 20th Anniversary celebration in 1983 and the emerging phenomenon of *Doctor Who* conventions. And there were the many fan clubs around the world created in the wake of the (relatively new) Doctor Who Appreciation Society's decision to only serve Britain.

And, of course, there were fanzines. But you already knew that.

With the TV series off the air, the question of fan identity really took hold. What made us who were are? Why did we love a defunct TV show so much? What was it that inspired us so? What made us special? Why were so many of us so different, in all the various forms of difference that exist?

Somewhere in the middle of our first decade of figuring this out, *Doctor Who* came back for one night only with a gorgeous console room set and a great actor in a dodgy wig playing the Doctor. There were car chases and kissing and it was made in Vancouver. And then it was gone, leaving fans with the gift of something new to debate.

Only there was always something new. That's the great thing about being a fan of *Doctor Who*. Even if you restricted yourself to the TV show (and during that time many did not; itself a source of debate to which we will return in Volume 4 of this series), there was always something wonderful to experience or discover.

Because, when it comes down to it, *Doctor Who* is the hobby that keeps on giving. There will always be something you haven't seen before, some detail you didn't know. There will be an opinion you never heard. There is some detail that will capture your imagination.

There is always something *new*.

"There are worlds out there..." the Doctor says in the final moments of *Survival*. He's absolutely right.

We were left to ourselves. *Doctor Who* fans, watching our beautiful, funny, absurd, wonderful TV show that we had always watched. We lived in hope that we would see the TARDIS again on our TV screens. And, on 26th March, 2005, our hope was rewarded.

But that is another story. Another world.

# We the Asthmatics!

**by Matt Jones**
*From Doctor Who Magazine #350, December 2004*

"Are you *the* Matt Jones?"

The question throws me. Being neither a celebrity nor having been convicted of a listed crime, I immediately assume that this particular "Matt Jones" cannot possibly be me. My questioner is a very young, very drunk gay runner on the drama series I'm producing. He leans forward, slightly unsteadily, in the black cab we're sharing with several other drunk colleagues on our first Work's Night Out.

"Did you used to write Fluid Links?"

Ah. Gay *Doctor Who* fans. Throw a Dapol Dalek in the world of TV and you're bound to hit at least three of us.

"I couldn't believe that someone wrote about being gay in *DWM!*" he slurs, more than just slightly. I try to be all modest and cool as if this sort of thing happens to me all the time, but the runner is undeniably cute and, I must shamefully confess, I'm rather enjoying the attention. "It meant so much," he continues, "I was fourteen and in the closet when I read that."

*Fourteen?!* My intoxicated smile dies on my face. I suddenly feel 250 years old. Oh *DWM*, my dear old thing, has it really been so long?

The wheel turns, civilisation grows, as Panna from *Kinda* would say. It seems unfathomable today, that only eight years ago a closeted 14-year-old might find some comfort in a magazine contributor coming out. But it brought an old puzzle to mind: what is it about *Doctor Who* that seems to so completely capture a young gay boy's heart? Why, in short, are so many *Doctor Who* fans gay?

Now, I am not the first person to ask this question. But the usual answers – that the Doctor doesn't have much sexual interest in women and isn't very macho – don't really stand up to more than a cursory inspection. After all, the good Doctor doesn't exhibit any sexual interest in men either. And lots of gay men like *Star Trek* and aren't remotely put off by Captain Kirk's liking of skirt and skirmishes.

The more I think about it, the more I suspect we've been asking the wrong question. Perhaps what we should asking is why so many straight boys stop being fans. Back in my school, all the boys were *Doctor Who* fans. At least, they were until puberty kicked in. It was only after the first flush of hormones that things changed. Suddenly, the playground game was flirting – and knowing the difference between Mondas and Telos wasn't exactly an advantage.

Those of us who couldn't or wouldn't compete in the new world of impressing girls carried on talking about *Doctor Who*, because with no girls to impress there was no reason not to talk about all the things we always had. We were the fat kids, the wheezing asthmatics, the effeminate boys; lurking in the library and computer room, keeping out of direct sunlight and the hormonal battleground that was the common room and dining hall. And it was we who grew up to be lifelong fans.

You see, I don't think *Doctor Who* has a specific appeal to gay men; I just think it strikes a particularly strong chord with anyone who's ever felt like an outsider, who's had a whiff of discrimination, bullying or being ostracised from the mainstream. And that unfortunately just happens to include more than its fair share of gay boys.

I'm not trying to offend anyone, really I'm not, but I do think there's a kernel of truth behind the image of the *Doctor Who* fan as an anorak-clad, runny-nosed wimp, because that's just a sneering stereotype of someone who doesn't fit in.

Perhaps I'm wrong, perhaps it was just me and my friends. Perhaps the rest of you were the cool kids, the stars of track and field I feared and so secretly desired. Perhaps you scored a hat-trick on the football pitch, then snogged the prettiest girl in the school before racing home to lovingly type up your critique of established Dalek continuity. But, you know, somehow I doubt it.

For those of us for whom conformity (and goal scoring) wasn't an option, the Doctor was there to say it was okay. The Doctor wouldn't care if you were podgy, geeky or fey; after all, he let Adric travel with him! This was a man who respectfully introduced himself to chickens, who picked up the telephone and announced cheerfully to the operator, "I'll speak to anyone!"

And whilst, looking back, it's not hard to see why he had such appeal to closeted gay teenagers like me, it'd be a mistake to try to make an exclusive claim for the Doctor's affections. The whole point of the character is that he's willing to intervene to help anyone in trouble, anyone on the outside. The Doctor's ongoing battle – whether against the Daleks, the Cybermen or Helen A – has always been against those who stamp down on unsuitable feelings, who hate people who are different or don't fit in. Whoever – whatever – they are. And, as Russell T Davies so eloquently argued in *Bob & Rose*, that's a good fight. For anyone. For everyone.

I've no idea what it's like to be gay and fourteen these days. From a couple of decades away, it certainly looks easier. There are out gay presenters on Saturday morning TV and gay boys snog on *Corrie*, the last known proper *Doctor Who* timeslot! I sure as hell hope that the world has turned and that civilisation has grown. And, if things haven't changed that much, then it's particularly welcome that the Doctor – in the safest of hands – is poised ready to return.

A new Doctor to capture the hearts of a new generation of outsiders, who might still need the reassurance that, whilst school is a battlefield, at least there's one man on our side.

So let's pull on our anoraks, fire up our inhalers. For the adventure begins again...

# Full Metal Frock Coat

**by Tat Wood**

*From Circus #9, early 2002.*

They've finally gone and done it. A video retrospective of Longleat, 1983. I haven't seen it, that would involve me having money, but its mere existence is scary enough.

You know what it means? It means that the majority of fandom don't remember it.

I do: I keep having flashbacks, remembering the time Beesie nearly bought it, the mud, the tents, the tannoy, those boys in uniform, some of them only twelve, goddammit. I remember the unlikely friendships made in adversity, the camaraderie formed by facing insurmountable odds and yet coming out on top. How having that gun in my hand changed me. The horror, the horror. Yet somehow, through all the squalor and pain, a terrible beauty was born that Easter.

It had all seemed so different when we signed up. I was resitting an A-level and hanging with a new crowd, kids a year or two below me. We were in a dreadful production of *The Crucible* when Wyke came up to me and asked if I'd seen the announcement after *The King's Demons*. They were doing a celebration at Longleat and he was going. Now, if you aren't from Kettering, you won't know Jon Wyke, but if you ever go there, as I did, and stand out from the mass in any way, as I definitely did, people would go up to you and ask "like, d'you know Jon Wyke?" If you did, they'd look at you in awe and terror, and run away, pointing you out to their friends. It was a *Doctor Who* event, so obviously I wanted to go, but Wyke was arranging a trip on School facilities, so I was definitely going.

So we went. We went in the school van, driven by Jeff Moran, economics teacher and playboy (too many stories there to get into now); me; Wyke; David Beese and Colin Macklin, who seemed to be joined at the hip; Dominic Divine (yes, really), an Adric-like ponce who worshipped Sting; and Jeff's son, aged six. We had to be up stupidly early on Easter Sunday morning to get there at any reasonable time, so we did, and I took a packed lunch of a sausage sandwich, a can of something and a banana. When I got downstairs, there was an Easter egg as well. En route, we stopped at Avebury for a stretch and a wee (no, not on the stones; we feared the Ogri too much for that). We swapped favourite stories, argued about whether Ainley was crap and bitched about Alan Clarkson (don't bother to ask, he's really not worth it). I tried to stay out of a potential blood feud about the relative merits of Big Country and The Alarm. By the time we arrived, we were as tight as any platoon. The full extent of what we were in for would not have daunted us even if we could have imagined it.

From a distance, Longleat's grounds looked like an angler's pail of maggots. The fishing analogy extended when we stepped from the Minibus Falcon (as we'd dubbed it) into the quagmire and wished for waders and waxed jackets. The tents in the distance gave it an air of Agincourt, mixed with 4077 M*A*S*H. Approaching nearer, the latter seemed to dominate. The tannoy sounded desperate and chirpy and oddly familiar. Eventually, one of us voiced the suspicion.

"That's K-bloody-9!"

John Leeson was, apparently, shut away in a cupboard and left to do announcements all weekend. He lost the plot early on Sunday afternoon and started reciting Monopoly cards ("Do not attend the video tent, do not pass Go, do not collect £200") and wittering about "enjoyment factor". At least he was dry. It soon became equally apparent that nobody had expected anyone to come and were all desperately trying to deal with incoming visitors. Unable to enlist the army, they had cadets with UNIT badges to herd us around. Pressure of numbers was making some tents unvisitable, such as the set for the forthcoming top-secret *The Five Doctors*, although word of the contents was filtering through. All the Doctors in a place called the Death Zone. Five of One, One, in Five...

And, when I turned around, I was alone apart from 20,000 strangers. I kept running into the rest individually during the afternoon. I made my way, against a sea of people (mainly bored dads) towards the Radiophonic Workshop tent. There, a video clip of Peter Howell explained things, but Dick Mills was there in the interactive flesh. "It's

Peter's birthday today, he'll be here tomorrow." Uncle Dick managed to keep cheerful being asked the same three questions by every kid, so I asked him a different one. Would they rather be thought of as artists or technicians? He'd obviously had that one before too: technicians, because "the word 'Workshop' isn't there by accident". He then proceeded to flog me their two new albums, one being the advertised *Doctor Who: The Music* with the hideous cover, the other Radiophonic Rock, complete with limited edition sticks of rock with "BBC Radiophonic Workshop" written all the way through. I'm sure mine would have been collectable if I hadn't eaten it. The rock, dummy!

When I'd seen the clip a couple of times, a commotion came from outside. Tom! Here! Elvis was in the building. You have to recall that this was 1983 and he'd severed all links with his old life. The transhumance outside almost physically sucked me out of the tent. I found myself on the cold hillside. At the house itself, the mass of humanity was approaching Schwarzschild radius; no chance of getting in without air cover. Another, smaller swarm surrounded a tent nearby. A sign outside promised screenings of old stories. It was bulging, filled with people sacrificing the ability to breathe for a glimpse of *The Dalek Invasion of Earth*, which had been running for about an hour. I didn't so much approach as slow down and find a crowd behind me and in front of me, accreting. A woman dressed as Basil Brush was forced to the rope barrier next to me; a chap in a suit on the other side. She was an American fan. (They had fans of *Doctor Who* in America? They had *Doctor Who* in America?) She had a voodoo doll of Tom Baker to prove it. He was someone who was later a bigshot in fan circles and then vanished.

I was cold, wet and squashed. Under the circumstances, I was impressed with my own aplomb in striking up conversations with them. Something I've noticed thousands of times since but which impressed me then was that, as one's interlocutors already know the most embarrassing thing about you simply because it's why you're there, you can talk to anyone about anything among fans. Your conversation is pre-cringed. This was my first experience of the phenomenon.

Then, just as in real life, a mundane approaches and spoils it all. He was a local army cadet ("local" as in both geographic and Royston Vasey senses; his parents had obviously been related) and about old enough to put on his uniform unaided. For an hour, he glared at us and shoved the press of people back from his tent. It wasn't his fault; they'd put the uniform on the boy, told him he'd get some shore leave, score some poontang; nobody mentioned the possibility of going missing in action, captured by fanatics. Who could tell what terrors he'd seen that day?

People eventually stopped joining the queue, leaving a hardcore of about fifty of us. "You might as well go," said the kid in UNIT drag, "you'll not get in." I importuned him. "But we're already inured to the disappointment. If we go, you'll have to apologise all over again to whoever replaces us. They might not be such good sports about it." John Leeson was getting frantic about the volume of traffic. In the opinion of whoever was ordering the almost-literal infantry around, making us move from our shell-hole might have seemed sensible.

There was nowhere else to go. I'd seen everything I stood a chance of seeing, and at least here I was among friends. If you'd told me a day earlier that I would have the chance to talk about *Doctor Who* to people I'd never met, including this strange American woman with the doll and the cape, and just bond with people over a silly TV show we all loved enough to squelch through tents and sit in a van for hours to come and pay homage, that would have been enough. I'd met Dick Mills ninety minutes earlier, how much better could it get?

I got out my packed lunch (or "piece", as we call it in Corby, hence loads of gags about American gangster movies: "He's packing a piece" / "Make sure he puts in a satsuma for pudding"; that sort of thing). Future Big-Shot Fan said, "You fan! A sausage sandwich. How very Amelia Rumford!" I'd never heard "fan" used as an insult before, but as he then produced a stick of celery from a tupperware tub I could hardly comment. Inspiration struck. I offered a piece of Easter egg to soldier-boy. "At least we're here voluntarily," I consoled him.

Just like the football match in 1917, this truce gesture brought about a new respect. Baby Benton had his orders not to let anyone else in and not to let the crush get dangerous. We were staying put, so he was doing his job and we were all happy. We were as close to seeing Daleks taking holiday snaps of one another as anyone would ever get, unless they somehow got these stories back on screen or out on video. "Smell that, son?' said Big-Name Fan. "That's Terry Nation. I love the—"

Then, abruptly, the Wiltshire Homunculus let us in to a newly empty cinema tent.

A hush fell as the once-terrifying Troughton titles began: it was *The Dominators*. For most of us, the only Troughton we'd seen since the first time was *The Krotons*, so we were prepared to be indulgent. It's funny, but on a big screen with an uncritical but attentive audience, the "zap" effect in episode one is actually rather gruesome. In fact, all the effects, under those circumstances, are given the benefit of the doubt, like a 30s *Flash Gordon*. Astonishing as it might seem, *The Dominators* cast a spell over us. Until episode three. Suddenly and terribly, to the bafflement of the US contingent, the charm wore off. Brian Cant in a Janet Reger nightie is hard to take seriously at any time, but in a packed cinema the result was explosive. Muttered explanations to the Yanks could be heard. The arrival of a Quark in the Council chamber was greeted by some wag with the words "through the... Round Window". Yet, incredibly, the special sound, the set design and the sheer weirdness of the Quarks won us over again (and let's not forget the rudest joke ever in episode five). You will never persuade me that *The Dominators* is anything less than thoroughly entertaining.

We emerged, blinking and astonished, into the daylight. The sun had come out. The queues had vanished. Quickly, I slid my way to the set-design tent. *The Five Doctors* was to be set partly on Gallifrey and partly in 1973 (if the desk calendar and phone book in UNIT HQ were to be believed). Over in another part was a display of effects and the queues had forced the barriers back. I high-fived Marvin the Paranoid Android, hefted a surprisingly heavy Gaztak gun (and decided that *Meglos* was an underrated gem) and then—

An *Earthshock* handgun. You press a button and the blue chamber lights up. I took aim, steadied my nerves, and shot K9. That tannoy was really winding me up. Nobody was around. I could have waltzed off with it, but that would have been betraying something. I didn't know quite what, but it was part of why I'd bothered to come. The copyright-threatening EBGB from *The Goodies* was there, as was the Heart of Gold. (I never understood why it was called that. You name spaceships after Grateful Dead records, not Neil Young.) All just objects. The gun, even though it lit up and did things, even though it had been used on screen, possibly by Peter Davison, was a bit of metal and plastic. It had been transubstantiated back into something mundane because I was in the room with it. *Doctor Who* wasn't about actors, sets or props, it was about us. Standing in the drizzle in the vain hope of seeing a story which we'd heard wasn't much cop was more exciting than firing the gun; no wonder I've enjoyed fandom more since 1990.

There was a costume exhibit nearby, so I went there next. They had Hecate from *K9 and Company*, and you might have seen it in subsequent exhibitions. They had Gundans. Gundans? I recalled something; as I'd missed episode four of *Warriors' Gate* (mum told me "Oh, Romana left" by way of synopsis), I had promised myself a copy of the hard-to-find-in-shitkicker-towns-like-Corby novelisation. I tracked down the merchandise stall (only the one; how unlike conventions as we know them). They had it, but it was by some hack, not Steve Gallagher as I'd hoped. They also had copies of *The Programme Guide*, in two volumes, and fliers for membership of the Doctor Who Appreciation Society. I grabbed three of those.

David Beese was outside, looking lost, as he always did when Colin wasn't around. He clocked the vinyl in my bag. "I thought about getting that, but it's probably crap." He collected Style Council 12" singles. I passed him a flier. "Smart," he said. We tried a reconnaissance sweep for our fallen comrades, past topiary devastated by passers-by. All hint of grass has been removed from the plain, as if Agent Orange had been sprayed. We could see no trace of the rest of our party and it is hard to miss Wyke, short though he is. Finally, we returned to base camp, the bus, before trench-foot set in.

They were there waiting for us. The Top 40 was playing "Snot Rap" by Kenny Everett. The others all had their stories to tell: how Tom, his head shaved, had set himself up as a god among the easily impressed natives; how Wyke's obsessive need to see Sarah Sutton in the flesh had almost led to him being torn limb from tiny limb; how Colin had, like me, noticed that the mist left, taking thousands of people with it, like the Angel of Mons.

We drove home, exchanging tales and testing each other with the *Programme Guides*. We were not the boys who had set out before dawn. I gave Wyke the last of the fliers. For the next five years, we would be together, through unemployment, crap jobs, the Boomtown Rats splitting up, an amputation, a pregnancy and *The Trial of a Time Lord*. But we didn't know that then. We went home that night still thinking that the 1980s had potential.

We all sent off our fivers and joined DWAS on the same day. It was that or get tattoos.

# The Unbearable Lightness of Being (a Doctor Who fan)

**by Scott Clarke**
*From Enlightenment #98, May / June 2000*


Oh, the agony of being a 13-year-old *Doctor Who* fan in North America. 'Tis truly to be an outsider amongst outsiders. Has anyone ever devised a crueller punishment? Not only do we watch a cult science fiction series, but it's British and they made it for their children. Indefensible.

I'm still haunted by a memory of setting the Beta machine to tape *Robot* back in 1982. It was 11:30 PM on a Sunday and I wasn't allowed to stay up. Excitedly, I popped in the tape, hit the record button and scurried off to my bunk bed.

The next day I raced home from school, anticipating my prize. Dad greeted me on the front steps, his hands covered in transmission grease.

"What the hell was that you taped last night," he cracked, brushing his greasy forefinger against his chin.

It was the way he said it. I suddenly felt like I'd peed the bed. And this is a man who has gladly sat down and watched *Star Trek* or *Quantum Leap*.

I would be revisited by a myriad of similar comments over the years: "Is that the one with the googlely-eyed guy?" "Those robots with the toilet plungers are really lame!" or the ever popular, "I can't understand a word they're saying!" (BBC English indeed.)

Simply put, a lot of people just didn't get it.

Now, *Star Trek* fans have some divinely ordered place in North American society. Sure, the mainstream perceives them as geeks, but there's an ownership there. When viewers see Dr McCoy use a salt shaker as a medical scanner there's a kind of wink, wink, nod, nod. Borg catch-phrases such as "resistance is futile", etc, are uttered from sterile cubicles across North America and beyond. By comparison, *Doctor Who* doesn't even show up on the collective radar screen, except perhaps in the occasional *Simpsons* episode or a surprising *TV Guide* poll which places *Doctor Who* up there in the top ten science-fiction shows of all time.

*Doctor Who* is different. Not only is the content alien, but the container is too. As Canadians, we view *Doctor Who* through an extra lens of the outsider. At the same time we're dreaming of Peladon or Androzani Minor, we're also experiencing London or the Home Counties countryside. It's no wonder that so many youthful *Doctor Who* fans grow up yearning to visit or live in England (and many do just that).

Heck, I don't know how many addictions I have to various English television programs that sprouted from recognising a *Who* guest star. From the moment that remote control rests on your lap, you're hooked. As has been noted by too many people to count, it's the very Britishness of the programme that serves as its allure.

But here we are in the year 2000, the show has been cancelled for over ten years and I have to ask myself: what are we pining for? While I've never been very interested in the tie-in books or audio tapes – or, for that matter, fan-fiction at all – I do hold a little spot in my heart that will always be interested in keeping my love of this programme alive. Even if it means finding fewer and fewer of those who I can share it with.

The glory days of the mid-eighties, where every PBS station from Bangor, Maine to Sacramento, California could give you a healthy dose of *Who* are gone. Inevitably, I find myself buying the blasted videos, priced not to sell as they are. As I slap my bank card down on the counter at Sam the Record Man's (the most reasonable prices in Toronto), I'm often told that they sell like Viagra. Yet, who's buying them? Apparently, I'm not alone. There are other poor, lost souls with IKEA shelves full of these things.

It's with this in mind that I maintain *Doctor Who* fandom is best suited for the quiet, intimate places of this life; sitting around in the local pub or a get together on a Saturday in someone's condo. I'm reminded of Sarah Jane and the Brigadier at the end of *Planet of the Spiders*, desperately waiting for the Doctor to return from his confrontation with The Great One. Scenes we didn't see probably had them all sitting around the officer's mess, or sunken into chairs in the Brigadier's office chatting away about the Doctor, of past adventures, wondering if they would ever see him again. Sound familiar?

When *Star Trek* went off the air, there were massive letter writing campaigns. Conventions followed. And then the massive moneymaking, culture-busting phenomenon we have today. I'd have been more surprised if *Star Trek: The Motion (-Sickness) Picture* had not happened. On the other tentacle, I'm still shocked that *The TV Movie* ever got off the ground.

Flash forward to 2000. Showcase (a Canadian channel that highlights gritty imports and past Canuck glories) is currently running *Queer as Folk*. Echoing that Sunday night (now Monday) of so long ago, I pop in a fresh new VHS tape (Beta RIP) and screw around with the timer for a good five minutes. The next morning I rush off to work with an Irish Cream in one hand and my carry case in the other.

Upon returning later that evening, my roommate is sitting at the kitchen table, his fingers covered in the juice of a dozen Buffalo Wings (okay, that's not true, but I'm trying to be literary here)!

"That show you taped last night," – he makes a face – "was so banal." He then proceeds to critique it, mercilessly.

Later I watch it and quite enjoy it. The *Pyramids of Mars* scene is quite funny.

I like my *Doctor Who* served up with a pint of Rickard's Red and a healthy dose of irony.

# Eight Wonderful Things About The TV Movie

by Jonathan Blum

**1) The eighth Doctor.** Remember when we thought he would never exist? Look at how this film defines its hero: whirling about under a starry sky, enthusing about a meteor shower. Seeing into a jaded woman's soul, appealing to her childish dreams. Carrying on two simultaneous trains of thought at once. Both visual and verbal sleight-of-hand: turning Grace's "I thought you were a Doctor!" back at her, trapping the Master in his own admissions. Looking a man in the eye, confiding a secret to him, and picking his pocket at the same time. Stealing a gun to threaten himself with. "I can't make your dream come true forever, but I can make it come true today." Sincerity and flim-flam side-by-side.

More than any Doctor since Troughton, *The TV Movie* presents the Doctor as a hero whose M.O. is to do an end run around evil, to value sneakiness over steeliness or punch-ups.

**2) Matthew Jacobs.** Phil Segal once described writer Matthew Jacobs as "a very hopeful, wishing person", and that's why he nails the ethos of *Doctor Who*. Because even when it's being grim and sophisticated, there's always lightness played against that.

The sense of glee and range is way more important to capture in a redefinition of *Doctor Who* than exposition about Time Lords or Daleks – and Jacobs gets them both in side by side, in the wonderful sequence where within minutes the Doctor is dancing his way through memories of a meteor shower, delightedly snogging Grace, and then crashing straight into the plot explanations. The fact that he's a skillful enough writer that the plot exposition also advances the emotional story – the Doctor's infodump convinces Grace the man she's just kissed is a fruit-cake – and that in turn twists the action story (by turning her against him), is just icing on the cake.

Jacobs ensures the story is defined not just by events, but by images; it may be built around a dot-to-dot brief, separate elements handed down from above like a JN-T/Letts acid trip, but he's found the common ground of meaning which ties them together. For the first time since *Planet of the Spiders* two decades back, the Doctor's regeneration is an outright rebirth: a redemption, a resurrection, a new burst of youth and energy, Jacobs' optimism made flesh. And everything comes back to that central image; not just the messiah imagery, but all the other characters' stories, from the contrast of the Master's bitter clinging to life, to Grace's journey from burnt-out to sure of her purpose in life, to Chang Lee liter-ally being delivered from death in the alleyway.

**3) Geoffrey Sax.** With a story built around images, Sax runs with them at every opportunity; he seizes on Jacobs' use of the Eye of Harmony and the various eyes of the Doctor, Master and Grace, and adds loads more eyes everywhere you look: from the dissolve from the Master's eyes to the eye-like top view of his restraints, down to the gleefully gratuitous close-up of the eye of a dead fish just before it gets its head chopped off (minutes before Lee faces a similar fate). Jacobs mentions Ted watching a horror movie in the morgue; Sax built the whole sequence around *Frankenstein*, playing both with and against Jacobs' scripted Christ imagery, and drawing out a whole series of images to question the Doctor's rebirth, as monster or messiah.

Even straightforward scenes like the Doctor picking Wagg's pocket gain grace notes; at the end of the shot, a waiter brings a tray of champagne glasses right into focus in the foreground, just so Grace can attempt to pick one up as an extra little punchline. These things don't happen by accident. Neither do the stray bits of feathers and stuffing flying around in the gun battle in the alleyway – specifically set up so that when the TARDIS begins to land, Sax can set them swirling about to visually sell the idea that the ship creates a windstorm as it materialises. The climax of this film largely consists of cutting quickly back and forth between two men standing in a room – but Sax pulls out all the stops and gives every shot a tremendous sense of variety and momentum.

**4) Grace Holloway.** Grace's choice to hop on the back of that motorbike is the moment the action story and the emotional story both depend on – and, again, it's all woven in with those wonderful motifs of holding back death and holding on to childhood dreams.

And what a companion she is! Grown-up, sophisticated, unashamedly upper class but unsnobbish about it: an American aspirational figure free of British hang-ups about class and "street cred". When she thinks the Doctor's a paranoid schizophrenic, she handles him smoothly with her send-up of the "Eye of Destruction". Daphne Ashbrook has lightning-quick timing in the "He likes me to call him Doctor" exchange. Once in his world, she keeps up with him; in her first TARDIS scene, she can rattle off not just dead-on *Star Trek* technospoofing, but challenges the Doctor to help solve the problem; their ping-ponging back-and-forth across the console is a joy. And ultimately, she's sure enough of herself that she can ask the Doctor to stay with her, and mean it; after everything she's been through, she knows her life is worth living in its own right.

**5) Two heroes for the price of one.** The cosmic threat in this film may be in the Doctor's world, but the advancing story is Grace's: it hits all the beats of that Campbellian hero's journey, from her initial refusal of the call to adventure, to her turning point on the threshold in the traffic jam, to her own death and rebirth after she's saved the planet from under the TARDIS console. And again, just as Campbell would have it, back into the ordinary world afterwards, with new knowledge of who she is and what she's there for.

And the story does all this while introducing the Doctor as the hero too! In Campbellian terms, he's serving as a mentor figure to Grace, but he also gets his own share of the action. It's pretty much the first time since the Hartnell days that a story splits the role of the primary hero. Here, it's the Doctor who's left hanging in the Cloister Room playing for time while Grace does the world-saving. His heroic role is polishing off the villain, but she's defeated his actual plan.

**6) The way the Doctor kisses.** I was convinced beforehand they couldn't pull it off. But they did! They made the first two kisses in particular an expression not of lust, but of the Doctor's sheer joy in life.

**7) The TARDIS.** At last, a ship that looks like it's been lived in for hundreds of years! In the past, all the big whimsical TARDIS stuff on screen had to be confined to glimpses spread out over decades: a CSO boot cupboard, the same brick-lined tunnel over and over, all those lovely props which disappeared after the Hartnell years. Suddenly, it's all there at once – and even more, thanks to those tantalising shadowy edges around the console room.

Any shot of the old console shows you how quickly the cutting-edge gets blunted. The TV movie console bypasses this by mixing all sorts of time periods: steampunk iron and brass, a Bakelite TV set, and the huge spacey Perspex-and-crystal time rotor. It shows you every moment except five minutes ago.

**8) Telling the unexpected story.** The TV movie doesn't quite follow any one person's set of rules about how *Doctor Who* should be reintroduced. Oh, it covers a lot of them – all the Campbellian stuff I mentioned – but never in the most straightforward way. It was planned as a *Spearhead*-style introduction from outside, but then they added the prologue showing us the TARDIS from inside first. It's Grace's journey, but it begins with the Doctor, then Chang Lee.

However, not doing quite what you expect is a wonderful thing. The beautiful accident with all these different cooks stirring the pot gave us something a bit odd and chaotic and idiosyncratic... and that's *Doctor Who*. So it isn't perfectly formed? Being a *Doctor Who* fan is all about knowing that imperfect stories can still work, regardless.

And it did work, for lots of people! There's no sign that its odd approaches actually alienated the US audience; the problem wasn't that they tuned out, it's that they never tuned in in the first place. And judging by the appreciation scores, the UK audience liked it about the same as *Rose*! We have no idea how a follow-on series would have done, but as a movie in its own right – which is all it was commissioned to be – it performed just fine.

The trend these days is to say that you'd have to be mad to relaunch the show with a regeneration story. Sure, that's true in 2005, when there hadn't been a regular Doctor for fifteen years; that's a wildly different landscape from when the TVM was made, barely two years after fourteen million people saw five different Doctors in *Dimensions in Time*. In one market, the Doctor was a known character; in the other, to people who don't know him, it's a wonderful expression of his unique character that he's someone who is reborn.

And that's the heart of this story: becoming young again. It's a hymn to the power of childish dreams, from the script down to the sheer love which making *Doctor Who* has inspired in the prop boys. It's about shedding your old skin and your old preconceptions. It's bold and brave and wholehearted. It's about an opera-loving, jelly-baby-strewing, trickster running rings around bad guys (and dull ones too). It's about hopping on the back of a motorbike with an impossible man and going for the ride of your life.

What's not to love?

# Blowing Kisses to the Past, Making Love to the Future

by **Eric Briggs**
*From Enlightenment #104, June / July 2001*


*"No. Not really, I don't think so. Not unless it comes back in a completely new way."*

—Jon Pertwee,
on whether or not *Doctor Who*
ought to be brought back (1995)


*Doctor Who*'s TV movie was first broadcast five years ago this month. *The TV Movie* bypassed most of the preconceptions most fans had about the old television series. Traditional aspects of the series were signposted, but there was no strictness about its continuity, character and plot references.

On the one hand, there was strict adherence to the mystique of the Doctor. It goes without saying that he is an eccentric man with voluminous pockets who travels through time and space in a police telephone box. And, in fact, this is the only necessary premise for a new series of *Doctor Who*. There didn't need to be lengthy explanations of Gallifrey, the Daleks, the Gell Guards, and so on. There was more continuity than just the basics: the busts of Rassilon, the Prydonian Seal, the TARDIS toolkit. But it was all window-dressing, kisses blown to the past. The Doctor doesn't even know who he is until the epiphany with Grace on a beach in Sausalito. When he remembers that he is a Time Lord from the planet

Gallifrey, the first thing he recalls is spending a summer's evening stargazing with his father. Of course, then he gets caught up in a huge tornado of an info-dump about the Master being pure evil and wanting to turn the Eye of Harmony inside out... Come to think of it, if they wanted to use the Master, they could have gone to the trouble of giving him some simple motivation for once in a lifetime. Huge info-dumps are a characteristic of *Doctor Who* we'd all like to forget, ironically.

The Master deserves to be mentioned as well. Originally designed as a Professor Moriarty for Jon Pertwee's Holmesian Doctor, the Master died along with Roger Delgado, the actor who played him. All of the Masters since Delgado have been caricatures of evil and increasingly silly. In *The TV Movie*, Eric Roberts played the role as a cartoon villain without aping the usual Master tropes. His Master is American, he corrects people's grammar and he's a little fey. There are many things that can be said about his role as the villain in this story, and some of them are complimentary.

Right from the start of the show, with the Master being executed by the Daleks for "his evil crimes", fans from you and I all the way up to Terrance Dicks knew that the plot of this show was too heavy. The style, by way of consolation, was fabulous.

The redesign of the TARDIS was a function of cash. Back in 1963, when Peter Brachacki designed the huge, powerful control room, it seemed almost cavernous. But over the years it had become physically smaller as well as more metaphorically confining. It was all white and had no carpets, no sofas and no wallpaper. *The TV Movie* gave us a TARDIS much more in line with the Doctor's nineteenth century fashions: a cross between 221B Baker Street and the Batcave. HG Wells is a more famous time traveller than *Doctor Who* and we needed a Wellsian or Holmesian mystique to re-establish the Doctor as an old-fashioned pulp hero.

The eighth Doctor who emerges in *The TV Movie* is the most passionate Doctor in the history of the series. He leaps around the frame eagerly, trying to express himself to his companions. He experiences extreme sadness about Puccini's opera. He is the only Doctor who can convincingly say, "Yeah, I'm the guy with two hearts." And he snogs his companion.

McGann's Doctor is like a cosmic crocodile wrangler, a galactic Steve Irwin. He wanders through millennial San Francisco, pointing and chuckling at humans and their funny, dangerous games and occasionally putting his head between the jaws of the monster. For some of *The TV Movie*, he has an air of the congenital idiot about him. He is the sexiest Doctor ever. Kissing the companion was a fun thing to put in *The TV Movie*, an admittance that, deep down, the Doctor is at least half-human.

The Doctor's been human before. Between 1963 and 1969 he might as well have been human, albeit with amazing science and technology at his forgetful fingertips. Calling him a Time Lord was self-evident even before the details of his derivation began to be laid out. And, although the plot of *The TV Movie* involved both the Daleks and Gallifrey, these aspects were pushed to the margins to focus on the consequently motiveless plot. There was a paradox to be dealt with: without enough *Doctor Who* references it's not *Doctor Who*, with too many it's rubbish.

The introduction stories of most of the different Doctors have been flawed, with the exception of Jon Pertwee's *Spearhead from Space*. As it happened, *The TV Movie*'s plot was wrong. But what did it offer? A continuing series of light entertainment circa Tom Baker 1979, or a gothic horror-romance serial circa 1976? Perhaps a bit of both. But probably not a bunch of technological stories with burbling electronic music and tacky clothes. *The TV Movie* was darkly lit and the music, although synthesised, had a more original take on Ron Grainer's theme than this year's arrangement by David Arnold in the Big Finish audios. The gossip about the Doctor being half-human may have been expanded upon, although the Doctor's usually not described as a Pinocchio who wants to be a real boy. There probably would have been another Gallifrey story eventually, no doubt involving some treachery on the High Council.

As it happened, *The TV Movie* didn't lead anywhere by a direct route. A lot of the fans couldn't deal with its novelty or its failings, and high ratings in other countries couldn't overcome its failure in American television's May sweeps. The BBC novels produced since 1997 tried at first to recapture McGann's frenetic energy with inconsistent results. The eighth Doctor's since been put through the wringer several times; he has now destroyed Gallifrey and wiped his memory of it. He could have just not gone back home; that's always left the narrative uncluttered in the past.

The new Paul McGann audios from Big Finish may provide an easier continuation for the eighth Doctor's adventures. With Paul McGann's own sexy voice and a more leisurely series of plots, the audio adventures haven't resorted to blowing up any important planets at all. There are a couple of possible complaints and some more ambiguous details. Some of the McGann audios are retreads of 15-year-old fan scripts. McGann has already come up against the Cybermen; adventures with the Daleks and the Time Lords are in the pipeline. It ought to be mentioned, though, that most of the upcoming McGanns don't feature returning villains.

McGann's first four audios are being billed as Season Twenty-Seven of *Doctor Who*, which they oughtn't. If McGann had gone on to a new series of *Doctor Who* after the TV Movie, it would have been Season One all over again, both literally and metaphorically.

# The Re-Awakening
# of Mediocre Who

by Ben Hakala
*From Enlightenment #69, July / August 1995*

Despite the often unmerciful dissections by most fans, I would argue that there are almost no truly bad *Doctor Who* stories. Many are simply mediocre, but quite enjoyable; why be a fan of a series that you only like a small percentage of, say, twenty "classics"? Thus, instead of dealing with the pinnacles such as *Warriors' Gate*, *Genesis of the Daleks* and *Spearhead from Space*, I intend to recall those lesser stories that are the meat of the series. Further, I'm intentionally mentioning stories I appreciate, not underrated ones that I love. I think *The Ribos Operation* and *The Leisure Hive* are just such stories, but this is a personal assessment; my argument is that a certain recognition is due to those episodes that never aspire to be better than average.

One of my favourite mediocre stories is *The Power of Kroll*. Admittedly, the split-screen effects were never convincing and the Swampies' tribal dance is ludicrous, but such things should be subordinate to the merits of the story. Effects are easily the least important aspect of any production, though sadly most Hollywood audiences would rather lap up *Jurassic Park* or *Terminator 2* (with their sickening $100 million budgets) over quiet gems such as *Husbands and Wives* or *Bob Roberts*. Presumably this is why *Kroll* seems drab and unimaginative to most, when actually it is unusually subtle and serious for its era, with moments of bone-dry humour. It has a marvellously complex script that is remarkably well informed of the plight of the North American native peoples yet, typically of Robert Holmes, refuses to hit us over the head with the message. Instead, John Abineri's restrained performance as Ranquin perfectly conveys the honour and turmoil of the Swampies. Much of the acting is equally impressive, with Philip Madoc playing against type superbly in a minor role and Glyn Owen as Rohm Dutt displaying an excellent, dry, deadpan delivery (his banter with Romana is well worth rewatching). As a whole, the story is noteworthy for its uniqueness within the sixteenth season; its restraint stands out when placed between the farcical *The Androids of Tara* and the epic (and often silly) *The Armageddon Factor*.

Often dismissed as tedious viewing is *The Space Museum*, a story crying for defenders. I find it well-paced and full of postmodern touches that challenge viewer's expectations. For instance, it toys with the accepted television conventions that most take for granted: one scene has

Ian and Vicki in the foreground while two people pass several feet behind them, carrying out a conversation we cannot hear. This seems natural, as TV and film have accustomed us to selective hearing; yet in this instance, it turns out that the conversation really is inaudible. Later, when Vicki sneezes as the villain passes (an intentional cliché), it seems a cheat when he doesn't hear. However, it soon becomes apparent that this is the point: he cannot hear her! Also of note is the characterisation, which is refreshingly natural for a Hartnell tale. There are subtle hints in the dialogue that the Moroks are going to seed; Lobos in particular is given many sardonic lines.

A selective journey through the worlds of mediocre *Who* will, I hope, illustrate the wide range the programme spans and the treasures that can be found across the spectrum. Look at *Destiny of the Daleks*, with perhaps the eeriest scenes ever shot in bright sunlight and an almost absolute lack of music. Or *Colony in Space*'s superbly cynical depiction of humanity's future, where huge corporations dominate a weak and corrupt government. The classic TARDIS within a TARDIS scenes in *The Time Monster*. The allegorical *Paradise Towers*, with its horrific picture of a society that has regressed to anarchy (a twist on JG Ballard's *High Rise*). Sarah, indignant at Harry's presumption to carry her, unaware that he has just saved her life, in *Revenge of the Cybermen* – and, of course, "Harry Sullivan is an imbecile!" The gritty Telosian exteriors in *Attack of the Cybermen*. The fascinating marriage of drug-smuggling, a hyper-space collision and a projection that can be entered in *Nightmare of Eden*. The commentary on inept politicians and bureaucrats in *The Claws of Axos*. That classic episode three cliffhanger in *The Face of Evil*: "Who am I? Who am I? Who am I?" The pleasantly literate and refreshingly inconsequential *The King's Demons*. Christopher Barry's tight and atmospheric direction of the silly and sketchy *The Romans*; in terms of visual design, at least, it is worthy of comparison to *I, Claudius*. The blackly humorous breaks in the otherwise unrelenting depression of *Terminus*: Bor, who is dying of radiation sickness, frets that "Hmm, short term memory's always the first to go!"

Perhaps this will encourage some fans to rewatch *Who* they'd left for dead. Too often, fans end up stagnating by only watching a handful of personal favourites. There are those who only watch a few episodes a year. Opinions can and should change; I once voted *Image of the Fendahl* my worst-ever story and now quite enjoy it. So put on your hiking boots and a durable Khaki jacket, and prepare to rediscover the merits of *Meglos*, *The Horns of Nimon*, *The Monster of Peladon* and many other stories you have intentionally avoided. You may be in for a shock.

# INTERLUDE

## The Key to a Time Lord - 6
by Scott Clarke
*From Enlightenment #124, November 2004*

### Episode Six: Resolutions
*"One perfect crystal and it will be complete. That is the crystal I need."*

I'm a sucker for a good ending. A satisfying finish should fulfil an idea
that was established at the beginning of the drama. Chekhov – the play-
wright, not the helmsman, dummy – was adamant: "If there is a gun
hanging on the wall in the first act, it must fire in the last."
   The resolution to any reliable *Doctor Who* story should offer a payoff to
themes, character development and plot points set up from the get-go. It
should benefit from the careful buildup of its theme and plot over a number of episodes, heightening expectations. And then, ultimately, it will
reveal the essential Doctor-ness of the central character by offering a
solution to the problem that defines the character and the underlying
ethos of the series.
   That's my *Norton Anthology of English Literature* answer anyway. The
last episode of a *Doctor Who* story should also be exciting, exciting, exciting – and full of surprises!
   *Planet of the Spiders* may well be one the most padded stories in *Doctor
Who* history (with some of the weakest effects), but it does have one hell
of an ending, that fulfils a number of thematic and plot threads developed early on. Designed as a Buddhist parable, the Doctor is forced to
confront his fear, take responsibility for his intellectual arrogance, and in
the end pay with one of his lives. He is then re-incarnated – becoming a
new man (neatly fitting in with the end of the era, the regeneration
mythos and Buddhist myth). The seeds of these events are carefully
planted in the first episode of the story, in the form of the Doctor's
actions towards Professor Clegg, causing his death, in the name of science.
   Throughout the story, that pesky blue crystal (actually introduced a
year earlier) is a symbol of power, both destructive and reconciling:

wealth for wimpy Lupton, conquest for the plastic spiders, the manifestation of pure control for the Great One and knowledge for the Doctor. Alternatively, it offers redemption to Mike Yates, freedom to Sarah Jane and healing to Tommy. In many ways, it is the "gun" that Chekhov spoke of, which helps to propel the story to its ultimate climax.

But *Planet of the Spiders* itself is a larger resolution, a mega-mix if you will, of everything the Pertwee era was about: morality, gadgets, action and CSO up the wazoo.

The third Doctor was always presented as a character in complete control. Ward Cleaver for the fourth dimension; he had all the answers, whether anyone else cared to listen or not. Science was paramount, as he frequently espoused to Jo. The pursuit of knowledge must take priority over everything (whether it was getting up close and personal with the Silurians or trying to remember where the hell the on-switch was for his TARDIS). But how far would the Doctor go?

Look at how the Pertwee era unfolded: forcibly exiled to Earth, nothing to eat but wine and cheese, he expended most of his energy trying to hightail it to the stars. After being granted his parole by the Time Lords, he sets his sights (almost obsessively) on getting to Metebelis 3, pilfers a crystal and sets in motion a nasty series of events that lead to his own death by CSO irradiation.

The Doctor's treatment of Professor Clegg is nothing short of scandalous. Does he enlist the hapless psychic to help the poor man? No, he does so to satisfy his own curiosity. He presses the man to confess to his true ability and then exploits the admission. There are echoes of the Doctor's often-patronising attitude towards Jo implicit in his behaviour. Don't be afraid, science offers the answers. Clearly it didn't, in this case, and an innocent got scotched. What is wonderful about episode six of *Planet of the Spiders* is that it clearly calls the Doctor to account for the consequences of his actions. No, he wasn't malicious, but the Time Lord's shortsightedness still had tragic ramifications.

There is something tragically inevitable about that final confrontation with the Great One. The Doctor couldn't avoid the seeds he'd sown; he was left only with the choice to confront his fear and by extension his true nature. Brilliant stuff.

In *The Caves of Androzani*, the theme of the Doctor's curiosity is revisited, with the Doctor blatantly acknowledging that his inquisitiveness always gets him in trouble. His life is once again forfeit, this time for friendship and Peri's scabby legs.

Many of the best *Doctor Who* stories operate in a similar fashion, illustrating the consequences of actions. The themes of racism and intolerance are developed through the Daleks and the character of Mike Smith in *Remembrance of the Daleks*, juxtaposing the choices of an everyman (Mike) with those of the most evil creatures in the universe. Little touches, like the "no coloureds" sign in the window and comments Mike makes to Ace, carry the viewer through to the ultimate conclusion: where do we stand, and will we let our choices lead us to violence and destruction? We all knew Mike Smith had to die in the end; a finger-wagging from the Doctor wouldn't have cut it.

*The Talons of Weng-Chiang* offers a much more straightforward plot execution, but is no less satisfying. Greel, the villain, wants his time cabinet back so he can return to the future and presumably corner the market on frozen fish sticks and semi-detached igloos. All his resources (giant rats, Chinese magicians, young English girls, etc) are employed to this end. When he finally gets the darned thing back, he uses it, to his ultimate, smoky demise. Simple. Robert Holmes may frustrate the goal in high style over six episodes, but ultimately he knows what his audience must have by the end. But let's not downplay the importance of that build-up to an important finale.

Noah's transformation in *The Ark in Space* and his battle to maintain his identity is kept in question until the last moment. Ultimately, his self-sacrifice to save the human race is made all the more potent because we have lived through his wrestling to take control of his will. The moment we witness his bubble-wrapped hand, we're committed to seeing out his fate; a fate which will say much about the Doctor's faith in humanity.

Whether or not you were duly impressed by the long-awaited appearance of the Great One, the buildup to her arrival is significant: it's the final trump card in the writer's basket (not unlike the Black Guardian in *The Armageddon Factor* or the Emperor in *The Evil of the Daleks*). We hear about the Great One, but we don't see her until the climax. She is the ultimate baddie the Doctor can't overcome. Unusually for the programme, there is even a little flashback to the Doctor's first encounter with the Great One after K'Anpo – the hermit of the Doctor's "daisiest daisy" speech in *The Time Monster* – reminds the Doctor of what he must do.

Because there is so much buildup in the serial/episodic format, our expectations are greatly heightened in terms of resolution. This is doubly so with a regeneration story, as the anticipation of "change" and regeneration are so great. When you get to kill off your main character every several years, make the most of it! You have to make the audience believe the threat to the Doctor is insurmountable. It makes his solution and his sacrifice all the more potent.

When K'Anpo tells the Doctor he has only one choice, at first the Time Lord doesn't even recognise it; then, when he does, the fear in his face is evident. What I've always found intriguing, though, is not that the

Doctor saves the day, but that he acknowledges that he's powerless, that nothing he can do can change the outcome; it's pre-ordained. And so, he returns to accept his fate. A truly poignant, Doctorish moment.

The Doctor frequently uses the truth to save the day. Witness his defeat of the Dalek Supreme in *Remembrance of the Daleks*. He forces it to see the ultimate reality of what the Daleks have wrought. Dalek go boom.

Alas, when a finale falls flat on its keester, it's painfully evident. *The Armageddon Factor* illustrates the point all too well, failing utterly to realise the potential of the stories that proceeded it. The story itself is okay, introducing the wonderfully realised Shadow, and the tragic conflict between Zeos and Atrios (I don't even mind the eleventh-hour insertion of Drax). As an end to the programme's first major season-long arc, though, it wastes all of the intriguing elements promised at its outset. Where is the ultimate battle between the Black and White Guardians? In the first episode, the quest is clearly stated: the Doctor is to collect the pieces of the Key so they can be assembled, and the White Guardian can restore order to a chaotic universe. Hello?! When exactly did that happen? Was I consistently on bathroom breaks? Is there a Missing Adventure out there I haven't heard about?

And knowing when to end a story or episode is equally essential. Imagine if *Vengeance on Varos* had ended with a cheery console room scene (as was indeed scripted), or if *Warriors' Gate* had ended with the Doctor trying to explain the plot to Adric.

Early signs of the new programme show strong signs that Russell T Davies is already set to introduce themes, characters and plot points that will weave their way throughout the first season. Some fans have arched their backs with cries of "soap opera" or "complicated continuity", but I say "bah"! This is a man who brought us *Bob and Rose*, an intricately devised drama, which presented a controversial (some would say implausible) scenario, and then made it real by developing believable characters and important themes into a resolution that was unmistakably human and hopeful.

And so, dear friends, as we wait out these last few months until *Rose* graces our television screens, speculating, second guessing and dreaming, remember that it ain't over 'til it's over. And if you listen carefully, one ear to the wind, you may heard me utter, through a fluted champagne glass, "That's the Key to a Time Lord."

# ACKNOWLEDGEMENTS

And now the thanking part.

This volume would have been a lot less substantial were it not for the contributions of so many people. Mad Norwegian Press publisher Lars Pearson's drive and vision has been invaluable to us and we have been grateful for his passion to see *Doctor Who* fan writing reach a wider audience. We would like to thank the executive of the Doctor Who Information Network for allowing us to reprint material from *Enlightenment*. Also enormously helpful were the various people behind *Shockeye's Kitchen* and we'd like to especially thank Steve Hatcher, Simon Kinnear and Gary Finney for their efforts above and beyond. Also going far beyond the call of duty was Matthew Kilburn, who kept sending us more and more material from his collection of archives. This collection would have been a lot poorer without his help.

We would also like to thank Lance Parkin, Rupert Booth, Simon Forward, Phil Purser-Hallard, Jim Mortimore, Paul Cornell, Peter Anghelides, Stuart Douglas, Shannon Sullivan, Joe Ford and Neil Hogan. We should also apologise to all those potential contributors whose work we wanted to include, but we just couldn't find you. We did our best, but there were far too many of you and the magic of Facebook could only take us so far.

Lastly, we would like to thank you, the reader. Because it's your willingness to read and engage with opinions on *Doctor Who* that has kept *Doctor Who* fan writing alive over the past forty years. We're grateful to you for that, because not only do we think it has made *Doctor Who* fandom so vital and so essential, we also think it has made the enjoyment of our beloved television series that much more special.

# TIME

## NINCORPORATED

### E DOCTOR WHO FANZINE ARCHIVES

Vol. 3: Writings on the New Series

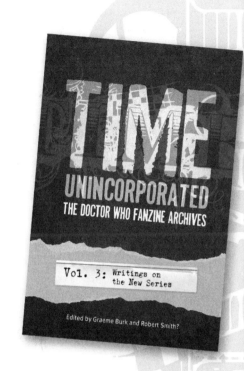

*ming soon...*

*ne, Unincorporated 3* compliments its predessor by presenting an astounding array of zine material on the new *Doctor Who* – including essays on Matt Smith's first season, *rchwood*, *The Sarah Jane Adventures* and *re*.

*rks* included in this volume stem from such *olications* as *Enlightenment*, *Tides of Time*, *ockeye's Kitchen*, *Mistfall* and more. Also luded are a number of essays on new *Doctor o* that were written exclusively for this vol*ne*, from such writers as Andrew Cartmel, Jon *m*, Kate Orman, Lloyd Rose, Steve Lyons and *re*.

3N: 978-1935234036
tail Price TBD

**www.madnorwegian.com**
1150 46th St, Des Moines, IA 50311 . madnorwegian@gmail.com

# Graeme Burk

... is a writer and *Doctor Who* fan. From 2000 to 2010, he was the editor of *Enlightenment*, the fanzine of Doctor Who Information Network, North America's oldest and largest *Doctor Who* fan club. He is the author of three *Doctor Who* short stories in the *Short Trips* anthologies, and was also a contributing reviewer for the first two volumes of Telos Publishing's *Back to the Vortex* guides to the new series of *Doctor Who*. A finalist for a new screenwriting prize with the Writers Guild of Canada, he has had his work published by magazines, websites and small presses throughout North America. He lives, sometimes, in Ottawa.

# Robert Smith?

... is a professor of biomathematics at the University of Ottawa who researches eradication of diseases such as HIV, malaria and human papillomavirus. In his spare time, he writes a column for *Enlightenment* and runs the online *Doctor Who Ratings Guide*. Oh, and he's also the braaaaaiiiiinnnnnnnssssss behind the recent academic paper on mathematical modelling of zombies that achieved worldwide fame and massive media attention by combining two incredibly geeky things in his life. Trust us, he was as surprised by this as anyone.

**Publisher / Editor-in-Chief**
Lars Pearson

**Senior Editor / Design Manager**
Christa Dickson

**Associate Editor**
Joshua Wilson

**Technical Support**
Marc Eby

*The publisher wishes to thank...*
Graeme and Robert, for proving the rule that the best strategy is to hire the right people for a task, then do everything in your power to stand back and let them get on with it; the wide range of contributors to this volume; Michael and Lynne Thomas; Shawne Kleckner; Jeremy Bement; Jim Boyd; George Krstic; and that nice lady who sends me newspaper articles.

1150 46th Street
Des Moines, Iowa 50311
info@madnorwegian.com
**www.madnorwegian.com**